A Vengeful Harvest

Alec Cattanach 1

Lexie Conyngham

A Vengeful Harvest

Lexie Conyngham

The Kellas Cat Press

ISBN: 978-1-910926-86-4

Two days after the Second World War was declared, on Tuesday, 5th September, 1939, a lorry crashed into a tram on Great Northern Road in Woodside, Aberdeen. No one was killed, though one man was knocked from his bicycle by an attending ambulance and broke his leg. On the same morning, a boy was run over and killed by a lorry on King Street, Aberdeen: his address was given as Seaton Drive.

These are historical facts, which inspired this book. In all other respects, none of the people involved in these two accidents, or serving in the City force at any time, are intended to be represented at all in this book. Any resemblance is purely accidental.

Dramatis Personae

The Police:
Lieutenant Moffat
Inspector Alec Cattanach
Inspector Cochrane
Sergeant McAulay
Constable Frankie Cooper
Constable Gildart Gauld
Constable Stewart
Constable Leggatt
Constable Anderson
Sundry officers of the County force

The Campbell brothers:
Robert, a trawlerman, Mabel, and her son Billy
Tommy, a shipbuilder, and Lizzie
Edward, in the harbourmaster's office, and Isabel
Sammy, on the liners, Betty, and family
Arthur, also a shipbuilder

Inhabitants of Aberdeen:
Gladys Hawthorne and Maggie, a promising child
Albert Lovie, jeweller
Dr. Mackay, his wife and daughter
Jock McKinstry
Ronald Sutherland, antique dealer
Stevie Tennant and his father
Mrs. Walker, owner of dogs

Outwith Aberdeen:
Frank Fraser, hairdresser, Peterhead
Gordon of Glenfindie and his ghillie
Harry Sandison, lorry driver
Tommy Wilson
Muckle Eck

1

'HI, MISS! MISS!'

She had to get to work. Mr. Robertson would be cross if she was late again.

'Miss! Stop!'

Who were they shouting at? She needed to get to work. And where was her respirator? Where had she put it? She couldn't have left it at home. She had got into the habit, already, of leaving it looped over her coat when she came home each evening, ready to be slung over her shoulder in the morning. Where was it? Could she have left it on the tram?

The tram …

She had caught the tram. Why was she walking?

'Hi, miss!'

Maybe she had dropped it. Maybe it had slipped off her shoulder when she climbed off the tram. But why had she come off the tram so early? It was miles to work from here. She would be late. Mr. Robertson would be cross.

'Miss, please stop!'

If she had dropped it, maybe that man was calling out to her. Maybe he had her respirator. Maybe she should stop and look round …

'That's it, miss, steady, there,' said the man. It was a kindly voice, young, about her own age. She looked up. He was tall. Taller with the hat. And a navy blue suit … uniform – oh, he was a policeman. She should have stopped. 'Are you all right? You look lost.'

'I have to get to work. I'll be late. They don't like it if you're late.'

'You'd be better not going to work today,' he said. 'I think they'd understand.'

'They wouldn't!' What did he know?

'Is this your gas mask?' he asked, holding up a familiar box on a strap. She reached out for it at once. 'Wait, now,' he said. 'You were on the tram, were you no?'

She nodded, suddenly unable to speak.

'Then you'd better wait for the ambulance,' he said. 'They can take a look over you, see you're all right.'

'I'm – I'm all right,' she said, conscious that she was echoing him. 'I'm grand.'

'Oh, miss,' he said, 'I dinna think so. Look at your poor feet.'

She looked down. Both her shoes were missing, and her feet were a mass of blood and dirt, her stockings torn to shreds.

'My new stockings!' she gasped in alarm. Then, as if she needed to see her feet to feel it, the pain hit her. 'Oh!'

'I'll get someone to come and help you,' said the policeman. 'Here, sit yourself down on this wee wall. There'll be someone with you in just a mintie.' He turned and hurried off, back the way she had come, the way he had followed her. She blinked after him, sucking in her lips at the agony of her feet. Along the pavement was a line of bloody footprints. She traced it with her eyes, step by step, back along the street lined with its low granite tenements, to where a dozen people were milling round – what was it? A great lump of a thing in the middle of the road, just where North Anderson Drive came down to Great Northern Road – she loved that bit where the tram came down the hill and swept right towards the city. She had been on the tram …

And then she saw it, saw what it was. The lorry must have been coming out of the city. It had hit the tram fair and square, and now the two vehicles were one – one that was not going to be going anywhere for a good, long while.

How was she here? How had anything come living out of that?

The man had been up since first light, or maybe before. He did not want to miss a moment of this, particularly not now. Of course it was never possible to know what the future would hold, but just now it seemed more uncertain than ever.

Season of mists ... here, at the door of his little tent, he watched as the mist lifted slowly, so slowly, off the land below. The man's heart seemed to beat with the same lack of urgency, barely perceptible, the only part of him that could be said to move at all. No need to move: here he was sheltered, and warm, and all he needed to entertain him was being revealed gradually without his having to do anything. The dark purple-brown of the heather, bright green of the late summer grass, salmon-pink of the dying bracken – a few deer in the distance, an early skein of geese overhead, calling to each other, then a hare much closer, unbothered by him as it would be unbothered by any other part of the landscape. The gold and cream of a scattering of birches slid out of the mist, then a ragged line of stone wall, the glint of a burn slithering down the hillside, cutting through black, peaty soil.

The man watched patiently, gratefully, as the mist finally dispersed, back to wherever mists came from. He drew a long, steady breath, more steady than he had hoped. Breakfast now. He leaned back into the tent, and pulled out his little stove, lit it, and tipped into a blackened pan his last slices of bacon and his last two eggs, and, shoving the pieces around with an old knife, he added a large, floury, tattie scone. The hare, unimpressed, loped off. The man ate his breakfast straight from the pan, used a brush of heather to scrape out the worst of the mess when he had finished, and packed everything away, finishing with the rolled-up tent. With all he had on his back, he stood, and stared down the hillside to a small clump of gorse by a stone wall. Beyond it, he could just see a dark, flattish surface. The roof of his car. He sighed, wondered what world he would be driving back to, and began a slow, careful descent of the hill.

'That's been a terrible morning,' said the red-headed constable. He had taken off his helmet, leaving an indented line across his freckled forehead, and a faint whiff of fresh sweat from his curly hair. He took a draft of tea that would have drowned an ox, and sat back to stretch out his long legs.

'No the best, aye,' agreed his companion, who must have been on tiptoes when he passed the test for the regulation height. He, too, though, spread his legs out as far as they could go. Taking the weight off the feet now and again, that was the trick. He sipped his tea more genteelly, even going to far as to remove the spoon first. His eyes were suspiciously moist, but then he had been the one to attend the accident in King Street.

'How did the lorry driver fare?' asked the bigger constable.

'Och, he was gey upset, a course,' said the smaller. His father had had him christened Gildart, but he went by Gil. Gil Gauld. 'Kept saying it was all his fault, he couldna stop in time, all that. But the lad just stepped out, by all accounts. Ken the pavement was gey busy, that time of the day. Students, and workers, and the bairns fooling about with no school to go to. The wee lad came out of nowhere, and the lorry just … well, you ken.' Gil had a couple of nephews himself: what had happened to the lad when the lorry just – it would stay with him for a while, he knew.

'Have you heard any more word about the tram thing? It's no a good day to be driving a lorry in Aberdeen,' said the big constable. He pulled out a flattened packet of cigarettes, and went through the daily formality of offering one to Gil, who, as usual, refused.

'Och, Frankie, the world's just gone to hell,' said Gil. 'Plenty injured, that's what I heard, plenty injured. One fellow knocked out of his senses. That time of the morning, they were all heading to their work, a' course. The tram was near full. The tram driver was in an awful state, and the lorry driver – well, I think he was half-asleep when he hit. I mean, who needs a war when we've all this happening? And then a fellow was knocked off his bike by one of the ambulances, broke his leg, they say.'

'Aye, you're dead right about the world,' said Frankie, emptying his cup with a resounding slurp. He lit his cigarette. 'What age are you, then?'

'Twenty,' said Gil mournfully. 'You?'

'Twenty-two,' said Frankie, nodding. 'The twa ends of the same thing.'

'Aye, for now,' said Gil. 'Twenty to twenty-two year olds for now, that's what they're saying, but it'll soon be more, twenty-five, twenty-eight, maybe even thirty. And younger, too – my cousin's just turned seventeen. When will they call him up? A' course, we're in a reserved occupation. But that'll be all our school friends, all lining up to register for the army. That'll be gey strange. The place'll be empty.'

'Aye, the ones that havena joined the reserve already,' said Frankie. 'Half of the ones I know are in the Gordon Highlanders.'

'And three quarters of my beat's in the R.N.R.,' agreed Gil. 'If they're no already on the trawlers. Yon wee lad, Billy Campbell, his step-faither's away to sea.'

'Is he? Do you ken the mother?'

'I ken her to see. She's got some family around, but it'll be a lonely time for her.'

'That's a fact.' Frankie watched Gil still sipping at his cup. 'Have you no that finished yet?'

'It's awfa hot.'

Frankie looked around for something to entertain him while he waited, twiddling large fingers on his cigarette.

'Is the Inspector no due back this afternoon? Cattanach, I mean.'

'That's what I heard, aye.'

'He'll be here soon, then, no doubt. What a day to come back to!'

'You'd better tell me about it, then, Cooper. Good day to you both,' came a new, familiar voice. Both constables pulled in their legs, and made to stand up. 'No, I've interrupted your dinner,' said the Inspector. 'Don't bother standing. But you can tell me the news.'

'Aye, sir. Will you take a fly cup?'

'I will.' Inspector Alec Cattanach, a slim, muscled man with sandy hair greying at the temples, found a cleanish cup, and held it out while Frankie Cooper filled it with something from the pot that looked as if it had been run through a peat bog. But Cattanach was used to it. He propped himself against the counter where the cups were lined up, and surveyed the two constables without much optimism. 'Go on, then.'

'A bad crash up Woodside direction. Where Great Northern Road meets Anderson Drive. A lorry went into a tram this morning.'

'Fatalities?'

'None, we think, sir,' said Gil. 'Neither of us was up there, mind, but that's what they're saying. Bad injuries, though.'

'Right. Anyone arrested?'

'The lorry driver, but he's up at the hospital. Constable

Stewart is with him.'

'Road cleared?'

'No yet, sir. They needed to bring in some big lorry thing from the tram place, or so I'm told. But the traffic can get round it except when they're actually lifting the thing. The road's wide there.'

'Of course. What else?'

He could see Gil swallowing.

'A wee lad knocked down by a lorry on King Street, up Seaton way.'

'Your beat? Badly hurt?'

'Killed, sir,' said Gil, his voice cracking again.

Cattanach gave a nod.

'Next of kin?'

'Mother, sir, in Seaton Drive. She knows – a wheen of folks that knew the lad were about the place, and they must have tellt her. Husband's at sea, but his brothers are around, she says.'

'Right. What about the lorry driver this time?'

'Blames himself, sir, but it wasna his fault, from all I could tell. The boy just fell off the pavement in front of him. A'body said so.'

'But you've taken his details?'

'Oh, aye, sir. In my notebook.'

'Good. Good.' He took a mouthful of the tea, containing a shudder as it scraped its way down his throat. 'And now, men, I've been away since Friday, so tell me – are we at war, or not?'

Gil and Frankie exchanged looks, and Gil set his cup down on the battered table. He cleared his throat.

'Aye, sir, we are.'

2

ALEC CATTANACH SAT at his desk for a long moment, his head in his hands. The office he shared with another inspector was mercifully empty for the time being, but beyond the window he could hear – could not avoid hearing – the racket of the building work that was extending Police Headquarters into Lodge Walk. More granite blocks arrived on the site daily, but had to be trimmed into place with howling saws that set his teeth on edge. Surely they had enough by now? Black holes gaped where the windows should be fitted soon. He stared out analytically. Had they made any progress at all in the time he had been away? It barely looked like it. The builders had been at the job since June, but now at least there would be a new impetus to finish. The extension was intended to house the new staff that were to train the Air Raid Protection officers.

Cattanach surveyed his in-tray and stuck his tongue out at the height of the pile there – the punishment for four days off. No doubt something in there, some slip of paper, would explain the function of the Air Raid Protection officers. Cattanach was not sure that he could describe it yet – it was a mystery to him. They seemed to be acquiring all sorts of powers, with the exception of making sure people were covering over any visible lights. That thankless task would be left to the police. But air raid protection? What were they supposed to do if bombs started dropping? Open umbrellas? And who would they recruit for this peculiar work? All the fit young men would soon be off fighting.

He drew a handful of the papers from the in-tray out on to the desk, and flicked through to see if there was anything that could be dealt with quickly. Registration, petrol rationing, blackout … if truth was the first victim of war, then paper manufacturers were the first winners. Plenty of paper manufacturers around Aberdeen: perhaps there would be some benefit. But it would hardly outweigh the bad side.

There was already a preliminary report in on the tram crash that morning – he would have to remember to compliment the constable who had finished it so quickly. Constable Leggatt - oh, yes, he was keen. He had the names and addresses of both drivers, almost all the injured, the remaining passengers, witnesses in the street who had seen or heard the collision. A girl who had lost her shoes and her respirator – glass picked out of her feet, state of shock. No wonder. Leggatt had recovered her shoes from the wreckage, but only one was good enough to wear and it would not fit over the bandages. The only thing he had had no success with – and Cattanach could almost sense Leggatt's frustration at his own failure – was that one injured man, knocked out cold, had not been identified. He had had no wallet, nor diary, nor even his initials stitched inside his hat. No one at the scene had recognised him, either. Roll on registration, thought Cattanach. Carry your identity cards, ye masses! It will make our lives much easier all round.

No doubt the man's wife was at home making the tea, wondering why he was late, ready to tease him about once again leaving his wallet on the hallstand. Or perhaps news of the accident had already reached her and she was bracing herself to call the hospital, to ask for him by name, to describe him and what he was wearing, to hear the news. How much easier for her if he had had a card with his name and address. She could have had the bad news so much sooner.

He glanced over at Inspector Cochrane's desk – they were the same rank, but he would never have thought of calling the other man anything but Inspector Cochrane. His in-tray was empty. Inspector Cochrane was going to love registration. All those cards to check! The day they had introduced a speed limit in the city, five years ago, Inspector Cochrane had spent his entire weekend off on Union Street, stopping anyone even accelerating sharply. You would have thought it had been done just to please him – he could barely contain himself.

Cattanach was grinning at the memory when there came a quick chap on the door, and Sergeant McAulay stuck his head round.

'Sir, you're wanted in – um – Loch Street, if you're available.'

'What's the problem?'

'A fire, sir.'

Cattanach, already on his feet, frowned.

'What kind of a fire? Surely the fire brigade are better at that kind of thing?'

'Well, sir, it was the fire brigade that called us, now that it's mostly out. It's round the back of the flats, in the drying green.'

'Bonfire out of control?'

'No, sir, a petrol fire.'

'A petrol …? Oh! Oh, I see. All right, I'm on my way.'

The little man who lived in the ground floor flat, the flat with direct access to the square of rough grass beside the washhouse that all the flats shared, was plump, and bald, and agitated, with a startlingly white collar to his shirt. The constable whose beat included Loch Street was hovering, ready to snatch him if he tried to abscond, but happy to hand him over to Cattanach with a smart salute. The little man jerked back, as though the constable had aimed a blow at him.

'I never thought!' he said. His name, apparently, was Ronald Sutherland. His little eyes flickered from the blackened stonework of the covered lane that led to the drying green, to the group of his neighbours, red-eyed and resentful, glaring at him from across the street where the fire brigade had sent them for safety. The stink of petrol must have been enough to drive them back, in any case. The small man could not, though, apparently, meet Cattanach's eye.

'So what was the plan?' Cattanach asked.

'Oh, aye, well, the plan was to get the place tidied up for the war, ken? The wallpaper and the paintwork inside, and the windows and the doors outside. These fellows'll be away fighting soon, and then who'll keep my place looking smart, eh?'

'Aye,' said Cattanach, 'it's a major question, right enough, at times like these.'

The little man eyed him for a moment, but failed to detect

any outright sarcasm. He really looked almost inflated, as if someone had been at him with a bicycle pump. Cattanach wondered if the coming war would slim him down.

'And they were on their dinner, you see, the painters. Well, of course, I don't smoke: I find it leaves a nasty smell, and it yellows the walls so quickly.'

Cattanach was beginning to wonder if he had been summoned for a talk on home decorating.

'But the painters smoke, and of course they didn't know …'

'They didn't know that you had a small, but fragrant, barrel of petrol tucked in by your kitchen door?'

'That's it,' said Mr. Sutherland. 'You'd have thought they could have smelled it, right enough.'

'Perhaps with all the paint, though,' said Cattanach.

'Aye, maybe. Anyway, the next thing I ken is there's a bang, and a great light up the back of the house! Well, of course, my first thought was the blackout,' he said dutifully.

'Not so much of an issue at dinner time,' Cattanach pointed out.

'No … maybe not. Then I realised what must have happened, for the painters had run through the lanie to the street, yelling, and of course I went out the front door to see what was going on, and there's smoke and flames, and the neighbours are screaming …' He cast an apologetic look in their direction, but there was little gratitude in return. In fact, the constable took a few slow steps forward, just to remind the neighbours that now was not a good time for any kind of mob attack. There was a big fellow among them with yellow hair who looked more than ready for a rammie.

'Did you call the fire brigade?'

The man shook his head.

'One of the painters did it – there's a box at the end of the street.'

'And was anyone hurt, do you know?'

'Hurt?' He looked bewildered, and lost a sizeable portion of Cattanach's sympathy, which had not been great to start with. 'I have no idea.'

'Well, with glass flying about and sheets of flame, there's the off-chance,' said Cattanach. 'I'll make enquiries.'

There was a pause.

'Does that mean you're away? Have you finished with me?' asked the little man, his eyes suddenly hopeful.

'Not yet, sir, I'm afraid. You see, I'll need to ask you how long that barrel of petrol has been in your drying green?'

'How long …? Oh … I'm not sure. I mean, ages, probably. I'd quite forgotten it was there.'

'Had you indeed? Have you a car, sir?'

'I … yes, I suppose I do.'

'So the petrol was for your own personal use? In the car?'

'It …' he swallowed, then swallowed again. 'It might have been.' His tiny eyes darted around the street again – looking for his car? Or for someone who might contradict his story?

'I see.'

'Petrol's not rationed yet, though, is it?' asked the little man, in a bold moment. Cattanach looked down at him thoughtfully.

'No, it's not, not yet. But hoarding it is already an offence, and the fine will depend on how long you've had that petrol there. So perhaps you might tax your memory a little more, sir – or shall I ask your neighbours when they saw it arrive?'

The little man began to bluster.

'It's really – it's not that long. Maybe yesterday? Or at most the day before?'

'And then there's the matter of all your neighbours' windows, right up the back of the tenement – and the tenement behind you, too, I'd say. That's a gey lot of broken glass, don't you think? Never mind the extra painting – assuming you want to employ the same painters again.'

'All of the windows? I'll have to pay for all of them?'

'Well, your neighbours know who was responsible. I suspect they'll be having words with you, don't you, sir?'

'Oh, my, oh, my! Oh, michty! How am I to afford all that?'

The constable, who had been hovering throughout, leaned forward helpfully.

'If you don't need your car, sir, maybe now would be a good time to sell it?'

'Do you think the petrol was for himself, sir, or was he planning to sell it on?' asked the constable when they had walked away from the scene.

'No idea, constable. I shouldn't have thought many in this area would have a car for their own use, but perhaps he has it for his business, whatever it might be.'

'He's an antique dealer, sir. On a small scale.'

'Well, then, he might need to scale it down further. Down to antiques he can carry on the bus, perhaps,' said Cattanach. 'But not cans of hoarded petrol. Make sure you get a few witnesses from the neighbours to say how long that barrel was at the back of the flat.'

Selling his car.

Later, in his house near Kittybrewster, with his suit still reeking of petrol smoke, Cattanach stood in his shirtsleeves with his hands in his pockets, and stared out at his car parked in the street. It was not the only one there – here, where relatively comfortable shopkeepers had their modest terraced houses and little private gardens, there were four or five cars parked under roadside trees, and his navy Baby Austin did not stand out. At seven horsepower, he did not think it would use up much of the petrol ration. According to some of the paperwork in his in-tray, he had eleven days before the rationing would start – he would have to register himself, and the car, with some office in Dundee. And then what? How far would he be able to travel, and how often?

Suddenly, like the little man in Loch Street, with his white collar and his small-scale antiques, he felt like filling a barrel in the back garden.

That car, and all it meant, was his lifeline.

3

CATTANACH WALKED TO work on Wednesday morning. He usually did, but today the walk was spoiled by the thought of petrol rationing – and then a sense of guilt that he was more anxious about petrol rationing than about the war itself.

The builders had already started when he arrived, and he was sure that Inspector Cochrane would already be at his desk, hard at his paperwork, probably with the window open for fresh air. So it came as a bit of a relief when the sergeant at the desk stopped him, and made a discreet gesture towards the benches in the waiting room behind him.

'Woman and her daughter,' he murmured. 'Something about yon wee laddie killed by the lorry on King Street – yesterday morning, mind?'

'I thought that was an accident,' said Cattanach, just as quietly. The sergeant shook his head as if to say he had no clue, either, and left Cattanach to it. Cattanach turned and took his first look at the visitors.

'Good morning,' he said. 'Would you like to come into this room here? Sergeant, will you bring some tea, please?'

'Och, no!' the woman objected. 'No, we dinna want to bother you! It'll only take a mintie, I'm sure.'

'We'll be much more comfortable in here,' said Cattanach. 'And, you see, that will leave space in the waiting room for anyone else coming in.'

'Oh!' The woman looked about her, as if expecting to see

hordes of the general public queuing eagerly for a space. 'Well, if you're sure we won't be in the way at all …'

She was a thin, hunched woman with a green coat several years old, pulled tight to a narrow waist. Her hat was brown, and had been out on many a rainy day, by the look of it: there was an over-felted, misshapenness to it, and the felt flower that had graced the band was sorrowful and saggy. The child she propelled before her, though, aged about ten, was a much less apologetic being. She gave Cattanach a steady look before taking her seat in the interview room, then stared about her as if taking notes. Cattanach was sure they would be detailed and accurate.

'Now, then, Mrs. - ?'

'Hawthorne,' said the woman. 'Gladys Hawthorne.'

'Very good,' said Cattanach. 'And you are?'

'Maggie Hawthorne,' said the girl clearly. 'Are you no going to make a note of our names, sir?'

'My memory's not that bad!' Cattanach smiled. 'But I'll write them down when I'm ready. My name is Alec Cattanach – Inspector. Will you take some tea?' The sergeant had appeared in good time, which probably meant that the tea had been stewing. 'I recommend some sugar with it.'

Mrs. Hawthorne shook her head quickly, but Maggie took her cup and solemnly added three heaped teaspoons of sugar. She stirred it slowly, sitting up very straight, her cardigan buttoned up to the collar of her fresh-looking blouse.

'I gather,' said Cattanach, 'that you've come here because you have something to tell me about the terrible accident yesterday. William Campbell, isn't that right?'

'Terrible,' repeated Mrs. Hawthorne, clutching the word for reassurance. 'It was terrible. Bad enough that there's a war on.'

'Were you present at the scene, Mrs. Hawthorne?'

'Me? No! Not at all. What would I be doing out on King Street at that hour of the morning?' She made it sound like the middle of the night. 'No, Maggie and her brother were away out– like she should be the day with no school to go to – and Mr. Hawthorne had gone off to the graniteworks, so I was making the beds and redding up the breakfast dishes.' She stopped, taken aback at how much she had said all in one go.

'So did you see the accident, Maggie?' he asked gently.

Constable Gauld had shuddered when he had talked about it. But Maggie gave a decisive shake of her shiny bobbed head.

'No, sir, I didna. But I saw Billy the day before.'

'I'm sorry, sir,' said Mrs. Hawthorne, interrupting Maggie. 'It'll be nothing, I'm sure. But she was that determined to come here and tell you – tell someone. I'm sure the mannie on the desk would have been enough. You'll have more important things to be getting on with than listening to a wee lassie.'

'Well, let's see,' said Cattanach, trying to placate both at once. He had the feeling he had failed in both cases. 'Go on, then, Maggie. Where did you see Billy? This is Billy Campbell, is it?'

'A' course!' said Maggie, as if there were no other Williams in the world. 'Billy lives next door to us – well, nearly. Old Mr. Slebarski lives in between, but he's deaf.' And therefore, clearly, did not count. 'So Billy and me are – well, no friends, ken, because he's a boy. But we've kent each other since he came here. And whiles he comes and talks to me, ken, when there's things he doesna want to talk to boys about. Because, ken, when you're a boy and you dinna want to say a'thing to a'body, it's all right if you tell a girl. It's like not telling a'body.'

Cattanach thought this was an astute observation, but merely nodded.

'Stop wasting the gentleman's time, Maggie!' hissed her mother, but Maggie was set on her story.

'And Monday was a blithe day and I was in our drying green, and after a whilie there he was at the wee holie in the fence, ken.'

'What holie in the fence?' demanded her mother. Maggie sighed.

'There's a wee holie, Ma, it's always been there. That's how we get from Mr. Slebarski's green into ours. And then there's the ither one into Billy's.'

Mrs. Hawthorne's well-ordered world, where fences had no holes, had received a blow, and she fell silent. Maggie took full advantage.

'So we sat there, him in Mr. Slebarski's green and me in ours, and he telt me what was going on. Well, he didna, really, he just – he just said things.'

'What kind of things?' Cattanach nudged her as she hesitated.

'When you say it, you wonder if it's a'thing. He said – he said that he didna much like having a criminal in the family.'

There was a pause.

'Those exact words, Maggie?' asked Cattanach.

'Exactly,' said Maggie, with certainty. 'Billy aye sounded old for his years,' she added, sounding ancient for her own. 'I waited to see if he would say a'thing else, and when he didna, I said I thought I wouldna much fancy it myself. And then I asked him if it was someone close, and he said well, it wasna his mother nor his stepfather – there's no one but him, ken – and I thought he wouldna say a'thing more. But then he was just saying something about his uncle, when Mr. Slebarski came to his back door and he scooted off to the holie in the other fence.'

'His uncle?'

Maggie nodded firmly.

'Aye, that's what he said. His uncle.'

'Do you know his family?' asked Cattanach. 'What uncles has he?'

'Och, he has a wheen of uncles,' said Mrs. Hawthorne, recovering from the revelation about holes in fences. 'His stepfather – he's away with the trawlers – he has, oh, it must be three brothers? Maybe four? And they're all about the place. Is that all? Can we go now?'

'Wait just a minute,' said Cattanach. 'This is when I want to write a few things down, Maggie, to make sure I remember them. And then maybe you could give it a read through, to make sure I've got it all right?'

'Aye, I'll do that for you,' said Maggie confidently. 'You dinna want to be making mistakes. A wee lad said his uncle was a criminal, and then the next day he's dead. That's no very good, is it?'

'But tell me first,' said Cattanach, acknowledging her point with a nod, 'what like of a lad was he?' With another girl of her age, he might have made some suggestions, but he felt he could rely on Maggie.

'He was a quiet loon,' she said, after a moment's thought. 'He likes to think about things afore he does them.'

'Did he like to tell stories?'

'Only ones that were true,' said Maggie, surprisingly. 'The

other lads'll tell you all sorts – their uncle in America's that rich he's built a house with fifteen bedrooms, or their big brother won the Victoria Cross at the Somme, and you ken fine it's all rubbish. But Billy wasna like that at all. He didna say that much, but what he said you could tell was true. And that's why I wanted to come here, Ma – the polisman needs to know about Billy's uncle and his crimes! And anyway, he was my friend. Even if he was a boy.' She stopped abruptly and focussed hard on the table.

'Right, well, Maggie, let's get this all down on a bit of paper, and you can get back to – whatever you were doing.' He had to keep reminding himself the schools were shut. A relief for the teacher, perhaps – he had no doubt that Maggie kept hers very much in line. He liked Maggie.

And perhaps because he liked Maggie, and thought she had more sense than many of the adults he came across, he decided to look further into the tragic death of William Campbell. When Maggie and her mother had gone – her mother hurrying her out of the station with much head-bobbing and mutters of apology – he made sure he had the right address, and took a tram up King Street to the best stop for Seaton.

King Street was the road carved over a hundred years ago to take Aberdonians north, up the coast. Once the city tenements were past, it opened wide, with one half of the ancient university – King's College – in behind its playing fields to the left, and new council housing off to the right, between the road and the sea. As he walked from King Street down amongst the new houses, he could see they had left room to spread still, a green expanse of machair up to where the ground was raised for the road that ran along above the beach. Here, small tents and huts had been erected, he was not sure why. The beach itself was long, and flat, and perfect for invasion. One of the memoranda on his desk mentioned tank traps and lookout posts and fortifications. These modern houses with their neat green gardens could soon be on the front line.

He found the Campbell house without difficulty, though he watched from a distance for a moment or two, hoping that he would not embarrass Mrs. Hawthorne by appearing outside her house so soon after her visit to the police station. Now he knew who lived in the three houses, he observed them with interest.

The Hawthornes' house was, as he would have expected, clean and neat and plain, unchallenging, eager, he would even have said, not to cause offence – though perhaps here he was thinking too much of Mrs. Hawthorne herself. The next, then, would be the home of the Pole, Mr. Slebarski – a tailor, apparently. He would most likely be out and at work – Cattanach had not asked whether or not he lived alone. His garden, even at the front, was productive – rows of cabbage of different kinds were flourishing, and netting showed where peas or beans had grown and been cleared away – further than that Cattanach could not identify, but he was impressed. The next house, then, must belong to the Campbells.

The garden here was full of autumn colour, late roses, ornamental leaves tinged with red, pretty stones collected perhaps from the beach and used to line the path to the fresh, bright front door. The curtains at the windows were frilled, and there were elaborate ornaments on the window sills inside. A rather different woman from Mrs. Hawthorne, then, he thought. Only the fact that the frilled curtains were closed, at this time of day, gave any hint that this might be a house in mourning.

His respectful knock on the door brought a harassed-looking woman to answer it.

'Mrs. Campbell?' he asked. She looked him quickly up and down, and frowned.

'Aye, but no the one you're looking, I'd guess. Who are you?'

'Inspector Cattanach, Aberdeen Police, Mrs. Campbell. Do you think your … sister-in-law?' – the woman nodded sharply – 'would be willing to answer a few questions about the accident?'

'Inspector?' queried the woman, giving him another inspection. 'You dinna look like one.' She tilted her head for a moment, then, as if she had heard some distant instruction, nodded again. 'Aye, come on in. Though yon constable from down the street has already been round.'

'Thank you,' he said, removed his hat, and stepped inside.

4

THE INSIDE OF the house was as frilly and colourful as one would expect. The Mrs. Campbell who had answered the door – who looked like the kind of woman who would haul your boat up from the beach, pull your boots off, and then gut a crate of herring in the time it took you to change your socks – showed Cattanach into a parlour, dim with the curtains closed, where a young woman sat on one of two easy chairs by a small unlit fire.

'Mabel,' she said, an edge to her voice, 'this loon says he's fra the pollis. About Billy, ken.' She turned to Cattanach. 'A fly cup?' she asked.

Cattanach hesitated, then nodded.

'Thank you.'

'How?'

'Milk, no sugar, thanks.' She left the room. On the other side of the fireplace was a similar easy chair, but it looked as if it had a name on it. Not wanting to offend, he found a hard chair, and pulled it up to sit fairly close to Mabel Campbell, who was watching him with curiosity. A smile touched the corner of her bright red lips.

'What's your name, then?' she asked, as if she had just met him at a party. But grief took people different ways.

'Alec Cattanach, Mrs. Campbell. Just to make sure – you're Billy's mother, yes?'

'Aye, I suppose,' she said. 'Even though he's dead. Poor wee lad,' she added, almost as an afterthought. 'And you're a polisman? You dinna look like one.'

'We don't all wear uniform, Mrs. Campbell.'

'Aye, but even in a uniform you'd no look right. Now, maybe an officer's uniform …' She tilted her head to one side, and her glossy hair caught a stray light from the window and glinted. 'Aye, like they posh ones at the barracks - that would suit you very well! I like a man who looks smart.'

Cattanach blinked.

'I wondered if I might ask a few questions, Mrs. Campbell? Where was Billy off to? Was he on his own?'

'I should think he was. He usually was. I don't know where he was away to – he packed up a piece in his schoolbag and away for the day, I suppose.' She frowned, very slightly. 'But it was an accident, was it no? They told me the lorry driver was blaming himself, but it wasna his fault. That's what they said.'

'That's what I've heard, too,' said Cattanach. He kept his voice low, calming, he hoped, though she did not look as if she needed calming. Mrs. Campbell sat sideways on the chair with her legs crossed, her hands folded on her lap, her head turned coquettishly slightly away from him. She wore a plain black dress, but with it were two chains that looked like gold, several rings, and a brooch with red stones in it that might have been garnets. Fine feathers for a woman in Seaton, perhaps.

'Then why are you here?' The other Mrs. Campbell was back, a cup and saucer in each hand. 'We've no fancy pieces. She doesna bake,' she explained, jerking her head at Mabel.

'May I ask which Mrs. Campbell you are, then?' He smiled. 'Just for the sake of clarity.'

'I'm Tommy Campbell's wifie,' she said. 'Lizzie's my name. She's Robbie Campbell's wifie. Then there's Edward – his wife's Isabel – and Sammy – she's Betty – and then there's Arthur. He's no married yet.'

The four uncles, then. Mentally, Cattanach noted the names.

'And all the men are at the fishing, are they?'

'Och, no!' Lizzie Campbell chuckled. 'Och, dearie me, no. Robbie does the fishing. My man's in the shipbuilding, and so's Arthur. Edward works in the harbourmaster's office. Sammy's away on yon big liners, ken? I think he's halfway to New York just now. The dear only knows what'll happen now there's a war, though. You'd think, after the last one, people would have more wit than to try that again.'

'But all connected with the sea,' said Cattanach, focussing on the family. More mental notes.

'So that's your questions answered, Inspector. Why are you here?'

'That's not all my questions, I'm afraid. You're right we have no reason to think that the lorry driver was to blame.' He took a breath. 'I'm sorry to have to distress you any more than you must be already, Mrs. Campbell, but can you tell me if Billy was worried about anything recently? Did he mention, perhaps, anyone he was scared of? Someone he had fought with in the playground, maybe?'

'Billy? Fighting in the playground?' Mabel gave a quick, breathy laugh. 'I never heard about it, then!'

'Was anything worrying him?'

'No!'

'Not that you'd be able to tell,' put in Lizzie Campbell. 'Billy wasna much of a one for telling you how he was feeling, ken.'

'Ach, boys dinna talk,' said Mabel, but Lizzie was shaking her head.

'They talk more than yon one. He was a quiet lad, Inspector. Never into anything that you'd call mischief, never cheeky, never sly, either. He was a serious wee fellow. He'd read the paper, take it all in. Not just the sports pages, either.'

Cattanach glanced at Mabel, but Lizzie seemed the one more likely to talk – the one who knew Billy better, oddly.

'Did you see much of him?'

'We all live hereabouts, well, this side of the town,' said Lizzie. 'He's ages with my youngest. I thought when Billy came they would play together, but Billy's not – not one for playing much, either.'

'What were his interests?'

Both women stared at each other.

'I have no idea,' said Lizzie, but Mabel just shook her head.

'He was aye out, or in his room. I dinna ken what he got up to.'

You could have asked, thought Cattanach, suddenly irate on Billy's behalf. You could have shown a bit of interest.

'Would you mind if I took a look at his room? Did he have his own room?'

'Oh, aye,' said Mabel with a sigh. 'Lizzie, would you … I'm sorry, Inspector, I'm that bone-tired …'

'Grief,' said Lizzie, as she led the way to the back of the house. It formed one downstairs flat of the small block. 'He was an odd one, and she's no the motherly type, but she's grieving all the same. Here's his room. Dinna worry, he's in the front room, himself.'

It was the small back bedroom, but well arranged and comfortable. The quilt on the bed, with two blankets underneath, looked warm, and there was a square of carpet on the floor – more than Cattanach had had in his boyhood bedroom. The room was orderly, more than clean and tidy. There were more books than he would have expected to see, and they were lined with precision along their shelf, spines touching the edge and no more. He was not surprised, on closer inspection, to see that they were arranged according to subject – plants and animals, apparently, including a couple of small white volumes in the Observer's books series. The only picture on the wall was an embroidered Bible text, taking Cattanach by surprise. It read 'Go now, and sin no more'.

'My sister-in-law's gey religious,' said Lizzie, noting his interest.

'Which one?'

'Isabel, Edward's wife.'

'Nicely worked, though.'

'She's the one with the time for that kind of thing,' said Lizzie, with a hint of resentment. Isabel's husband worked in the harbourmaster's office, Cattanach remembered. What scope for crime was there in the harbourmaster's office? But he would look into all of them.

'Tell me about the family,' he said. Lizzie hesitated.

'The three of them, or the whole boiling of us?'

'Start with the three of them.'

'Is there something wrong? Something wrong about the way Billy died?'

'We don't know. There might be. Would that surprise you?'

'Well aye, aye, it would. I mean … och, I liked the boy. He didna come out and tell you things, or not much, but there was something – decent about him. I ken he was only ten, but you felt you could rely on him, d'you see?'

Cattanach nodded.

'And, well, what?' She was asking herself, and he said nothing. 'Robbie's the second oldest of the boys – my Tommy's the oldest. Robbie had a sweetheart at school, but she died of scarlet fever. They all thought he would get over her, but he seemed not to. He just fished, and made his money, and kept it, and fished more. Then one day he said he was to marry, and he brought her home.' She jerked her head towards the stairs.

'You think she married him for the money?'

'No, not a bit of it, for I found out later she had more money than he had. Billy would have been comfortably off when it came to it, so I gather. But she's an odd one. We could never make out where Robbie found her, really. And she never talks about where she was, who her folks are, who Billy's faither was, where the money came from … She's never really fitted in with us, but then, I dinna think she's that bothered. She's friendly enough, and she remembers the bairns' birthdays and such, a wee gift or two at Hogmanay, but she's no someone you'd sit down with for a good gossip, ken? Whereas Betty and I – and even Isabel, for all her airs and graces – the three of us get on grand, and you'd put the kettle on in each other's kitchens and all without thinking about it. But I think today's the first I've ever been in Mabel's kitchen. It's all parlour with her.'

She stopped, and looked sideways at Cattanach as if she felt she had said too much.

'This could be very helpful, thank you, Mrs. Campbell. If we can find out anything that will help us –'

'If a'body touched that poor wee lad, I'll skin and bone him myself,' said Lizzie firmly. 'So I dinna ken where you're going with this, but if there's anything I can say or do that'll help, I will. So what else do you want here?'

The boy's schoolbag lay on the floor by his bed, presumably returned there from the street where he had died. School or not, Billy needed something to carry his dinner in. There was a splatter of dark blood across the fake leather case – you would hardly see it if you did not know. Cattanach nodded at it.

'May I look inside?'

'Go on,' said Lizzie. She was propped now, arms folded, against the doorpost. Her black dress had seen a few funerals, he thought, but if he offended her in any way she would probably throw him out single-handed. He picked the bag up delicately, and set it on the bed, opening the buckles one by one.

Inside was a brown paper bag, a little greasy at the corners, a notebook, and a small black tube. He lifted out the bag.

'His dinner?'

'Aye, I'd better take that,' agreed Lizzie. They opened the bag and peered inside to make sure. A cheese sandwich, scented with pickle, sat soggy at the bottom.

Fortunately the grease had not marked the notebook, which was wrapped in waxed cloth anyway. A pencil had been stuck inside it, and a loop of elastic held it shut. Cattanach set it on the bed beside the bag, and pulled out the black tube. It was a little telescope.

'For looking at birds, and such,' said Lizzie. 'He carried it with him everywhere. It's a wonder it wasna in his pocket.'

'It's a nice one,' said Cattanach, running it out to its full length. Not large, just the right size for small arms to support, just the right size for a pocket.

'I think his faither brought it back last time he was home.' There was a catch in Lizzie's voice.

'Has anyone managed to get word to Mr. Campbell?' he asked.

'Aye, by the radio, in a roundabout way. But he'll be back … oh, a fortnight, maybe.'

'Deep sea fishing, then?'

'Oh, aye. None of your lobster pots for Robbie! Off for weeks at a time, up Greenland or thereabouts …'

'It'll be lonely for her, now,' he remarked, with a gesture to the stairs.

'Och,' said Lizzie, rousing herself, 'we're all close by. We'll make sure she's all right. Aye, that's what we'll do. Whatever …'

'May I take this? The notebook, I mean,' he said, laying the telescope back in the bag. 'I'll make sure it's returned.'

'I doubt she'll miss it,' said Lizzie sadly. 'But I'll tell her if she does. She did love him, ken. She's just not the motherly kind.'

5

NOT THE MOTHERLY kind – she had said it twice. But families were like that, he knew: there was often a kind of catchphrase for each member, a summing up for those who were well aware of all the complexities of everyone's character, but needed a shorthand for them. 'He has no sense of direction – couldn't find his way out of a paper bag.' 'See her? She'd forget her head if it wasna screwed on.' 'Aye, Mabel, well, she loves him. But she's just not the motherly kind, is she?' And heads would nod around the kitchen table.

He walked back out on to King Street, and met there Constable Gauld walking his beat.

'Can you show me where the boy was killed, Gauld?'

'Aye, sir, no far fra here.' He began to walk at beat pace up King Street. Cattanach fell in beside him.

'Where was he off to, do you think?'

'Who knows, sir? Nobody's said. He had his schoolbag with him.'

'It's at his home now.' He could feel the notebook stiff in his coat pocket, the pencil still inside.

'Here, sir.'

They stopped at an ordinary bit of the pavement, by an ordinary bit of the road, where an ordinary little boy had lost his life. Someone had been out and scrubbed it clean, for a piece a couple of yards across was paler than the rest, and there was a faint tang of bleach.

'See the way I think it happened, sir, was the lorry driver was looking ahead to the busy junction. He wanted to turn in to St. Machar Drive, but he couldn't get out because the traffic was coming past, so he was watching his mirror. And from all the witnesses say, he would have had no chance anyway, for the lad just stepped off the pavement. He'll maybe have been crossing to the school gate there, sir.' He pointed across the street. 'But whether he was ready to cross, or just tripped, or what … What's your interest, sir, if I can ask?'

'Someone came to tell us that the boy said something odd, the day before he died. Something that made me wonder if it was all entirely straightforward. You're a neighbour, aren't you? How well do you know the family?'

But Gauld was shaking his head.

'Not well, sir. I ken his mother to see – I'm no sure I would even recognise his father, for he's away with the trawlers more than he's home.'

'There are uncles, apparently?'

'Oh, aye, sir. Well, they were older than me and their children are younger, so I'd maybe know … let me think. Edward's the grand one, he works at the harbourmaster's office. Oh, Arthur was the year above me at school, so I remember him. He's at the shipbuilding, sir.'

'What is he like?'

'Arthur likes a party, sir, and a pretty girl.'

'Anything we would be interested in?'

'I've never heard it said, sir.'

'And the rest of the family? Their reputation?'

Constable Gauld wrinkled his forehead under the brim of his helmet.

'They're a respectable lot, from all I've heard, sir. Arthur would be the wildest, and he's no that wild.'

'Hm. I'll go and see if I can have a word with his class teacher. I wonder how?'

'That'd be Miss Meston, sir. She's no bad.'

'I'll tell her you said so, Constable,' said Cattanach with a grin.

But if he had hoped for much in the way of revelation from Miss Meston, he was to be disappointed. The school office directed him to an empty classroom, rather than to Miss Meston's home.

'We don't think the schools will be closed for long,' said the secretary, 'and there's always work to be done.'

A kindly, tired-looking woman set aside a pile of books she was mending to speak with him, but could tell him nothing more than he had heard already. Billy was quiet, diligent, disliked rule-breaking, kept his word, and somehow, despite being a little strange, had not been the kind to attract the attention of bullies or playground roughs.

'I hope you don't believe that one of his classmates pushed him, Inspector,' she said. 'I should like to think that if someone in the class had done such a thing, with such terrible consequences, that it would be obvious in their behaviour. None of them could be so heartless as to keep it hidden, surely?'

'This may well be a wild goose chase, Miss Meston. I hope it is.'

She glanced about her classroom, perhaps picturing her pupils at their desks, wondering about Billy and his friends. He wondered where Maggie Hawthorne sat. The lofty windows were crisscrossed with tape, and it took him a moment to think what it was for. Air raids, he realised. To stop the glass going everywhere.

He took Billy's notebook back to the police station. He had not even glanced inside it before he asked to borrow it: it could be blank, for all he knew. But the pages on one side of the inserted pencil looked used, greyer than the ones on the other side. If it was notes for his arithmetic homework, then serve Cattanach right.

But it was not arithmetic: it was more in the way of a nature diary. Billy had kept notes on several expeditions he had made, apparently on his own, and on all he had seen. Judging by the dates of the expeditions, the notebook had been a birthday present, or bought with a birthday sixpence, for the notes began in May and as far as Cattanach remembered that had been around his birthday. Ten years and four months.

The expedition notes were meticulous, the identification of the various birds, animals and plants he had seen on them impressive and accurate. On most pages he had tried to draw something he had seen: these sketches, sadly, were lamentable. His descriptions, though, were accomplished for his age. He did not seem to have ventured too far: he had gone to the beach and watched sanderlings ('early', Billy had written beside the account), down to the tree-bordered playing fields at the university and seen foxes, rabbits, badgers, and rooks, up to the Don estuary to the north, and seen seals and wading birds and gulls, and even a pod of harbour dolphins. He had kept himself busy. Cattanach wished he could have met him. He had done much the same thing himself, at Billy's age. And later.

He busied himself for a moment retrieving from his memory the four Campbell uncles and their wives and occupations. Robbie the fisherman, his wife Mabel, and son Billy. Edward in the harbourmaster's office and his religious wife Isabel – did they have children? Why did Isabel have time to do embroideries? Tommy and Arthur, shipbuilders – at Hall Russell, perhaps, or another yard. Tommy was Lizzie's husband, and they had at least two children, one of them the same age as Billy. Sammy was Betty's husband, and he was on the liners – what did Betty do with herself, when her husband was halfway to New York? And Arthur was single. He'd put the word out, check the lists, see if any of them had been up to anything of interest to the police in the past.

'Any word on the unconscious man from the tram crash?'

Sergeant McAulay looked up at him from his copy of the *Evening Express*. The front office was quiet, and Cattanach was not going to grudge him a catch-up on the news.

'Still unconscious, sir, so I hear.'

'And no identification yet?'

'Nothing, sir.'

'Odd. You'd have thought a wife or a mother would have come looking by now.'

'Maybe glad enough to be rid of him, sir.'

'Cheerful thought.'

He went up to his office, and tried to stop his heart sinking at the sight of Inspector Cochrane at the other desk. Inspector Cochrane nodded solemnly at him, pressed one finger to his lips and pointed down at his paperwork, indicating that he required silence. Cattanach wondered if anyone would come looking for Inspector Cochrane if he were knocked unconscious in a road accident.

On Friday, Billy Campbell was to be buried in the rambling St. Peter's Cemetery, down King Street from where he had died.

Cattanach, escaping from yet more memoranda threatening to slide down from his in-tray and smother him, went to pay his respects, making sure he reached the house well before the coffin left so that he could see the aunts, as well as the uncles. Mrs. Hawthorne, Maggie's mother, gaped when she saw him, but reluctantly helped him with the identification of the family members: plump, red-faced Isabel clinging to the arm of smartly dressed Edward, dabbing her eyes constantly; Tommy and Arthur, hands scrubbed and best suits on but still somehow giving off the aroma of oil; Lizzie there with Tommy and with a boy, older than Billy had been, but not quite a man – just about old enough to come to his cousin's funeral. No Sammy, of course, nor Robbie, Billy's stepfather. But Betty, Sammy's wife, was there, with a grown-up daughter slightly over-made-up, unpractised at grooming. Mrs. Hawthorne, disapproving, told Cattanach that the daughter worked in Woolworths on the cosmetics. Betty and Lizzie saw to the food with tight-lipped efficiency, while Mabel, in a new black dress and different jewellery, sat in splendour in the parlour, receiving her guests like a queen. A typical family on an atypical day, mourning for a little boy who should have been there with them – even if he would probably have slipped out to the garden to watch a wren, or to talk to his little friend Maggie two gardens away.

None of the uncles set bells ringing in Cattanach's head, none called to mind any 'Wanted' pictures he had seen recently, or any paragraphs in the *Police Gazette*. His memory for faces was good, but he could not say he had seen any of them before. Arthur's hair was slicked back in the latest fashion and his suit was new and neat. Edward wore his suit as if it were his second skin. Tommy was more uncomfortable, Cattanach would have said: this was his Sunday best, not his Friday shipbuilding gear. Nevertheless Tommy had an authority that even Edward lacked: while the women dealt with the food and drink, he was directing his brothers in a more solemn ceremony, the arrangements for the walk to the burial ground.

More neighbours arrived, more unfamiliar faces – Mrs. Hawthorne pointed out Mr. Slebarski, the tailor from next door. They came to pay their respects to the little boy, and then to Mabel Campbell. Constable Gil Gauld, a neighbour himself, slipped in, saw Cattanach, and nodded to him. He was off duty, and not in uniform. Lizzie, along with Betty and, reluctantly, Isabel, made enough pots of tea to float all five of the Campbell brothers, and kept pouring. Mismatched china pointed to borrowed cups and saucers, plenty of fancy pieces showed that even if Mabel did not bake, her family and friends certainly did. Away from the direct proximity of Mabel, there was debate about the war – was the Government to blame? How long would it last? What would happen to the fishing? Chatter, discussion and gossip, though maybe not so much as with many funerals. This was no place for long-familiar anecdotes of a long, well-lived life, or discussions over what would happen to the business, or who would inherit the land. Billy had been too young for conventional funeral talk.

At last the minister came, and said his prayers over the little coffin in the other front room, the main bedroom. The uncles, Tommy, Arthur and Edward, and Tommy's son, pale as rice pudding, lifted the coffin and made for the door, the women parting a way for them, then following after the procession of men to wave a final farewell.

Cattanach and Constable Gauld joined the men at the tail of the procession. As they assembled themselves on the roadway, he glanced back at the women clustered around the bright-painted front door, around the grieving mother, all their eyes on the coffin.

Except for Mabel. Mabel was not looking at the coffin at all. She was staring at someone – someone in the procession. And the look on her face was no longer one of grief. No: it was the look of someone just beginning to realise something quite, quite terrifying.

6

CATTANACH LOOKED QUICKLY about him. A funeral procession should not have been an easy place to hide, he would have thought, but he could see no obvious reason for Mabel Campbell's fearful stare. He checked – no, he had not been mistaken. She was very frightened, but the women made a kind of block around her and she could not move, nor could he have easily approached.

No one that he could see amongst the mourners was looking anywhere near her, and even as he tried to make out exactly who was in the line of that stare, he realised they were all in constant movement, angling themselves into the right positions, not too far to the front in case they should usurp the family's position, not too far to the rear where they might be left behind. There must have been around fifty men now, from the family, from the neighbourhood - perhaps from the Campbells' church, or friends and colleagues of the uncles, too. They moved off like a slow murmuration of starlings, already trying to negotiate a corner in good order. Cattanach allowed himself to slide to the back, where he could watch everyone else – who had Mabel Campbell seen? – and found himself joined by Constable Gauld.

'Is there anyone here you don't know?' Cattanach murmured. 'Anyone who wasn't at the house?'

Gauld looked ahead.

'Loads of people, sir. You ken what it's like – you take a quick hour out of work, and you want to get to the interment, so you skip on the scones.'

'But men you don't know?'

'Aye, a good few, sir. I ken the ones in our street, and the uncles a bittie, like I said. But that's all.'

'No faces you recognise from, er, work?'

Gil Gauld gave a half-smile.

'I dinna think so, sir. But I'll keep my eyes open.'

They paced steadily along the street and out, with care, on to busy King Street. Traffic slowed around them. Pedestrians stopped, men removing their hats, women with heads bowed, all noting, no doubt, the size of the coffin. Cattanach scanned the crowds discreetly. He did not enjoy funerals, not this part. He felt like an actor in a peculiarly dull play, someone with no right to be on this particular stage, either. False pretences – he thought horribly that someone would point him out, cry out, 'That's no someone that knew Billy Campbell! That's a polis!'

It seemed a terribly long walk, this one, down past the university playing fields, the decent grey houses, to the stern railing-topped walls of St. Peter's Cemetery. The grand central gate stood open, the caretaker ready to direct them, for the cemetery was large and, in places, old and wild. But it was to the more modern area they went, to a grave with a headstone already in place, propped for safety, and a grave neatly dug. When the coffin was interred – a quick but decent process – the mourners stood for a moment, then began the inevitable tots of whisky at a respectful distance from the open grave. Cattanach took a moment to read the headstone: Billy's step-grandparents, and great grandparents, to judge by the names and dates. An established family in the area. All those uncles, just nearby. What was one of them up to? What had upset Billy, the day before he died?

Some of the men were heading back to the Campbell house, to collect their wives or to indulge in a last cup of tea. Others bade farewell and walked off to whatever yards or offices they had left to come here. None of them looked particularly frightening.

Gil Gauld managed not to salute, and disappeared to enjoy the rest of his day off in whatever manner he chose – the cinemas were shut, of course, for the duration, so he would miss that. Cattanach was not much of a cinema goer himself, but he had already noticed how much quieter the streets were at night now: people were cautious.

He caught a tram back down into town, staring out at the grey houses with their little gardens, then at the tenements, thinking of Billy Campbell. When he himself had been that age he had been interested in wildlife, too – somewhere he even had a similar notebook. He had been an observant boy. Many boys were, like Billy, and some made sure to cultivate it and use it in later life, as he himself did. What would Billy have done when he had grown up? Did he have ambitions or dreams? Had he told his friend Maggie? Perhaps he would have made a good polis.

Perhaps a good polis would have spotted the man in the funeral procession who had scared Mabel Campbell – unless that had been some kind of illusion. Perhaps he had misread her look. Perhaps it had been a sudden realisation of her loss.

He let the tram take him past his usual stop and round the corner into Union Street, where he joined the sudden crowd in the aisle and made his way slowly to the doors. He was still pondering as the passengers dispersed, the tram drew away, and the Town House was revealed, in all its Victorian glory. An elderly Bentley was stopped outside, and as he watched the driver climbed out and went to open the rear passenger door. A tall, white-haired man emerged, had a word with the driver, and was about to approach the revolving doors of the Town House when something made him stop, and turn. He scanned the road, and in a moment spotted Cattanach. He raised a hand in greeting. Cattanach paused, then crossed the busy street to meet him.

'Good day to you, Alec!' the man said. 'You look sombre.'

'I've just come from a funeral, sir,' Cattanach said. 'Work, but it was a young lad. Sad.'

'Very sad,' agreed the old man. 'I'm late for a meeting. Summoned to do our bit! But we forgot about the harvest traffic, so I must dash.'

'I'd better get back to work, too,' said Cattanach. They stood for a second, awkward, then the older man put out a gloved hand, and Cattanach shook it. With a nod of their heads, they parted. The old man vanished into the building, and Cattanach walked on round its bulk into Broad Street, where he could complete his circuit and get back to Queen Street and the police station.

In his office, mercifully unoccupied, he spent several hours trying to make sense of all the new paperwork that had appeared on his desk, enough of it to bury the old paperwork that he had still not managed to arrange. Cinemas. Street lighting. Telegraph poles. Luminous paint on the pavement. Shipping movements – what did he know about shipping movements? But in a town like this, where they had fished and whaled and built ships since they knew ships could be built, many of the police officers knew a great deal about shipping movements. Air raid protection for the shipyards – of course. The Germans, if they had any aeroplanes, any bombs, and any sense, would make for the shipyards. Aberdeen might be in for a bad time of it, unless the Germans kept their focus down south. And how many aeroplanes did Britain have? He had no idea. How many ships? How many soldiers? He felt suddenly adrift. If they were planning something in the police, at least he had some idea of how many officers he had at his disposal, how many cars, bicycles and radios. Now he was in the middle of someone else's plan, and he had no notion what was happening.

He turned his attention to the real work on his desk – the tram crash. According to a note from the inestimable Constable Leggatt, the driver was still in a ward at the Infirmary, with a broken leg. Leggatt had gathered up the man's address and the registration of what had been his lorry, but not much else, having had a deal of work to do with the rest of the casualties – the tram driver was badly injured, and his wife had decided to take out her anger on poor Leggatt. His black eye was the talk of the station, and was now keeping him off his beat. No member of the public likes to see their local policeman with a black eye. Cattanach, picking up the note, went to find him.

Leggatt had been put to work in the evidence store, a place that looked like the last resting place for all the city's least successful jumble sales. Leggatt himself had a dejected air as he tried to make a list of objects on a shelf. He brightened at once when Cattanach came in.

'Sir! Can I help you, sir?'

'I think so. Can you give me the latest news on the tram crash?'

'Maybe not the latest, sir. I've been out of action since yesterday dinner time.' He pointed to his eye. Black was not the word for it: it was a rainbow of delight.

'That was from the tram driver's wife?'

'That's right, sir. Is there any opening on the force for a police matron? She'd be fair and handy when the pubs close on a Saturday, sir.'

'Perhaps we should look into it. How is the tram driver?'

Leggatt's face turned sorrowful.

'It looks like a broken neck and back, sir, not to mention various other bits and pieces. He'll likely no work again. She was right to be angry.'

'And the other injured?'

'None so bad as that, sir. The lassie with the cut feet is away home, though she's no walking too far. The man that was knocked out is still out, so far as I know.'

'And there is still no information about him? No one has come forward to claim him?'

Leggatt shrugged.

'Again, sir, not as far as I know. There wasn't so much as a laundry mark on his shirt, though, so far as I can hear.'

'Hm. Mysterious. And the lorry driver?'

'Just the broken leg, and a bit of a knock on the head. He was a bit muddled when he spoke to me.'

'But he said he was from Dundee?'

'That's what he said, sir. He seemed sure enough about that.'

'Any idea what he was doing in Aberdeen?'

'None, sir.'

Cattanach paused, thinking.

'What was in the lorry?'

'Nothing, sir.'

'An empty lorry?'

'Aye, sir. Not a thing in it.'

The hospital was so new that it still smelled of fresh plaster and paint, almost as strongly as the usual hospital smell. Cattanach could still not visit it without thinking of Edward VIII, who had been supposed to open it but instead had nipped off to meet Mrs. Simpson – his brother, now the King, had stepped in at the last minute with his wife. The policing operation that morning had been complex, to say the least.

'Mr. Sandison?' Cattanach approached the bed that the sister had directed him to. 'Much brighter now,' she had said. 'Quite on his toes – or he would be, if he hadn't broken his leg.'

'Aye, doctor, that's me.' The man struggled to sit up a little, but the plaster on his leg looked particularly heavy.

'No driving for you for a bit, then, eh?' said Cattanach, taking a seat on the one hard chair. There were a few others in the ward, but they paid him no attention: it was not visiting time and they probably assumed, too, that he was a doctor. 'I gather you're from Dundee? You'll be keen to get back, somehow.'

'I'm as well here,' said the man comfortably. 'I'm no looking forward to telling the boss about his lorry.'

'Yes – it's in a worse state than you, certainly,' Cattanach agreed. 'You hadn't driven straight up here, had you? Overnight?'

'Naw,' said the man. He scratched his head, rearranging coarse black curls. 'I drove up the Monday, and I slept the night in the cab. It's no so bad, if it's no too cold.'

'Where were you heading?'

'Inverness,' said the man quickly.

'Taking a delivery?'

'Naw, I was away up to fetch something back.'

'What was that, then?'

'I dinna ken,' said Sandison, with an expansive gesture implying he would have made Cattanach a gift of his knowledge if he had had any. 'I pick up all sorts. It's that kind of a useful wee lorry, ken?'

'Well, it was,' qualified Cattanach. 'It's not going anywhere now, of course. And you are aware that you are under arrest?'

'Wait, now,' said Sandison, suddenly wary. 'I dinna mind seeing you around here afore, do I? I've been that confused.'

'The sister says you're much better now, Mr. Sandison. Quite well enough to have a chat with me. I'm Inspector Cattanach, of the City Police.'

'Och, be damned to it,' said Sandison, and slumped back on his pillows.

7

'DO I TAKE it, Mr. Sandison, that you have something to tell me?'

Sandison groaned.

'Not a bit of it,' he said. 'I've lost my boss's lorry, and I've bust my leg. What else do you want from me?'

'A good few people were injured in that crash,' said Cattanach. 'The tram driver isn't likely to drive again. There's another man hasn't come round yet – might never.'

'Aye, well, I'm sorry about them and all. But it wasna my fault.'

'That's not how the witnesses tell it,' said Cattanach, who had read all of Constable Leggatt's carefully gathered statements. He quoted from one of them: '"It was as if he had no idea the tram was there. He just kept going, straight on and into it." That's what they say, you know.'

'I braked. Maybe the brakes didna work properly.'

'There's no sign of braking. No one says they heard brakes, or saw you slow.'

'That's what I say. They didna work.'

'Perhaps you'd like us to contact our colleagues on the Dundee City force and ask them to have a word with your boss about the maintenance of his vehicle? What's his name?' Constable Leggatt had already made a note of the registration of the lorry, and the Dundee City force had already been told. But perhaps it was worth a further call, just to be sure.

Sandison paused, then grunted.

'Aye, well,' he said. 'Maybe there was something on the road.'

'It's left no trace, then.'

'Huh.'

'How well did you sleep, Mr. Sandison, in your cab? When did you settle down for the night? When did you waken up?'

'I slept all right,' he grumbled. 'It was a warm night. I had a blanket and a Thermos flask.'

'Of what?'

'Cocoa.'

'Anything else?' Sandison looked surly. 'A tot of whisky, perhaps?'

This time the expression on Sandison's face was one of alarm.

'Whisky? What makes you say that?'

'I'm trying to establish, Mr. Sandison, what makes a driver drive his lorry straight into the side of a tram in broad daylight. It looks to me as if you might have fallen asleep, but on the other hand you might have been inebriated. I'm wondering which it was.'

'There was no whisky in the flask. It was plain cocoa,' said Sandison firmly.

'I'm glad to hear it,' said Cattanach, 'for your sake. I daresay we have it somewhere, and we can check.'

'There was no whisky in it,' Sandison insisted. Cattanach was inclined to believe him, but he would still check.

'Now, then, you told me there was nothing in the back of the lorry.'

'That's right. You should be able to check that, too,' said Sandison, sarcastically. 'That shouldna be difficult.'

'We've already checked,' said Cattanach. 'Where did you say you were going, again?'

'Inverness.'

'Well, you were on the right road, at least. Have you done the drive before?'

'Not this one. I dinna ken Aberdeen that well. I've only been here twa-three times afore – and I'm not that keen to come back, either.'

'That's understandable. Where were you going in Inverness,

then?'

Sandison hesitated.

'I canna just mind …'

'Somewhere you had been before?' Cattanach suggested helpfully.

'No, not a bit of it. I had the address in my head …'

'And now you've forgotten it?'

'Aye, that's right.' Sandison snatched at the suggestion. 'That's a pity, now, for I could have told you, if I hadna forgotten it.'

'But your boss would know where you were going, presumably. He would have the address.'

'Aye, I'd have called him, I suppose. But what does it matter?' Sandison assumed an air of hopelessness. 'I'm no going to get there now, anyway.'

'Was it urgent?'

'Urgent?'

'Well, you were pushing yourself on a bit, weren't you? In late, up early …'

'Who said I was in late?'

'Well, was it urgent?'

'My boss is the kind likes things done smartly, ken? If he tells you to do it tomorrow, you'd better get on and have it done yesterday.' He was clearly pleased with this little joke, and smiled to himself. 'Aye, so in that sense I guess it was urgent, but it wasna a matter of life or death …' He trailed away there, and the smile faded. Perhaps he was at last thinking of the people he had injured. 'I was up early and I thought I should just get going.'

'Where did you park for the night?'

'Down by the beach.'

'That's off your route, if you're coming from Dundee and going to Inverness.'

'Aye, well, it's quiet there, and I like the sound of the sea.'

'Did your boss tell you you could find space to park down there?'

Sandison blinked.

'Aye, aye, that's right. That's where he told me to park.'

Aye, aye, that's right, thought Cattanach. Sandison knew Aberdeen better than he was pretending to. He would like a word with Sandison's boss before Sandison had the chance to speak with him. It looked as if there was more to this story than a bit of careless driving, and he hoped they had not agreed their stories beforehand. Where else could Sandison have been heading along that road? Inverurie, Keith, Huntly, all points northwest. It could have been anywhere. Without knowing what Sandison was to pick up, it was hard to guess where he might have been planning to do it.

He left Sandison with reminders about the charges against him, and wandered out of the hospital, thanking the ward sister as he went. The air was fresh outside, healthy: that had been one of the reasons for choosing this site on its broad, south-facing slope. It felt almost like the countryside, but not quite enough. He set off downhill to catch a bus that would take him back to the police station and a telephone call to Dundee.

'Well, I'd no trust him with my cash box while my back was turned,' was the Dundee inspector's verdict on James Kitchener, owner of one fewer lorry than a week ago. 'He has twa-three – no, I think it was maybe four lorries, though three again now if what you're telling me's right. Dear only knows what's in them half the time. A wise man wouldna enquire.'

'And a policeman?'

'Well, now, aye,' said the Dundee inspector. 'Let's say that any time we've stopped him and taken a wee look, everything's been fine. But you ken what it's like – there's that look in his eye that just says he has the good stuff round the back, in the one place you've no searched, or it was gone out of the yard while you were getting on your bicycle back at the station. You ken?'

'Oh, yes, completely. And Harry Sandison, is he one of Kitchener's regulars?'

'He is, aye. You say he was injured in this accident?'

'Broken leg. Maybe concussion, or maybe he's pretending to be confused.'

'Och, that one's confused enough without being hit on the head. It'll no do him lasting damage. But I take it he'll no be driving for a while?'

'No, and the lorry's unrecognisable.'

'And the crash was his fault?'

'That's what it looks like.'

'He's never been the best driver in the world, any road. Ha! Any road?'

'Very good! Then why does Kitchener use him?'

'He does what he's told, I suppose. Asks no questions – well, beyond the simple ones, any road.'

'Any idea what he might have been doing up here? He was heading out on the road to Inverness, but he told me too quickly that that was where he was going, and he had no address. Said he was picking stuff up – the lorry was empty.'

There was the sound of the Dundee inspector clicking his tongue thoughtfully.

'I dinna think Kitchener has any pals up that way, that I've heard tell of. His contacts are more to the south. Let me ask around, see if anybody has any bright ideas.'

'Thanks.'

'And if you've the space for him in your hospital, or in your jail, feel free to keep Harry Sandison up there for as long as you like. I'll make you a personal present of him,' he said with a laugh.

'Oh, no, I'd not like to see you deprived of him for long! We'll get him back down to you as soon as we can. Poor fellow.'

The Dundee inspector laughed again, and they agreed to keep each other posted.

Cattanach sat back at his desk, and contemplated his shuffled heaps of memoranda. Inspector Cochrane must have taken himself out to enforce something. This was probably the moment, when he had some peace and quiet, that he himself should go through the memoranda and pay some attention to them.

But it was Friday afternoon, and the sun was shining. The walls were closing in on him. He took his hat from the hatstand, waved his paperwork goodbye, and left the office.

The junction of Great Northern Road and North Anderson Drive was a major one, and still being treated warily by drivers as they negotiated it. The scars of the tram and lorry crash were still visible, not least on the road surface itself. The tram rails had been repaired more swiftly to allow the trams to pass again. Anderson Drive was a great broad sweep of a road that almost marked the outer edge of Aberdeen from the River Dee in the south (where it was South Anderson Drive), crossing all the main routes out of the city and swinging round to end here, in the north, just by the suburb of Woodside. The tram would have picked up a whole crowd of people going to work in the centre of the city. He could picture it, running smoothly down the hill in its secure rails, confident of a clear turn on to the main road and into the terraced street, until Sandison failed to stop. He could almost see the impact, the jerking tram, the passengers shaken from their seats, the upstairs ones tumbling down, the tram driver flung broken from the wreck. The noise alone must have been dreadful. He had seen the stark photographs of the mangled lorry and tram combined, horrific from every angle. They were incredibly lucky that no one had been killed.

Great Northern Road, the lorry's intended path, led out from here past Bucksburn and Dyce to Inverurie and points northwest, just as Sandison had said. It was quite a distance from the beach road where he said he had spent the night. He could easily have joined Anderson Drive further south, and cut out the centre of the city completely, made more progress on his way to wherever. Had he fallen asleep after a cold night and an early start? The Dundee inspector had said he was a careless driver. Had he also been drinking? Constable Leggatt, careful man, had not mentioned any smell of spirits. Perhaps it had just been careless stupidity.

But where was Sandison going? Not Inverness, Cattanach was sure of that. Maybe Dundee would turn up some contact of Kitchener's up north, solve the mystery.

He stood at the junction for a while, watching the traffic, trams sliding round the corner, lorries coming into the city and leaving, cars and bicycles and carts. After five minutes or so, he realised that someone else was staring at the traffic, too. A hunched figure, supported by a stick, stood on the opposite side of North Anderson Drive, wearing, he suddenly noticed, soft slippers. He took in the rest of the figure, and saw that she was unexpectedly young for the stick and the slippers. But in another few minutes she turned, and hobbled painfully away, so slowly he could easily have crossed the road and caught her up. But why would he?

8

ON SATURDAY, CATTANACH was summoned by a loud double thump on his kitchen wall. He set aside the dishes he was washing, dried his hands, and headed to the house next door. He knocked, and pushed the door open.

'All well?' he called.

'Aye, Alec, come on in,' came his neighbour's voice.

He made his way, in a mirror-image of his own house's layout, to the kitchen at the back. Mrs. Walker was cooking breakfast. She was a sturdy individual, grey hair scraped back into a practical bun, apron over a dark, sensible dress.

'I'm behind,' she explained. 'A fly cup?'

'I've just had breakfast,' he said, 'thanks.'

Two small dogs, white Scotties, pattered across the lino to greet him, and he bent to rub their ears.

'You want me to take them out?' he asked.

'Would you?' She turned gratefully, as though surprised.

'You know I'll always do it if I can, Mrs. Walker.'

She jerked her head upwards.

'He had a bad night, and I doubt it'll be a bad day, too.'

Mrs. Walker had lost one son in the war. The other was upstairs, and had fought too, and come home, though sometimes Cattanach wondered if it might not have been kinder if he had been killed outright, too.

'I'll take them now, if you like, and then again later.'

'Are you no working the day?'

'I might go in later.'

'You'll be busy the now,' she remarked with certainty. 'Yon petrol rationing's going to cause trouble, if you look at the letters in the paper. What are you going to do with your motor car?' Mrs. Walker did not run one.

'I'm not sure yet.'

'You'll miss your wee trips out by,' she remarked, sagely. He said nothing. 'Aye, no doubt it'll just be the first of the rationing,' she went on. 'A'thing that comes from abroad, that'll be next.'

'I suppose you're right.'

'My William would have been pleased not to see it. Not to see another war.'

'I should think most would agree.'

'I wonder if they'll ration whisky, and all?' she pondered.

'That's where Mr. Walker worked, wasn't it?'

'Aye, he was brewer in a few distilleries, over the years. Always in the trade, from when he was a boy. But the last war did the distilling no good at all – so many places closed, and some never opened again. Aye, it was tragic.' She heaved a weighty sigh. 'That was when we came into the town at last, that and so as to be nearer the Infirmary.'

He took the dogs out for an hour, around about the streets, down towards the University and back. Having the dogs almost made up for not heading out of the town this weekend. He had been brought up with dogs about the place, and missed them. Should he go in to the office this afternoon, or not? He had such a strong feeling of being on the brink, of knowing that things were going to be bad, that made him want to linger as long as possible on the edge here, away from it all. No, he would stay away until Monday morning, unless they called him in.

But they did not, and the weekend was strangely peaceful.

'Anything new?' he asked Sergeant McAulay on Monday morning. The sergeant shrugged.

'We had yon wee man with the petrol fire in, sir – said his neighbours were threatening him.'

'I'm not surprised. Any particular reason?'

'He's a bittie slow paying for their windows, I think.'

'Tell the constable there to pay a call and see how things are – we don't want any more trouble, even if he deserved it.'

'Already done, sir,' said Sergeant McAulay.

'Of course. Just think of it as me reminding myself what should have been done, if you hadn't already had it well in hand.'

'Aye, sir, that's what I do.' McAulay grinned at him, and returned to his paper, but Cattanach was not quite finished.

'Any word on the tram crash? Has the lorry driver been charged?'

'Now that I dinna ken, sir,' said the sergeant, surprised at himself. 'I'll find out.'

'Thank you, Sergeant,' said Cattanach, quietly pleased at having caught the sergeant out in something, at least.

The quiet pleasure faded when he walked into his office, and found that Inspector Cochrane was already there, solemnly pasting papers into a thickly bound ledger. As far as Cattanach could see, the papers were a collection of the various missives they were being sent regarding war regulations – a complete collection, if he knew Inspector Cochrane.

'Are you going to index them?' he found himself asking.

'Of course,' said Inspector Cochrane. 'How else would we be able to look one up in an emergency?'

'Very sensible,' said Cattanach. He sank into his office chair, already exhausted at the thought.

'Lieutenant Moffat left you a message,' said Inspector Cochrane. Cattanach looked about his desk, but the paper coverage seemed to be much the same as it had been when he had left.

'Where?'

'It was a verbal communication,' said Inspector Cochrane. 'Though a written one would, of course, have been more secure: what if I had been called out suddenly, or had to wait until your return?' He seemed to settle into a little cushion of dissatisfaction.

'Perhaps, then, we should take this opportunity for you to pass the message on now?' suggested Cattanach. 'In case you should indeed be called away before you have the chance?'

'Well, yes,' said Inspector Cochrane. 'Of course. It was to ask you to call on a Miss Mackay, in Albyn Place, with regard to a report of a missing person.'

'A missing person?' Cattanach's mind made a leap to the

unknown, unconscious victim of the tram crash. 'A man or a woman?'

'I have no idea,' said Inspector Cochrane. 'He asked me to ask you to go.'

Of course, an inspector would be required. In Albyn Place he imagined that any Misses Mackay of any standing would not expect to be called on by anyone less than an inspector. He wondered why, if Inspector Cochrane had been readily available, Lieutenant Moffat had not simply sent him. But what if the missing person really was the tram crash victim? There seemed to him to be a good chance that it was, and he was eager to find out.

In Union Street, broader even than King Street but heading resolutely west, he caught another tram and sat on the top deck, enjoying the feel of the autumn sun on his skin. Close your eyes and pretend there is no such thing as war. Open your eyes and look at the shops, busy, bustling. A glimpse of the docks down Marischal Street showed him ships in the harbour, and on his right the kirkyard of St. Nicholas was leafy and green still. But the closed cinemas, the crisscrossed tape on so many windows, the adverts for black-out cloth, kept nipping at him, reminding him. What would it be like? Zeppelins and trenches, like the last lot? Europe torn up again? Would they go marching across a continent, looking for Adolf Hitler, or would Hitler come looking for them?

At Holburn Junction the tram slowed to turn, and he slithered down the stairs to alight, nodding to the clippie. It was not far to Albyn Place from here, though in a few paces he was a world away from Union Street with its shops and banks and hotels. Here he was in the west end: the houses, the couthy abodes of bankers, professors or advocates, were grander, sometimes in imposing terraces, sometimes detached with fanciful granite details, flowers or turrets or curlicues about the windows. Once the Victorians had learned the skills of carving granite, it seemed to have gone to their heads.

The Mackay house managed to look both imposing and comfortable, with a broad porch that sheltered visitors while they waited for, in this case, a ruddy-cheeked maid to answer the bell.

'Miss Mackay asked for someone to call,' he explained. 'My name is Cattanach.'

The maid, with an air of being surprised by nothing these

days, took his card and brought him into a dark hallway, panelled and scented with polish and late roses. Cattanach pictured Miss Mackay – an elderly spinster, he thought, well to do, anxious perhaps about a nephew who had been allowed one too many nights on the tiles, and was sleeping it off in a room over a cheap pub. Or was he unconscious and unidentified in the Infirmary?

'Please come this way,' said the maid. A country voice clipped into a town accent. He warmed to her, and wondered what part of the shire she was from.

The drawing room was on the first floor, up the broad, carpeted staircase. The maid announced him, and withdrew slightly, and a figure, which had been seated, rose effortlessly and turned to greet him. Not an old maid, then.

'Anna Mackay,' she said, extending her hand.

'Alec Cattanach,' he responded. 'Inspector with the City Police.'

'How very good of you to come,' she said. 'Agnes, some tea for the Inspector, please. Please make yourself comfortable.'

He sat after she did, and for a moment cast his gaze about the room, hiding his surprise at her appearance.

Heavy velvet curtains – good for the blackout.

Soft brown hair, fashionably but neatly styled, catching the light from the broad bay window.

A couple of good portraits, probably her parents, nicely done.

A face less pretty than handsome – she would age well, judging by her parents' faces.

Photographs in silver frames, silk lamp shades, embroidered footstools and a basket of embroidery silks.

Intelligent eyes, settled hands, lips ready to express opinions – or smile.

'I'm sure that the current unpleasant situation must be making extra work for you, Inspector, so I am particularly appreciative of your visit. Ah, Agnes, thank you. Milk, Inspector? Sugar?'

Agnes arranged the tea things, and curtseyed as she left. Miss Mackay poured two cups and handed one to Cattanach, self-assured for a young woman.

'A matter of a missing person, I'm told?' he prompted her,

though he suspected she needed no prompt.

'That's right.' Here it comes, he thought. A youngish, dark-haired man. Maybe a brother, if not the nephew he had hypothesised? But had the unconscious man looked as if he might belong here, in this house? Cattanach had not seen him himself, but the description of his clothing had not, in his memory, seemed to fit.

'I should explain, Inspector, that I am a medical student at the University. My father is a doctor, of course. He has had occasion to help the police in the past. At present I am also a volunteer recruiting blood donors – you'll have heard of our blood bank?'

'I have, yes. That's valuable work.'

Aberdeen held one of the major blood banks for Scotland, but he had read in the *Press & Journal* of the search for more volunteer donors.

'Vital, if a little pedestrian. I hope you donate?'

He nodded quickly. He did, but he was glad he could answer truthfully. He suspected she would check.

'We go about in pairs – I work with another woman, who calls and interviews, and I take the blood sample and answer any medical questions. Except that when I went to meet her for work today, she did not appear.'

'Perhaps she was ill? Or there was a misunderstanding?'

'There should be no misunderstanding: we both had copies of the worksheet. And I know where she lives – it was near where we were to work – so I went to see if she was there, and there was no answer. The neighbour, a foreign gentleman, said she had not been there all weekend.'

'Has she disappeared before?'

'Not in my experience, no.'

'Right,' said Cattanach, laying down his cup and saucer and producing his notebook and pencil. 'I'd better take some information, if you have it. Let us start, please, with her name.'

'That at least I know,' said Anna Mackay, with confidence. 'Her name is Mabel Campbell, and she lives in Seaton Drive.'

9

THERE COULD BE two Mabel Campbells in Seaton. Even ones with foreign gentlemen next door.

'Slim, well turned out, husband works on trawlers?' he asked.

'That's right.'

'Do you know her son was killed in an accident last week? Perhaps she has been allowed time off.'

'No, I knew about that,' said Miss Mackay. 'She telephoned me, and said she was keen to get back to work.'

That at least did not seem out of character, given what he had seen of Mabel Campbell so far. She would not want to sit about an empty house, and she did not socialise much with her sisters-in-law. Did she have any other friends? It seemed he was going to have to find out.

'When was that?'

'Last Wednesday evening. We should have been doing rounds on Thursday and Friday. She told me that the funeral was to be on Friday, but after the weekend she would be quite ready to work. She sounded –' Miss Mackay tilted her head, analytical – 'She sounded quite normal. I was a little surprised. But when she couldn't be found this morning … my father tells me that it can take a little while for the police to start searches for adults who could well have left of their own accord, but with the death of her son … I thought perhaps she was one of those people who go through death and grieving visitors and funeral in a daydream, and then suddenly the shock hits them. And so,' she said with a deep breath, 'I wondered if she might have wandered off, distressed.'

'She has a lot of family about.'

'Her husband's family, yes.' Anna's tone summed up the relationship very economically.

'Has she spoken with you of friends? Anyone she might have turned to?'

Anna Mackay frowned. A question to which she did not know the answer.

'She never mentioned anyone specifically …'

The drawing room door shot open, and a small, smartly-dressed woman marched in, a fine cairngorm glowing at her shoulder. A quick comparison with the portrait on the wall confirmed that this was Mrs. Mackay. He rose politely to his feet.

'Anna, my dear, can you believe it? Agnes has given her notice!'

'Mother, this is Inspector Cattanach. Inspector, my mother.

'How do you do, Mrs. Mackay?' said Cattanach, when Mrs. Mackay turned to look at him. He saw a quick calculation behind her eyes.

'Mr. Cattanach, how do you do? I'm so sorry – domestic problems. The maid – her brother has volunteered, and she wants to go and help her father with the harvest. At such short notice!'

Well, the harvest would not wait, Cattanach thought, but gave her a sympathetic smile.

'But no matter – are you a friend of Anna's, then? I don't believe we've met before …'

'I don't believe so, no.'

'Mother, he's here because I'm worried about Mabel Campbell. Remember, I told you about her?'

'Mabel – oh, yes. The blood person. We are going to need so many volunteers before this is over, don't you think, Mr. Cattanach? Doing all kinds of things.'

'My mother is very much involved in the W.V.S.,' Anna Mackay explained, her tone flat.

'Did you know Mrs. Campbell?' Mrs. Mackay asked him.

'We had met, briefly, after her son died.'

'He's with the police, Mother.'

'With the police, yes, of course. But surely you're not …' She eyed him, again with that quick calculation. 'That is, surely your *father* was not a policeman?'

Anna's eyes widened.

'No, my father was not a policeman,' Cattanach replied, trying not to laugh. Mrs. Mackay looked satisfied. 'But my uncle was.'

'Oh! Oh, goodness …' Mrs. Mackay visibly adjusted herself. She sat on a Queen Anne chair, her back very straight, perhaps ready to defend her daughter from the mere presence of a real police officer. 'Then you are taking this quite seriously? You really think she has disappeared?'

'Miss Mackay has only just given me the details, Mrs. Mackay,' said Cattanach, 'so as yet we have only one account to go on. I shall be talking to her neighbours and relatives, of course. As Miss Mackay pointed out, Mrs. Campbell was likely to be in a state of some considerable distress. It is possible that she has become confused, or sought comfort with friends she has not mentioned.' Friends – he had asked Miss Mackay about friends just before her mother came in. She should have had time to think by now. 'Miss Mackay, I asked you if Mrs. Campbell had mentioned any friends, or you might know of someone she might confide in. Have you thought of anyone?'

But this time Anna was sure of her answer.

'No, she never mentioned anybody, that I can remember. No one at all – just her husband's family. And from what she said, I don't think she would have gone to them.'

He would have to check – it was the obvious place, after all.

'What did she say about them?'

Anna for once looked uncomfortable.

'She … she gave the impression that they were not … that they did not have much in common.'

'I know it is an unpleasant subject to discuss, but did you think she was happy in her marriage? Or happy generally?'

'Happy … that's perhaps too strong a word. I didn't know her very well, Mr. Cattanach – we had been walking about our given routes together for maybe a month, but not every day. I have studies, of course.'

'She has to work very hard, Mr. Cattanach,' put in Mrs.

Mackay, still perching on her chair.

'Of course, Mrs. Mackay. But if you'll both forgive me, I should say that Miss Mackay is an astute judge of people, a skill I daresay she is honing in her chosen profession. Any impression she can give me, that might lead to information on Mrs. Campbell's whereabouts and help us to ensure her safety will be most valuable.'

'Hm,' said Mrs. Mackay, raising her eyebrows at her daughter. Anna did not respond.

'I should say, Mr. Cattanach, that she was content. Occasionally she was in a higher mood than usual – perhaps three times. On one of those occasions she told me that her husband had reached home safely the night before, after a risky voyage. Based on that, and one or two comments she made about the loneliness of being on her own with a child in the house, I should say that she was happy in her marriage.' But there was a hint of something in Anna Mackay's tone, and Cattanach looked up to meet her eyes. 'Based on that evidence,' she said again, nodding.

But she held his gaze, as if driving home the significance of what she had just said. Based on that evidence – did she have other, contradictory evidence? If so, why would she only hint at it, and not tell him?

'And the last time you heard from her was last Wednesday evening?'

'That's right.'

'She rang here?'

'She did. She had no telephone herself, but there is a call box at the end of the road. She had called and left a message once before, when she was going to be late. She was an organised woman in that respect, Mr. Cattanach, and considerate. I should be very surprised if she had deliberately not told me she was not coming this morning.'

'Is there a central office? Someone she might have told there, hoping that they could pass the word on to you?'

'There is a clerk,' said Anna Mackay. 'Of course I rang him, but he had heard nothing, either.'

'At Foresterhill?'

'Yes, where the blood bank is,' Anna angled her head slightly, as if pointing to Foresterhill. The large hospital site on the outskirts of the city accommodated the Infirmary, the Children's Hospital and the Maternity Hospital, and a random collection of other medical establishments. Eventually it was hoped that the old infirmary building at Woolmanhill in the centre of town, and the city hospital by the sea, could be emptied and moved out to join the rest, but for now medical provision could be scattered in an often illogical way. No doubt Anna spent much of her time there on the wards, and at Marischal College, where the bulk of medicine was still taught. She would be busy enough: he wondered why she had volunteered for the blood collection. Why, too, had Mabel Campbell thought it a good way to spend her time? He would have expected her to choose something more glamorous, somehow.

'I hope nothing alarming has become of her,' said Mrs. Mackay, as if reading his thoughts. 'So very sad for that poor man, to come home to a dead son and a missing wife.'

'Well, then, allow me to see if I can at least clear up one of those.' Robert Campbell was due back in a week, weather permitting. Mrs. Mackay was right: they would have to do their best for him.

But what had Anna Mackay meant about that evidence?

Whatever it was, he was not intended to find out today. Mrs. Mackay had decided that the interview was at an end.

'Indeed,' she said, 'we must not keep you back any longer, Mr. Cattanach. It was very good of you to come and – and gather your information.'

'You have both been most generous with your time,' he countered. 'I hope we shall have good news soon.'

'I'll see you out, Mr. Cattanach,' said Anna Mackay, rising gracefully. He noticed that she wore a simple single string of pearls over her rose-coloured twinset – more understated than Mabel Campbell's array of jewellery. He wondered how the two women had got on on their walks. Well enough, evidently, for Miss Mackay to be concerned about her. Mrs. Mackay made to rise, too, but Anna waved her back. 'No, no, Mother, I'll do it. I daresay Agnes is packing, and you've been so busy.'

She led Cattanach back downstairs to the panelled hall.

'She really does work hard, you know. The W.V.S. have a great deal to do just now.'

'I know,' said Cattanach, 'and all of it valuable. You didn't think to join there, if you wanted to volunteer?'

'I can use my medical skills in the blood volunteers,' she

said, 'such as they are yet.' He waited for more, but they had reached the heavy wooden door and she had swung it open before she added, in a quieter voice, 'I saw her in town, you know. Mabel Campbell. When her husband was away. She was with a man, and let's say that had I not known her husband was away I would have assumed it was he.'

'When was this?'

'About a fortnight ago, I think. I had been working late and had supper with a couple of the other students. We were walking back along Union Street, towards here. She was on the other side, with him.'

'What did he look like?'

'Oh, goodness – I tried not to look, if you see what I mean.' She made a frustrated sound. 'I couldn't tell you upstairs, not in front of Mother. She has almost accepted that I am to be a doctor – not quite in the same way that my older brothers are, apparently, but just until I find a nice husband – but she still believes that the real world is not for people like us.'

He smiled gently.

'It must be difficult.'

'Anyway,' she went on, staring out into the rosebeds in front of the house, 'I almost didn't look at him, but I wanted – I wanted to make sure that my impression was correct. So I did see a little of what he was like. A little taller than she, rather fat, and smartly dressed. So was she. I wondered where they could be going. If I had seen them in London, I might have assumed they were off to a smart restaurant and then on to a club.' She gave a little grin. 'But not at the west end of Union Street, I think.'

'Thank you. That is something to pursue.' He stepped outside, and put his hat on. 'Again, thank you for your time.'

'Not at all. Please, please do find her. I find – I find I quite like her.'

10

'LIEUTENANT MOFFAT WANTS to see you, sir,' said Sergeant McAulay on his return.

'Oh, yes? Is he in or about?' The senior officer had a habit of wandering the breadth of his domain, and appearing unexpectedly. He had been particularly fascinated by the building work, and Cattanach had been summoned to see him several times over the last few months where he was standing outside, watching lumps of granite being lifted and laid.

'He's up the stair. Not long out of a meeting at the Town House.' The sergeant nodded slowly and significantly. Town House meetings depressed the Lieutenant, and gave him indigestion: he had said he was neither senior enough to be useful, nor junior enough to be missed.

'I'll try not to provoke him,' said Cattanach, and set off to the stairs.

'Inspector Cattanach, come in,' said the big man, when Cattanach knocked and put his head round the door. 'Have you been to see Miss Mackay?'

'Just back from there, sir.'

'Her father's a fine doctor. I gather she has the makings, too – shame.'

'Shame, sir?'

'She'll marry and give it all up, no doubt. A good-looking girl, as I recall.'

Cattanach opened his mouth and shut it again, not sure why he felt an urge to defend Miss Mackay. She had looked in no need of help from him.

'She wanted to report a missing person, sir.'

'She did, aye. Who was it – a servant? A boyfriend standing her up? Though I canna imagine a boy having the nerve, in her case.'

'Miss Mackay is involved in recruiting volunteers to contribute to the blood bank, sir. She goes about with another woman – the other woman does the interviews, and Miss Mackay collects blood samples. It's the other woman who has gone missing.'

'Another medical student? Another student?'

'No, a woman who lives in Seaton.'

'In Seaton? Not someone Miss Mackay is likely to have met socially, then, or at the University. What is Miss Mackay's concern?'

'The woman has proved herself reliable in the past, and then has gone missing without explanation. Miss Mackay went to the woman's home and found she had not been seen since Friday.'

'Miss Mackay went to her house?'

'She says she liked the woman: she trusted her, and they rubbed along well.'

The Lieutenant raised his badger eyebrows in disbelief.

'I suppose if she comes to be a doctor she'll see all sorts. Still, on her own? My, my.' For a moment he seemed to contemplate the rashness of youth. Cattanach contained a smile. Seaton was perfectly pleasant, even if it were not quite the West End. 'And her family and friends? What do they say?'

'She is presently living alone, sir. Her husband is on the trawlers, and – well, it was her son who was killed by the lorry on King Street last week.'

Moffat sat back in his chair, pulling his woven fingers on to his ample stomach as if he had forgotten about them.

'What was her name again?'

'Mabel Campbell, sir.'

'Mabel Campbell. And the wee lad was killed – it was an accident, was it no?'

'That's what was thought, sir.'

'At the time, aye. But then, was there no someone came here to say there was more to it?'

Cattanach had not yet written any kind of report on the matter of Billy Campbell's funeral, but Lieutenant Moffat could rarely be accused of missing what went on in his own station.

'There was, sir, a friend of Billy's came in with her mother, and said that Billy had been concerned that one of his uncles was involved in some kind of crime. Constable Gauld is helping me to look into it.'

'Oh, aye, he's a Seaton loon and all, is he no?'

'He is, sir, but he didn't know the family well. Seaton's so newly built: it's not as if families have known each other for generations.'

'No like the tenements,' said Moffat, with a sigh. He had a bent for nostalgia. 'But I suppose the most likely thing is she's gone to friends for a few days. Was Friday no the wee lad's funeral?'

'It was.'

'Then she'll have been upset. Are the uncles around? Are there aunts?'

'There are, sir. I thought I'd ask them first if they know where she's gone.'

'That'd be best, aye. What like of a family is it?'

'Trawlermen, shipbuilders, fishermen – all sailors, sir. That's on the husband's side. We don't know much about her family.' He should have asked Miss Mackay if Mabel Campbell had ever spoken of parents, or a sister, or any other relations. Where had she and Robert Campbell married? What was her maiden name? Had anyone else been at the wedding? If they wanted to try to find Mabel Campbell, there were plenty of questions that could be asked, plenty of leads to follow.

'Take Gauld with you,' said the Lieutenant. 'His folk are sailors. And it's time he saw a bit more of life.'

'I'll do that, sir,' Cattanach agreed happily. He had thought himself that Gauld and Leggatt were due a bit of more interesting work: they both had brains. And some help from someone who knew the sea and the ways of those who worked with it would indeed be very useful.

It did delay things, however. When Cattanach found Gauld in the canteen and told him he was to come and talk to the Campbells, Gauld retrieved the ancient clothes brush from the stationery cupboard and brushed his uniform from top to bottom, then polished his boots. He walked in reverent silence slightly behind Cattanach all the way to the home of Tommy and Lizzie Campbell, in a good old-fashioned tenement off the south end of King Street. Here the wind from the sea scoured the grey streets, and the street names themselves called to mind a number of nasty murders and other crimes in their fifty years or so of existence – the most recent less than five years before. But though the terraces looked glumly uniform, the interiors varied a great deal. Lizzie Campbell's stair was clean and bright and freshly painted, and each door was smartly polished.

'This is one of the shipbuilding uncles,' Cattanach had to say over his shoulder. 'The older one – it's Arthur you know, isn't it?'

'Aye, sir. Tommy's the oldest, I think.'

'I think so. He certainly seemed to be in charge at the funeral, didn't he?'

'What do you want me to do when we get there, sir? Do you want me to stand at the door?'

'No, no. Come in and either sit or stand somewhere unobtrusive, but where I can see you. If anything catches your attention, nod to me, but don't interrupt straightaway. I think we'll just see what happens – we're here to find out where Mabel Campbell is, not to investigate a crime.'

'Aye, sir,' said Gauld. He looked as if he would rather be anywhere else.

'It's all right. You won't have to do any more than say hello and goodbye.'

But there Cattanach was wrong.

'I ken you from the funeral, do I no?' Lizzie Campbell asked Gauld straightaway. 'But you were no in uniform then. Do you live nearby?'

Gauld admitted that he did, and was then subject to a full-scale interrogation on his mother, father, grandparents, and great grandparents, punctuated with little nods of satisfaction as Lizzie Campbell identified a street or a ship or a cousin they had in common. Cattanach sat back and watched in astonishment. Had the family tried to do this with Mabel when she married Robert Campbell? Had there been any little nods of satisfaction then? He hoped to find out.

Lizzie had not been standing idle during her interrogation: the kettle had boiled and she poured them tea – somehow Constable Gauld had ended up at the table with them, his notebook now aligned with the pattern on the oil cloth. Lizzie offered round a plate of butteries. The room was as Cattanach had expected: orderly, busy, comfortable, a little overwarm from the stove.

'You'll have to eat them now,' she said, 'for the dear knows what the war will do to them. Now, what can I do for you?'

'How is Mrs. Robert Campbell? Your sister-in-law?'

Lizzie shifted in her chair.

'To be honest, I havena seen her since Friday. Since we cleared up after the funeral, ken?'

Lizzie had said the family would be keeping an eye on Mabel. What had gone wrong? Cattanach sat, silently waiting. Lizzie cleared her throat.

'I said to her she could come and stay here, or I would be up in the morn to see how she was. Well, she near took my head off. Said she could manage well enough on her own: she didn't need me sticking my nose in.' Lizzie repeated the words stiffly, the hurt clear in her face. 'And she said the same went for Betty and Isabel, we were all to clear off and let her – and then she caught herself up and tried to be nice – let her mourn in peace. Well, ken what funerals is like, Mr. Cattanach. We just decided to let her be for a day or two, for we were in no great form ourselves.'

'And none of you has seen her since Friday evening?'

'Not a bit of it,' said Lizzie. 'Isabel said she'd go round after church yesterday morning. Betty and I told her she was on a hiding to nothing, but there's no stopping Isabel when she has a notion in her head – she took a cake, and all. But she came back to us after, and said there was no sign of Mabel in the house, so she thought she must have gone out for a walk, or something. Not that we ever knew Mabel to go out for a walk.'

'Did you know that Mabel was volunteering with the blood bank?'

Lizzie's eyebrows rose.

'To give blood?'

'No,' said Cattanach, 'to recruit more volunteers to give blood.'

'Oh! That makes more sense,' said Lizzie. 'I couldna see

Mabel with needles in her arms. She was a bittie sensitive like that.'

'But you didn't know she was recruiting?'

'No, not at all.'

'Does it surprise you? Was it the kind of thing you would expect her to do?'

'Not really, no,' said Lizzie, without having to reflect. 'Now, if you paid her to go about meeting people, that'd be one thing. Maybe she was just bored.'

'Did she ever mention a Miss Mackay? Miss Anna Mackay?'

'I dinna think so.' Lizzie frowned. 'What's the matter, Inspector? Am I being slow here? What's wrong with Mabel?'

'Miss Mackay, another blood bank volunteer, has reported Mabel missing, Mrs. Campbell. And no one seems to have seen her since Friday after the funeral. Can you think of anywhere she might have gone? Did she mention any friends? I think you said she had not talked much of her family, but did you even have an impression of where she might go?'

There was a pause, then Lizzie stood up abruptly.

'I'll put more water in this,' she said, grabbing the teapot. 'It's gone cold.'

Cattanach let her top up the teapot from the kettle on the stove. Constable Gauld continued writing in his notebook: he seemed to be recording the whole conversation.

'I shouldna have listened to her, should I?' Lizzie turned back to them, but her gaze was lowered. 'I should have kept an eye on her. If she's gone and done something stupid …'

'There's no reason to suspect that yet,' said Cattanach gently, though it was his first thought, too. 'She's probably with friends.'

'But what friends?' asked Lizzie. 'What friends that werena at the funeral? Because we were the last to leave, and she was still there then!'

'They might have offered to come back for her. Waited until she had packed some things.' A thought struck him. 'If she had packed a bag, taken things from the house, would you know? If you had a look around.'

Lizzie gave this her full consideration for a moment, then shook her head.

'I have no idea,' she said. 'She had that much stuff, but there's nothing I could even say well, she'd no leave that behind. She liked her things, ken, but she wasna that attached to any one bit of them, as far as I could ever see.' She shook her head again. 'I'm sorry. I'm that sorry. I should have stayed. I shouldna have listened to her nonsense. I should have brought her back here.'

11

CATTANACH HAD DELIBERATELY chosen Lizzie first, as the Campbell he felt he knew best and the one, perhaps, most likely to talk to him. Now he had the rest of them, the ones he had only previously seen at the funeral. He glanced at his watch. Lizzie's husband Tommy, the head of the family by all accounts, should be about to leave work at the shipyard just now, along with his brother Arthur.

'Come on,' he said to Constable Gauld, 'let's see if we can catch the gates at Hall Russell.'

It was an industrial area, in between the terraces of tenements: the men employed in graniteworks and slaughterhouses and gasworks mingled, weary, on the streets as they made their way home, distinguishable only by the stains or dust on their clothing. The City Hospital was here, ostensibly for treating fever patients in the good sea air, but there was little enough of that air to be had until they were well down into Footdee and could glimpse the harbour waters between the buildings. Cattanach thought they would be late, and perhaps miss the men, but the wave of shipbuilders leaving the yard to join the tramp homewards had only just begun by the time they reached there. Tommy Campbell, tall and authoritative, was easy enough to spot. Cattanach waited in the mouth of a lane until Campbell was passing them, and fell into step with him. Gauld scurried behind. Just beyond Tommy Campbell, almost hidden by him, was Arthur. Both men were blackened and greasy, and Cattanach noted that Gauld kept a safe distance from them.

'Mr. Campbell, could I have a word, please? It's about Mrs.

Robert Campbell.'

Tommy strode on a couple of steps, hesitated, and turned. Cattanach edged to the side of the street, out of the way, and Tommy followed.

'Mrs. Robert Campbell? Mabel?' He frowned. 'Is she all right?'

'When did you last see her? Or you, sir?' he directed his question to Arthur Campbell who had stopped to see what was happening. The two brothers looked at each other, no answer ready. The flow of workers diverted itself around them like salmon.

'I suppose it would have been Friday, at the funeral,' said Tommy. 'My wife said she asked her to come and stay with us, after that – ken her son died.'

'These folks were at the funeral, Tommy,' said Arthur, and Tommy looked at them again.

'Polis?' He studied Gil Gauld. 'Aye, yous were at the funeral, right enough. You're a neighbour,' he jerked his head at Gauld, 'but I wondered about you at the time,' he added, turning back to Cattanach. 'Lizzie telt me who you were. Aye, Lizzie said she was to come and stay with us, but she never.'

'And I think she wasna very gracious in her refusal – Lizzie wasna too happy with her,' added Arthur with the start of a grin.

'Aye, well,' said Tommy, in a tone that told Arthur to fall silent. 'So no, I've no seen her since then. We come back to that wee flat of hers – of Robert's – and had just the fly cup, but there wasna much chat.'

'No one felt like it,' put in Arthur. 'Not after wee Billy.'

'And so we all just went home. The women stayed to help tidy up, I suppose.'

'I thought she might come for her dinner after church yesterday, but there was no sign of her. Lizzie gives me my dinner on the Sabbath,' Arthur explained.

'She's no – is she all right, like?' asked Tommy.

'All right?' queried Arthur, frowning at his brother.

'I mean, you've no found her …'

'No one has seen her at all, Mr. Campbell,' said Cattanach quickly, saving him finding the words. 'She seems to have disappeared.'

'Oh, aye?' Arthur was less dismayed than Tommy, a hint of

his ready grin reappearing. 'Has she, indeed?'

'Arthur, that's enough,' said Tommy. 'Have you asked the neighbours? Oh, I suppose you are a neighbour,' he said to Gil Gauld.

'We believe the neighbours have not seen her either, sir,' said Cattanach, 'but they will be asked again.' He took a step to the side that let the two men move again, and they joined the end of the flow of workers in the street. 'You were out late today – yard busy?'

'Oh, aye,' said Tommy, 'busy enough. Plenty to get done.'

'But we canna talk about it,' said Arthur, with a wink. 'War work.'

'Of course.' A little prick of awkwardness hit Cattanach, as though he had caught himself out in a lapse of manners. He cast a sideways glance at the two brothers, quite different in their appearance even in their similar working gear. Tommy was a big man, with a solid face – unimaginative, Cattanach thought, but not stupid. His hands were large and practical, his pace sure and unwavering. Arthur was smaller, leaner, and walked like a dancer, like a cat, ready to deviate if it might amuse him. He wondered what Robert, Mabel's husband, was like.

'When is Mr. Robert Campbell due home?' he asked.

'End of this week, if the weather holds,' said Tommy. 'I think it will. If she's no back by then …' He gave a little shake of the head, not wanting to imagine it.

'Ah, she'll be back, Tommy, never worry,' said Arthur cheerfully.

'That's enough, Arthur,' said Tommy firmly. 'Right, well, Inspector, this is our road here. I hope you find her. If I hear anything I'll let you know.'

Confirming himself in his place of authority, he nodded his head at Cattanach, then at Gauld, and turned up the road to where Lizzie no doubt had the tea waiting. Arthur followed obediently, waving back at them one last time.

'I'd like a word with Arthur on his own, some time,' said Cattanach quietly, watching them go. 'He seems to think he knows where Mabel is, or who she is with, perhaps.'

'Who she is with, sir? Who would she be with, if not with her family?'

'Well, for one thing, Gauld, we know nothing of her own

family, not even whether or not they exist. This is her husband's family, and she doesn't seem close to them, despite their best efforts. And then, for another thing, Miss Mackay, who reported her missing, told me that she had seen Mabel Campbell with a man who was not her husband – a smart, well-dressed man, one evening at the west end of Union Street.'

'A man who was not her husband, sir? When her husband was at sea?'

'I believe so.'

'Oh, that's no right, sir,' said Gauld. 'Unless he was like her father or her brother or something.'

'According to Miss Mackay, that was not what it looked like. I did not ask for details,' he added.

Gauld looked somewhere between shocked and puzzled, as if he were trying to picture exactly what 'it' had looked like. Cattanach glanced down once more after Tommy and Arthur, and took the other street at the junction, checking to see that Gauld was following.

'Who's next, sir?' Gauld asked in an effort to recover.

'There's the harbourmaster's office,' said Cattanach, pointing to a squat tower on the edge of the harbour, 'but I suspect his assistant has gone home for the evening. I think we need to go back up the hill a little, and see if Edward Campbell is in – unless the harbourmaster's assistant has urgent war work, too. In which case, perhaps we can chat with Isabel Campbell.'

Another tenement, another well-kept stair, and this time a smart black front door with a doormat outside it. Cattanach knocked, and as if she had been waiting behind the door Isabel Campbell flung it open, then stopped.

'I'm sorry, were you expecting someone?' asked Cattanach politely.

'Oh! Oh, my husband – it's Inspector … Chattan, is it not?'

'Cattanach,' said Cattanach, nodding. 'And this is Constable Gauld. May we come in and ask a couple of questions? I'm sure you're about to eat, but it's about your sister-in-law, Mrs. Robert Campbell.'

'About Mabel?' Isabel Campbell waited for them to wipe their boots on the doormat, then backed into the narrow hall so that they could follow. The scent of cooking food was in the air here, too, but she had already removed her apron, and her hair was freshly brushed and arranged and she wore a smart dress, as if she had changed for dinner. Cattanach was fairly sure that Lizzie Campbell would not have. Isabel led them into a parlour where the little round table was already laid for tea. There were a couple of miscoloured religious prints on the wall, several embroideries of religious texts like the one in Billy's bedroom, a very small piano – Cattanach wondered how they had managed to haul it up the common stairs – and two easy chairs by the fire. She gestured to one of them, and perched like a well-fed partridge in the other, leaving Constable Gauld to take his stand by the table. 'Please, do take a seat, Inspector. I hope Mabel is not in any kind of trouble. How can I help?'

Cattanach sat, noting the tension in her, in her plump fingers. What trouble did she think that Mabel might be in?

'When did you last see Mrs. Campbell?' he asked.

'Ah, well, now, that's *rather* strange,' she said, emphasising 'rather' as though she liked the word. 'I suppose I last saw her on Friday, at the funeral, of course. We all helped to clear up afterwards - by 'all', I mean Lizzie and Betty and I – and Lizzie asked Mabel if she wanted to come and stay with her and Tommy. Well, of course Mabel had no *notion* of staying there. The flat is tiny, and then there are the children, and Arthur's there too, more often than not. So of course Mabel wanted to stay at home, and Lizzie was put out, and went off *very* crossly. Lizzie does like to organise people,' she added with a sigh. 'So I was going to ask her if she would like to come here – much nicer for her, I thought, and quieter – alas, we have no children, you see, Inspector.'

'I see.'

'But Mabel was clearly impatient to have us gone – she must have been *exhausted*, poor dear – and so Betty and I left her in peace. I thought I would let her rest for a day or so, and then go back and see if she wanted to come. But when I went on Sunday, after church, she was out.'

'No sign of her at all?'

'Nothing. I looked through all the windows –' she broke off and glanced furtively at him – 'I was suddenly *worried*, you see? But there was no sign of her.'

'Did you ask around?'

'Well, no. I wasn't keen to linger, and the old man next door, well, he's … he's a *Catholic*. Not that I have anything against Catholics, you understand, but, well, I'm not quite sure what they do on a Sunday, and I would never want to *interrupt*.'

'Would you say you were close to Mabel?'

'Well, she is my sister-in-law,' said Isabel, after just the least hesitation.

'Would you sit down with her for a news? Drop in for a fly cup?' asked Cattanach, but already Isabel was shaking her head.

'Oh, no, I should usually wait for an invitation. I am not the kind of person who likes to *intrude*, Inspector.'

'Of course.' He smiled encouragingly. 'But if you were invited – or if you invited her here – would you expect her to confide in you? Did she tell you, for example, anything about her background? About her own family?'

'Oh! You think she might be with them?' She frowned, considering. 'Well, of course, she must have had some family. And perhaps family from her first husband, too, from Billy's father.'

'And did she say anything about them at all?

'Not a thing, Inspector. She just *appeared*, just like that.'

12

ISABEL SEEMED READY to say something else, then jumped at the sound of the flat door opening. She pushed herself out of her seat and hurried off, straightening her dress as she went. They could hear her clearly in the hall, as Cattanach rather thought they were meant to.

'Edward dear, welcome home!' As if he had been on a long sea voyage, rather than just in an office along the road. 'We have visitors, and I'm afraid it's not good news. Mabel has disappeared!'

'Disappeared?' Edward's response was not wholly surprised.

'Here, let me take your coat, dear,' Isabel continued. 'That's it. Now, dinner is almost ready, but perhaps you'd like to say good evening to the *visitors*, first? One of them is that nice police inspector who was at poor little Billy's funeral.'

Thus depriving them of any chance of seeing Edward's first reaction to the news, Isabel led her husband into the parlour. Cattanach rose to shake his hand, with which Edward seemed quite comfortable.

'There, now, sit down, Edward! Do sit down, Inspector. I'm sure Edward doesn't know *any* more than I do, but I'm sure you'd like to hear it from him! The Inspector had no *idea* that Mabel had just appeared from *nowhere*, can you believe it?'

Edward, sitting very upright as though his tight collar were hooked to something behind him, gave a little shrug.

'Robert always treated them well,' he said, 'both of them. He was fond of Billy.'

'Do you know who his father was?' Cattanach asked. 'We're trying to find anyone Mrs. Campbell might have gone to stay with – we're concerned, as you can imagine, for her safety.'

'I don't know who his father was,' said Edward precisely.

'Mabel's first husband, dear,' Isabel reminded him.

Edward met Cattanach's eye, then flicked a glance at his wife. Edward, then, did not wholly believe that there had been a first husband. Well, it would not have been the first time that a woman who had, perhaps through no fault of her own, acquired a child out of wedlock, invented a widowhood to make herself acceptable again in the eyes of society – and to give the child a good start, too.

'Do you have any idea where Mrs. Campbell might have come from? She never said anything that made you think, or maybe your brother Robert mentioned something?'

'I didn't pay much attention to what she said,' said Edward Campbell. 'She was not the kind of person whose opinions I much valued. And Robert doesn't say much, anyway.'

'I see. But you were prepared to take her in, look after her while she was in need, before her husband came back. After Billy died.'

'Were we?' asked Edward, and Isabel flushed.

'Of course we were – she was *family*! And you wouldn't want her in poor Lizzie's flat. There wouldn't be *room*.'

'Of course, we would have more room for her. But she never – she never asked. She never came to stay here.' Edward was confused, and did not like to be. He straightened his cuffs, and then his tie. A man on his way up in the world, but not entirely sure of his footing.

'I'm afraid our dinner is ready, Inspector,' said Isabel sweetly. 'Would you mind very much?'

'Anything you found interesting about that, Gauld?' Cattanach asked, as they made their way back up the street and out of Footdee.

'He didna like her much, anyway, sir,' said Gauld. It was impossible to argue with that on the evidence presented.

'No, you're right there. And I think it would have come as

surprise to him if Isabel had managed to bring Mabel home – that was Isabel's idea and she had not told him. But something else.'

'She calls their tea their dinner?' Gauld tried. Cattanach hid a smile. If Edward was going up in the world, Isabel was right behind him – possibly pushing.

'Neither of them was concerned that Mabel might have committed suicide. Lizzie and Tommy both thought that, and Miss Mackay feared it. Both of those two, Edward and Isabel, went straight to the conclusion that she was in trouble of some kind, and probably of her own making. Interesting. Right, let's see now – we have one Campbell household left to go – the absent Samuel on his ocean liner, and his wife Betty. Hanover Street, I think, by the school.'

It was uphill again. For a few paces Cattanach closed his eyes and tried to imagine that he was out on an open hillside, not surrounded by streets and works and people. It was not entirely successful: he could not stop up his ears and his nose, after all.

He had not seen much of Betty Campbell at the funeral: she had been busy with food and cups of tea, quietly efficient, and he had rather assumed that she was just a twin of Lizzie, her namesake. Certainly their flats were similar, busy but orderly, full of the smell of tea, though in this case the meal had already been served and Betty's children had almost finished eating. Cattanach, ushered in at once to the kitchen and given a seat alongside Gauld, took a look at them: the lad who had taken his share with the coffin, a younger boy, and a girl – the one who worked in Woolworths, that was it. She was clearly just back from work, too. The boys were in school uniform, which surprised him: they were both at Robert Gordon's College, in the middle of the city. Betty went to the fire to make fresh tea, with a wave at the table.

'This is Barbara, and Andy, and young Sam. I hope you dinna mind them, Inspector – they're aye starving when they get back, but they'll soon have finished. Are you here about Mabel? Lizzie came round for a mintie and tellt me. That's terrible. I hope she hasna – well, you ken,' she finished, with a glance at the younger boy. Cattanach saw out of the corner of his eye that Gauld had made a mark in his notebook at this – Betty and Lizzie both thought of suicide.

'We're concerned for her safety, anyway, Mrs. Campbell,' said Cattanach.

'Oh, aye, you would be. We are, and all. Have you no idea where she might be? I havena seen her since we redd up after the funeral – och, the poor wee lad,' she added.

'No one seems to have any idea,' said Cattanach. 'Did she ever speak to you of her family? Or Billy's father's family?'

'She never spoke about herself at all, only if she'd a new hat, or a new ornament,' said Betty.

'Or new makeup,' put in the daughter Barbara, confident enough to join the conversation. The boys concentrated on finishing their tea. 'She talked to me sometimes about makeup, because I work on the makeup counter at Woollies.'

'Oh, of course,' said Cattanach, smiling at her. 'You'd have had a shared interest.'

The girl looked pleased at the thought, though her mother was less impressed.

'Not that she would buy much of her makeup in Woollies,' she said. 'Esslemont & McIntosh is more her kind of shop.' The department store stood on Union Street in discreet splendour, for a rather more select clientele. It was not the place Cattanach would have pictured Mabel Campbell.

'Does she – would you call her extravagant, then?' Cattanach asked. Betty smiled and Barbara chuckled.

'She's no spending all of Robert's money, if that's what you mean,' said Betty. 'She brought plenty of her own money to the marriage, from all I heard at the time. Oh, aye, wherever she's from, she brought a good bit of it with her.' She fetched two cups and saucers, and poured tea for both the policemen without asking. Cattanach winced at the sugar, but hid it well. Gauld seemed to enjoy his. 'That and Billy, and a nicer lad you couldna find – though quiet, mind,' she added, with a thoughtful look at her own two. 'If you've finished, lads, run along and do your homework.'

The boys left without reluctance, not interested in the conversation at all. Barbara, though, showed no sign of shifting.

'But no,' said Betty with a sigh, as the boys shut the door behind them, 'no, she never says much, or a'thing, about where she came from. And after the first couple of times I didna ask. I mean, it's nice to know where your family comes from, and all, but with her … well, I had the idea she'd no been happy, afore, and that now maybe she was. And that is not something I want to be responsible for disturbing, ever. I mean, she isna the kind of person I could feel comfortable with, no like Lizzie. She's that bit different, ken? But I'd no wish her harm, and if I thought we'd left her when she needed us – well, then, it'll take me a long time to forgive myself.'

'Did she seem to want you to stay? Any or all of you, after the funeral?'

'No! Not a bit of it. In fact, I'd say she was dead keen for us to go. She maybe just wanted a good greet, and the same way I wasna comfortable with her, she was likely no comfortable with us, and didna want to cry in front of us. That'd be it. Aye, she fairly chased us out the door, in the end, the minute the work was done.' She grinned. 'She'd no have chased us till we'd finished, a' course. Not the domesticated kind. The dear knows what the place'll be like when poor Robert gets home! But there,' she turned sombre again, 'they'll have worse things to think about than a bit of dust, the Lord save them.'

'Is it a happy marriage, would you say?' Cattanach asked after a respectful pause. 'I hear it hasn't been a long one.'

'No, not that long,' agreed Betty. She glanced at her daughter. 'Ah … I'm not that keen to talk about others' marriages, when it comes down to it.'

'It's more to give us an idea of how she might be feeling just now. Mr. Robert Campbell is due home at the end of the week, isn't he? Will she be looking forward to that?'

'Oh, aye, a' course,' said Betty at once. 'Aye, we're all pleased when they come home. For a bittie, anyway!' She laughed again. 'Until they get under our feet! But no, I daresay she'll be happy to see him. Though Robert's no the brother I would have married, anyway – well, obviously. But Robert's got a surly way to him, sometimes. I fancy he's the jealous kind. If she's no there when he gets back – well, a' course, if she's away she might no be there. I hadna thought of that. He'll no be pleased, I should say.'

Cattanach hesitated, thinking of what Anna Mackay had told him.

'Do you think – have you ever had the impression – that he might have grounds for jealousy?'

Betty looked sharply at him.

'Another man, do you mean?'

'Did you ever have that impression?'

Betty's mouth twisted, as though she was not sure whether or not to let something out.

'She never told me anything of that kind,' she said at last.

'But did you suspect, nonetheless?'

'She'd be the type,' muttered Betty, tight-lipped.

'She's more than the type,' said her daughter suddenly. 'I saw her. Saw them! I did!'

'Dinna be daft, lass,' said her mother at once. 'You never saw anything of the sort.'

'But I did,' said Barbara. 'I saw them in Woolworths. Not at the makeup counter, of course,' she added, with a look at her mother. 'They were at the sweets. You canna get those in Esslemont & McIntosh, can you?'

'When was this?' asked Cattanach.

'Och, a couple months ago. The start of the summer – not long after I started working there. I saw her and I thought to myself, 'Oh, there's Auntie Mabel – I can say hello and she'll be all surprised to find me working here!' But then I saw the mannie, and I thought 'That's no Uncle Robert', and my first thought was to wonder if it was someone from her family, ken. But he had her by the arm and they were – well, they were laughing, and I thought to myself, 'Best just shift out the way, Barbara,' and I went off to my own counter and let them be.'

'You should have said!' cried Betty, shocked more at her daughter's discretion than at Mabel's behaviour, Cattanach was sure.

'I don't suppose you have any idea who he was?' asked Cattanach.

'I do, as it happens,' said Barbara with pride – and a dismissive look at her mother. 'The lassie that was on the makeup counter with me then, she knew who he was – a neighbour of hers in Littlejohn Street. A skinny, black-haired man he was – I didna like the look of him at all. She called him Jock.'

13

'SO WE HAVE a Christian name – or a nickname – and part of an address. How well do you know Littlejohn Street, Gauld?'

'It's the one down the side of Marischal College, sir. Long way from my beat.'

'True, but not far from the police station. A short street, but overcrowded: I suspect there are plenty of men called Jock around there.'

'It's no exactly unusual, sir.'

'No. Right, time we went back to the station anyway. I'll find out whose beat it is and talk to them. You go home. Thank you for your help today.'

Gauld, looking solemn, saluted.

'I hope we do find her, sir, before …'

'Well. We'll see.'

Back at the station, he discovered that the man on the day shift whose beat covered Littlejohn Street was already gone for the night, and the night man was out. He fetched himself a cup of tea from the canteen, and went to sit in his office. Inspector Cochrane must not have been in, for the latest swathe of memoranda, copies on his desk, copies on Cattanach's, remained unglued.

It was useful to believe, or have others believe, that Mabel Campbell might do herself harm – might commit suicide, the crime itself, in grief at the death of her son. It meant that he had a reason to go and ask people questions, find out more about her. But in his heart, somehow, Cattanach could not imagine the Mabel Campbell he had met doing anything like that. Granted, he had only seen her in the shock of the news of Billy's death. People who had known her better than he did feared the worst. But then, even they admitted they did not know her well.

What did he have? He drew over a sheet of paper and considered.

Billy was not Robert Campbell's son.

Robert and Mabel had married – or had they? No one he had met had been to the ceremony – had become associated with one another three or four years ago. Billy would have been six or seven.

Mabel had her own money, and spent it.

Mabel had been eager to get her sisters-in-law out of the house after the funeral.

Mabel had been seen in the West End recently with a man who was not her husband, and in Woolworths with a thin, dark-haired man called Jock who lived in Littlejohn Street, at the beginning of the summer.

Robert was the jealous type.

Mabel had not been seen, by anyone he had found, since just after the funeral on Friday.

It was not much.

He looked at his watch. It was eight o'clock, and he was hungry. He took his hat from the hatstand, and went home.

Mrs. Walker had left him a jar of rich broth, with a saucer over the top, on his doorstep – her way of thanking him for walking the dogs, which he was more than happy to do. There was half a loaf in the bread bin, and some early apples his grandfather had sent him. What more could he want? He turned on the wireless, and the soft glow was enough to counter the late dusk as he sat by the kitchen stove, and thought about trams, and lorries, and Inverness, and Mabel Campbell.

He had come to no startling revelations by the time he reached his desk the following morning.

'You have two notes,' said Inspector Cochrane, with disapproval. He presumably thought it was untidy. 'One from

Lieutenant Moffat.'

'So I see. Thank you,' he added, determined to be meticulously polite.

The other note was from Sergeant McAulay, passing on a telephone message from Anna Mackay. He wondered if she had remembered anything useful about the elusive Mabel Campbell. How could anyone talk so little about themselves? Give so little away?

There was nothing from the constable who walked Littlejohn Street – he would be the same man, Cattanach remembered, who had attended the petrol fire in Loch Street. A sensible fellow, if eager for excitement. He wondered how the petrol hoarder was getting on with his neighbours now.

'I'll go and see the Lieutenant,' he announced. Inspector Cochrane made a face, as if Cattanach were an irritating pupil who had, for once, given a sensible answer.

Lieutenant Moffat was outside watching the workmen fitting windows to some of the holes in the new extension.

'Neat work, Cattanach, don't you think?'

Cattanach nodded. There was less banging today, but it seemed the workmen could not function without whistling, singing, and shouting at each other, to make up for the want of machinery.

'How did the call to Dundee go? Do you need any help?'

'Not just yet, sir. I'll be talking to them again shortly.' Moffat turned to take a stroll about the building, and Cattanach followed. 'They're to go and have a word with the boss of the man we have in hospital, see if they can find out what he might have been up to.'

'But we have him for the driving offence.'

'Yes, indeed, that's strong. But there's something more to it, clearly. The man in hospital, Sandison, is not what you'd call the Napoleon of Crime, but he's up to something.'

'Of course it might have nothing to do with us, in the end,' said Moffat. 'It could be between the Highland and Dundee forces, or the County, if, as you say, you don't think he was really going to Inverness. Have his bits and pieces been recovered from the lorry?'

'Up to a point, sir. The Thermos flask is broken, but we have his change of clothes and the remains of a pillow and blanket, so it does look as if he spent the night in the cab as he claims. They couldn't find any papers, though, sir. He claims he has forgotten the address, and would have had to call his boss for an address when he reached Inverness.'

'Hm,' said the Lieutenant. They had strolled away from the building work now, and were out on West North Street, near its junction with King Street. This end of the street was a long way from where Billy had died, but it seemed to put Moffat in mind of it.

'What about that missing woman? Campbell?'

'Not much, sir. I may be wrong, but I don't think it's suicide, anyway. We have two sources telling us she had been seen in town with a man who was not her husband, and we have a Christian name and a partial address for the man, in Littlejohn Street.' He gestured: from where they stood, they could just about see the end of Littlejohn Street round the back of Marischal College. The college, with its grand granite façade, stood two storeys tall at the front, but much taller at the rear where it extended both upwards and downwards on the hill. Littlejohn Street was short but steep.

'A slum waiting to be cleared,' said Moffat sadly. 'You could have a long hunt there.'

'I'll ask the constable, but we also have a possible person who recognised him, someone who saw him in Woolworth's and named him to a niece of the missing woman.'

'And you believe that this Campbell woman might be with him?'

Cattanach shrugged.

'I don't know, sir. I just hope he might have some information. She's not the kind – I can't see her leaving her comfortable flat in Seaton for a hole in Littlejohn Street. And her husband is due back on Friday, and apparently he is the jealous type.'

'Could she have left him? No longer needed to stay for the sake of the boy? They could both be off, together, this man in Littlejohn Street and the Campbell woman. Have they any means of support?'

'She has money, apparently.'

'But has she? Has she taken it with her?'

'I'm hoping to talk to her bank manager this afternoon, if I can find out where she banked. This morning I want to take a look inside her flat, if I'm able.'

'I suppose someone has checked to see she's not lying there, dead?' asked the Lieutenant, jocular but wary. Mistakes did happen.

'I believe so, sir. But who knows, she might have turned up by now.'

'Save us all a deal of trouble,' said Moffat, nodding sagely.

Back in his office, Cattanach examined the other note, the one, via Sergeant McAulay, from Anna Mackay. It simply said that she had called, no promises of further information. He sighed.

'Is that the young lady in Albyn Place?' asked Inspector Cochrane. He was not above looking at other people's messages – he probably thought of it as making sure he had a clear idea of what was happening in the station.

'It is,' said Cattanach briefly.

'I hear her father's Dr. Mackay. The medical man.'

'I believe so,' said Cattanach.

'I've worked with him myself a few times,' said Inspector Cochrane nonchalantly. 'Not a bad fellow, on the whole.'

'I'm glad to hear it,' said Cattanach. 'I'd better return this call, though.'

'Oh, aye. You don't want to keep the young lady waiting, do you?'

Cattanach made a conscious effort not to grit his teeth, and put the call through. In a moment or two he heard the maid Agnes' distinctive accent – she must not have managed to leave for her father's farm straightaway.

'Oh, yes, Mr. Cattanach,' she said. 'Miss Mackay left a message for you – she's had to go up to the hospital. She asks if you could meet her there at one o'clock, by the main entrance – that's the one up the hill, she says.'

'At one o'clock, thank you, yes.' He put the receiver down.

'One o'clock,' mused Inspector Cochrane. 'You might have to take her out for lunch.'

'I doubt it,' said Cattanach. 'That's me off. Enjoy your morning.'

'Oh, I daresay I shall,' said Inspector Cochrane, smiling tightly, and returned to his perusal of the *Press & Journal*.

The little flat in Seaton, with its colourful garden, already looked deserted.

'You can sort of tell she hasna come back, sir, eh?' said Gauld, back on his home beat. 'Even the flowers look sort of dead.'

'Well, let's hope she isn't, anyway. Was it you who looked round the house yesterday? No, it can't have been.'

'No, it was Constable Cooper, sir.'

'Oh, yes. Did he go inside?'

'I think he shone his torch through the windows, sir. They're good and wide – you can see almost everything from them.'

'Well,' said Cattanach, with a degree of misgiving – mistakes could be made – 'let's take a proper look inside now. All right, Mr. Mathieson?'

A small man, in a suit made for a large man, had agreed to come from the Council's housing department, bringing with him a sheaf of paperwork and a bunch of keys.

'Are you sure she's no in there? Are you sure we'll no find a body? See, I was there when they found one once, and I couldna face my food for weeks after.'

'If you open the door for us, we'll go first,' Cattanach assured him. 'That way you won't have to see it – if there is a body.'

Mr. Mathieson fiddled with his keys, selected one, considered it, changed his mind and applied a different one to the lock. The door opened.

The air that lay inside was stale, nothing more. Memories of the cigarette smoke from the funeral lingered about the furniture. A faint, cold aroma of scones ventured out of the kitchen. Cattanach looked quickly into each room, including Billy's bedroom, and under the beds, inside the wardrobes, in the cupboard under the stairs.

'You're safe, Mr. Mathieson, no bodies in here.'

The man stepped cautiously into the flat, and looked about him.

'Aye, they keep it well. We just need a few more of these up here now, ken.'

'More housing? In Seaton?' Cattanach had thought the building was finished.

'Aye, sir, there's plenty that need it,' put in Constable Gauld. 'There's folk down the end of this, between the houses and the sea, living in tents and huts and the like. They're out of the slums but there's nowhere to put them yet.'

'And now there's a war on,' said Mr. Mathieson, as though it were purely an impediment to Council progress. 'So when's that going to be done, eh?'

'Can you look around the main bedroom for any papers, Constable? I'll check the parlour.'

'Aye, sir,' said Gauld.

There was nothing of interest in the parlour, arranged just as it had been for the funeral. It was Gauld instead who found the deedbox.

14

THE DEEDBOX WAS small and battered, and Gil Gauld had found it on the floor of the wardrobe, half-hidden by an old shawl. There were no markings on it. The lid had a sturdy hasp, but the box was barely closed. Using the end of his pen, Cattanach opened it.

Inside there was hardly anything. A few loose papers lay on the gleaming base. One was clearly Billy Campbell's death certificate, still crisp and unfolded. Beneath it, when Cattanach flicked it aside with his pen, was a rent book.

'That'd be ours,' said Mr. Mathieson, peering between their shoulders. 'They've never been in arrears – I checked before I came out.'

'Coal deliveries and grocery account,' said Cattanach, reading the titles of two more small, dark red books. 'I suppose there might be more to them than meets the eye, but I doubt it. No bank book. And a good deal of empty space.'

'Would she have taken a bank book with her, sir?'

'She might. If she left here on Friday afternoon, a bank book would have been no use to her till yesterday morning. Was she planning to go far? Would she have needed cash, or would she be relying on someone else?'

'She maybe had cash in the box, sir.'

Cattanach stared down at the empty space. Mabel Campbell had had this box out in the last week, anyway, to place her son's death certificate inside it. There was no birth certificate, he realised.

No marriage certificate, either. He would put word round the banks in the town, see if she had had an account with any of them. He had a feeling she would not, if possible, have simply deposited the money she had brought to her marriage into her husband Robert's account.

'Can you find a suitcase, Gauld?' he asked.

'I've no seen one yet, sir. There's plenty clothes, though.'

'That's not to say she hasn't taken some with her. Keep looking.'

He himself examined the cupboard under the stairs – the stairs themselves belonged to the upper flat, of course. This seemed to be Robert Campbell's domain: he kept a variety of tools here, though nothing out of the ordinary. In one corner, by the floor, were a small garden fork and trowel, meticulously clean. Longer garden spades and so on must be outside somewhere.

The kitchen held nothing but kitchen things, some of them barely used. The bathroom – these new council houses each had their own bathroom and W.C., not like the tenements in town with the shared W.C. on each landing and a tin bath for Saturdays – the bathroom was spotless, but full of soaps and flannels and towels of all kinds, stuffed into two small cupboards. Thoughtful, Cattanach returned to the main bedroom and, as Gauld completed his search of the wardrobe and bedside cabinets, he went to the dressing table.

There was very little in the way of makeup on it or in it, and no hairbrush. The closest he could find was an old, broken comb, shoved to the back of a drawer.

'Did you find any jewellery?' he asked over his shoulder.

'No, nothing,' said Gauld.

'And no suitcase?'

'Only this one,' said Gauld, producing a small fake leather thing with two of the corners ripped off. 'It was under the bed. It's Robert Campbell's things, nothing in it to do with Mrs. Campbell.'

Cattanach thought back to both his meetings with Mabel Campbell. Each time she had been made up to within an inch of her life, and wore at least four striking pieces of jewellery.

A burglar might take the jewellery, might take cash or a bank book. He was much less likely to take makeup and a hairbrush.

He was sure, now: Mabel Campbell had left her house of her own accord, with time to pack, almost certainly on Friday afternoon.

He was even more sure, now, that she had no intention of taking her own life. She might not be committing any other kind of crime, either. But, if that look he had seen on her face as the funeral procession formed was anything to go by, she had been afraid, and she was running away. But from what? From whom?

He had driven his own car to Seaton, which was just as well: driving, he only just reached the hospital entrance at Foresterhill in time to meet Miss Mackay. The bus would have taken ages. The new buildings in their exposed, empty grassland setting were enormous: he was glad she had named a clear meeting place. But then, she seemed an efficient kind of person.

She arrived at the entrance a moment after he did. He was relieved she had not been standing waiting for him. If Anna Mackay had been the image of a well-bred respectable daughter yesterday, today she was very much the efficient doctor at work. Her gleaming bobbed hair was pinned back at either side, there was no jewellery to be seen, and her neat tweed suit and flat black shoes proclaimed business. She would not have tolerated lateness.

'Oh, thank goodness that's that morning over,' she said at once. 'Thank you for coming – it will be a relief to think about something else for a change, beyond – well, medical matters.'

'What do you do for lunch here?' Cattanach asked. He had never yet seen any place to eat at the new hospital, though he supposed there must be some kind of canteen.

'Agnes usually makes up sandwiches for me,' she said, 'but what with her giving her notice, I think she forgot this morning. I'm glad she remembered my message to you, at least.'

'Can I take you somewhere?' Cattanach could hear Inspector Cochrane's voice in his head, telling him what to do. He ignored it.

'I don't have long,' she warned him.

'I have a car here.'

'In that case could we go somewhere? I'll pay my share.'

'A fair offer,' he said, smiling, and led the way to his little Austin. He was glad it was clean, and put petrol rationing out of his mind. After all, this was police business.

There was a decent tea shop near the west end of Union Street, and space to park outside it. She nodded approval.

'We come here sometimes,' she said, 'some of the students. The coffee is good.'

They ordered soup and bread, and it came quickly and hot. He had a feeling she was watching how he used his cutlery, but she ate fast and they said little until their plates were cleared, and he had asked the waitress for a pot of coffee.

'That will see me through the afternoon,' said Miss Mackay with a sigh. 'Thank you for bringing me. But I shall pay my own way, as I said.'

'If you insist,' said Cattanach.

'After all, I summoned you,' she said, but not over-seriously. 'I want to know if you've found anything. Or found Mabel Campbell. Have you? Is she all right?'

He shook his head, tipping back to let the waitress set the coffee pot down. Anna Mackay poured out two cups of the fragrant liquid, and both of them leaned in again, serious now.

'No? You've not found her, or she's not all right?'

'No one that I can find has seen her since Friday, after the funeral.'

'No one at all?' She sat back in dismay. 'I had hoped … I had thought maybe she was just … No, I didn't really,' she admitted sadly. 'I might have hoped, but I didn't really think she would have told me to meet her, and not shown up. She just isn't like that.'

'What is she like, then?' he asked. He had heard all Mabel's in-laws' verdicts: it was time to hear a colleague's.

'Reliable, as I said. Personable. The people we speak to like her, and they want to volunteer because she smiles at them and asks them. In the areas we've been visiting, I think they see her as someone just a little better than them, someone to aspire to being – she is always well turned out, well made up – perhaps a little too much, but it makes a good impression.'

'Has she been chatty? Quiet? Well-informed?'

'She is chatty, but not about herself. She'll talk about the weather, about things she has seen in the papers, or heard on the wireless – popular music, the cinema. I've never heard her talk about politics, I don't think. Not even much about the war, even though that's why we've been doing what we've been doing, in preparation. Anything to put people at their ease – maybe chat about the fishing, too, to make a connexion. She's good at that.'

'But she's never talked about anything going on in her own life? You said something about her missing her husband when he's away.'

'Casual remarks, really, that's all.'

'But she did tell you that her son Billy had been killed.'

'Well, yes. That's something rather more serious, don't you think? And anyway, she had to tell me why she would not be at work last week. Of course she sounded shaken, more than I had ever heard her before. It's only what you would expect.'

Cattanach considered, and stirred another lump of sugar into his coffee. It was powerful stuff.

'Can you think of anything more you might be able to tell me about the man you saw her with? The one you thought was not her husband.'

'Well, he certainly was not her husband – her husband was at sea. And if anyone told me he was her brother or her uncle I'd have been rather shocked. There was something quite definite about the way she was clinging to his arm and looking up at him that was not the least bit sisterly.'

'Describe him again, if you would.'

'Well polished. Stout, well-dressed, pleased with himself. Pleased with her, too. Smiling a lot, looking down at her proudly. It was hard to tell in the dusk, and of course he was wearing a hat, but I think dark-haired.'

The man that Barbara Campbell had described in Woolworth's had had black hair.

'He looked like a prosperous shopkeeper,' Anna Mackay went on. 'But I think – I had the impression – that you would want to go to his shop. He looked … I don't know. Kind.'

'Kind?'

'Well-meaning. That's a horrible phrase – you mean well but it goes wrong, somehow, and you're not strong enough to fix it. Benevolent? Now he sounds like a charity. No, he looked kind. He looked as if he would treat her well, because he liked her and because he was a decent human being. There, that's the best I can do,' she said, and lifted the coffee pot, weighing it. 'More?'

'Thanks.' He thought back again to Barbara's description of the man in Woolworth's. She had not been so sympathetic to him. And she had said that he was thin. 'Are you sure he was stout?'

Anna Mackay laughed a little, and finished her coffee again before replying.

'I'm at the stage of constant diagnosis,' she said. 'I looked at him and thought, "Overweight, sweaty - heart problems".' She glanced at her watch. 'Could I prevail upon you to run me back up to Foresterhill? It would just crown everything if I turned up late this afternoon.'

Cattanach agreed, but as they paid – separately – and went out to the car his mind was still on Mabel and her friend. He might have more than heart problems if Robert Campbell found out about him, Cattanach thought. Betty had said that Campbell was a jealous man. Strange that Mabel seemed to have been so open about it – strolling down Union Street, shopping in Woolworth's. Did she really not care, or was she trying to provoke a reaction in her husband? Was that what running away was all about? Or had someone threatened to tell him when he came home – and that was why she had fled?

15

HE DROVE HIS car home after taking Miss Mackay back to the hospital. Already traffic seemed to be lighter, as people saved their petrol, but around Kittybrewster Station it was still busy with vans and lorries manoeuvring about the railway bridges as he tried to turn into Bedford Road. Even when the cattle market was not on, it was a congested corner. He followed a lorry over the bridge and down towards the university. Tuesday – it was only a week ago today that the lorry had hit the tram, and the second lorry had hit Billy Campbell. And still plenty of questions to be answered about both incidents.

Constable Anderson was the man who had attended the petrol fire in Loch Street. He had his elbows on the table in the canteen and was reading what was left of the sports pages of the *Evening Express*, but swung himself up willingly to his full height when Cattanach came in looking for him.

'Aye, I cover Littlejohn Street an' all, sir. Gil Gauld said you'd be looking for me.'

'Did he say why?'

'You're looking a man named Jock, he said.'

'That's right, who lives in Littlejohn Street. Or did live there in about June last.'

'Well,' said Anderson, 'I can think of at least a dozen men called Jock in Littlejohn Street, sir, and from what Gil Gauld says, near half of them would fit the description you have. Thin and black-haired and the kind of fellow you'd cross the street to avoid?'

'That's not word-for-word what the girl said,' said Cattanach, 'but it covers the sentiments, I think. And you've half a dozen of them?'

'At least, sir. There's more folk in Littlejohn Street than you would think.'

'I'll see if I can narrow it down, at all. Thanks, Constable.'

'Aye, sir.'

'How is our antiques dealer with the petrol barrel?'

Anderson grinned.

'Gey sorry for himself, sir. But the neighbours is all getting lovely new windows.'

'Good. If I find out anything more about our mysterious Jock, I'll let you know.'

Woolworth's was the obvious place to start – it was mid-afternoon, and Barbara Campbell was likely to be working. He had not thought to ask her which branch she worked in, though. The St. Nicholas Street one was closer but smaller: it did not take long to find a manager and discover that Barbara worked in the huge branch on Union Street. The St. Nicholas Street branch had been quiet, but the Union Street one was thick with mothers and children filling the aisles and emptying the sweet jars.

His height was useful, but really he followed his nose as best he could to the perfume and make-up counter. Barbara, her hair pinned up and her maroon uniform neat, turned a beaming smile on him that faltered at once as she recognised him.

'Inspector?' she whispered across the counter, with an uneasy glance at her colleague.

'It's all right, Miss Campbell, I'm not here to arrest you!' This, if anything, made Barbara look more alarmed. 'I just want to speak to your friend who recognised the man that your aunt was with, back in June.'

'Oh!' Barbara's eyes went straightaway to the Weigh-Out Sweets section, as if the man and Mabel might still be there. 'Oh, that was Patricia Hall. But she's gone now.'

'Gone?'

'She got married not long after that – a June wedding, it

was!' Barbara gave a little sigh. 'And so she left. You don't really stay on, you see, when you get married.'

'Of course not.' It was the usual thing. 'Do you know, by any chance, her married name? Or where she might be living?'

Barbara shrugged, then took a sustaining deep breath and turned to the other girl on the counter.

'Fiona, do you know where Patricia Hall went?'

'Patricia Hall? She got married. Who wants to know?' She had looked Cattanach up and down in a second. He felt filleted.

'This gentleman's a policeman. An Inspector.'

'Is he, indeed?' Fiona clearly had no truck with such stories.

'No, he is, really. He's trying to find my aunt Mabel. She's disappeared.'

Fiona looked far from reassured.

'Inspector Alec Cattanach, of the City Police,' said Cattanach, feeling he lacked authority. She studied him closely for a moment, then seemed to accept him.

'She's Patricia Hamilton now,' she informed him. 'She lives up in Back Hilton, in one of those new bungalows.' There was a little sigh behind the words. Fiona would have liked a new bungalow in Back Hilton, he thought. After a moment's thought, she gave him the street number.

'Thank you,' he said.

'Do you think this man Jock has something to do with Auntie Mabel disappearing?' asked Barbara, concerned. 'Should I have stopped him, or something?'

'I don't know what you could have stopped him doing, at that stage,' said Cattanach, 'and I don't really know if he's involved. I'd just like to have a word with him.' He looked at her, saw a dampness in her eyes. 'You're fond of her, aren't you?'

'Well, she's my auntie,' said Barbara.

'Doesn't follow,' said Fiona shortly.

'No, but she likes make-up and perfume and things. Pretty things,' she explained, waving a hand at the merchandise before her. 'Mammy and Auntie Isabel and Auntie Lizzie don't really care about all that, but I like it, too.'

'Did she ever tell you anything about herself? Where she came from, or who her first husband was? Or just say anything like – I don't know – 'Oh, yes, my brother used to do that too' or 'Yes, my father worked in a shop' – anything, anything at all?'

'I dinna think she did, not ever,' said Barbara, after a moment of ferocious concentration. 'She just talked about now. Now or next week, nothing further away than that.'

'But she had money, money of her own, didn't she?'

'Oh, well, now, she did say something about that, once. She didn't really say it to me: she was more talking to herself. Mammy and I were there, and Auntie Mabel had gone into the bedroom for something. For money, in fact, to pay the coalman. And I – I dinna ken why, for she was in a bad mood – I just wandered after her. She was at the wardrobe, down on her knees, at some box or other, I think. And I heard her muttering, and it sounded like "So it's not mine", she said, "maybe it's not mine, but I deserve it!" And then she turned round and I thought she was going to see me, so I ducked away out the door again and back to the front room. It's sort of stuck with me. I think maybe because it was a rare thing for her to be in a bad mood, and it just made me curious, you ken?'

'That's very useful, thank you, Miss Campbell. I'll not disturb your work any more, but if you do happen to think of anything else about your aunt, will you let me know?' He handed her a card, and she took it reverently, slipping it into her uniform pocket. 'Thank you both very much.'

Fiona nodded reluctantly at him, and he was conscious of both girls watching him pick his way through the crowds of children, and find his way back to the street.

Hilton, appropriate to the name, was on a steep incline to the northwest of the city, north of the new hospital site. The bungalows on Back Hilton Road were privately owned, but built to one design like little toy houses in a railway set. All was new and modern and organised: it did not take long to find the new Mrs. Hamilton in her new house, newly come from the kitchen by the look of her floury hands. Cattanach did not keep her long: indeed, as soon as he mentioned Littlejohn Street she was keen to see the back of him. Patricia Hamilton had left all that behind.

'I canna mind his surname,' she said swiftly. 'He was only someone you saw around, ken.'

'Can you remember anything at all about him?'

'Look, I have a cake in the oven,' she said, annoyed. 'If it gets burned …'

'Anything at all that might help us to find him.'

'I daresay you'd have seen him afore, anyway. He was the kind of fellow the polis would have their eye on.'

'For anything in particular?'

'Look, I dinna ken! It was just what folks said, ken?'

'Did he have any family? Where did he work?' Mrs. Hamilton was their only source of information: he was not going to let her go easily, not unless smoke started billowing from the kitchen.

'I dinna ken! He was just Jock, that was all.' She glared down at her flour-covered hands, wiping them on her apron. Then a thought struck her. 'He must have worked at the granite. He was aye covered in dust.'

'Stone dust?'

'Of course. Gritty, the way it is.'

'Thank you.'

'The granite works? Aye, there are twa-three of them on up West North Street, not that far from Littlejohn Street,' Constable Anderson confirmed. 'But Jock who works there … let me think.'

It took him a good few sips of tea before he spoke again.

'See, the thing is, if he's skinny like you say, what's he doing in a granite works? I dinna mind any Jock going about looking like a granite worker. But there's a fellow, Jock McKinstry, that does a bit of work sometimes around the granite places – not with the stonework, but working on the pneumatic machines, things like that. I doubt he's gey skilled or he'd have a better job, mind. But he drinks with the granite workers.'

'He must have a strong head, then.' The granite workers had a bit of a reputation. 'Has he come to our attention before?'

'He has, an' all,' said Constable Anderson. 'He has a reputation for using his fists – put his mother in the hospital once, and she's not been right since. But she wouldn't clype on him so we never got him.'

'Annoying. Anything else?'

Constable Anderson made a face.

'Nothing you could lay your hand on him for, sir. He can put on the airs and graces when he likes - he's cunning. And, well, I say he does the odd bit of work for the granite yards, and here and there, but he's never short of a bob or two. He can pay for the drinks very nicely when it suits him, even before the end of the week and any pay he might have legitimately earned.'

'I see. Yes, suspicious. Any other family?'

'None that I've ever heard tell of, sir. Just the mother and himself, and she's in the asylum now.'

'Well,' said Cattanach, 'the granite yards will be shut for the day. I'd better look for him at home.'

'I'll come with you, sir, if it's all the same with you.'

'Isn't your shift over?'

'Aye, but like I say, he's handy with his fists. And his temper's not always what you'd call serene, at the best of times, never mind when a polis wants to talk to him.'

It was five minutes' walk from the station to Littlejohn Street, passing the back of Marischal College again. The nights were drawing in: it felt later than it was, and the back of the college rose like a great black stump into the dulling sky. Constable Anderson, confident now that he had the right Jock identified, led the way to an ill-kept doorway smelling strongly of cats and ashes, pushed the door open with one large boot, and headed for the stone stairs to the first floor. They were sticky underfoot, dark and not remotely welcoming. The landing above was no better, but at least Anderson seemed disinclined to go further. He went to the nearest flat door, and knocked it sharply.

'Jock McKinstry!' he called, managing to make his voice resound about the little landing. There was a cry of alarm from one of the other flats, and a tousle-haired woman stuck her head out.

'He's no there. He's away to the pub.'

'Which one?' asked Cattanach.

'The foot of the road,' said the woman, as though he should have known. She slammed the door, and a baby somewhere beyond it began to cry. Anderson leaned an ear cautiously towards McKinstry's door, just to make sure, then shrugged at Cattanach.

'The pub, then,' said Cattanach.

'The pub, sir,' Anderson agreed.

The pub, however, was not what fate had in mind for them that evening. Following Anderson down the narrow stair again,

Cattanach heard a noise from the dark depths beyond the foot of the stairs, the place where prams and bicycles lurked. He spun just in time to see a wiry figure shoot out of the darkness, ready to grab Anderson and pull him around.

Cattanach stuck out a foot. The figure went sprawling with a heavy grunt, face down on the filthy floor. Anderson turned in alarm, tripped over the man's arm, and fell in turn, staggering across the foot of the stair and blocking Cattanach's way. The man, seizing his opportunity, scrambled to his feet, and ran.

16

RUNNING FOOTSTEPS FADED, as Anderson, swearing softly and apologetically, tried to push himself to his feet without touching the floor or the walls.

'Was that him? Did you get a chance to see?' asked Cattanach.

'Aye, Jock McKinstry,' Anderson nodded. 'The very man. Sorry, sir.'

'It was a joint effort, Constable. Never mind. He's well away now, and I think, given why we're looking for him, we'd have a fine excuse to take a look in his flat. His mother's in the Mental Hospital, you say?'

'Aye, sir, he lives alone.'

'That's a wonder in itself in Littlejohn Street, isn't it? Not sharing with another family?'

'As I say, sir, there's nothing you could put your finger on, but he's no quite right, either.' He shook himself like a dog, trying to shed the dirt of the floor, then grinned. Cattanach could see the glint of his teeth in the dark. 'I'd love to take a look inside his place, sir!'

'Come on, then.'

As it turned out, McKinstry must have left in too much of a hurry to lock his door. Cattanach had worried about attracting the attention of the young woman across the landing again, but they simply let themselves in, and flicked the light switch to illuminate a single room, dull in the green-yellowish light of a single uncovered bulb.

'He'd have trouble hiding Mabel Campbell in here,' Cattanach remarked.

'Unless she's behind those boxes, sir,' said Anderson, looming behind him.

'It's possible.' The room contained a table, two hard chairs, a small cold stove with a dented kettle on top of it, a very narrow bed with a very warm, new-looking, eiderdown, and three pairs of boots, all the same size, by the door. They were well-kept and gleaming.

And the boxes. They stood along one wall, up to waist height, reducing the workable size of the room by a couple of feet.

'About a van load, wouldn't you say?' asked Cattanach. 'Have we heard of anything going astray recently?'

'There was a van stolen near Keith,' said Anderson tentatively.

'What did it have?' The story rang a bell.

'Bottles of whisky,' said Anderson. 'Going to some big hotel in the Highlands.'

'There's a thing,' said Cattanach with interest. The boxes looked uniform and sturdy. He opened the nearest one, and peered inside at a dozen sealed whisky bottles, their golden glow given an undersea look by the single lightbulb. 'Well, now.'

'Do you think it's the same whisky?' asked Anderson.

'As to that, I have no idea,' said Cattanach, 'but I doubt that McKinstry came by – how many … three dozen crates of it by honest means. Go quick and fetch a team from the station, Anderson: we'll need to take this in tonight, before our friend Jock comes back.'

Poor Anderson, he thought, listening to the man's big boots on the stone stair. He was long past the end of his shift now. Cattanach took the chance to look more carefully round the little room. McKinstry's clothes were hung on a few hooks over the boots by the door, and he went through the pockets, finding nothing but a clean handkerchief. The clothes were of surprisingly good quality, and like the boots seemed fairly new. McKinstry must like to preserve his outdoors appearance, anyway – a little vain, perhaps? A curtained alcove contained shelves for a saucepan and some tins of food, a lump of cheese, some bread and butter. No wireless, Cattanach noted. No running water, in this little flat. And no sign of any female occupation – no forgotten lipstick, or trace of perfume, or dropped handkie with a telling lace border. He grinned. Life was never quite like a Penguin crime novel.

The team from the police station, equipped with their own van for removing their exciting prize, were in high good humour despite the lateness of the hour. Fingerprints and photographs were dealt with, and the tousle-haired woman across the landing came and watched in grim satisfaction as the officers in an orderly line carried the three dozen cases down the stair.

'What's in them, then?' she asked. 'Is it knives? Nasty wee man,' she added, without waiting for confirmation. 'See what he did to his mother? Nasty.'

Anderson had already been sent home to wash off the detritus of the tenement's floor, and now, paperwork completed, Cattanach longed for a bath, too. He headed home, hoping that this was the day his cleaning woman left hot water for him.

She had: he ran it until the angular little bathroom under the stairs was filled with steam, and lay almost completely submerged, staring up at the sloping ceiling above him. He wanted to relax, but his mind was still busy. He had taken the time, before he had left the station, to read the thin file they had on Jock McKinstry – it would be fatter by tomorrow. No known family, no known connexions outwith Aberdeen. No very definite associates – except, perhaps, Mabel Campbell. But he had not disappeared when she disappeared. He had a strong feeling that McKinstry had not left the city. He would turn up. And then they could hold him for the whisky, and ask him about Mabel Campbell.

He wondered, not for the first time, if his uncle had lain in this same bath and thought about his police work. His uncle had been a sergeant, but had died in an accident at the end of the war. His aunt, his father's sister, had lived on here, childless, and invited Cattanach to stay with her when he moved into the city. In turn, she had left him the house. It was too big for his needs, but at least it was a house. He was not living in a tent in Seaton – with no bath.

Mabel Campbell … where was she? Not dead, not by her own hand, he was sure. But Billy was dead, and there was a chance that had been deliberate. He assumed there was a connexion – was he wrong? Not the lorry driver's fault, though, not that one.

The tram crash … He thought of the poor tram driver, so badly injured, and the unconscious man, still not identified. And the fool of a lorry driver, with his empty lorry and his unknown destination in Inverness. What was he up to? Well, nothing much now, not with a broken leg. He would have to call the Dundee police tomorrow, he thought, and see if they had discovered anything. And the county police, to see if they could identify the whisky.

Two accidents, just a week ago. Two investigations that had seemed entirely straightforward, if tragic – and now they had grown legs and were trotting down the road away from him. What would his uncle have said? Cattanach had barely known him, could not imagine what he might have said. His aunt, though, would have told him to get a good night's sleep, and examine it all again in the morning. For himself, he would rather get away for a day or two. He had been on call last weekend, and he had been mindful of petrol, anyway. Next Saturday seemed a long way away.

If Sandison was lying – and Cattanach was sure he was – where was he heading, out along that road, if not Inverness? Plenty of other places. Dyce, Inverurie, Kintore, Kemnay, Insch, Oyne, Huntly, Keith …

Keith.

The van with the whisky had been stolen in Keith. Keith had a distillery, maybe two. There were distilleries all over the place in that direction.

What was it his neighbour Mrs. Walker had said? Never mind petrol, soon they'll ration whisky, was that it? And if people were prepared to hoard petrol, then many would hoard whisky – and sell it later.

Having made the leap to hoarding whisky, Cattanach slept surprisingly well and walked, refreshed, to the station in the morning. Most of the window frames now seemed to be fitted in the new extension: someone high up must have told the builders to get a move on. Lieutenant Moffat was out watching the progress. He, at least, would miss the work when it was finished.

'Morning, Inspector Cattanach,' he said, turning at the sound of Cattanach's approach.

'Good morning, sir.'

'Nice work last night. I daresay you'll be calling the County police this morning? While I feel a cell full of whisky is an asset to the station, it does make me uneasy.'

'We wanted to make sure it was well locked up, sir, yes. I hope it's the missing vanload, or there might be more abroad.'

'A sign of things to come.' The Lieutenant nodded. Perhaps he had a neighbour, too, telling him about the distilleries. 'What about Jock McKinstry? It would be very satisfying to have him locked up, judging by his file, don't you think?'

'I hope we'll pick him up soon, sir,' said Cattanach. 'You'll have seen he seems to be entirely based in the town – we have no record of him ever venturing past Anderson Drive, I think.'

'Ah, there be dragons out there,' said Moffat, unexpectedly.

'Yes, sir. So I'm not sure he would have fled too far. It was my fault we missed him, but I think we'll catch him soon enough.'

'But alas, no sign of Mrs. Campbell, I gather. I wonder if she has any fear of dragons. There was no trace of her at McKinstry's flat?'

'None at all – nothing in the least feminine, not even that might have belonged to his mother. You know he beat her, and she's in the Mental Hospital now.'

'I had heard,' said Moffat with distaste. 'But you don't think that he has taken, or is hiding, Mrs. Campbell?'

Cattanach frowned.

'It looks as if she waited – impatiently – for everyone to leave after the funeral, then packed a few things, including, possibly, some cash, and left. No one seems to have seen her leave, and I can't find any taxi driver that claims to have picked her up.' Constable Stewart had been working on it, unsuccessfully. 'But in any case, if she was in such a hurry going out to the public telephone and calling a taxi and waiting for it to come out from the middle of the town might have felt like an unnecessary delay. If she could easily carry what she was taking, I think she would just have gone.'

'Unless a friend came and picked her up,' suggested Lieutenant Moffat

'It's not a road where you see many cars,' said Cattanach. 'Constable Gauld is going to talk to the neighbours again today. But I think a taxi or a private car would have been noticed.'

'Then a tram, or a bus? Out on to King Street, and away?'

'That's my guess.'

'But whither, Inspector? Whither?'

'That's the question, sir. That and why.'

'Indeed. Indeed.' Moffat sighed, and began to walk slowly back towards the station's main door. 'No word from Dundee yet?' he asked.

'No, but I'm going to give them a call today. I wondered – after last night – if perhaps Sandison had been going north to collect a lorryload of whisky?'

'That's a notion.' Moffat turned in the doorway, heavy eyebrows raised. 'A very good notion, I should say. Put it to your Dundee friend, see what he thinks. Dundee was always a place where the illicit whisky was sold. Following a fine tradition, perhaps.'

'Perhaps, sir. Anyway, I'll see what he says.'

'Good. It seems you have quite a bit to keep you occupied just now, Inspector Cattanach.'

'Yes, it's quite busy, sir.' Would Lieutenant Moffat suggest that Inspector Cochrane should take over one or other of the cases?

'Well, I'm sure you're more than capable,' said the Lieutenant comfortably. 'Gauld pulling together all right?'

'Yes, sir.' No threat of Cochrane, then.

'Good, good. Keep me posted.'

Moffat vanished towards the stairs, and Cattanach turned to Sergeant McAulay. The sergeant had a mock stern expression on his face.

'Dinna arrest too many folk today, sir,' he said. 'Remember we're one cell down – someone's using it as a bonded warehouse.'

Cattanach grinned, and headed up to his own office. Inspector Cochrane was at his desk, examining his respirator.

'Something wrong with it?' asked Cattanach.

'I sincerely hope not,' said Inspector Cochrane. Cattanach hung up his hat and his own respirator case. He wondered what cases Inspector Cochrane was working on at the moment. He was hard put to think of an answer.

'There was a message for you,' said Inspector Cochrane, 'some time ago.' He shifted the respirator, and produced a small piece of paper. 'I suspect it is of very little importance.' He held it until Cattanach came over to fetch it. The note had a time and date on it: half past four, last Thursday.

'Have you had this since last Thursday?' he asked.

'I imagine so,' said Inspector Cochrane, unbothered. Cattanach tried to find words, and then chose not to use them – not out loud, anyway. He unfolded the note, and read it quickly.

'Sister Knox rang from Infirmary.' Sergeant McAulay's writing was broad and clear. 'Man from tram crash woke up, discharged himself before further information obtained.'

17

CATTANACH ROSE SLOWLY from his chair, folding the piece of paper in half. Then, without looking at Inspector Cochrane, he left the office, and walked the length of the short corridor outside. Then he unfolded the note again, and reread it. After all, he told himself, what difference would it have made if he had received it when it first arrived? The man, and all his mystery, had already gone.

He ought, however, to pay Sister Knox the courtesy of calling back. Or perhaps a brisk walk up to Foresterhill would do him good … no. He had other calls to make first.

The Dundee City inspector received the suggestion of whisky with enthusiasm.

'That sounds very much like the kind of a thing our friend Mr. Kitchener would be involved in,' he said. 'And you've a whole cell full of the stuff? My!'

'Firmly locked,' said Cattanach. He caught Inspector Cochrane watching him, and gave him a generous smile. 'The man with the key is teetotal.'

'That's a terrible waste,' said the Dundee man with lugubrious humour.

'I've no proof that it's the stuff that was stolen in Keith,' Cattanach reminded him. 'But it's an expensive enough one, and local to Keith – Chivas Regal. But it was the idea of whisky that struck me then – what else would Sandison have been driving all that way to collect? It wasn't exactly the kind of lorry to take timber.'

'No, I think you might have the right of it,' said the Dundee man. 'We'll do a wee bit of poking around at this end. Will you talk to someone in Aberdeen County?'

'We'll be talking to the fellows in Keith, anyway. I'll see where it goes from there.'

The sergeant at Keith was less content.

'Have I to go all the way to Aberdeen to look at the stuff, sir?' he asked.

'That's up to you,' said Cattanach. 'But if you want to find out if it's yours, that would be the best way, surely?'

'Aye, I suppose,' said the sergeant. 'I'll have to get a train.'

'You'll have to get someone to take it away, if it's yours,' said Cattanach. 'We can't store it here indefinitely.'

'And who's the fellow that had the stuff, then?' asked the sergeant shrewdly. 'Do you no have him in your cell with the whisky?'

'Not yet,' said Cattanach, doing his best to sound confident.

'Would you no be better to keep the whisky there till you get him? Confront him with it?'

'We don't need a whole cell full for that,' Cattanach countered. 'One bottle would do. A photograph, even, and we have enough of those.'

'See, we've no really the room here for – how many cases did you say?'

'How many are you missing?'

'The round three dozen, sir.'

'And by a remarkable coincidence that's what we have here. And we really don't have the room for them, either.'

'But what are we supposed to do with them?'

'Well, you're pretty much surrounded by bonded warehouses up there, aren't you? Ask one of the distilleries to hold on to it for you.'

'Off police premises?' The sergeant was shocked.

'Better than off altogether,' said Cattanach. 'You'll know yourself that whisky's going to get scarce if the war goes on – that's what happened last time. By the time you get down here with a van, that three dozen boxes could have doubled in value in some underhand dealing.'

'Oh my,' said the sergeant, even more concerned. 'I'd better give you a receipt for it, an' all, sir.'

'I think you better had,' agreed Cattanach.

'I'll away and talk to the distillery manager down the road,' the sergeant muttered, 'and maybe I'll see if they can lend us a van, an' all. I'll send you a message when I ken when I'm coming, aye?'

'That would be best, Sergeant. We don't want some clever person impersonating you and intercepting the load, do we?'

'Oh my,' the sergeant repeated. 'No, indeed, sir.'

'All organised?' asked Inspector Cochrane, as Cattanach replaced the receiver gently. 'Or have you not found Jock McKinstry yet?'

'Do you know him?' asked Cattanach, surprised.

'There are those whose reputation goes before them,' said Inspector Cochrane, primly.

'And what have you heard about McKinstry?'

'Oh, that he's a nasty little man,' said Inspector Cochrane. 'That he put his mother in hospital. Now she's in the Mental Hospital, poor thing.'

'Do you know anything about any other family?'

'Other family?' Inspector Cochrane looked – what? Uneasy?

'Known associates, that kind of thing.'

'I shouldn't think so,' said Inspector Cochrane, though his shoulders were still a little hunched. 'Who would want to associate with him?'

Someone who wanted his three dozen cases of whisky, Cattanach thought suddenly. The whisky, if it was the same whisky, had been stolen in Keith. McKinstry never ventured outside Aberdeen. It seemed unlikely that he had been working alone.

Not wanting to give Inspector Cochrane the satisfaction of hearing him speaking to Sister Knox, Cattanach decided he would now go to Foresterhill in person and speak to her – to apologise, at least, for his tardy response to her information. And the walk would be much more conducive to his thoughts about whisky than would sitting in an office watching Inspector Cochrane examining his respirator, or whatever he had found to spend his time on.

He chose to avoid Union Street this time with all its busyness, and instead walked along West North Street, through

Mounthooly and into Powis Place, then on between the railway lines before they converged at Kittybrewster, near his home. Turning in to Ashgrove Road, he was conscious of skirting the lands of the Mental Hospital, where poor Mrs. McKinstry was after her son's treatment. Some people feared asylums, maybe with justification: it seemed easier to go in than to come out, often. Was that what had made Inspector Cochrane look unsettled when they were talking about Jock's mother?

The road to the Infirmary from here was a long, gentle climb, a good stretch of the legs as the air grew clearer out of the city's smoke and traffic. McKinstry must have been working with someone, and that someone, no doubt, would be back for the whisky for its onward distribution – unless they intended to use Jock's flat as a depot for the duration, which seemed unlikely. Had McKinstry been able to warn them to stay away? Or would Constable Anderson, now keeping an eye on the flat in case of Jock's return, need some help? He kicked himself for not thinking of it earlier. And if McKinstry had been able to contact his associates, had he also taken refuge there? He wondered if the stolen van had been spotted yet. Whoever the thieves were, they must have had a good reason for emptying it of the three dozen cases of whisky and lugging them up to the first floor and Jock's flat. He frowned. The van, he thought, was either miles away or at the bottom of the harbour. They wanted the whisky, and they were going to split it up in Littlejohn Street.

Three dozen cases, though, was not a large amount. Jock McKinstry and his associate, or associates, he sensed, were not anything big, though they might be thinking of a more glorious criminal future. Best to nip that kind of ambition in the bud. But the war, he thought, was going to bring that kind of person out: those for whom the misfortune of others, or any kind of calamity, was just an opportunity waiting to be explored. He sighed, and thought of all those memoranda being pasted into Inspector Cochrane's mighty ledger. With new rules as well as new criminals, they were going to be busy.

The clear air and open land eased his mind, though, before he saw the bulky blocks of the Sick Children's Hospital down to his left, and then the sprawling Infirmary further ahead. Like any other policeman, he was used to frequent hospital calls. It had been much handier when the Infirmary was at Woolmanhill, in the middle of the city, but he thought he could come to relish striding up here, stopping to stare down over the west of the city and feeling the wind from the hills meet the wind from the sea. A healthy place, he thought. He wondered if the medical students felt the same, for like him they had to shuffle now between Marischal College, almost next door to the police station, and the hospital. He pictured Anna Mackay striding authoritatively up the hill with her classmates, shook his head, and wondered if he would see her today. He hoped not. It would be awkward. Too many times in one week.

Sister Knox was instructing an orderly in the sluice room when Cattanach arrived. The nurse who led him to the door advised him to wait outside.

'Yes?' said Sister Knox when she saw him. She was a beefy individual, with strong arms and a red face. 'I beg your pardon, sir, are you the new doctor?'

'No,' said Cattanach, 'I'm from the City Police. You kindly left me a message last week and I'm afraid for various reasons it only reached me this morning.'

'Oh, aye?' He could see he had been downgraded in her eyes. There would be no begging his pardon now.

'About the unconscious man from the tram crash in Woodside,' he reminded her.

'Oh, aye, yes. You're Inspector Cattanach, I daresay. Come to my desk,' she said, abandoning the orderly and the sluice room.

He followed her to a table at the head of an open ward – not, fortunately, the one where Sandison presumably still lay with his broken leg. There was an extra chair, and she permitted him to take it.

'I sent that last Thursday,' she said, quietly enough not to be heard by the nearest patients.

'I know, and I'm very grateful,' said Cattanach. 'I really came to apologise that I had not thanked you earlier. It was good of you to pass on the information.'

'Well, you did ask us to,' said the sister, a little resentful. 'Anyway, I'm pleased you got it.'

'Is that unusual?' he asked. 'Do unconscious men suddenly come to and leave?'

'They're not usually up to it,' she said. 'If they come to and they're confused, you might find them wandering round the ward, trying to work out where they are. But this man just upped and left, without, it seems, anybody seeing him.'

'In daylight?'

'That's right. It's probably easier in daylight. There would be more people moving around, so staff are less likely to ask questions.'

'And …' Cattanach tried to picture what might have happened. 'I suppose you had put him into pyjamas?'

'Of course.'

'So his clothes and anything that had come in with him, that would have been – in the little cupboard by his bed?'

'Yes. He had taken the lot, by the way. We clean the cupboards after every patient. It was empty.'

'But surely he could not have walked out of the hospital in his pyjamas?'

'That would certainly have been unusual. But no, he did not do that.'

'You have a doorman, of course.'

'We have a doorman, yes. But also, Inspector, we're not above a little investigation ourselves. He left his pyjamas in one of the bathrooms.'

'Changed and left. Very impressive for a man who had been unconscious for two days, and had just woken up.'

'Well, indeed, Inspector. And we're tempted, my colleagues and I, to draw the conclusion that he was not, in fact, unconscious for as long as we thought he was. That he was, in fact, biding his time.'

'Did you go after him?'

'We are not the police!'

'I meant for medical reasons – in case he was still unwell. If he had, as you say, been wandering in confusion around the ward, you would have put him back to bed, would you not?'

'We would, of course. And yes, we did look for him. But there was no sign of him anywhere. It was visiting time, and he must just have dressed and gone out amongst the crowd. So I rang the police station.'

And encountered the obstacle of Inspector Cochrane, thought Cattanach with a sigh.

18

'AND HE NEVER showed any signs of consciousness before that?'

'Nothing,' said Sister Knox.

'And no clue at all to his identity?'

'His clothes were perfectly ordinary. Not a labouring man – maybe a clerk? He didn't have any obvious scars, or tattoos, or anything like that. I think someone came from the police and took a photograph of his face when he was first brought in.'

'That's right,' said Cattanach. It had not, he suspected, been a good likeness – shadowy and surly, the skin slumped as it does when someone is lying on their back. 'Has Sandison taken any interest in him?'

Sister Knox made a face.

'I'd have to ask my nurses that. It's not something that would be on either of their notes.'

'No, I suppose not. I just wondered if perhaps they knew each other.'

'I've heard nothing about that, certainly. But Mr. Sandison is – well, a thug, I'm afraid, and clearly our other patient was not completely honest, so perhaps they were able to hide any association they might have had?'

'Would you mind if I had a word with Sandison? And perhaps with one of the nurses who looks after him?'

'No, go ahead with Mr. Sandison, certainly. And any time you'd like to take him away, when you find a nice cell for him, please don't hesitate. We'll even help you carry him out.'

She gave him an unexpected and mostly unsisterly grin.

'We'll be happy to take him off your hands, when the time comes,' he agreed. 'I take it he can't walk anywhere unaided just now?'

'No,' said Sister Knox definitely. 'He won't be walking out without anyone noticing.'

Sandison was toying with a copy of the *Evening Express* from, as far as Cattanach could see, some time several weeks ago, when Cattanach approached his bed.

'Oh!' he said, instantly taking on a hunted look. 'It's you.'

'Our friends in Dundee are having a word with your boss, Sandison,' said Cattanach, perching one hip at the end of the bed comfortably. 'Can I send on any greetings? News? Apologies for crashing his lorry?'

'He'll be worried about me,' said Sandison, unconvincingly.

'He'll be worried about the job he sent you on, no doubt,' said Cattanach. 'Where did you say you were going again?'

'Inverness,' muttered Sandison, not looking at him. He began folding the paper up layer by layer at one side, and focussed on that.

'Well, now, we'll see if Mr. Kitchener remembers it the same way, won't we?'

'The Dundee polis might tell you lies. The wrong thing, anyway. What would they ken about Inverness?'

'Do you miss your pal?'

'What pal?' Sandison looked confused.

'The fellow in the bed across there. The one that left last Thursday.'

'I dinna ken what you mean. The fellow that was across there, he wasna awake, I dinna think. I thought he was dead a long time and they just hadna taken him away. He never said nothing to a'body.'

'Had you seen him before?'

'I couldna see him then,' Sandison pointed out. 'He was flat on his back, and I'm stuck here. For all I know he could have been my ain brother.'

'Maybe he was,' said Cattanach, but he thought that Sandison was speaking the truth. But who had the man been? 'Tell me, have you any friends in Aberdeen at all?'

'I dinna ken a'body here.'

'What about Jock McKinstry? Smallish, thin, handy with his fists?'

But Sandison shook his head, puzzled. He was not, Cattanach thought, a very good actor. The name Jock McKinstry was not familiar to him.

Sister Knox had sent an older nurse over to speak to him when he had finished with Sandison.

'Aye, we'd be that pleased if you took him away,' she said. 'There's none of the young ones wants to go near him. His leg may be broken but there's nothing wrong with his hands – nothing that a good slap wouldna fix, anyway.'

'Overfamiliar?'

'That's putting it mildly,' she said, nodding hard.

'Has he had any visitors?'

'Not a one.'

'What about the man that was unconscious? Did anyone come to see him?'

'No, not him either. Of course, they'd have been hard put to know he was here, if none of us knew who he was.'

'What was your impression of him?'

The nurse considered.

'Indoorsy. His hands were clean, and his skin was a bit grey, not reddened. His clothes were plain, not fancy – I suppose he'd have been off to work on that poor tram, and I'd have said he was heading for an office in the town.'

'Manager or clerk?'

'Clerk,' she said at once. 'Nothing expensive about him, except his watch. It was quite good.'

'No one has mentioned a watch. I heard there was no wallet, no letters or papers of any kind.'

'Not that I saw, and I was the one changed him and folded his clothes away. Aye, the watch was one a bit like my brother's that he got when he was promoted – he's in the paperworks at Peterculter. A nice Ingersoll, he has.'

'Did you notice anything engraved on it?'

'Aye, for I was looking for anything that would tell us who

he was. Did Sister Knox not pass it on?'

'We've had some problems with messages recently, unfortunately,' said Cattanach apologetically. Specifically a problem called Inspector Cochrane, he thought. Unaccountably his heart gave a little skip of excitement as he asked, 'What did it say?'

'It said,' and she closed her eyes to picture it clearly again, 'it said "To T, from your Belle".'

'"Your bell?"'

'"Belle",' she repeated, 'like the belle of the ball, only with a capital B. It's French, is it no?'

'It is, yes.'

'So I'm guessing it was from a lassie, and no his mother nor his sister, either.'

'Just "T"?' he said, sadly.

'Aye, just that. Thomas, likely enough,' she said, with a brisk nod.

Tony, Toby, Terence, he added in his head. Well, it was mildly exciting. A man whose name probably began with T had run away from a hospital, perhaps with concussion, perhaps smitten with a sudden guilty desire to rush back to his stool in an office somewhere in the town. Somewhere a woman he called Belle may or may not be missing him – or perhaps he had gone home.

Cattanach was making his way out through the main entrance of the hospital again when someone called his name. He knew before turning round that it was Anna Mackay.

'Good morning, Miss Mackay,' he said, hat already in his hands anyway.

'Good morning, Mr. Cattanach. Were you looking for me?'

'Ah, no, I was speaking with some of the nurses about something else.'

'You're not looking for Mabel Campbell?' she asked in alarm.

'We don't always have the luxury of concentrating solely on one case at a time, I'm afraid,' he explained, 'and unfortunately we haven't made much progress since yesterday.' Apart from scaring off her old boyfriend and finding three gross of whisky bottles in his flat, he thought. 'We're still making enquiries.'

'Father says you say that when cases go quiet,' she said, a

little sharply.

'The case has not gone quiet,' he said. 'But I reserve the right to say that as often as it's true,' he added, with a polite smile.

'Of course,' she said after a moment, almost apologetic. Today her suit was a lavender tweed, with a pretty blouse, slightly softer than yesterday's appearance.

'I remembered something else about Mabel,' she said. 'It may be nothing, but it came to me at dinner yesterday. My mother – you remember, she does a good deal at the Women's Volunteers?'

'Yes, indeed.' And found me a puzzle, he thought, smiling inwardly.

'She was talking about registration, you know? Identity cards and all that horrid stuff?'

'Yes, I know.'

'And it reminded me. Mabel was always asking me about it. Once she knew that Mother was helping there, she came back to it several times.'

'To registration?'

'Yes. You know there'll be a kind of census at the end of the month, to get all the information for registration, and the Women's Volunteers are helping with it. Mabel kept wanting to know what was to be asked, and how many questions, and what kind of details they would want, and – and this she came back to three or four times – who would be able to see it when it was done. I think she has the idea that it will be in the local library for anyone to look up – I don't suppose it will be, though. But she seemed very anxious about it. It was odd, for generally she was quite a calm person.'

'That's very interesting, thank you, Miss Mackay.'

'I wondered, when I thought about it after dinner, if she thought someone was going to use it to find her?'

'Did you think she was hiding from someone?' he asked.

'It never occurred to me. Not until last night, when I was thinking about her questions.'

'Well, I shall make a note of it,' he said. 'Thank you again.'

'Right,' she said. 'You're welcome.'

But she stood there for a moment longer, not quite releasing him from the conversation. Only when the door behind them swung open and a group of other well-dressed young people clattered their way through did she show any sign of moving, when one of the men, broad-shouldered and handsomely sportsmanlike, called her name.

'Anna! Coming?'

'Oh! Yes,' she said. 'Yes, of course. Good bye, Mr. Cattanach.'

'Good bye, Miss Mackay.'

And she was swept away with them, out into the autumn sunshine. He watched her go, but of course she did not look back.

Could there be any other reason why Mabel Campbell was so anxiously curious about registration? She was, by Anna's account, an organised, responsible person: carrying an identity card was unlikely to hold any fears for her. But Anna's idea that Mabel might fear that someone was looking for her might explain her disappearance, not to mention that look of terror at the funeral. Whoever it was she thought was looking for her, to judge by that, had found her. But who could it be? Without knowing more about her past, it was hard to guess.

But there was one other possibility that crossed his mind. Robert Campbell was a jealous man, and Mabel Campbell, when he was at sea, was going about with another man, a man with at least one crime to his name and probably more. Did that man know her by the name of Mabel Campbell? Or was Mabel Campbell, perhaps, leading a double life?

He had let Anna Mackay and her friends get well clear of the doorway before he himself left the hospital and began the easy walk back down the hill into the town, taking the Westburn Road route this time, past parks and the front of the Mental Hospital, and then the factories and slaughterhouses of George Street and Hutcheon Street. The one thing he missed about his time as a constable was walking the beat, getting to know an area in all its intimate detail. But he had quickly realised that the only way he was going to be free to make the excursions into the countryside that he needed was promotion, promotion he was quite capable of achieving. After all, if Inspector Cochrane had risen to that rank, then he could.

Constable Leggatt was still hiding his black eye in the evidence store. Cattanach thought he looked pleased to have company for a minute or two.

'The unconscious man,' he said.

'Aye, sir? Have you found out who he is?'

'I'm afraid not, and I discovered this morning that he absconded from the hospital – well, he was hardly under arrest – last Thursday, without saying anything to anyone.'

'Concussion?' asked Leggatt, in sympathetic tones.

'No idea. He had not shown any signs of being conscious before he left. He took everything with him. I just wanted to check, though: are you absolutely sure he was in the tram? He wasn't on the street, for example, or even in the lorry?'

'He was definitely in the tram, sir. I got all the passengers to make a list of everyone they had seen on it, so we could make sure no one was unaccounted for. He was on several of their lists, but no one knew his name, nor who he was.'

19

USUALLY AS HE approached the police station, one question in his mind was the whereabouts of Inspector Cochrane. Now, he found, he was more concerned not with Inspector Cochrane's whereabouts, but what he might have been doing while Cattanach was out. He would have to make sure, each time he returned, to check with Sergeant McAulay or his equivalents to see if they had left any messages for him that Inspector Cochrane might have chosen to – to what? He left it at 'interfere with'. No doubt Inspector Cochrane had some strange motives of his own: Cattanach, for the moment, had no particular wish to delve into them. Instead he would check as he passed the reception desk.

But when he pushed through the doors into reception, he found much of the space taken up by Constable Anderson and a small, skinny man with a nasty smell coming from him. Constable Anderson, far from looking dismayed, had a very satisfied expression on his round face.

'Inspector, this is Jock McKinstry, sir,' said Anderson. Cattanach, well used to dogs, recognised a stick when he saw one, and metaphorically patted Anderson on the head.

'Well done – where did you find him?'

'He didna find me,' Jock McKinstry objected at once. 'I was in my ain hallway, gangin' up till my ain flat, and yon great monster leps out from under the stair and grabs me by the collar. What was I doing wrang? Not a thing!'

'He'll have learned that leaping out from under the stair from you, no doubt,' said Cattanach. 'I'm very pleased to see you, Mr. McKinstry. Sergeant, is the interviewing room free?'

'It is, aye, sir.'

'Then please step this way, Mr. McKinstry.' Cattanach opened the door and gestured to him to go and sit at the other side of the table there. 'Constable, perhaps you could stand by the door here – if we can avoid closing it altogether I think that would be preferable.'

'I've a bucket of bleach standing ready,' said Sergeant McAulay, a little pink around the gills from not breathing properly.

'Good man. Right, now, Mr. McKinstry.' Cattanach pushed the door almost closed, and took a seat opposite the man. He had quite a keen sense of smell, himself, and hoped this would not take too long. Either that or they would have to take the man into the yard and hose him down. 'Perhaps you could account for your movements yesterday evening.'

'Yesterday?' asked Jock.

'Yes. The twelfth of September, starting, shall we say, at about seven?'

'I was in the pub,' said Jock. 'With my pals.'

'When did you leave?'

'Late. Aye, it was late.'

'How late? Was the pub closing when you left?'

'Aye, aye, it was.'

'And were you there all the time? Was this the pub at the bottom of Littlejohn Street?'

'Aye. Aye, I was there the whole time.'

Cattanach looked at him. There was almost no point in telling him he was lying – they both knew.

'That's a decent suit, Mr. McKinstry,' he said, 'or it has been. I wonder if the steam laundry could take away some of that – er, odour for you?'

'I fell in some sharn,' said McKinstry, glancing down at his filthy sleeves.

'Did you? Where was that, then?'

'In a street,' said Jock, after a pause.

'Unfortunate. Where did you sleep last night, Mr. McKinstry?'

'In my flat.' It was a bold lie. McKinstry did not look the type to stay in stinking clothes longer than necessary.

'And that flat is …' Cattanach recited the address from memory. Jock McKinstry hesitated.

'Aye, that's it. That's the one.'

'Quite small, isn't it?'

'It's no big, right enough,' Jock conceded, though his gaze was fixed on Cattanach like a mouse watching a cat.

'Did you ever bring Mabel Campbell back to it?' asked Cattanach. Jock's jaw dropped.

'No! I never,' he said. 'Her? There?'

That made sense, Cattanach thought.

'So where did you meet her, then?'

Jock's tongue slipped out, and moistened his lips furtively.

'Meet who?' he asked.

'Mabel Campbell.'

'I don't know anybody called Mabel Campbell,' said Jock, not quite looking at Cattanach now.

'Oh, come on, now, Mr. McKinstry. You know, the woman you didn't bring back to your dingy flat. You must have met her somewhere else, then. Do you meet her regularly?'

'I tell you, I don't know her.'

'I think you do, Mr. McKinstry. You were seen together. When did you last see her?'

'If you know so much about her, Inspector, you tell me!'

'Maybe you saw her the day she disappeared? Maybe you've seen her since she disappeared?'

'Wait, wait now,' said Jock McKinstry. 'Disappeared? What are you on about?'

'Mabel Campbell has disappeared,' said Cattanach kindly.

'When?'

'Well, if you don't know her, I don't think it's any concern of yours, really, do you?'

'It's just – it's just – just a common human concern for another human being,' said Jock desperately.

'That's very good of you, Mr. McKinstry. If I knew where she was, I could pass on your best wishes.'

'Does … has she really disappeared?'

'When did you last see her, Mr. McKinstry?'

Jock exhaled weightily, and Cattanach could almost see him change before his eyes. Jock pulled his shoulders back, tilted his head a little, pursed his lips.

'I haven't seen her since July. The beginning of July. She told me she didn't want to see me anymore.' His accent had neatened itself up, too.

'You'd have taken that badly,' suggested Cattanach. 'No man wants to hear something like that.'

'I was more sad than anything,' Jock admitted. 'She was nice to go about with. I liked fine being seen with her on my arm.'

'You knew she was married?'

'Aye, but we never went to the kind of places her husband's family would go. She made sure of that,' he said.

'Her husband's the jealous type, did she tell you?'

'I can look after myself,' said Jock McKinstry, and his eyes narrowed.

'Of course you can – I've heard that,' said Cattanach. 'I've heard you've a bit of a temper, Mr. McKinstry. Tell me – did you lose your temper with Mabel Campbell?'

'No – I told you, I was a bit sad. That's all.'

'You didn't, by any chance, hit her? Hurt her?'

'A woman? I'd never hit a woman!'

'You hit your mother,' said Cattanach. 'I hear she's in a bad way.'

'That's different,' said McKinstry. 'I liked Mabel. I'd never have hit her. Has she really disappeared?'

'Yes,' said Cattanach. 'Last Friday. After her little boy's funeral.'

'Her what? The wee lad?' McKinstry was genuinely shocked. 'I never knew. Och, that's terrible.'

Whoever had frightened Mabel Campbell that afternoon would have known it was her son's funeral, surely. Cattanach rubbed his face, and sighed. On the good side, he had almost stopped noticing the smell.

'Now, then: why were there three dozen cases of whisky in your flat?'

This time the shock on McKinstry's face had been bought and paid for weeks ago.

'Were there?' he asked.

'Where did it come from, Mr. McKinstry? Keith, by any chance?'

'I've never been to Keith,' said McKinstry, probably honestly.

'Then someone brought you back a very fine present. We've a sergeant coming in from Keith to tell us all about it, and about the van it came in. Maybe you'd like to get your story in first? I'll tell you, by the way, that the whisky is no longer in your flat, and we're checking the boxes and bottles for fingerprints.'

'Oh, aye, that whisky. The stuff in the boxes,' said McKinstry. He looked up at Cattanach from beneath thin brows. 'I was doing a favour for a friend.'

'Good of you. I bet you're known for your generosity, aren't you?'

'I like to think I can do things for others,' said Jock, lifting his shoulders a little. 'In my small way.' The gentility was still hovering over him.

'Maybe you'd like to do something for us,' Cattanach suggested.

'If I can, of course,' said Jock.

'Maybe you could tell us the name of your friend? The one that brought the whisky.'

'I've forgotten it,' said McKinstry simply.

'Yet to do a favour like that – I'd have thought he would have been quite a close friend.'

'Call him more a friend of a friend,' said McKinstry after a moment.

'Then tell us the name of the friend. Your friend, whose friend brought the whisky.'

'I've forgotten that, too,' said Jock, with an air of melancholy.

'I think,' said Cattanach, 'that you've been under a good deal of strain, haven't you?'

'I have,' said Jock.

'That'll be why you're forgetting things, I daresay.'

'More than likely, Mr. Cattanach.'

'You need rest. Rest, and maybe a change of clothes. A wash, at least.'

'That would probably help, aye. See what I've been told is I need to look after myself more. Put myself first for a change.'

'Very true, Mr. McKinstry,' said Cattanach warmly. 'And in that regard, I think we can be of some assistance. Our sergeant here, out at the desk, he can show you to a nice peaceful room with a bed, and he can provide a change of clothes and some water – I'm not sure it will be hot water, but I should imagine it will at least be clean. And you can have a rest, and let your memory go to work on those names. I'm sure you'll find it very refreshing.'

'You're no locking me up!'

'I think you'll find we are, Mr. McKinstry. Take advantage of the break.'

Cattanach rose, bade Jock a polite farewell, and left the room, nodding to Sergeant McAulay.

'That'll be two cells full, then,' said McAulay, keeping a reproachful tally.

'I'm sure they'll be down from Keith soon to clear that cell out.' He thought of Inspector Cochrane. 'Any messages for me?'

'Aye, Constable Gauld rang no long ago – while you were in with Jock there. Said he's been going round Seaton chapping on the doors.'

'Good.'

'And he thinks he has something, and that you won't want to wait till the end of his shift, so he wondered if you would want to go there yourself? He gave a name, now, let me see ... it was a Mrs. Hawthorne. Gladys Hawthorne, he said. Lives near Mrs. Campbell's house.'

'She does indeed,' said Cattanach, picturing the dull little house. He wondered what on earth could have tempted the mousy, apologetic woman to bother Constable Gauld and waste the time of the police. 'Right. Nothing else for me just now?'

'Not a thing.'

'Inspector Cochrane in?'

'He's away out, sir. He said he was going to inspect the blackout blinds on the shops in George Street.'

'Good for him,' said Cattanach without emphasis. 'I'll go to Seaton. If Gauld calls back, tell him I'm on my way.'

Constable Gauld, guessing correctly how Cattanach might travel, was waiting near the tram stop at St. Machar Drive, improving the shining hour by updating his notebook.

'You left a message about Gladys Hawthorne,' said Cattanach.

'Aye, sir,' said Gauld. 'I thought when you heard what she told me you might want to have a word with her yourself.'

'And what did she tell you?' asked Cattanach, beginning a slow walk back down the road towards the Hawthornes' house. If Gauld were promoted, he would have to learn to walk faster than beat-pace.

'Well, she and twa-three others said they'd seen a couple of men hanging around the place. From what I can tell, we're talking about from the Friday evening, the day young Billy was laid to rest, on down to yesterday or maybe Monday: the one report I had of someone seeing them yesterday it was a bittie down the road and they werena sure.'

'Two men? Did the descriptions match each other?'

'Oh, aye, sir,' said Gauld, and read from a place his finger had marked in his notebook. 'One was a fair big fellow, with yellowy hair and working clothes, though no sign of what he might work at – no big waterproof boots for a fisherman, say, nor dust from the granite works, nor whatever. The other was smaller, smartly dressed, like a fellow from the Council, one of them said. Dark hair, and pale.'

'Always together? It couldn't just be chance?'

'Well,' said Gil Gauld, 'always together till the one time that Mrs. Hawthorne told me about. And that would be Monday, in the late afternoon. That's the time that has got her worried.'

20

'GO ON, THEN, Constable.'

'Aye, well, she said her wee lassie was just in and having a piece of toast when there was a knock on the door. Mrs. Hawthorne tellt me she went to open it and there was the smart man, the wee-er one, on the doorstep, his hat off and looking all polite. Mrs. Hawthorne thought he was very respectable looking. And he was asking questions about Mrs. Campbell.'

'What kind of questions?' asked Cattanach, with a glance at Gil Gauld's serious face.

'About where she might be, sir. And about her friends and her family.'

Cattanach drew to a halt, thinking.

'And did she answer him?'

'That's what's worrying her – she says she did, and now she says she doesna know why, and it's preying on her mind that maybe she should have kept her mouth shut. She says,' he added, distancing himself from the coarse phrase.

'Right,' said Cattanach, 'yes, I think I'd like a word with the lady. Are you in the middle of something else, Constable, or will you come too? I'd like to make sure she tells me the same thing she told you.'

'A' course, sir.'

Mrs. Hawthorne answered the door in a wriggle of wretched embarrassment.

'Och no, Inspector, I'd no idea of taking up any more of your time! No!'

'I think we need to have a word about what you've told the Constable here, Mrs. Hawthorne,' said Cattanach, trying to sound reassuring. 'I hope it won't take long. I'm sure you're a very busy woman.'

'But I told him everything!' She jerked her head at Constable Gauld. 'Can he no tell you, if you think it's important? He'll have the right words for it, and a'thing.'

'I'd really like to hear it from you, Mrs. Hawthorne. May we come in?'

'In?' You might have thought he had offered to bring his pet elephant with him. Her eyes darted, carrying out a frantic inspection of the strip of carpet, the frame of a colourless picture, the shine on the bakelite door handles. 'I – I dinna ken …'

'Of course, not if it disturbs you,' said Cattanach smoothly, 'but it might be preferable to standing out here in the street. Where almost anyone might see you,' he added innocently.

Mrs. Hawthorne swallowed hard, and pulled back the door to let them in.

'All right, then,' she said. 'Come on in.'

The parlour was cold, and showed little sign of much use. Cattanach wondered if Constable Gauld had been admitted to the sanctuary of the kitchen, and felt briefly envious. He was invited to perch on a chair that looked soft and was not, while Mrs. Hawthorne took up a fraction of a hard-backed chair by a small table. Constable Gauld arranged himself by the door, producing his notebook again behind Mrs. Hawthorne's head.

'I gather that you've seen a couple of men in the neighbourhood,' Cattanach began, 'and then one of them called on you on Monday, is that right?' She nodded sharply, keen to get this over with. 'Tell me what he said to you.'

'He said good afternoon, and he took his hat off,' she said, and he could already see that she had been impressed. 'He had very nice manners.'

'That's always a good thing, isn't it?'

'Mmhm. Then he asked if I knew the lady who lived two doors down, in the ground floor flat. I said I did, it was Mrs. Campbell. He said he had thought the minute he saw me that I was just the kind of sensible, noticing person he had hoped to find, because he was trying to find Mrs. Campbell, and did I know where she had gone. Well, I didn't know she had gone at all – I just knew she hadn't been around much since – since Friday.' Mrs. Hawthorne glanced at the wall, as if she could see through it to the kitchen. The distant sound of a wireless tickled the edge of hearing. He wondered if she had intended to switch it off, or if young Maggie was in there listening.

'Perhaps you thought she was with her family.'

'Her husband's family, yes. I suppose if I'd thought at all then that's what I would have thought.'

'Did you tell him that?'

'I did. He seemed very pleased with that and I thought he might go away then. As far as I could see he was on his own – that big man wasn't with him, thank goodness, for I never liked the look of him. I was going to ask the man in –' (he really must have been charming, thought Cattanach, still wondering about his pet elephant) – 'but then he said he thought Mrs. Campbell had had some friends visit, or colleagues, or something, and asked me about that. So I tried to remember anyone she had come to visit her, or whatever, and I told him about the mannie in the big black car.'

Constable Gauld looked across the top of Mrs. Hawthorne's combed head at Cattanach, and nodded significantly. This was what he had wanted the Inspector to hear.

'Well, then, tell me about him,' said Cattanach encouragingly.

'Well,' said Mrs. Hawthorne, rubbing her skirt along her thin thighs, 'I don't know that I should.'

'Why would you not?'

'I suppose …' She tried to think of a reason. 'I suppose it's no really police business.'

'We're very good at ignoring stuff that isn't police business,' he told her.

'And I dinna think she would like me telling you.'

'Well, for one thing,' said Cattanach reasonably, 'you've already told the man who came to the door – and I suppose you didn't ask him his name?'

'No,' she said wretchedly. 'But I could see he was a respectable man.'

'And for another thing,' Cattanach went on, assuming for the sake of argument that he himself did not look like a respectable man, 'if it helps us to find Mrs. Campbell, and bring her home safely, then would it not be better to tell us?'

'I suppose,' she said slowly.

'Well, then,' said Cattanach again, and waited.

'I never saw him very clear.' She cleared her throat, not looking at him. 'I mean, I only ever saw him after dark. I saw the car – there's never that many cars round here – and I saw it stop, and then he got out and he came round and opened the door for her, and out she got, too. And then she went in home.'

'When did you see this?'

'Maybe three times, over the summer?'

'Always after dark?'

'That's right,' she said, nodding quickly.

'How were they dressed?'

She cast him an uncertain look.

'Nice. I mean, kind of grand. Like when you see them in the flicks, when they're out for the evening to somewhere posh.'

'I see.' This did not sound much like Jock McKinstry. And Jock said he had not seen her for months. Had Mabel moved on to another man? 'Long dress?'

'Oh, yes.'

There had not been one in her wardrobe. He wondered if she had taken it with her, along with her jewellery.

'Could you describe the man at all?

She shook her head.

'No.'

'You probably noticed more than you think. Was it definitely the same man, all three times?'

'Oh yes.' Unhesitating.

'Then there was something about his shape, or his height, that you must have seen. Was he taller than her?

'Only a bit. But she was in high heeled shoes.'

'Was he stouter than her?'

She gave a brief laugh.

'Oh aye, he was that. I remember thinking he looked gey well fed, an' all.' There was a hint of resentment there: Cattanach wondered how well stocked the larder was in this flat.

'Older? Younger?'

'Older, a bit, I think. Just the way he moved.'

'Any idea of his colouring, at all?'

She thought hard now, encouraged by what she had seen without realising, but in the end she shook her head again.

'No. It was that almost-dark light – colours go all wrong then. I said the car was black, but it could have been dark green, or navy blue, if I'm honest.'

'And you told the smart man all this?'

'Not all that!' she said. 'I couldna have told him all that! Anyway, he didna seem much interested in him. He just said aye, yes, and then he asked if Mrs. Campbell had any other callers, friends, or people maybe from where she worked. Well, of course, I said she didn't go out to work, not at all, and then I remembered that she's been volunteering. We'll all have to, won't we?' she added unexpectedly, looking anxious.

'I expect so,' said Cattanach. She gave him an assessing glance, maybe still concerned that she was wasting his time, but he showed no sign of leaving.

'Well, she'd got in early on the volunteering, then,' she went on, 'for she likes to be out and about. So I told the man that Mabel Campbell had been doing some work for that blood bank thing, and he was all interested, for he said he had read about it in the newspaper. And he asked what kind of a thing did she do, did she work in an office or what, and I told him what I'd seen her do – going round people's houses with another woman, looking for volunteers. They even came here,' she said, and sniffed. 'My husband told them he would think about it.'

'That must have pleased the man, all that information,' said Cattanach encouragingly.

'Oh, yes. And I told him about the lassie that was with Mabel Campbell and all, for they seemed friendly, though she was – well, she was much grander than Mabel Campbell, with all her jewellery. You could see. She had a way about her, even if she never opened her mouth. And the man was gey interested in her, too. So maybe that's where Mrs. Campbell is – she's off staying in some grand house in the West End, living in the style she's always wanted.'

'Well, what did you think, Constable?' asked Cattanach as they returned to the street.

'She doesna really approve of Mrs. Campbell, does she, sir?'

said Gauld.

'I don't think so, no.' Cattanach smiled. 'Was there any hint, anywhere, that anyone knew who these two men were? Can you remember any other references to them? A big fellow with yellow hair, and a smaller, darker, smarter one.'

'He'll be the brains, sir, no doubt. But no, I couldna call to mind anyone like them I'd seen or heard of, and they were strangers to anyone who told me about them. That was why they remembered them. There's no so many houses up in this bit yet, and strangers are noticed.'

'What about the tents and huts you told me about, along the road here? Between the houses and the sea.'

'Just on the edge of the links, sir, that's where they are. I always make sure that's part of my beat,' he said earnestly. 'When people are no happy they're more likely to cause trouble, I think. So I go and see that they've all they need. Apart from a solid roof over their heads – that's a wee bit outside the power of a constable, I think, sir.'

Impressed, Cattanach nodded.

'But no sign of two men like that, I take it?'

'No, not at all. Nor even three.'

'Three?'

'One of the neighbours, he thought he'd seen another man with them, whiles. But not this last week or so.'

'But more than once?'

'Oh, aye. He'd called them the Three Musketeers, in his head, he said. And he said "thick as thieves", looking at me like I might ken they were thieves. He'd been in two minds about calling me in about them, he said.'

'Pity he hadn't,' said Cattanach. 'Could he tell you what the third man looked like?'

'A bit, sir,' said Gauld. 'Fair, but not so yellow as the other big loon. And he had a moustache, a wee narrow one, he said, two shades darker than his hair. A solid fellow, he said, not so tall, but tougher looking.'

'Good,' said Cattanach. 'That's useful. Now, I wonder where he's gone?'

21

THURSDAY MORNING. ONLY two more days until he could head for the hills, literally. But should he? How far would he be able to get with his petrol ration? Should he keep it for emergencies?

He was shaving in the crooked little bathroom when he heard distantly, through the open window, a goods train creeping past along the line at the top of the road. The line from the station there went to Inverness – where the lorry driver, Sandison, had definitely not been going – and the local trains stopped at a variety of small stations, some of which might get him somewhere useful. He resolved to give it some thought, and walked to work.

He reached the office before Inspector Cochrane, and spent a blissful moment or two simply appreciating the emptiness of Inspector Cochrane's desk chair. A new set of memoranda had appeared in both their in-trays, which would give his colleague some happy gluing to do. He was tempted to pass the memoranda from his own in-tray to Inspector Cochrane's in-tray, to double his work. But he was sure that Inspector Cochrane would notice the duplication. He was probably the only man in the police station who actually read the wretched things from top to bottom. He wondered if the ledger included annotations and cross-referencing. He imagined it probably did.

He had skimmed most of his own copies and very occasionally added one to a small heap in his desk drawer for future use, when Constable Stewart appeared at his door.

'Sir, Sergeant says that Jock McKinstry's had – an improvement in his memory, sir, and would like a word when you're free.'

'How very obliging of him,' said Cattanach with a grin. 'Tell the Sergeant I shall be down in a moment.'

Jock McKinstry had been moved back to the interview room, dressed in clean workman's trousers and a collarless shirt. He looked smaller, somehow, but a good deal more wholesome. There was still a lingering odour, but that might have been Cattanach's imagination.

'Mr. McKinstry,' he said, taking a seat while Constable Stewart took up a place by the door. 'How very nice to see you again – and looking so much better. I hope you slept well?'

'I did, Inspector, I slept affa well. That's the thing with a guilty conscience, I'm told – it's gey bad for you sleeping.'

'So I believe, yes. Well, did your good night's sleep improve your memory at all?'

'It did indeed, sir. I minded that the friend of a friend was really no a friend at all. He wasna a very nice person – he really forced me into storing the boxes at my flat. I'm no sure I even knew there was whisky in them, Inspector.'

'Your fingerprints were found on some of the bottles, Mr. McKinstry,' said Cattanach helpfully.

'Oh, aye. I mean, I didna know there was whisky in them when he brought them, ken. It was only after he left me with them I took a wee look inside. Well, you would, would you no? In your ain flat?'

'I daresay. And he forced you to store it?'

'He did, Inspector,' said Jock, sadly. 'He made it very clear that if I didna take it in – and it was only to be for a wee whilie, no long, he promised – if I didna take it in, it would be the worse for me.'

'In what way?' Cattanach sounded interested. Jock blinked, and hesitated.

'He didna specify, Inspector. He didna specify.'

'Goodness,' said Cattanach. 'Well, now, then, Mr. McKinstry, have you remembered the name of this unpleasant character?'

'I have an' all,' he said eagerly. 'His name's Stevie Tennant, and I'll tell you more – he lives down off a street off Union Street, up a wee lanie.'

'You'll have to be a little more specific,' said Cattanach, and McKinstry described the place. Cattanach nodded. 'Do you know – did he happen to mention where he had found the whisky?'

'It came in a wee van, Mr. Cattanach. He drove it to the door of the flats, and he made me help him carry it up the stair, an' all.'

'Didn't he have anyone else to help him?'

'Not a bit of it. It was just the two of us. My knees was killing me by the end of it.' He sighed heavily. 'Am I going home now, Mr. Cattanach?'

'I'm afraid not, Mr. McKinstry.' And Cattanach explained politely about charges and magistrates, and Jock McKinstry's face, all clean and freshly shaved, grew resigned.

The alley off a street off Union Street – a 'lanie', in the local parlance – looked not much more promising a neighbourhood than had Littlejohn Street. Council scaffies no doubt ventured in to scrape off the cobbles, but it was naturally dark and grim and Cattanach wondered what it must be like to be brought up in such a place, gloomy from the start. Or perhaps some found it cosy, sheltered, welcoming. He tried to picture it. There would be good families here as well as bad, he was sure. It was the same everywhere.

'Can you see a van, at all, Constable?' he asked Stewart. Constable Stewart gave him a look, and shook his head. The only way a van could have been hidden there would have been in pieces – though it would not have been the first time.

The address they had been given was at the top of one of the tenements, up a fairly clean and tidy stair. Two little boys, who should have been at school, took one look at them and hissed 'Germans!' before scuttling off into one of the flats. The door they were looking for, right at the top, was unadorned except for a small label saying 'Tennant', just over the letterbox. It was good when criminals declared where they lived, Cattanach thought, and knocked.

It was several minutes, and he had raised his hand to knock again, before they heard footsteps somewhere inside. After some fumbling, the door opened a crack and they were surveyed by someone breathing noisily. Eventually the door swung open.

'Aye?'

He was a tall man, but frail-looking, and there was a stick

propped against the wall beside him. Whether he used it as he walked about the flat or not was moot, as one of his sleeves was pinned up and empty. He was in shirtsleeves and a knitted, sleeveless jersey with a poorly-mended rip across the front – but then who could mend well with one arm?

'Mr. Tennant?' said Cattanach. 'We're from the City Police – I'd like a word with Steven Tennant, please.'

'Aye, that's me,' said the man. He leaned against the doorpost, and Cattanach could see he was taking the weight off one foot. Surely this was not their whisky thief?

'Have you a son lives here, Mr. Tennant? Known as Stevie?'

'Stevie?' His eyes, more alert now, skipped from one to the other of them. 'You're looking for Stevie Tennant?'

'That's right. Does he live here?'

'Well,' said the man. Either he had just woken up, or thinking fast no longer came very naturally to him. His thin hair stood on end, inclining Cattanach to the first theory. 'Well, aye, I have a son Stevie.' He considered. 'And aye, he bides here.'

He glanced quickly at Cattanach, as if gauging to see if he had made a mistake, admitted too much. An honest man trying to protect a dishonest son, perhaps.

'Can we have a word with Stevie, then, Mr. Tennant?'

'Well … truth is, I've no seen Stevie for a week.'

'A week?'

'Aye. I thought maybe, there, you were coming to tell me …'

'Tell you what, Mr. Tennant?'

'I dinna ken. A'thing.' The man's eyes were damp. Cattanach frowned.

'Are you able to get out and about, Mr. Tennant? Does anyone bring you your messages?'

'Aye, aye. Stevie does. I canna get far, ken.' He made a vague gesture towards his feet. 'Them stairs is awful steep.'

'So you've had no messages for a week?'

'I've tea,' said Mr. Tennant, trying to be defiant and failing. 'With a bittie sugar. And I made the bread last till – fit day's this?'

'Thursday.'

'Aye, I made the bread last till …'

Cattanach turned to Constable Stewart, and quickly handed

him a few shillings.

'Go on to the corner shop. See what you can get – bread, milk, sugar, maybe some tinned meat and jam. Sharpish.'

Constable Stewart pattered off down the stairs.

'You should go and sit down, Mr. Tennant,' said Cattanach. 'Is the fire lit?'

'Oh, aye, I can do that if I take it steady,' said Tennant, turning back into the flat and expecting Cattanach to follow. 'I'm fine, ken. We had worse in the trenches.'

He leaned on walls and furniture to get back into the little kitchen. It was here he seemed to have been sleeping: there was a box bed, but a Windsor chair was covered in knitted blankets and looked just vacated. Tennant made straight for it.

'I'll put the kettle on, then,' said Cattanach. 'Have you a tap?'

'Oh, aye, got everything here,' said the man. 'And I seen what you gave your constable there. There's money in that tin over the stove – take what I owe you.'

'Thank you,' said Cattanach, doing so. He would have stayed unpaid happily, but there was no point in offending the old man – and the tin was quite full.

Constable Stewart was back remarkably fast, dropping an armful of groceries on to the table by the window. He set to slicing bread and spreading it thick with butter and jam, and Cattanach found a plate and handed the food to the old man. He fell on it with delight, drank his milky tea when it was ready, and sat back, a much healthier colour.

'You're a good man, sir,' he said.

'What can you tell us about Stevie?' asked Cattanach. 'Where do you think he might have gone?'

'I have no idea,' said Tennant. 'None at all. See, he told me he had the use of a van for a few days, but he had some work to do, so he would be busy.'

'Do you know where he parked the van?'

Tennant shook his head.

'Must be somewhere nearby,' he said, 'if he had that much to do. He said if he had time when he finished, he would take me for a wee run in it. I'd like that fine – I've no been in a car since the war.'

'What kind of a job was it, do you think?'

'Oh, I suppose he was taking things here and there. With a van, see.'

'Good point. Does he work regularly for anybody in particular?'

The old man took a swig of tea, not looking at Cattanach.

'I think he works for different people. He never really tells me their names. He works hard, Stevie: there's always a bit of money coming in, and he'll bring me wee treats like a good rich fruitcake, or a half-bottle of whisky. And he says "There you are, Dad, that'll keep you going," and we have a wee laugh, ken?'

'He sounds like a good son,' said Cattanach. 'Do you know the names of any of his friends?'

'Not since he was a wee lad, no. I mean, whiles he goes out on a Friday night, and he says it's with his pals, but he doesna tell me their names. And he always comes home by eleven. He's a good lad.'

'Well, we'll keep an eye open for him,' said Cattanach, though he dreaded the news he might have to bring this old man. 'Have you a neighbour I could ask to bring you anything you need? Just until Stevie's back, in case he's delayed.'

He knocked on a door on their way back down the stair, and a muscly, capable woman nodded and said she would do whatever was required.

'I didna ken he was on his own just now,' she said. 'I'll pop up for a news. Dinna worry, sir, I'll keep an eye on him.'

22

'SO YOU HAVE another missing person, then?' Lieutenant Moffat looked put out.

'Last seen by his father last Thursday, sir,' said Cattanach, resisting the temptation to protest that it was not his fault.

'Remind me why we are interested in him?'

Cattanach was sure the Lieutenant knew exactly why.

'Jock McKinstry named him as the man who persuaded him, or told him, or asked him, to keep three dozen cases of whisky in his flat in Littlejohn Street. The whisky which we believe was stolen along with a van in Keith. Stevie Tennant told his father he had the use of a van this week. Presumably he wanted to distribute the whisky from the flat.'

'Why not just keep the boxes in the van?'

'Well, sir, I imagine that he had no place to hide the van, and it could be identified at any time as having been stolen. They could easily lose the whisky that way.'

Moffat nodded.

'And in the meantime, you're waiting for some evidence that your lorry driver that went into the tram was also intending to smuggle whisky?'

'Possibly not to steal it, though, sir.'

Moffat waved a dismissive hand.

'Any known connexion between the driver and this Stevie Tennant? Or Jock McKinstry?'

'We're checking, sir.' Well, Constable Leggatt was

checking, a marginal improvement on tidying the evidence store. 'Offhand, no one can think of one. Sandison, the driver, doesn't seem to have any contacts locally.'

'Right ... Now, again, remind me why we were interested in Jock McKinstry in the first place? We had no idea he had a year's supply of whisky in his flat, did we?'

A quick calculation made Cattanach wonder about the Lieutenant's whisky consumption.

'No, sir. He had been seen in the company of the missing woman, Mabel Campbell, though it seems that information might have been a bit out of date.'

Moffat made a face.

'This Jock McKinstry – he hasn't come to our attention much, has he?'

'Not fully, if you know what I mean, sir. From what Constable Anderson says, there has always been a suspicion that he was up to something, but he had never been caught. He's a bit of an actor, I think. I'd say he's enjoying being the centre of attention down in the cells.'

'But it's a bit of a coincidence, isn't it? A woman he's been seen with has disappeared, and about the same time – isn't that right? Within a day of each other? – his partner in crime also vanished. You don't think there's any chance that they have gone together? Perhaps this Tennant has taken her, or perhaps they have gone off, well, together?'

'When you put it like that, sir, it's worth looking into. I'll see if we have any links between them. But it's odd: Mabel Campbell lived an outwardly very respectable life in Seaton, and her husband's family seem to be above reproach. Yet she was seen going about with Jock McKinstry, and now we're wondering about a connexion with Stevie Tennant. Where did she meet these people? She seemed to like the finer things in life, not shabby tenements in Littlejohn Street or flats shared with crippled parents down alleys off Union Street.'

'Have you found out anything more at all about her background?' asked Moffat. Cattanach shook his head.

'Nothing. Not even her marriage certificate to Robert Campbell. Billy Campbell's death certificate has Robert named as his father – I don't know if Campbell was his real name or if he adopted Robert's surname when Mabel remarried. The family don't know where they married or where she came from. Robert doesn't seem the talkative type, and Billy was a quiet boy. Yet the answer must be there somewhere in her past, surely?'

'What about Robert Campbell? Is he ever coming home?'

'Yes, sir, they're due into harbour tomorrow. I hope to be there to meet the ship.'

'A hard homecoming for him.'

'Yes. But at least it won't be a shock: he's been warned in advance.'

'I hope he has something to tell you, Cattanach. She's been gone six days now. We've had no reports of sightings from the city or the County force, either. Whether she's with Stevie Tennant or not, where on earth has she gone?'

Cattanach added to Constable Leggatt's workload with a request to look out for links between Stevie Tennant and Mabel Campbell, before heading back upstairs. As he approached his own office, he could hear voices – well, specifically Inspector Cochrane's voice. The man had assumed his very best accent, the one Cattanach had once, excruciatingly, heard him use when presented to the Lord Lieutenant. He hoped it was not the Lord Lieutenant in the office, or Inspector Cochrane would be unbearable for weeks.

Cautiously he opened the door. Inspector Cochrane was on his own in the room, but mercifully was speaking into Cattanach's telephone. He turned slightly as Cattanach appeared, nodded, and held up a hand, apparently to the person on the other end of the line.

'Yes, yes, Miss Mackay, I can assure you that the whole force is working to its utmost to find the lady. And I am quite sure that Cattanach will be more than grateful for any information you are able to give him. I must tell you that I am now in a position to summon him to the telephone, if there is anything else you might wish to impart to him directly.' He listened for a moment, ignoring Cattanach's outstretched hand and smiling like an insurance salesman. 'Of course. And my very best wishes to your father, of course. A very good day to you, Miss Mackay, a very good day.'

He handed the receiver to Cattanach and returned to his desk, where he sat, beaming at Cattanach as if he had now shown him what to do. Cattanach tried to hold the receiver a little way from his mouth, conscious of how warm Inspector Cochrane's eager breath had made it.

'Miss Mackay? Good afternoon.'

'Is that Mr. Cattanach? It is you, isn't it?'

'Yes, it is. Inspector Cochrane said you had some information?'

'Yes … I told him, but I think I should perhaps repeat it.'

'By all means,' he said, appreciating her perception. He found a pencil and paper on his desk, but stayed standing, with his back to Inspector Cochrane. 'Go ahead when you're ready.'

The receiver caught a little huff of breath.

'I'd almost rather do this in person, but I'm sure you're very busy – working for Inspector Cochrane.' He could hear the grin in her voice. 'Anyway, I saw the man again – the one I saw with Mabel Campbell on Union Street that night.'

'You're sure?'

'Absolutely positive, Mr. Cattanach. I had the same immediate thought about heart trouble, and then realised it was him.'

'I hope you didn't approach him,' he said, suddenly concerned by her confidence.

'Well, I spoke to him, yes.'

'You did?'

'I could hardly avoid it. My mother and I were in his shop.'

'His shop?'

'I told you he looked like a prosperous businessman – I was right!' She sounded pleased with herself. His alarm deepened. Was she one of those people excited by the thought of police investigations, wanting to be involved? That could be annoying, and obstructive – and sometimes very dangerous.

'Well, that's very interesting,' he said, trying to sound as bland as possible. 'Can you give me more details?'

'Inspector Cochrane's still there, isn't he?' she said. 'Well, the man has a little jewellery shop in Rose Street. Small, but some good things, very tasteful. My mother occasionally pops in for presents for friends, which is what she was doing today. I don't think I had done more than glance in the window before, but we had had lunch and I went with her. And there he was, behind the counter.'

'Do you know his name?'

'Yes: he's Albert Lovie.'

'Thank you.'

'Well dressed, very smooth, but … well, I'd have said he was a nice man. Kindly. The same impression I had when I saw them together. I'd be so surprised if he had done her any harm.'

'Perhaps he hasn't,' said Cattanach. 'He may well have nothing to do with her disappearance.' And appearances can be deceptive, he thought to himself. 'I'm just hoping to find out a little more about her – perhaps even a hint as to where she might have gone on her own.' He had not mentioned to Miss Mackay his strong impression that Mabel Campbell was running away from something. She might have run to Albert Lovie.

'Well, I hope it helps.' There was a pause. He wondered if she was expecting him to say something specific.

'I'm sure it will. Thank you very much for taking the time to contact us.'

'No trouble at all. I hope we shall see you soon, Mr. Cattanach.'

He wondered, as he reached for a Post Office directory, who 'we' was. She and her mother? She and her father, working with the police? He took his seat behind his desk, aware that Inspector Cochrane had barely moved and was still watching him with benevolent interest.

Lovie, Albert N., jeweller, had a work address in Rose Street and a home address in King Street. The number of the King Street property was high, but Cattanach was not sure just how far up King Street it might be. It could be near Seaton. He would start with the shop.

Rose Street was one of a number of neat little streets just north of the west end of Union Street. The shops were small and varied, the buildings not particularly tall or imposing, and it took him less than five minutes to find the discreet door and elegant window with 'A. Lovie' in white letters on black above it. The shop was open, as he had expected, and when he entered he found it was also empty. Perfect.

The soft ting of the shop bell summoned Albert Lovie from behind a black velvet curtain at the back of the shop. His smile was automatic, but his eyes were warm.

'Good afternoon, sir! What may I do for you?' He spread plump fingers across the counter. His cuffs were spotless, his tie silk and precise. He so fitted Anna Mackay's description that for a moment Cattanach was tempted to think she had invented him. He introduced himself.

'The City Police?' repeated Lovie. 'Is it jewel theft? I don't buy from anyone I don't know and trust, Inspector.'

'Very wise,' Cattanach agreed. 'But I'm afraid it's nothing to do with your business.'

'My car?'

'No, not that, either.' He had checked that, too: Lovie was the registered owner of a bullnose Morris Oxford, dark green. Cattanach had noticed it parked at the end of the street: presumably the jeweller wanted to leave space for his customers just outside the shop. 'Mr. Lovie, are you acquainted with a Mabel Campbell?'

Dismayed embarrassment slid down Lovie's face from top to bottom, starting with his eyes and finishing by turning down his lips.

'I'm – I'm not sure, Inspector, that my acquaintance with Mrs. Campbell is strictly police business. Surely what a couple do in – well, in their own time – is not against the law?'

'Probably not, no,' said Cattanach. 'Tell me, if you will, Mr. Lovie, when did you last see Mrs. Campbell?'

'Well, now,' said Lovie. He gave Cattanach an anxious look. 'I don't see her very often. In fact, I haven't really seen her that many times altogether. Not – not for want of enthusiasm on my part.'

'But when, please?'

'It was the twentieth of August, as a matter of fact.'

'You seem very sure.'

'I am, Inspector. I don't mind telling you, I look forward to our little evenings together very much. Very much indeed.'

'Have you had any contact with her at all since the twentieth of August?'

'No, not at all. You see – well, because of her unfortunate circumstances, it's always best if she contacts me, you see?'

'I see, yes.'

'Inspector.' Cattanach could see that the man was starting to shiver. 'Inspector, please tell me. Is something the matter? Is it – her husband?'

'Nothing to do with her husband, Mr. Lovie,' said Cattanach. 'No, the thing is, Mabel Campbell has disappeared. No one has seen her since last Friday afternoon.'

'Dis – disappeared?' stammered Lovie.

He was behind the counter. Cattanach could do nothing to save him when he fell to the floor in a dead faint.

23

THE WIDTH OF Lovie and the narrowness of the space behind the counter meant that Cattanach had no hope of laying the man out flat or hauling him on to a chair. But Lovie's eyelids were flickering again in a moment, and he struggled to his feet without help, rubbing over his mouth and the back of his neck, loosening his own tie a fraction.

'She's disappeared?' he asked, obviously keen to ignore his sudden weakness. Cattanach wondered what Anna Mackay would make of it, professionally.

'Yes, so you can see why we might be trying to find people who know her, who might know where she has gone. Her family are very worried about her.'

'I told her they were nicer than she thought,' he said, but his mind was not quite on the words. 'She's disappeared? But what about her husband? What about Billy?'

'Mr. Campbell is still at sea – he should be back tomorrow,' Cattanach explained. 'Obviously he was away when she disappeared, and we haven't had a chance to talk with him yet.'

'At sea?' Lovie's face was blank.

'Robert Campbell is at sea, yes. On a trawler, apparently.'

'Are you sure we have the right family, Inspector? Mabel Campbell and Robert Campbell, in Seaton Place?'

'Yes, that's right.'

'Little boy called Billy?'

'Yes …' It seemed he had some more bad news to break to

Albert Lovie. 'What did Mabel Campbell tell you about her family situation?'

'Well, her husband is a cripple, of course. She looks after him at home most of the time, but sometimes his sister takes him for a while to give her a break – and sometimes he has to go in for treatment.'

Lovie looked quite sure of himself.

'Did you meet any of his family?' asked Cattanach, just in case they really did have the wrong Campbells.

'No … Mabel said she didn't have very much in common with them, though they were decent people.'

'I've met,' said Cattanach carefully, 'three of Robert Campbell's brothers, and three of his sisters-in-law. They all tell me he is a trawlerman, currently on his way back to Aberdeen from fishing somewhere near Greenland.'

'No!' But Lovie had been brought up to trust policemen, clearly. His certainty was wavering.

'What about Billy?' asked Cattanach. 'Did Billy not mention his step-father was at sea?'

'Billy doesn't talk much,' said Lovie, still struggling to take in what Cattanach had told him. 'He's a quiet boy. I like him. He's interested in birds and plants and suchlike, not always knocking a ball around, or getting into fights. He calls me Uncle Albert,' he added, with a shy smile.

'Then I'm sorry, Mr. Lovie, I'm really sorry, but I have some very bad news for you – and it's not Mabel Campbell's disappearance. I'm afraid that Billy was involved in a very serious accident last week.'

'An accident?'

Cattanach thought that Lovie was going to pass out again, but he held the edge of the counter firmly, and took a deep breath.

'A serious accident,' he repeated. 'I'm afraid Billy was hit by a lorry on his way to school. He was killed instantly.'

'Oh … Oh, poor Billy. Poor boy.' Tears surged in Lovie's eyes, and he drew out a large, gleaming white handkerchief to dab them away. 'Poor Mabel. Oh, poor sweet Mabel! Oh, no. Oh, Inspector, you don't think she's – she wouldn't have done anything foolish, would she? You said she's been gone since last Friday!'

'The day of Billy's funeral,' Cattanach nodded. 'But for

various reasons I think she has not, as you put it, done anything foolish. I believe she saw someone at the funeral who frightened her, and after the mourners had left she packed a case, and left in a hurry. No one has seen her since.'

'Someone who frightened her? But who would that have been?'

'That's what I'm hoping to find out, Mr. Lovie,' said Cattanach, but if Mabel Campbell had not even told Lovie the truth about her present life, what chance did he have that she had told him anything useful about her past? 'Look, Mr. Lovie, you're someone who knew Mrs. Campbell well, and so I hope you'll realise there are certain things I have to check. I understand you live on King Street. Will you come with me now and show me your house?'

'My house?' Talking to Lovie was a little like talking in an echoey cave. 'It's only a flat,' he said, as if that would make a difference.

'I just need to see that it's not where Mrs. Campbell is taking refuge.'

'I see.' But Lovie almost certainly did not. He was in three different kinds of shock, and Cattanach felt cruel to be taking advantage of him when he was obviously not thinking straight.

'Have you a car here? I can drive you.'

'Well. Well, I suppose,' said Lovie. He blew his nose thoroughly. 'I suppose – the thought of keeping the shop open, under the circumstances … wee Billy, the poor wee lad … I think, perhaps, you are right. I should shut up the shop for the day, and just go home. Perhaps she has even been trying to telephone me. Perhaps she has, yes. Oh, poor Mabel! Such an unfortunate life!'

He seemed to have forgotten that Robert Campbell was not a cripple to be cared for.

'Would you like me to drive you?' said Cattanach. 'You'll not be feeling very steady.' Or looking very steady. Lovie nodded.

'I'll fetch my coat.'

The Morris Oxford was large, compared with his Austin. Cattanach drove with care on to Union Street, then left on to King Street.

'Whereabouts is your flat?' he asked.

'Oh, a long way, yet. Up past St. Machar Drive.'

'Far past?'

'No, not far. A little beyond Billy's school.'

He must not have been passing around the time of the accident. Cattanach drove all the way up, past the graveyard where Billy was buried. There were trees there: he hoped Billy would like them.

'Where did you meet Mrs. Campbell?' he asked, apparently casually.

'At a tea shop,' said Lovie. At once there was a smile on his face. 'Down near the harbour. She was on her own - one of the times her husband was in hospital.' Cattanach could feel his sideways glance. 'Or at sea.' Cattanach said nothing. 'She – she's very pretty. Quite lovely. The tea shop was busy and she – I asked – she said I could share her table. And things went from there, I suppose.' His shoulders crumpled into a shudder. 'I pray she's all right.'

At Lovie's direction they pulled into a lane off King Street beyond Billy's school, as he had said, and he led the way to a neat little stair in an old tenement. As Cattanach could have guessed by now, Mabel was not in the flat, with its tasteful furnishings, polished wireless and gramophone, fresh curtains and the breakfast dishes washed, more than Cattanach sometimes achieved before going out to work. Unlike Jock McKinstry's grubby little flat, this one did hold one or two signs of Mabel, though: a brooch she had dropped and he intended to return, a little bunch of roses from her garden, rather dried now but still in a cut glass posy vase.

'What else did she tell you about herself?' he asked. Lovie, watching him fixedly as he examined the place, sat on an armchair and stared at the brooch which he now turned over in his hands.

'Her husband has a large family. Fishing people, or at least boats. She always said we would be quite safe dining – where we usually dine, at the West End – because the Campbells would never be so sophisticated as to come there. Though she never really seems to worry much about them, anyway. She says they're not her kind of people.' He looked up at Cattanach, almost pleading. Cattanach nodded.

'That's all true, as far as I can tell,' he confirmed. Lovie frowned, concentrating on dividing up fact from fiction.

'She said she had married Campbell four or five years ago.'

'A little less, we think.'

'You think?' Lovie paused, but decided to let that one lie.

'Before that … I'm not sure she has said very much, ever. How strange: it had never occurred to me. I know she isn't from Aberdeen, of course: no shared childhood memories. And I don't think she comes from further north, either. I mentioned once an aunt in Ellon, and she didn't seem to know the place. And you don't have to go far north before you reach Ellon. No, I think my impression has always been she's from somewhere further south.'

'Did she tell you that Billy is not Robert Campbell's son?'

'Well, yes, of course. She said she'd been married before. But …'

'Yes?' Cattanach prompted, after a moment.

'Well, all right, I've often wondered. I mean, maybe, yes. But I do wonder if there was a former husband. She …' He squirmed, embarrassed. 'She's very fond of men's company.'

Free with her favours, thought Cattanach. It seemed that way, yes. He wondered, though, if she had dropped Jock McKinstry with all his apparent, but acted, polish, when she met Lovie and saw his potential to be the real thing.

He strolled to the window, thinking.

'I can't believe little Billy is dead,' said Lovie, perhaps to fill the silence. 'I just can't believe it. Poor lad.'

'A tragedy,' Cattanach agreed. From where he stood he could see the tail end of Lovie's car. 'Do you usually drive to work?'

'I do, yes,' said Lovie, relieved at the change of subject. 'I like to arrive fresh, you know, and ready for the day. The tram is handy, but usually very crowded.'

'It's a busy piece of road.'

'I do tend to get out before the rush. What with the university, too.'

'Of course. It's not going to be so easy soon, though, is it? With petrol rationing. What do you get with a nice car like yours - twenty, twenty-five miles to the gallon? I suppose you would be all right, if you weren't expecting to do more than drive to Rose Street and back each day.'

He heard a sound behind him, and turned. Lovie was sobbing uncontrollably in his chair, slumped over his handkerchief.

'Please – please just leave me, Inspector,' the man begged indistinctly. 'Please go. I'll tell you if I hear anything, I promise.'

And Cattanach did: he left the flat, and went to wait for a

tram back to the station.

Friday morning. This time tomorrow he could be on his way out of the city. Much as he wanted to make some progress in both the traffic cases, to find Mabel Campbell and Stevie Tennant, he prayed that nothing demanding would happen today that might mean he would have to give up his weekend. Robert Campbell's boat was due back today – that would surely be enough.

Wireless communication with the boat, the *Christina Mary*, had allowed them to break the news of Billy's death, but there had been some problems with the radio since, and beyond their expected arrival date they had heard little. And Robert Campbell did not yet know about his wife's disappearance.

'Anything nice planned for the weekend?' asked Inspector Cochrane, when Cattanach had settled at his desk. Inspector Cochrane had just surfaced from a close perusal of *Police Duties and Procedure*, perhaps memorising the latest amendments. Cattanach suspected Inspector Cochrane of sleeping with a copy under his pillow.

'Not much,' said Cattanach, casually. 'You?'

'Oh, you know,' said Inspector Cochrane. 'Golf with the Lieutenant tomorrow. Lunch with the family on Sunday.'

Golf with the Lieutenant? Cattanach suspected that this just meant both men would be playing the same course, somewhere. He knew he was supposed to ask, so he did not.

'The family all well?' he asked instead. Inspector Cochrane looked suddenly queasy.

'Yes, yes,' he said, slightly too quickly. 'Yes, yes, quite well.'

Well, he had been the one to mention them, thought Cattanach.

'Good,' he said, and turned to his in-tray. The telephone rang, and he picked it up in relief.

'Cattanach.'

'Aye, sir, we've just had word. The *Christina Mary*, Robert Campbell's boat. That's her just coming in now.'

24

CATTANACH TOOK A police car, and was lucky enough to find Constable Gauld free to accompany him. Gauld knew a good deal more about the sea and the fishing than Cattanach did, and even if it were not useful it was reassuring to have him there. They reached the berth at the harbour just as the ropes were flung over the side. Constable Gauld helped to secure them to great iron bollards.

They had a photograph of Robert Campbell from his house: it was easy to spot him amongst the small crew, all the more as he was the only man there without someone to welcome him back. He stood for a moment, looking about him in resignation, before Cattanach approached him.

'Robert Campbell?'

'Aye.' The man was guarded, his face closed to strangers.

'Inspector Cattanach, of the City Police.'

'Oh.' Campbell set his pack down on the cobbles and straightened to look Cattanach almost in the eye. He was not a tall man. 'I'm guessing this is about Billy? They got a message through, ken, before the wireless went funny.'

'So I believe,' said Cattanach, 'but as there has been some confusion I want to make sure: you know that Billy was killed when a lorry hit him, on the way to school on the Tuesday before last?'

'Aye.' Campbell gave a quick, sharp nod. 'Aye, that's what they said. Ken, he wasna my son, you'll have heard. But he was a good lad. A gey good lad.'

Cattanach remembered the generous gift of the telescope,

and was sure Campbell had cared for the boy.

'I haven't heard a word against him,' Cattanach assured him.

'You said there was some confusion? D'you just mean the wireless?'

'Well, no, Mr. Campbell. Look, will you come and sit in the car? It's not ideal, but it's a bit more private. Then we can take you home, if you like.'

'Private?' Campbell's eyes darted about the quay again, and he frowned. 'Where's my wife? Where's Mabel?'

'That's the question, I'm afraid, Mr. Campbell. Mrs. Campbell has not been seen since Friday afternoon – just after Billy's funeral.'

He thought they would have to lift Campbell bodily to get him into the car. He seemed to have stuck in place, feet spaced as though still steadying himself against the roll of the boat, one hand holding the rope of his pack. But his face was still expressionless. Cattanach wondered if he ever showed emotion. He nudged Campbell's elbow, then pushed it a little harder.

'Come along, now, Mr. Campbell. We'll take you home, and get a cup of tea, and have a chat about it. Maybe you'll be able to tell us straight off where she might have gone, and all this could be settled by dinner time.'

They stopped for Constable Gauld to hurry out of the car for a bottle of milk at a corner shop, but otherwise drove in silence, except when they passed St. Peter's Cemetery.

'Is he in there?' asked Campbell. 'My lad?'

'He is,' said Cattanach. 'I can show you later, if you like.'

'Aye.'

Campbell had a doorkey of his own. He stopped when he had opened the door, listening, perhaps, to the quiet house, perhaps still expecting Billy or Mabel to come and greet him. After a moment he gave up, and went on inside.

'Kettle on, Constable,' said Cattanach, and followed Campbell into the parlour. The odour of sweat and fish and saltwater, strong in the car, trailed through the house now. Presumably if Mabel had been at home there would have been hot water for a good bath.

Campbell did not seem to know what to do with himself in the parlour, though. He stood by the window, fingering one of

Mabel's ornamental figures, without looking at it. Then he went to stare at the cold fireplace, then almost sat at the table, then changed his mind. He glanced at the parlour door, as if he wanted to go and look around the rest of the flat, but he did not seem to be able to shift himself. Cattanach drew out his notebook, and from memory sketched the position of Billy's grave in St. Peter's Cemetery, relative to the main gate. He tore out the page and passed it to Campbell, who glared at it then nodded his thanks. He folded it and placed it on the mantelpiece.

'I know this is very difficult, Mr. Campbell,' said Cattanach, impatient for the cup of hot tea that would start the treatment of Campbell's shock. 'But can you think of anywhere Mrs. Campbell might have gone? To, let's say, take refuge?'

'Take refuge? What from?'

'From all that had happened, perhaps? Grief at Billy's death?'

'I suppose you've spoken to my brothers and the women?'

'So far as I can, yes.'

'None of them knows?'

'No, I don't believe so. They're all very worried about her.' He waited, but Campbell said nothing. 'What about friends? I'm afraid your family couldn't give me any names.'

'Don't know that she had any friends,' said Campbell. 'Not women friends.'

His voice was tight, and his face still had that private look. Constable Gauld, a little pink in the face, clattered in with a tray, nicely laid with two teacups and saucers, the milk in a jug and sugar in a bowl. There were even teaspoons. He laid the tray down on the table, and went to fetch the teapot.

'No one seems to think she will have attempted to harm herself, Mr. Campbell,' said Cattanach, for want of anything else. He would have sworn that the thought was quite far from Campbell's mind, too. Constable Gauld came back with the tea, and jiggled the pot a little before pouring it, milk first, into the two cups. He handed them out to the others, then went to stand by the parlour door. He was learning, Cattanach noted, to efface himself – it was a useful skill.

Campbell drew the cup towards himself without looking at it, and gulped the scalding liquid, shaking his head as if to help it down. He emptied the cup, and refilled it for himself. He was already a better colour, but his face still gave little away. Cattanach considered remaining silent to provoke Campbell to fill the blank, but he had a feeling that Campbell could sit there all day and never say anything.

'Where did you meet your wife, Mr. Campbell?'

Campbell looked at him at last, and for a moment Cattanach thought he was not going to answer. But at last he said,

'Montrose.'

'How did it happen?'

'Boat needed work. Montrose was nearest – Esk basin. We went in, had to stay twa-three days. Met her in a tea shop.'

As had Albert Lovie.

'Did she say anything about her family? Her background?'

'What's that got to do with it?'

'It might give us an idea of where she's gone – or where she hasn't gone. Mr. Campbell, I was at Billy's funeral. I saw your wife just as the procession was leaving the house. She had just seen something that scared her badly, I'd swear to it. After everyone returned to the house, your brother's wives stayed to help her clear up. She hurried them out. Then, it seems, she packed a suitcase with probably her jewellery and some cash, and left. She did not take a taxi, and no one saw a car. It seems likely she was in too much of a hurry to wait, or was too scared to stay still for long.'

'Why would she be scared? What would she be scared of?'

'We also have an account,' – he did not say it had come from a ten-year-old girl – 'that Billy, the evening before his death, was worried that his uncle was a criminal. Then he fell under a lorry the next morning. The lorry driver was not to blame, but there is some suspicion that he might have been pushed in front of it.'

'Billy? Billy said his uncle was a criminal?' Campbell's face had finally found an expression. He was baffled. 'Which uncle?'

'He didn't say. But he was very concerned. I gather he was upset by rule-breaking?'

'Aye, aye, he was. He liked things done right. He did.' He scowled. 'Which uncle?'

'Did your wife have any brothers? Married sisters?'

Campbell shook his head.

'Not that I knew of.'

'Did she tell you anything about herself?'

'Only that she'd been married before. To Billy's father, a' course.'

'Of course.' Or perhaps not, he thought. 'What about your marriage certificate? She must have put down the names of her parents, surely?'

Campbell looked at Cattanach from under dark brows.

'We never married,' he said, challenging Cattanach to object.

'Was she against the idea?'

'She was,' Campbell admitted. 'And it didna bother me. I just came back from Montrose and a week or so later she and Billy came up on the train, and I told the family we'd met and married. They didna ask many questions.'

Not to your face, thought Cattanach, no. They'd have liked answers, all the same.

'So she just called herself Campbell?'

'No, funny enough she was Campbell already. So was Billy. It made it easier.'

'Common enough name, of course.'

'Aye.'

'Do you think she was from Montrose?' It was not a large town, an hour on the train down the coast. Fishing and potato farming were the main industries – he could not see Mabel Campbell involved in either. Campbell frowned again.

'I never asked. But I thought she was maybe from somewhere further south. Not much, maybe, but Aberdeen seemed to be a strange place to her and I dinna think she belonged in Montrose, really. Billy didna seem to have any friends there, or go to school, or a'thing.'

Albert Lovie had also thought Mabel was heading north. From something, or to something?

'Did she ever seem scared of anything? Mention anyone who might threaten her? Anything criminal in her past? You must have wondered, I should think, why she told you so little about herself?'

'No' really,' said Campbell, shrugging. 'She was a gey attractive woman, and we got along well. She looked after me and Billy fine, and kept the house looking nice. If she didna want to say much about the past, who was I to ask her? I suppose I didna say much about myself, if it comes to that.'

Cattanach supposed he did not, indeed.

'You said she didn't have any women friends, Mr. Campbell. Did you mean, perhaps, that she had male friends?'

'Male friends?'

'Yes – some women simply get along better with men, don't they? Just as some men get along better with women.'

'Aye, and I ken what kind of men those are – and what kind of women, an' all. What are you saying?'

'I'm asking if you know of anybody at all that your wife might have gone to. She left deliberately, of her own free will, apparently. Where could she have gone?'

'I'm telling you this, Inspector. If I find Mabel's with a man, I'll tear his eyes out and use them as fishbait.'

He had hardly raised his voice, nor shifted his hands on the table, but his eyes glowed with a cold light that Cattanach did not like at all. But he had to press on just a little more.

'Have you any reason to think she might be with a man?'

'Have you? If you have, I want his name.'

'She's not with any man that I'm aware of,' said Cattanach. 'Look, you've had a shock, Mr. Campbell. We'll leave you in peace just now, but if you can think – if anything occurs to you from anything Mrs. Campbell said, or anything Billy said, that might help us to find her safe and well, then please tell us.'

'Safe and well? You really think something's happened to her, do you?'

'I think she feared it might. Which is not a good place to start, in my book.'

25

THE MILK CHURNS were arriving, with dull clanks, on the platform opposite as Cattanach waited at Kittybrewster Station on Saturday morning, and the chilly dawn rose pink, fading the already masked platform lights. The embankments of the surrounding roads cast a long shadow almost to the platform's edge as the north-bound train drew in through a fog of its own steam. There were not many waiting to catch it: one or two hoping to make the most of a day in Inverness, perhaps, or visiting family in the country. The train slowed and stopped, the locomotive snorting and hissing like a dissatisfied horse. It had started at the Joint Station down by the harbour, not far at all, so it was probably impatient to be getting on its way. You would hardly think there was a war on. But Cattanach was here saving petrol.

In the compartment he sat by the window, eager to see hills, but he had to be patient. And to be open to memories of work – in a few minutes they were at Woodside, a stone's throw from the site of the tram crash last week. This train would follow, very closely, the road to Inverness, the road that Sandison, the lorry driver, had claimed he would be taking. It would pass through Keith, where the van of whisky had been stolen by some associate of Jock McKinstry, though Cattanach did not plan to travel that far today.

The suburb of Woodside slid, with barely a green field and some allotments in between, into the village of Dyce. Cattanach looked out with an interest that was neither work nor countryside related – here was their nearest airfield, barely five years operational as a civil site and now taken over by the RAF. A mixture of aeroplanes of different sizes sat neatly among huge hangars, little dark green birds with their roundels bright. Cattanach had no idea what they all were, but the place looked reassuringly organised. It seemed very easy to look in and see what was going on: he wondered if they would soon put up a fence, for fear of German spies taking the train to Inverness.

Little stops – Kintore, Kemnay, farming land, a station and a couple of cottages with the smoke from breakfast stoves sneaking up from the chimneys.

Inverurie and the canal came next: the station was right behind the town hall but somehow the town itself had little presence from the railway side, overshadowed, perhaps, by the mighty locomotive works just beyond it. Like the airfield at Dyce, it already seemed to be a hive of industry even this early on a Saturday. Cattanach felt briefly guilty about leaving his desk for two days, but what was the point? Others were working on what they could work on, and he could clear his head and come back refreshed on Monday. He was beginning to feel an urgency about some people, as if they felt they needed to get on with something, hurry along, get the war work started. For his part, he thought he should be conserving his energies, mental and physical, along with his petrol. He was sure they would all be needed, before very long.

Proper countryside beyond Inverurie, though rather flat for his liking – Garioch farmland, with the Don curling through it down to Aberdeen. But up to his left the hills were starting to rise, the yellow of gorse and the purple of heather painting long slopes up to easy crests. When the line crossed the road towards Oyne, the land was growing more promising, and at the station he pushed open the door and stepped, long-legged, down to the platform, already eagerly drawing in the air even if it was still rich with smoke and steam. He reached back for his pack, swung it on to his shoulders, and barely gave the scattered settlements of Oyne a glance as he headed for the edge of the village and the lands of Bennachie.

So he could, he thought, as he sat over the remains of his dinner that evening. He could get out and away on the train, and if it was more restrictive than going by car, at least it could be done.

He wiped the last trace of gravy from the pan with a heel of bread, and chewed on it, staring out over the dimming landscape before him. He had seen deer and fox, stoats and weasels, and a pine marten, and any number of different birds, moving from hiding place to hiding place to angle his binoculars and study them. He had lunched by a stream, climbed to the top of Mither Tap and surveyed the county through layers of mist, gathered fir cones for a winter fire at home. Finally he had pitched his small brown tent with its back to a rise in the ground for shelter, its front looking over a gentle valley, and lit his stove. He wondered if Billy Campbell had ever come up here with his notebook and his telescope. He would have loved it, he thought.

He had brought Billy's notebook with him, but it was too dark to read it now and he did not bring it out of his bag. Instead he just watched the light fade over the world, listening to the high cries of birds heading for their roosts, the last duskish rustlings of small animals in the undergrowth, the steady sigh of the wind across the land. He prayed he would never have to leave here, to go overseas and fight and perhaps die, far from home. Let him die here, he thought, defending it.

A dram of whisky and a cup of cocoa from his flask, and it was time for bed.

His heart leapt when he emerged into the damp dawn of Sunday. A man was seated on a nearby rock, staring out over the same view that he had watched fade the previous evening. Two spaniels sat by him, but the moment they saw Cattanach appear at the tent flaps they trotted over, eagerly licking his outstretched fingers.

'Dad!' he said. 'Why didn't you wake me?'

'Might not have been you,' said the man, not looking round. Cattanach refrained from pointing out that the tent was exactly where he had told his father he would be. He pulled on his trousers, boots and jersey over the shirt he had slept in, and crawled properly out of the tent.

'Coffee?' he asked.

'Aye, that'd be fine.'

Cattanach lit the stove, and filled a pan with water he had collected the previous evening. He glanced from time to time at his father, sitting still in profile, one spaniel at his feet while the other hopefully attended Cattanach. The old man – old? How old was he? – wore country tweeds and a flat cap, a knitted mustard scarf his only concession to the chill of the morning. He looked exactly as he had always looked.

'All well?' Cattanach asked him.

'Aye. Busy enough.'

'Shooting?'

'No today. Tomorrow.'

Cattanach hesitated.

'I saw the laird in town the other day. Going into the Townhouse for a meeting.'

'Aye, that'd be him,' said his father, as if there might have been any danger of misidentification.

'He's looking well.'

'Well enough.'

'Good.'

There was silence while they waited for the water to boil. Cattanach added two spoons of sugar to his father's cup, and handed it to him.

'Ha! He wants me to go up to the house for Christmas,' said his father, holding the tin mug in heat-proof hands.

'You should go.'

'What would I do there?'

'Eat. Drink. Have conversations.'

His father made a dismissive sound. Cattanach tried not to sigh.

'Think of him. He's lonely, and he likes your company.' Another snort of disbelief. 'Now that his wife's dead …'

'Aye, well,' his father conceded. 'He'd no be asking me if she was there.'

'That's true. But it's all the more reason to go. Make more of a connexion.' He paused. 'You've a lot in common, when you think about it.'

'But who knows where we'll all be by Christmas?'

'That is also true.'

They fell silent again, two men and two dogs staring out over gorse and heather, rock and earth, trying to see even a little way into the future.

The spaniels escorted them on a convoluted path back towards Oyne.

'I daresay you're busy, there in the town,' said his father eventually.

'Yes, a couple of road accidents that turned out to be more complicated than we had thought.'

'I heard. Sad about the lad.'

'It was, yes. And now his mother has disappeared.'

'She'll be upset.'

'There seems to be more to it. I think she's afraid of someone. It's possible the boy was pushed out in front of the lorry.'

His father drew in a shocked breath, and tutted.

'His father was out on the trawlers. He only came back yesterday.'

'Aye, that's bad.'

'It wasn't good.'

His father stopped to pull a spaniel's nose out of a dead rabbit. Cattanach stooped to hold the second spaniel back and out of the way.

'What about the other accident?' his father asked. He always listened, even if he looked as if he were ignoring everything.

'Tram and lorry. The tram driver is in a bad way. I think the lorry driver was heading out this way for illicit whisky.'

His father nodded.

'Aye. There were problems with whisky in the war.'

'So Mrs. Walker said.'

'She'd know.' His father, as far as he could tell, had liked Mrs. Walker, on the rare occasions they had met. 'How are her dogs?'

'They're well. Getting old.'

His father sniffed. Getting old was for dogs and other people.

They came into Oyne station about an hour before dusk, earlier than Cattanach would have liked but in good time for the last useful train of the day. His father stood, his long stick in one weathered hand, with the spaniels at his heels, like a monument to rural life. Cattanach was taller, but dressed the same way: he wondered if anyone watching would take him for a tounser or a teuchter, a townie or a countryman. And which was he, anyway?

'You should go and see the laird,' said his father unexpectedly.

'That's what I've been telling you, Dad,' he said with a smile.

'Aye, but you should. He's no a young man.'

'No, he's not.' Cattanach called to mind the sight of him, stepping from his car outside the Townhouse. Never stooping, no, but thinner, his well-cut coat hanging more loosely, his face greyer. Maybe he should go and see him – maybe, if he were to be at more meetings in the town, meet him for dinner. All he had said about the old man to his father was true – the laird was lonely, trying to make a connexion. No use relying on his father: he would have to do it himself.

The rails below them started to sing, and they could hear the hiss and chug of the train approaching, thoughtful and steady, a bit of a countryman itself. But it was to take him back into the town, and work, and streets and buildings and buses and lorries and trams … oh, well. He had had his two days.

Once in a compartment he closed the door, opened the window and grinned at his father.

'Good to see you, Dad.'

'Good luck with those accidents,' said his father.

The stationmaster blew his whistle, and his father stepped back, lifting his cap in farewell. Cattanach waved until he could see him no longer, and sat back, thinking over the day. It had been a good one.

The compartment was empty apart from him. He pulled Billy Campbell's notebook out of his pack, and contemplated it, then thought he would rather look out of the window for a little longer. He was on the north side of the train this time, catching a last glimpse of farms and farmland. The track passed close to a steading, and he could see straight into the farmyard as the train slowed for one of those indefinable train reasons. A lorry stood in the farmyard, a couple of men loading metal barrels into the back. Farmhands, certainly. An older man stood watching, perhaps the farmer himself. And another man beside him, dressed more like a tounser – perhaps the lorry driver. He wondered absently what they were up to: would the driver set off now or would the farmer give him some supper first, or were they getting ready for an early start in the morning? The train drew him irresistibly past, where a car could stop and watch and ask and get answers. Could he manage without his car?

26

IN THE END he slipped Billy's notebook back, unread, into his pack again as the train edged into Kittybrewster. He would give it more thought very soon, though.

It was dusk as he shouldered his pack, picked up his cap, and climbed the short slope out of the station up to Bedford Road. Less than five minutes' walk to his house from here – maybe it was a reasonable solution, though he might grow tired of starting always at Oyne. He would have to think of other possibilities.

The street lights would normally have been starting to come on, lamps in windows illuminating the range of quiet, domestic Sunday evenings along the road, but there was nothing showing, and he could look up at the stars unimpeded, taking his last opportunity for peace before the weekend was over. But he had less time than he thought: as he approached his front door, he heard the telephone bell ringing from the hallway.

He flung his pack down and seized the receiver.

'Cattanach.'

'Oh, good, you're back, sir.' He knew at once the voice of the duty sergeant, and his mind came smartly back into the city. 'Been trying to get you.'

'What is it, Sergeant?'

'It's a body, sir. A dead one.'

'Where?'

'Nigg, sir, by the battery.'

Inspector Cochrane was the one who was supposed to be on

call this weekend: Cattanach tried to consider generously that he might be busy on something else, somewhere else. He changed quickly out of his muddy boots and socks, and into the clean shirt and suit he had already laid out for Monday morning. His shoes were already polished. The baby Austin, neglected on the street, mercifully started at the first turn. Though of course, the body was going nowhere fast.

Four years ago, a body found by Torry Battery would have been nothing to do with him. Nigg and Bridge of Dee, formerly in Kincardineshire south of the city, had been brought into the City force lock, stock and barrel, stations, officers and all. Cattanach wondered why one of the Nigg inspectors had not been called out to this one: he would have a better knowledge of the area.

The narrow road that skimmed the headland to the battery curled back and forth – in the daytime it would provide a fine view of the harbour, now in angular darkness. The battery would soon be in use again to protect it, no doubt: it had already seen service before and during the last war, but in the last few years it had been one of the sites pressed into use to help the city's housing crisis – the same situation that led to people camping in Seaton. The solid granite walls had contained, until recently, twenty families grateful enough for their own fireplace and sinks. He remembered reading in the paper that one of them, before being moved into the battery, had been living in a garden shed. But the place had quickly grown neglected and the Council had cleared the families out, just before the Army decided it could make good use of the defences again. Cattanach was not quite sure what stage the transition had reached. Would he have to deal with army officers, too? Was it a soldier who had died?

A constable with a small torch stopped him, and directed him up a steep little curl of road to a place outside the battery's walls, where he could park without blocking the main road. He stopped, and after a moment's thought removed his polished shoes after all, and tied on his muddy boots that he had remembered to throw into the car.

The wind whipped at him as he left the car and looked about, still trying to adjust to the light. The harbour lay down below, across the water, and the hill rose sharply behind him, gorse-covered and weather-beaten. He heard a shout from up the hill.

'Hi, is that the inspector?'

He turned, and clambered up towards the voice, brushing through the gorse until he found a makeshift shelter of thick black cloth, with a frozen-looking constable clutching one side of it against the wind lifting it. Inside, mercifully, there was light, a warm cocoon of lamplight. Briefly he was reminded of folk tales, of hillsides opening up to lure the unsuspecting down into the bright, glowing, beautiful land of faerie, never to be seen again. He crouched down and looked in: three men were neatly folded into it, one of them lying on the ground. None of them looked the least like a faerie: the two men standing were both slightly familiar, though, and one shuffled towards him at once, welcoming him in out of the darkness.

'Evening – Inspector Cattanach, isn't it?'

'It is. And you're Inspector Pithie?' He shook hands with the Nigg man. 'Good to see you.'

'You'll know Dr. Mackay, no doubt,' said Pithie, completing the niceties with a gesture.

'We've never met,' said Dr. Mackay, 'but of course I've heard of you. You're the one Anna called out to chase after that missing woman.'

Anna's father, of course, who sometimes helped out. Anna's father, whose portrait he had seen stately in their drawing room. Cattanach put out a hand again, and Mackay shook it.

'I've just cleaned my hands,' he explained. There was indeed a smell of disinfectant. 'Casualty surgeon's laid up with a broken leg,' Mackay went on. 'So here I am again, called out from my comfortable hearth.' But he grinned, and Cattanach could see Anna Mackay's intelligent eyes and bright face. Mackay's dark hair, though, was greying at the temples. He looked, against Cattanach's expectations, likeable. But now he turned sombre. 'Not that this fellow will know a comfortable hearth again.'

The man between them lay twisted on to his back, as if he had been crawling between gorse bushes and had half-turned to hear something behind him.

'He's been photographed,' said Pithie. 'He was lying face down when he was found, and we pulled him up after the photographer to take a look at his face. Cause of death likely to be the stab wound in his back, though, according to Dr. Mackay here.'

Cattanach craned round to see it. No weapon remained, but the man's dark suit was ripped ragged, and sticky-looking.

'It was a sharp knife, so far as I can see just now,' said Dr. Mackay. 'The cloth's torn like that because something's been at him since – animals, you know.'

'Of course.'

The expression on what was left of the man's face, so far as one could judge in the oddly cosy light, was surprise, and dismay, perhaps. It seemed reasonable. The knees of his trousers were filthy, as were the heels of his gloved hands. It looked as if he had indeed been crawling between the gorse bushes before falling down to provide dinner for the local wildlife. Cattanach looked more closely at his face, and was fairly sure, despite the lack of eyes and the grazing on the soft flesh, that he had not seen the fellow before. He was a large man, with fairish hair and a little, sharp moustache protecting what was left of his gnawed top lip.

'So how long has he been dead, then, if the animals have been after him?' he asked Mackay, who was showing no sign of impatience to return to his cosy fireside.

'I'd say about a week, maybe more,' said the doctor.

'I'm that pleased he's out in the fresh air,' said Pithie. 'Disinfectant's one thing.'

'If he's the man I'm looking for, a week fits well enough,' said Cattanach. 'No one seems to have seen him since Thursday or Friday of the week before last. I'll have to find someone to identify him: his father's not very fit, but if we can get him down his stairs and to the morgue he might be able to do it.' He took a careful peek outside the makeshift tent at the exposed hillside. The wind nipped at him at once. 'Who found him?'

'A young couple,' said Inspector Pithie, with a shrug. 'They'll no be courting around here again, I should think.'

'Enough to put anyone off,' said Dr. Mackay, eyeing Cattanach thoughtfully. Cattanach pushed all thoughts of Anna Mackay firmly to the back of his mind.

'I take it you haven't looked at the possibility of fingerprints yet?'

'Oh, aye, and checked them against the register, of course.' Pithie made a face. 'No, we've not looked – he's wearing gloves, as you see. We should be lucky, though it looks as if a fox has had a go at ripping one off. Otherwise his suit and his hair protected him from the larger vermin.'

'Anything in his pockets?'

'No means of identification,' said Pithie. 'Why do they not think to make it easier for us? There's a wee cheap notebook, but if there was anything written in it it's gone – the pages are ripped away. I think it's from Woollies, and there was the stub end of a pencil to go with it.'

'And a filthy handkerchief,' said Dr. Mackay, 'which on its own would keep a forensic team busy for months.'

'So there we are,' said Pithie cheerfully. 'Man matches the description of someone you were looking for, I think,'

'He does, doesn't he?' He could picture Stevie in that cheap suit and worn boots. 'Do you know him?'

'Well … not exactly.'

Cattanach smiled.

'Prepared to elaborate? I take it you won't be meeting him for drinks at Hogmanay.'

'Ha. A whilie ago we had news of someone in our area. Someone new, but still Kincardineshire.'

'Him? Stevie Tennant?'

'No, he's from your place, is he no? From the city?'

'If it's him, yes.'

'Aye, well, from what I heard it looks as if your friend Stevie here met my friends around here, with a view to some profitable business. When I saw your bit in the *Gazette* it was the Aberdeen mannie came to mind at once.'

'Interesting. And who are your friends, then?'

'I wish I had anything like a description,' said Pithie apologetically. 'A big yin and a wee yin, to quote our most reliable witness. Show me a man in the whole country who might not fit one or other of those descriptions.'

'I suppose it's a start. Stevie's likely been looking for somewhere to dispose of three dozen cases of decent Scotch – any hint that either of your men has a link to the licensed trade?'

'Not that I've heard, at all. Mind, I've heard that little they could own the Palace Hotel and run a distillery for all I would know to the contrary.'

'Well, gentlemen,' said Dr. Mackay, who had been bending

over to take a last look at the body on the ground, 'that's all I can do for you just now. If you don't mind, I'll be going – I'll try and arrange the post mortem for tomorrow some time, though.'

'Thank you for coming out, sir,' said Pithie.

'I won't say it's a pleasure, Inspector, but I'm pleased to be able to help. Good night to you. Good night, Mr. Cattanach.'

'Good night, sir.'

Mackay ducked out of the cocoon, and they heard him slither off down the hill into the wind.

'Seems a nice fellow, for a medic,' said Pithie.

'Seems so, yes. So you don't know anything more about these two fellows Stevie was meeting?'

'Just … you know, acting a bit suspicious. Nothing specific. Where they shouldn't really have any business being, doing nothing useful. Watching people. Nothing you could put your finger on.'

'That sounds like Stevie, right enough. Doing nothing useful, but nothing quite indictable, either. Poor Stevie.'

'Eh?'

'Well, he must have done something at last, I suppose. Something that got him killed.'

27

IT HAD BEEN a late night, by the time Pithie and he had overseen sending the body back to the morgue, talked again to the young couple, made sure everything was tidied up.

'I'd like fine a last dram with you,' said Pithie, 'for it's clear you've plenty on your mind. When I get like that I find it's good to go over with someone else. But I live in Stonehaven, and you're in the city – it would make it even later for both of us.'

'Maybe soon, though,' said Cattanach, shaking hands with him. 'Thanks for calling me in. I'd sooner have found him alive, but there we are: at least he's found.'

He acknowledged the truth of Pithie's words, but Cattanach was not much of a one for talking things over with others. And certainly not with Inspector Cochrane, who was the first available candidate when he arrived at the station on Monday morning.

'I hope you had a good weekend,' Cattanach said politely as he took off his coat. 'Not too many call outs?'

'What?' Inspector Cochrane looked up from his examination of the *Press & Journal*. 'No, no. It was a quiet weekend.'

Apart from the discovery of a body at Torry Battery, thought Cattanach, but decided not to say. Any weekend when Inspector Cochrane was on call seemed to be a quiet weekend. Perhaps he had an arrangement with the local criminals to take time off when he did.

He drew his ever-fruitful in-tray towards him and began to

flick through the contents, though his mind was chiefly on last night's discovery. The body certainly looked like that of Stevie Tennant: his father would have to make more permanent arrangements for the delivery of his messages and so on. So what had happened?

Stevie had been in Keith on – what – the second or third of September. The weekend that war was declared, though that was probably a coincidence. He had stolen a van with three dozen cases of whisky in it. Cattanach had read the report at last, brought from Keith when the sergeant had come to collect the boxes from their cells. It looked like an opportune theft: the van driver had stopped to go behind a bush, and almost immediately heard the van being driven off. He had had a vague recollection of seeing someone nearby but had paid them no attention in his haste for relief, and he had left the engine running as the van was elderly and unreliable to start.

Right, so Stevie, in Keith for reasons unknown, had spotted his chance and taken a van. He probably couldn't believe his luck when he found the whisky in the back. He brought it to Aberdeen, and persuaded Jock McKinstry, whether against his will or not, to take the whisky into his flat (that was on the third, the Sunday) and then he drove off in the van. Neither he nor the van had been seen since, as far as Cattanach knew, until last night. And according to Dr. Mackay – Cattanach shifted slightly uncomfortably at the thought of the man – according to the acting Casualty Surgeon, Stevie Tennant had been dead for about a week, maybe more, so the likelihood was that he had been killed not long after he had last been seen.

A falling-out amongst thieves? There was no evidence that anyone had been with Tennant when the van was stolen. Could McKinstry have killed him? Instinctively Cattanach thought not: Jock McKinstry was a chancer, and sometimes a thug, but not a killer. But he could be wrong, and it would have to be checked. Jock might have a sound alibi. He struck Cattanach as the kind of man who always had two or three sound alibis about his person, just in case.

He would have been surprised, too, to find McKinstry on the winning end of a punch-up, particularly with a large man like Stevie Tennant. But then there had been no punch-up, as far as they could see last night – he would know better after the post mortem. But one stab wound in the back, and Stevie's look of surprise, did not seem to add up to an ordinary fight. It looked as if Stevie had been ambushed. What had he been doing out at Torry Battery, anyway? Had he been lured there, or had he tried to lure someone else there, to a secluded spot for – for what? A conversation about the disposal of three dozen cases of whisky? Or had he been hiding out there anyway? A few years ago, when the accommodation in the Battery had been at its most neglected, Cattanach would have said that would have been a good place to hide, but now, with the army at work clearing the place out, it would be useless. And Stevie Tennant had not looked the kind to want to sleep rough amongst the gorse bushes.

He was almost at the end of his in-tray, with just two pieces of paper left. One, a hand-written note, was from Dr. Mackay, scheduling the post-mortem for that afternoon at four. He hoped they would be able to get old Mr. Tennant in and out for the identification well before that. The other was a circular about a billeting committee.

He had not thought about billeting, and for a moment he paused, fingering the note. He lived on his own in a house with three bedrooms. Would he have to take in half a dozen soldiers? It was not a happy thought.

He put it resolutely to the back of his mind for now, and went to see if Constable Gauld was about.

'It's a fine sight,' Gauld shouted across the wind. He gestured down the hill. In daylight, from here where Stevie Tennant was found, there was a good view of the mouth of the river Dee, the harbour, the little village of Footdee, the long beach beyond it where families picnicked and bathed in the summer, and on up the coast, dunes and golf links up to the estuary of the river Don and beyond to Balmedie. You could see why there had been a battery here for so long. There was a good deal to see, and to defend.

'This is where he was,' said Cattanach. The gorse had hardly taken much harm from last night's work, but the weather had been dry and there was blood on the ground between the bushes. He could see Gauld swallowing as he reluctantly took his attention from the sea, and looked down at it.

'He canna have been staying here, sir. He'd have been frozen.'

'There must be some shelter around. But I think he would have to have been desperate. I didn't have him down as the outdoor type.'

'I think they say it was cosy enough inside the Battery, out of the wind,' said Gauld. 'But then they were desperate, too, the folks they housed in there. I'd no fancy it much myself.'

'Not much chance now, unless you volunteer,' said Cattanach. There were already guards at the gate, and a bonfire inside tossed smoke up to be ripped apart by the wind. A few soldiers, surrounded by broken chairs and old mattresses, stood ready to feed it. Cattanach wondered where they were billeted.

'Are we looking for anything in particular, sir?' asked Gauld, rubbing his hands together against the wind. 'Apart from the van.'

'No, nothing specific. But in the dark it's easy to miss things.'

'Like the murder weapon?' Gauld sounded more uncomfortable than excited.

'A slim chance, I think,' said Cattanach, 'since the killer was careful enough to take it out of the body, I suspect he took it away with him.' Both of them were already casting about from the place where Tennant had been found, pressing aside the gorse bushes with their boots and trying to see underneath.

'Could it maybe be a woman, sir?'

'A woman? Well, it's possible, of course. Why do you ask?'

'Just thinking, sir. A courting couple found him, you said. Maybe he was up here with a sweetheart, and she – well, I dinna ken, sir, I'm making it up now, but they had a fight, or she was the jealous kind and he had another woman? Sorry, sir, I was just thinking.'

'Thinking is good, Constable. Yes, it's possible, but it would be unusual, I think. Speaking of which, why on earth would courting couples come up here, anyway? It's nothing but gorse bushes.'

'Aye, sir, but there's bits further up where it isna, and it's kind of sheltered. The couple that found him were likely going up there, or coming back down. Or if you've a car the place you've parked down there is grand – you can pretend you're stopped to look out at the sea, and then who knows what might happen? I'm told, sir,' he added quickly, and the pink of his ears was not caused by the cold wind. Cattanach grinned to himself, and kept looking among the bushes.

Larks sang above them, battling the wind, as they tried to keep methodical paths across the headland. Bottles and bottle tops seemed to be the rubbish of choice with the local courting couples, and greasy brown paper that had perhaps held sandwiches. Cattanach was the kind who always meticulously took his rubbish home, but as a policeman he appreciated the stories other people's leavings could sometimes tell. But there seemed to be few stories here beyond the obvious. The ground beneath the bushes was hard and sandy: any prints were shallow and fragile. Where they had all stood last night, looking down at the body, one could barely have said anybody had been there at all.

In the end it was Gauld who found their best discovery, and it was not even on the ground.

'Look at this, sir,' he called. He had wandered down the slope while Cattanach had gone upwards. Cattanach zigzagged back down towards where Gauld was pointing into a gorse bush.

'What is it?' he asked as soon as he was close enough.

'In there, sir.'

Dangling from a twig in the depths of the bush, like a secret Christmas tree ornament, was a pretty little penknife.

Resisting the temptation to reach in and seize it at once, Cattanach propped his hands on his knees and peered in.

'No visible rust, and it's delicately caught there - looks as if anybody brushing by might dislodge it. Yes, I'd say it hasn't been there very long.'

'Do you think it's the murder weapon, sir?'

'No,' said Cattanach. 'This is pretty small, and the wound was much larger. Of course it's folded up, so we might not be able to see any blood, but we'll get it looked at and make sure. But still … even if it wasn't used on Stevie Tennant, I wonder if it might be connected with him or his killer?' He reached in carefully now, with his gloved hands, and unhooked the knife from its twig. They both stared at it, lying on his palm. The sunlight played on the mother-of-pearl set into the side of the handle.

'It's … like you say, sir, it's delicate. Could it be a

woman's?'

'It could, indeed. But it wouldn't have to be. I think it's old, though. Victorian, at least.'

'How do you know, sir?'

'Just a feeling.' When you're brought up with old stuff, he thought, somehow you know. Old things tell you. 'Well spotted, anyway, Constable. Do you think there's anything else?'

'Fifty-eight bottle tops, sir,' said Gauld promptly. 'And an old bottle opener – I think it might be Victorian, too.'

Cattanach laughed. He was pleased that Gauld felt confident enough to make a joke.

'Well, I think we've achieved all we're going to achieve. Let's drive on towards the lighthouse. I still want to know where that van has gone.'

The road looped around the headland, past the lighthouse and round to the open land around the ruins of St. Fittick's Chapel. And there, tucked against the wall of the little graveyard, looking as if it had not been far in a while, was a van.

28

'YOU WOULDN'T PARK here and then walk your girl all the way back to the Battery for a beer and a sandwich,' said Cattanach, as they approached the van. 'Even the way the weather has been.'

'Do you think someone tried to hide it here after they'd killed him?' asked Constable Gauld.

'It seems likely. Either that or Tennant hid it here himself before going to meet – whoever it was.' He peered in through the passenger window. The front of the van was a mess, as if someone had decided to clear all the rubbish from the Battery and store it here. Crumbs and empty bottles and greasy papers littered the footwell, and a blanket was crumpled on the passenger seat. 'I think this might be where Tennant went when he left Jock McKinstry,' he said. 'Well, maybe not in this exact place, but I think he was living in the van at least for a night or two. The van was stolen on the Saturday, and he brought the whisky to McKinstry on the Sunday night … so that's one night, anyway. Probably Sunday night, too, for his father hadn't seen him.'

'Do you think he was hiding, sir?'

'He was probably hiding the van, yes. But also, there he was with three dozen cases of whisky. I imagine he'd be trying to find somewhere to sell it.'

'Would he not wait until the hue and cry had gone down, sir?'

'It would be sensible, but I don't think Stevie was that kind of criminal. He'd have wanted to get rid of it as quickly as he could.

So I suppose we're looking for pubs and shops that would turn a blind eye to the origins of a sudden and unexpected offer of whisky. I'm sure we have a list at the station.' He looked about him. It was a surprisingly lonely spot, though it was not far from the tenements of Torry.

'Stay here,' he said, 'and I'll go and report this and send the fingerprint people down. They can take a look at the penknife later. I'd better see if Tennant's father has been able to come in and see the body, too.'

'Aye, sir.' Gauld was flexing his shoulders and his feet, preparing himself for a long wait in the cold – the life of a lowly constable.

'Thanks for your help this morning, Constable – and well done for finding the knife.'

Gauld beamed.

'A pleasure, sir.'

It was the best he could do for now. Cattanach climbed back into his own car, and headed off to send the cavalry back to save him.

'Aye, that's my son – Steven Tennant,' said Mr. Tennant, when the morgue attendant lifted back the sheet. He seemed resigned. 'He'll have been dead since I saw him, then, or near enough?'

'Ah, yes, we believe so,' said Cattanach, taken aback. The smell of decay from the body was a lot stronger in here than it had been on the hillside. Mr. Tennant nodded.

'Seen them like that in the trenches. Ken, if they were caught on the wire and we couldna get to them. All swelled up and dribbling.' His words caught in his throat, and he wiped across his mouth abruptly with the back of his one hand.

'Would you like a cup of tea, Mr. Tennant?' asked Cattanach.

'I suppose you've nothing stronger? Aye, well, a decent cup of tea will be a treat an' all.'

Cattanach hoped it would be a decent cup of tea. He nodded to the assistant and guided Mr. Tennant slowly to a place where they could sit in peace for a few minutes. The morgue was not much designed with live visitors in mind. He was going to wait a moment, give Mr. Tennant time to recover from the initial shock, but Mr. Tennant plunged straight in.

'What way did he die?'

'He was stabbed in the back. We'll know more probably later today, though.'

Mr. Tennant nodded.

'Aye, well. I suppose it's no great surprise it should come to this. He was aye into the wrong things. He was aye interested in people, the wrong people, though, too. He always wanted to learn about them. Do him credit, when he made a bit of money he was always generous wi' it, and he always looked after me when he was at home. But I never wanted to ask where the money came from. Not if he wasna going to say of his own accord, ken?'

It was a kind of eulogy, Cattanach supposed, and probably the best that Stevie Tennant was going to get.

'Can you remember the names of any of his pals, or anyone who might know what happened?'

But already Mr. Tennant was shaking his head.

'I tellt you afore I had no idea who they were. Where was he found, did you say?'

'By Torry Battery.'

'There! He'd no call to be away there. Torry's away the other side of the Dee. I tell you, till I joined the Gordon Highlanders in 1914, I'd never been the other side of the Dee. No call for it.'

He was probably not alone. Now there would be another whole generation venturing south of the Dee, too, off to places they'd never heard of, maybe never to return.

'Can you just confirm when you last saw Stevie? Or heard from him?'

'Saturday morning a week ago. Ken, the day afore yon fellow said we were at war again. I thought to myself at the time, Stevie, boy, you'd better keep away from here or they'll have you in uniform afore you can say no. But I havena seen him since.'

'Did he say where he was going, that morning?'

For once, Mr. Tennant hesitated.

'I dinna think he did,' he said. 'And I canna rightly put a finger on it, but I've a notion he was going to catch a train.'

'A train? West? South? North?'

But Mr. Tennant was shaking his head again.

'I've no idea. I'm sorry, son, for I'd like fine for you to catch the fellow that did this. But I'm no even sure he was after a train. It's just a sort of notion.'

Well, a train to Keith and back in a stolen van, that made sense. But why Keith? Had he just fancied a run? Had he gone alone? Maybe it didn't even matter, but Cattanach thought he would send a man down to the Joint Station, and see if anyone remembered Stevie Tennant buying a ticket for Keith, or indeed anywhere else, on the second of September, or boarding the train. If he had thought, he might have asked the sergeant from Keith to make enquiries at that end.

Back at his desk, he took from his pocket a sketch he had made of the penknife before handing it in for examination. He was quite sure that it was not the murder weapon, but it had been an expensive little object in its day, and he suspected that most of the courting couples on the hill, with their beer and their sandwiches, could not have afforded such a thing. That was enough to make him interested in its origins. There had even been a hallmark on one side, and he had taken particular interest in that. He thought back to his conversation with his father at the weekend – only yesterday morning, he realised with a shock. He had sort of agreed to contact the laird, and this might be a good excuse. He knew the laird had in his library a book that listed hallmarks. It would be easy enough to call him and ask.

Inspector Cochrane was out: this might be a good time to do it.

He found he was hesitating, and shook himself. Get on with it, he thought. He picked up the receiver, and placed the call.

The switchboard, the operator, the butler – there seemed to be endless opportunities to change his mind. But before he could bring himself to put the receiver down, he heard the laird's voice.

'Alec? Is that you?'

'It is, sir. How are you?'

'What a pleasure! I'm very well, very well – busy with all this war nonsense! But then I daresay we all shall be, sooner or later. Have you seen your father recently?'

'Yesterday. We met on Bennachie. He said you wanted him to come up to the house for Christmas.'

'Of course I do, if we're all spared. Who knows what next year will bring? You, too, Alec, if you can get away. Imagine the three of us sitting round the fire – what tales!'

Imagine, thought Alec drily, but the laird had really sounded wistful. He was lonely, just as Cattanach had told his father. And just as his father was.

'I won't know till much nearer the time, sir,' said Cattanach, 'but thank you for the invitation. I was calling to ask you a favour. You have a book of hallmarks, don't you?'

'That's right. Do you want to borrow it? I could have it sent into town for you – I know you've always had an eye for antiques.'

'No, it's just one mark I want to look up, if it's not taking up too much of your time. I could call back later, if you prefer.'

'No, no, I'll fetch it just now. It's on my desk, so I shan't be a minute.'

There was a clatter as the laird laid down the receiver, and slightly uncertain footsteps fading away. Cattanach hoped the laird was not growing frail, not yet. He had always been a strong man – only the death of his wife had knocked him for six.

There was another clatter, and a moment's heavy breathing as the laird sorted himself out. Cattanach pictured the cold hallway and the ancient table and chair that had been selected to house the telephone when the laird's father had finally agreed to install one. Then the laird cleared his throat.

'Alec? You still there?'

'Yes, sir.'

'Right, here we are. You'd better tell me what mark you've found – you know what to look for.'

'It's a castle – you know, the three-tower one for Edinburgh, then a thistle and the plump man, and then an I.'

'What does the year letter look like?' Cattanach could hear pages being riffled.

'It's Gothic, I suppose.'

'Right … that seems to be Edinburgh, 1840,' said the laird. 'Does that help?'

'No idea, sir, to be honest!' He was pleased to hear the laird laugh. 'But it's a detail, and all details have the potential to be significant.'

'Your father said something about a missing woman in the

town. Are you involved in that?'

'Yes, I'm afraid so. No sign of her yet, unfortunately.'

'Then I'd better let you get on, and pray for a good outcome. Oh, by the way …' He sounded unsure of himself suddenly. 'By the way, I'll be in town for another of these interminable meetings tomorrow, but it should be over by seven. Could we – I mean, if you are not too busy – could we maybe meet and have a spot of dinner somewhere? You could come to the club, if you'd like: it might be simpler than trying to find somewhere.'

Cattanach knew he meant that if he had to cancel, the laird could still have his dinner in congenial surroundings. It was a sensible precaution to take – and the food at the club was pretty good.

'You know I can't promise, but I'd like that very much,' he said, and meant it.

'Then I shall look forward to it,' said the laird, at once happier. 'Good luck with the search!'

Cattanach sat back and wrote 'Edinburgh 1840' on his sketch of the knife. Almost antique, only just Victorian. A pretty little thing but not, he thought, with a silent apology to Constable Gauld, quite a woman's knife. But who would have been carrying such a thing up at Torry Battery, and did they have anything to do with Stevie Tennant's death?

He looked at his watch. It was a quarter to four: just time for him to head back to the morgue for the post mortem, and Dr. Mackay. He was not sure which he was looking forward to less.

29

COLD TILES, COLD floor, cold air. Cattanach had attended a number of post mortems over the years, though rarely of murder victims. He was inured to the sight of blood and the spilling of bodily fluids, and even the smell he could try to block, but the cold, unlike anything he had felt on a winter night in the hills, seemed to drive into his bones as if he could offer no resistance to it.

The morgue assistant, the one who had lifted the sheet for poor Mr. Tennant earlier, had a look about him that was equally cold. Cattanach was not sure if he was just a long-term sufferer, or played some part in the cold's generation: either way, he was almost completely frozen silent, going about doing Dr. Mackay's bidding with icy efficiency. Perhaps he was simply an enthusiastic supporter of the usual Casualty Surgeon, and resented Dr. Mackay's intrusion into his domain.

Stevie Tennant, stripped and washed and laid on the table, was not an attractive sight. As they had suspected, his hands and torso had not been readily accessible to predators and the white skin gleamed, stretched shiny by the gases building up inside his stomach. His legs were flabby and scarred – clearly smaller beasts had managed to crawl up inside his trousers, but had not troubled his feet. They had been safe in the muddy boots now set aside for later examination. His face still had that look of surprise, the little moustache an irrelevance under his distorted nose.

It took all three of them to turn him on to his stomach. The stab wound, a single neat slit, was horizontal.

'Nice work,' said Dr. Mackay appreciatively. 'You don't get caught on the ribs that way.'

'A professional job, you think?'

'Well, there's no wild hacking, anyway. And by the look on his face he was conscious – might have been stupid with alcohol, or something else, I suppose, but there's no smell of it from him.' He was all workmanlike today, barely looking at Cattanach, pushing on with the job. Now he was measuring the wound from side to side, and down into the body. 'Hit a rib before it could go through, though, on the front. Long blade.'

They turned the body again, and the serious work of dissection began.

'Well,' said Dr. Mackay, washing his hands in the bowl of steaming water presented by the assistant – in here the water was likely to be steaming at almost any temperature above hand-hot – 'the stab wound in the back is definitely the cause of death. A biggish blade, not your average kitchen knife, and long – it went straight through, as you saw, to hit a rib by the breastbone.'

'Single or double sided?' asked Cattanach. Mackay raised an eyebrow at him.

'Double. I'm an old man, Inspector Cattanach. My first thought was a bayonet – the old seventeen inch ones we strapped to our Lee Enfields.'

'Did you fight in the last war, Dr. Mackay?'

Mackay laughed.

'Fight? We were too busy patching them up. I saw enough bayonet wounds then – granted, more from German blades than our own – and it did make me wonder.'

'Just to confirm – a silly question, I know – but there is no possibility this wound was caused by a penknife?' Cattanach showed Dr. Mackay the sketch, with the dimensions noted. Dr. Mackay snorted.

'No. Not a penknife. Definitely not.'

'I had to ask.'

'It's a pretty thing,' granted Dr. Mackay. 'Where did it come from?'

'It was just a possibility – something that cropped up,' said Cattanach vaguely. 'No other injuries on the body?'

'No, nothing except bruises on the knees, probably from falling on to them when he was attacked.' He reiterated, noting on his fingers one by one. 'No defensive wounds, nothing to indicate he might have been knocked out or half-out before he was stabbed. Last meal involved bread and some kind of fish paste, probably a couple of hours before death – you understand he had been dead for some time, and what happens in the stomach can continue for a while after death. Dead, as I say, for some time – I'd say well over a week, in this weather. It's hard to say beyond that. Putrefaction … well, as you can see.'

Cattanach nodded, and thought he caught a glimpse of approval from Dr. Mackay. Undismayed by the mention of putrefaction. In any other world that would be bizarre.

'Do you have a confirmation of identity?'

'Yes: it's Stephen Tennant, as we thought. Confirmed by his father. Missing since the third of September, or at least there have been no sightings of him since then.'

'It's good to have a name,' said Dr. Mackay, and stood for a moment, hands folded, before the body. He nodded, and the morgue assistant drew a sheet over the whole corpse with business-like reverence.

'Any idea who killed him? I'm not asking for names, of course, just wondering how you're getting on.'

'We know what he was up to, and we have some known associates,' said Cattanach evasively.

'And Mabel Campbell? Is she connected with this?'

'I shouldn't think so,' said Cattanach with a smile. 'But we're concerned about her, certainly. We're still looking.'

'Good,' said Dr. Mackay.

The entrance hall at the station was busy when Cattanach went to see if he could speak to Jock McKinstry. He heard, vaguely, excitable constables talking about a break-in at a bank, and someone else saying heavily,

'Not a real bank, you fool!'

But his mind was set on Jock McKinstry and Stevie Tennant, and he paid little attention.

'What do you mean he's dead? How could he be dead?'

Jock McKinstry, Cattanach would swear, had known nothing of Stevie Tennant's death until Cattanach told him. And the news had caused him more than the simple grief of one for his fellow man. Jock was panicking.

'Why so worried, Mr. McKinstry?'

'Me? I'm not worried. Not at all. Why would I be worried? Sad, that's all. He was a friend of mine. Have you never lost a friend, Mr. Cattanach?'

'You seem worried. And you haven't asked very much about the circumstances. He could have died in a random accident.'

'Of course he could,' said Jock quickly. 'Did he?'

'No. He was stabbed.'

'In a fight?' Jock's voice was faint.

'In the back. No sign of a struggle.'

Jock considered this. He was not a good colour. He had been given back his own clothes and now had the look of a cut price undertaker, rather shiny and black. Why had Mabel gone about with him? What had attracted her? He made a mental note to talk again with Robert Campbell, then spontaneously asked:

'Where did you meet Mabel Campbell?'

'What?'

'Just wondering. You and she seem to move in different circles.'

'She was in a teashop, if you want to know. In Market Street – the harbour end. I don't only seek refreshment in bars, you know, Inspector.' But he needed to get back to Stevie. 'Where did you find him?'

'By Torry Battery.'

'Oh, aye,' said Jock surprisingly. 'He mentioned yon place a couple of times. He liked watching the boats, I think.'

'Did you two talk much? Just about general things?' Cattanach hoped he had caught McKinstry in a reminiscent moment.

'Aye, well, now and again, I suppose. He was young and enthusiastic. Thought he'd be rich one day.'

'You've told us he acquired the van and the whisky that disappeared in Keith. Do you know why he went up to Keith that day? He didn't seem to have planned anything, but it was the last time his father saw him, that morning, when he went for the train.'

'Oh, aye, his father. That'll be a sad miss for him. Just the one leg, has he no?'

'And just the one arm, too.'

'See … I dinna fancy much going to war,' said Jock, and for once he seemed entirely sincere. Cattanach allowed him a moment before going back.

'So why Keith?'

'He said he'd met a girl. I think she'd been visiting Aberdeen and he'd taken a fancy to her, and he thought, or so he told me when he brought the whisky, that she'd be impressed if he turned up on her doorstep, all the way from Aberdeen. I tell you, travelling to foreign parts is a waste of time. She turned her nose up at him, and he found himself kicking around in Keith till his train back. The van was by way of a consolation prize, and saved him waiting.'

Three dozen cases of whisky in payment for a date. Cattanach wondered if the girl would have been flattered.

'She must have been in the money, or her family was,' said Jock, idly. 'That was the one thing we always agreed on. If you're going to get involved with a girl, make sure she's financially worth it.' He was edging back to his grandiose attitude, when Cattanach knew he would be much less useful with information. He tried to divert him.

'Are you sure there was no one else involved in the theft?'

'Damn' sure,' said Jock. 'He'd gone up on his own and he'd come back on his own.'

'After he left you,' said Cattanach, 'no one has reported seeing him again until his body was found. We think he had been living in the van. It looks as if he was hiding. Have you any idea who he might have been hiding from?'

'Unless he tried selling the whisky in the wrong place,' said McKinstry thoughtfully.

'Could he have been working with someone? Working for someone, who didn't like him, ah, branching out on his own?'

Jock's eyes met his briefly, and flickered away. There was something.

'He usually worked on his own,' he said. 'Like, a job here and a job there. Not responsible to any one person, and no splitting the profits.'

'He brought you the whisky.'

'He needed somewhere to hide it. He kenned I lived on my

own, and that. And he could trust me.'

There was no talk now of having been bullied into taking in the boxes. Cattanach was impressed that Jock had not taken the opportunity of Stevie's death to blame him for everything, now that Stevie was not in a position to tell his own side of the story. It seemed they had actually been friends.

'Did you see him at all after he left the whisky with you? Hear from him? Even if he was in hiding, he must have been thinking of doing something with the stuff, or just telling you to sit quiet on it.'

'Never saw him again,' said Jock, addressing the remark to his own intertwined fingers on the table. But Cattanach had a feeling, and he kept quiet. 'Never saw him again,' repeated Jock, 'only the once … and that wasna really seeing him …'

Still Cattanach said nothing.

'It would have been the … what, now? The Tuesday night, I think. I was coming back from the pub. I heard my name from the end of a lanie. A' course I was away to walk on past, quick sharp, but then I heard it again and I recognised his voice.'

'Stevie's voice?'

'Aye, that's right. So I went back. I couldna see him, ken, but he put a hand on my arm and I kenned fine well it was him.' He hesitated, but Cattanach stayed silent. 'He said he had to go away for a whilie. He said it had nothing to do with the whisky, and I wasna to worry about that, just sit quiet. Like you say.'

He stopped, and cleared his throat mightily.

'Is there any cigarette I could have?'

Cattanach removed a packet from his pocket, and passed one to Jock, but when he offered him a light Jock shook his head. He toyed with the cigarette, turning it over in his fingers, squeezing it flat in the middle.

'He said he had done something he shouldna have done, a bad thing. And he reckoned he was going to be punished for it. So he was going to go away for a whilie, as I say.'

'Punished for it? You think he meant that he was going to be arrested?'

'Naw! I dinna think so, any road. That wasna the way he sounded, at all. No, he'd done something to annoy someone.'

'Did he say what?'

'Not a bit of it. He was in a hurry to be off. And he was dead scared, I can tell you.'

'Scared?'

'Terrified. I said he'd put his hand on my arm – and I tell you, he was shaking like a leaf.'

30

MRS. WALKER FROM next door had left a pot of stew on his doorstep when he reached home. She had an unerring knack of knowing when he had not managed to get to a shop. Inside all was order and cleanliness, as Monday was one of the days his cleaning woman came, polished and dusted, and took his clothes away to the steam laundry. He lit the oven and put the stew inside to heat, kicked off his shoes and exchanged his suit for slacks and a jersey. Peace.

The kitchen was not naturally a bright room, but he ignored the electricity and lit a hurricane lamp, casting the table into a pool of warm, comforting light. A pad of paper was always there, and a pencil, and he drew them across now. The last twenty-four hours had been all to do with Stevie Tennant, where he had been, where he had ended, and he felt he needed to stop and take stock not only of everything he had found out about Stevie, but also of the other puzzles he was trying to solve. He felt as if he had been clinging to the tail of a galloping horse for the last two weeks. He needed to stop, and review.

As far as he was concerned, all the stories began on the fifth of September, the day that Sandison had crashed his lorry into the Woodside tram and little Billy Campbell had fallen in front of another lorry in King Street. The tram crash was perhaps the easier place to start. It had happened about ten to eight in the morning, and Sandison had been driving to somewhere outside Aberdeen, to the north west, with an empty lorry. He was known to work for a Dundee man with a shady reputation. Currently he could not leave his bed, and Cattanach was waiting for Dundee to get back to him, but it was possible that Sandison had been going to get whisky. In addition, a man knocked unconscious in the crash, who had been on the tram, had not been identified and had later left the hospital without speaking to anyone. He had not been seen since, but might just have gone home and be living his life in a mild daze. It was possible that his first name began with T, Cattanach remembered, thinking of the description the nurse had made of the man's watch. That, he thought, was all that could be said of that case. It was unlikely that any further progress could be made without input from Dundee.

He set aside that piece of paper, and contemplated a fresh one. A more complicated matter altogether, though it had begun so simply.

Billy Campbell was killed on the fifth.

Billy was a quiet, solemn lad, who read the newspapers and was interested in wildlife. He had no noted enemies, and was not the kind of boy who got into trouble – on the contrary, rule-breaking upset him. Cattanach considered: he wanted to take a closer look at Billy's notebook, if only because of that fellow-feeling he had for the boy.

On the sixth, little Miss Hawthorne had come to tell them that Billy had been worried that his uncle was a criminal. None of Billy's uncles, his father's four brothers, seemed to have any criminal connexions. Constable Leggatt, slowly healing, had scoured the files for anything relating even tangentially to any of them, and come up with nothing.

Billy had been buried on Friday the eighth, and at the funeral Cattanach had seen Mabel Campbell catching sight of someone and looking scared. After the mourners had left, Mabel had packed a case and gone, and had not been seen since.

Mabel had been married for three or four years – no, she had been living with Robert Campbell, unmarried. Robert Campbell had met her in Montrose. Billy was the son of some former husband, lover, chance encounter … Cattanach had no idea. Robert Campbell did not seem to know much more about her past than that, either. But Mabel had money, at least, and a taste for the things that money could buy her.

The last man she seemed to have been associated with, apart

from Robert Campbell, was Albert Lovie, who lived within sight of where Billy had died. He was a jeweller, with an expensive car. He had believed, or chosen to believe, all Mabel had told him about Robert Campbell. He seemed to have been fond of Billy. Everyone seemed to be fond of Billy. And yet Billy was dead. Could it have been an accident, as they had all at first thought? But even if it had been, there was the mystery of Mabel Campbell's disappearance.

And that was where things became complicated.

The other man seen with Mabel Campbell had been Jock McKinstry – they had not been associated for long, perhaps, but they had known each other. Did they know how the two had met? He could not remember if he had asked McKinstry, a man with ideas above his station, who liked to play the sophisticate, even if he lived in a grubby flat in Littlejohn Street. Had Mabel seen through him, and moved on to the more obviously decorous Albert Lovie? She had found McKinstry in a tea shop, just as she had Lovie and Robert Campbell. Was that her method, or was it coincidence?

Mabel had led them to Jock McKinstry, and Jock McKinstry had led them to three dozen cases of whisky and Stevie Tennant, who was now dead.

He pictured Stevie Tennant lying there on the hillside at Torry Battery, the look of surprise on his face, that little moustache surviving where the flesh was eaten away around it.

The little moustache – he had been sure it was Stevie Tennant at once, because of that. But had Jock McKinstry actually mentioned that moustache? Or was he getting muddled?

He drew the shape of the moustache on his paper, and circled it. There was something wrong here, but he set it aside and pressed on with his thoughts, not to be side-tracked just yet.

He thought Mabel Campbell was probably safe somewhere. But he thought that because people still seemed to be looking for her – people who might be the men she had been fleeing from to start with. The man who had spoken to Mrs. Hawthorne, charmed and questioned her on her own doorstep. A well-dressed, smart man, who had been accompanied, in the area, by a large man and sometimes a third … sometimes a third. Who had said that?

He taxed his brain for a moment or two, running all his conversations for the last week through his head. Gauld, he thought. Gil Gauld had said something about an old man in Seaton and the

Three Musketeers, the smart smaller man, a large yellow-haired man, and a third – with a little narrow moustache, two shades darker than his fair hair.

Could it be that Stevie Tennant had been the third man?

He shook his head. He would need proof.

He would have to see if Mr. Tennant had a photograph of his son. There would be no sense in showing anyone one of the post mortem photographs, not for a reliable identification. Not if they didn't want to upset any witnesses. And then Constable Gauld would have to find the old man at Seaton again, and see if he recognised Stevie.

Stevie Tennant, helping to hunt for Mabel Campbell. No, he would not even start to think what that might mean: not until he had proof.

He sat back at the kitchen table, and noticed that the air was full of the rich smell of stew. His dinner was ready, and he realised suddenly that he was starving.

He turned on the wireless, and as it warmed up he spooned hot stew on to a plate he had left to heat, and put the kettle on to boil. When the meal was done, to the accompaniment of some unchallenging music, he used the hot water to wash his solitary plate and glass. Then with silence restored, he retrieved Billy's journal from his pack, settled in a deep armchair in the front room, and poured himself a whisky.

Before he opened the notebook, he wondered how he could have managed such an evening with soldiers billeted in his house. He would have to find out what the situation was, and soon.

Inspector Cochrane had the glue pot out again when he reached the office the following morning. He left his coat, respirator and hat on the hatstand, and went to find Constable Stewart.

'You fetched Mr. Tennant yesterday, didn't you?'

'Aye, sir.'

'Did you happen to notice any photographs of his son Stevie in the house?'

Constable Stewart screwed up his face in the effort of remembering.

'I think there was maybe one, sir, on the mantelpiece. A few years old, though, I'd have said.'

'It might be better than nothing, but if he's prepared to lend us a more recent one that would be good.'

'You want me to go and ask him, sir?'

'Yes, please, Constable, and see if he's all right, while you're there. The downstairs neighbour was supposed to be fetching him his messages. I don't want him starving.'

'Right, sir.' Stewart bustled off importantly. There was nothing else Cattanach could do in that line until Stewart had returned. Leggatt would have told him if he had found anything new – any criminal connexions of Billy's uncles, or links between Stevie Tennant and – and what? Stevie liked working alone, but he was eager to make money. Had he fallen in with someone a bit further up the criminal tree? But who, and what were they up to?

Trees made him think of Billy and his nature diary, or journal. He had enjoyed reading it last night, participating in the young lad's delight at the seals in the estuary, deer coming down from Seaton House, ducks and geese – the first early V of the barnacle geese ploughing their steady path overhead with their reassuring cries. An observant boy, as so many ten-year-olds are – much less concerned with themselves and more interested in the world around them. He wanted to go and see exactly the path he had taken and recorded that last night, though: not the night before his death, but the Sunday night. Perhaps it was something he had seen that night that had made him say what he had to Maggie Hawthorne – perhaps he had seen one of his uncles, involved in something he should not have been involved in. But what? And which uncle? And had it really led to his death?

He sighed. He had no wish to return to work in his office with Inspector Cochrane applying the adhesive across the room. He wanted to get out.

He ran back up the stairs, darted into the office to snatch his hat, coat and respirator, and fled, leaving, he hoped, the impression of urgent duties to be attended to. Then he trotted down the stairs, raised his hat to the sergeant, and left the building.

He headed on to Broad Street, past the granite cage of Marischal College and then down Schoolhill, past ironmongers and bakers and the strange brick spire of the Triple Kirks, unique in a city of granite. Robert Gordon's College lay behind the arched gateway to his right, a prim quadrangle leading to the old domed building. On each side of the doorway had been a black-painted cannon, left over from the Crimean War, but they had been taken now to be melted down into more modern weaponry. It seemed a shame to disarm the school just when they might need them.

Then there was the Art Gallery and the war memorial – what would happen to that? – and to his left the neat granite and ironwork fence that bordered Union Terrace Gardens. They lay beside the railway, the line he had taken on Saturday. Public grounds now, the houses they had once belonged to stood as Union Terrace, a rather grand assortment of prosperous buildings now mostly offices. He went to the one that served as the local headquarters of the Women's Voluntary Service, where he hoped he might find out more about billeting. What he did find, almost as soon as he had entered the cool, busy hallway, was Anna Mackay's mother.

31

MRS. MACKAY'S DARK heather tweed suit had the air of a uniform – an officer's uniform, of course. She was at the front desk, bending over to address the girl behind the desk: straight back, generous hips, hat firmly in place, gloved hand pointing authoritatively at something in a register. Cattanach held back, hoping not to be noticed, but at once Mrs. Mackay's head rotated towards him, and she stood upright, like a wooden doll pulled by strings. Cattanach thought she probably suffered a fair bit from back pain.

She hesitated, and he could see she was trying to decide whether to address him as 'Mr.' or 'Inspector'. The latter would, she would probably think, put him in his place, but one did not always want the police calling on a respectable establishment.

'Mr. Cattanach,' she conceded, and managed to make it sound as if he had come to see to the boiler. 'I'm afraid my daughter does not accompany me here.'

'I had a general enquiry to make, Mrs. Mackay,' he said innocently. 'I would not presume on the valuable time of either you or Miss Mackay.'

'I see.' She looked down at the receptionist behind the desk. The girl was decidedly pretty, and was already smiling at Cattanach helpfully. That would evidently not do. 'Come with me, Mr. Cattanach. Perhaps we may be of assistance.'

She turned and led the way without looking back. They passed the door of what had presumably been the dining room when the building was still a house: it was full of women, busy with heaps of paper around a large, polished table, exchanging information in low, quick voices.

'Preparing for registration,' she snapped, waving a hand. 'There is a significant amount to do. Where the authorities would be without us I have no idea.'

They passed a smaller room almost entirely full of boxes. One woman sat on the floor, solemnly labelling each box with something, moving it from one pile to another in an impossibly small space. They reached the foot of the stairs, and Mrs. Mackay led the way briskly to the first floor.

'My office,' she explained. Not hers alone: like Cattanach's, it was shared, here by two other women, each busy at her own desk. They glanced up and smiled at Mrs. Mackay, and nodded at Cattanach.

'Tea, Effie?' asked one. They both rose. 'Can we fetch you anything, Margaret? Or your guest?'

'He won't be staying long, thank you,' said Mrs. Mackay, and the two women left. 'Now, what did you want to know? Mrs. Campbell didn't volunteer here, if that's what it is.'

'No, it's nothing to do with Mrs. Campbell, though of course we are still pursuing a number of leads,' he said. 'No, I wanted to know what the situation is with billeting in the city.'

'Billeting? Why?'

'It has come up in the course of an enquiry,' he said smoothly. There was no point in making it clear to the authorities that he had two free rooms, not until he had to, anyway.

'Billeting,' repeated Mrs. Mackay. 'No … No, that seems to be one of the few things we are not handling here. It's the council that's organising that. With the military, of course.'

'Is it? Then you don't know anything about how it is being arranged?'

'Well …' It was clear she was reluctant to admit ignorance. 'I imagine …'

'No, that's fine, Mrs. Mackay. I understand – I shall enquire elsewhere.'

'Then you really didn't come here looking for Anna? For my daughter?'

'Not at all, Mrs. Mackay. Not that it isn't a pleasure to meet her when we chance to meet.'

She frowned.

'Your uncle was a policeman.'

'Yes, a sergeant,' he said.

'Yet you …' She tailed off. He smiled, a friendly smile.

'Well, I mustn't take up any more of your valuable time, Mrs. Mackay. Thank you so much for your assistance.'

He caught a tram on Union Street and sat on the top deck, thinking about billeting, and about Mrs. Mackay, and Dr. Mackay, and Anna. Were her parents always so protective of her? Did every fellow medical student in her class undergo interrogation? Or had he been unlucky enough to draw their particular attention? And what did Anna think about that?

She was certainly an attractive woman – those intelligent eyes, that sweep of shining hair, that neat figure. But he had no intention of thinking of her in that way, none at all. He was sure she felt the same way about him: in fact, she seemed to see him as someone who could serve her purpose, whether it was driving her into town for lunch or tracking down her erstwhile colleague, pursuing jewellers at the snap of her fingers.

He left the tram at its terminus, within sight of the Bridge of Don, and walked toward the river. From his pocket he drew Billy's notebook, stopped, and took stock.

On Sunday evening, after war had been declared, Billy had walked to the end of his road and up King Street to the bridge. Cattanach wondered how he had been feeling. Surely war was the biggest rule-breaker of all? Was he upset? Frightened? Or focussed on the world around him, the things he could see and touch and smell and hear? Had he gone out to find refuge?

King Street was busy at this time of the day, but on a Sunday evening it would be quieter, and here the land was opening out, reaching the edges of the city. There was a putting green, and some scrubby land that was probably a haven for wildlife. Billy had crossed the road and wandered about in it for a while, noting a shrew, a wren, a rock where a dog fox had marked his territory. Overhead there had been the honk of a heron, and herring gulls calling, and the urgent squawk of oystercatchers. Billy had noted them all, and drawn some in his usual clumsy fashion.

Then, wanting a change of territory, he had crossed back over King Street at the end of the bridge, and made his way down into the overgrown dunes at the estuary's edge. 'No seals', he had written, and Cattanach could picture him watching and waiting before coming to his conclusion. The bridge loomed above them here, and Cattanach moved, as Billy had, downstream, away from it. There was more cover here than there had been on the scrubland: hawthorns grew into sturdy little trees, and there was gorse and heath holding the sandy soil secure. A boy could vanish easily into the undergrowth, and watch what he wanted, unseen. The Don's waters, meeting the sea a hundred yards away, rumbled along and hissed on little beaches, masking sound. There would be waders to watch, and gulls. Billy had noted them. But waders and gulls had nothing to do with criminal uncles.

Cattanach pocketed the notebook again and considered. There was no obvious path for Billy to have taken: he could have wandered about, or squatted under a tree, or both in turn. He was not specifically descriptive about his route, and his account tailed off with no finishing time noted on it, as there had been on his other journal entries. Cattanach walked on, looking from right to left, trying to see anything that Billy might have seen, that might have concerned him. Then he found it.

The hut was of corrugated iron, a random pattern of old green paint and rust, almost invisible lying low amongst the bushes and trees. It had a wooden door that one might think would fall apart if anything touched it, but when Cattanach took a closer look, he saw that the hinges were sound and recently oiled, and the lock on the hasp was new. To add to his suspicions, he saw that someone had wiped mud over it, to make it less obvious. Someone had not wanted this hut to be noticed. Had Billy noticed it?

Cattanach walked slowly round the little structure – to call it a building would be taking it too far – and found that the door, shabby though it was, was possibly the strongest part. The corrugated iron sheets sagged at one of the back corners, making a slit two or three inches wide at its broadest. The ground was higher here, and a stray buddleia bush masked the hut from this angle and also, probably, made the slit less noticeable from the inside. Cattanach pressed the fading leaves and whippy branches to one side, crouched down, and took a look inside, giving his eyes a few minutes to become accustomed to the dark.

He knew what was in there before he could properly see it,

though. The smell gave it away, but there they were, solid in the dark, three large metal barrels. Another hoard of petrol.

He stood slowly, rearranging the branches of the buddleia and checking to see he had left no trace of his being there. Was this what Billy had seen? He read the newspapers, his aunt had said: he would have known that petrol hoarding was a crime. And if he had seen one of his uncles here, with the petrol – but which one? And was it really enough for his uncle to kill him?

He made his way back out on to the road, and stared out across the open ground, the putting green and the edge of the links, over to the row of new houses that constituted Seaton Drive. He could just make out the Campbell flat, and thought the curtains were still closed. He should speak again to Robert Campbell, and see if he had thought of anything further to say.

The road he was on led to the raised esplanade beyond the links, but there was a turn-off before the links that would take him round to the far end of Seaton Drive. He took it, letting his thoughts wander as he walked, for he knew that wandering thoughts sometimes found new and interesting paths to take, where focussed thoughts passed them by. Petrol hoarding, that was where his thoughts went now. Petrol hoarding, like that foolish man Sutherland in Loch Street. At least a hut in the middle of nowhere was a safer place to keep it.

Which uncle would it be? Young Arthur, with his slicked back hair and love of a good party? Tom, the leader? Sam, off on the liners – he had not even been here on Sunday, so was that him cleared? Or Edward, respectable Edward with his desk job and his smart suits? None of them seemed quite right. He was not even sure that any of them ran a car. Something else to ask Constable Leggatt to find out. At least the foolish man in Loch Street had claimed to have a car. Something to do with his business – antiques, wasn't it?

Antiques – like a pretty little penknife made in Edinburgh in 1840.

That was surely too much of a coincidence to run. Cattanach laughed at himself, tying threads together when there was no need. And if there were a connexion, what on earth was it? He tried to picture the man from Loch Street, little Mr. Sutherland, stabbing Stevie Tennant, professionally, without hitting the ribs. It really did not fit.

The road veered again, and he found himself passing the huts and tents at the end of Seaton Drive. The Council desperately needed to push on with new homes for these people, but what would happen now, in the face of another war? Money would be scarce. These people here, like the ones who had gone to live in Torry Battery, must be desperate to freeze here rather than live in whatever slum they had left. His mind wandered back to Jock McKinstry and his single grubby room in Littlejohn Street. His single room, which he occupied alone – positively luxurious. Constable Anderson had told him that most flats in that area were full to bursting. Jock must have more money than it seemed, or knew how to use his influence, whatever that might be. Some kind of blackmail?

He was just toying with that thought and where it might lead them, when he heard a shout, and someone call his name.

'Sir! Inspector Cattanach, sir! We've got it!'

32

IT WAS CONSTABLE Gauld, of course. Cattanach was once more on Gauld's beat.

'What have you got, Constable?'

Gauld trimmed the beaming smile on his face down to something more police-like, and waved a manila folder.

'Constable Stewart got the photograph of Stevie Tennant, sir, from Mr. Tennant. It's not great, but I've put together a few others to see if the mannie can pick him out.' He opened the file, keeping a careful grip on the edge in case anything might blow away. It took Cattanach himself a moment to pick Stevie Tennant out of the line-up: the picture was obviously a snap taken by someone probably on the beach nearby, with Stevie standing by his father, in shirt sleeves and a sleeveless pullover, squinting into the light. The image was small, but if you looked closely Stevie's face was fairly clear. The others were of a similar type, family photographs, in one of which Cattanach thought he could spot a younger Gil Gauld.

'Try to let him see just one person from each photograph,' said Cattanach. 'It'll make any identification clearer.'

'I've got some bits of paper to cover things up, sir,' said Gauld, clearly embarrassed at his own picture.

'Do you want to go in on your own? Make less of an occasion of it? If you like I'll wait out here,' he added, suddenly impatient to know if Stevie Tennant really had been one of the three men looking for Mabel Campbell. He had been trying to put it to the back of his mind until he had more information – now that information was within touching distance.

'I think he'd be awful pleased if you came in, sir. I think – well, he knows me just as a local loon. He'd think we were taking it gey seriously if an Inspector turned up an' all.'

'Excellent,' said Cattanach. 'Lead the way.'

The way led to an upstairs flat, the door opened by a pretty woman dabbing quickly at her mouth.

'Sorry,' she said, 'I'm having my dinner. It's Constable Gauld, is it no?'

'Aye, miss,' said Gauld, colouring slightly. 'And this is Inspector Cattanach.'

'Oh, my!' said the girl, but put out her hand to shake his. 'That sounds serious!'

'Can we have another word with your grandfather, please?' Constable Gauld asked.

'A' course! It'll make his day.' She stood back and ushered them in, taking them to a bright parlour where an old man sat by the window with a tray on his lap. Dinner was well in progress: he was tucking in to a bowl of broth, and a pot of tea sat by the girl's place at the table, ready to be poured. 'Here's your pal again, Grandad!' she sang out.

'Och, Gil! Grand to see you, son,' said the old man. 'Sit you down, you're gey tall for an old man like me.'

'And this is Inspector Cattanach,' added his granddaughter. 'My grandfather, Davie Allan.' The old man's eyes widened, and he beamed.

'You've the cavalry with you, an' all! Here, lass – take away my tray. A man canna do business with his elbows in a bowl of broth. Is there tea in the pot for these gentlemen?'

Cattanach smiled – the polis were not so welcome everywhere. He sat where he was directed, and gratefully accepted a cup of hot tea.

'I hear from my constable here you've been very helpful, watching what's going on in the street?' he said.

'I've nothing much else to do,' the old man admitted. 'It's no so entertaining as being up a stair in our old street, for you could see straight into other people's windows there, and there was great goings-on up and down the street. But the air's better here.' He gestured to the window beside him. His view took in the golf links, the putting green, the esplanade, and the best part of the street. 'And if there are strangers, it's not long till they're spotted.'

'I can see that,' said Cattanach. 'Constable Gauld says you remembered seeing one or two strangers recently?'

'Aye, that's right. The last week or so … let me think, now, and be sure. It would be maybe a day or so before that wee lad up the road was buried.'

'That was awful sad,' put in his granddaughter. 'Do you mind if I get on? I've to be back at the shop in twenty minutes.'

'You carry on,' said Cattanach, and turned back to Mr. Allan. 'So from say the sixth of September, maybe, until when?'

'What day's this?'

'This is Tuesday the nineteenth.' A fortnight now since the accidents.

'Aye,' said the old man, 'you're right. I havena seen them since maybe last Friday?'

'Not over this last weekend at all?'

'No, I'm sure.'

'I know you've already told Constable Gauld here,' said Cattanach, 'but would you mind going over again what they were doing and what they looked like? It's just we find that when people go over things again, they sometimes remember another little detail, perhaps, that might help.'

'Aye, aye, I ken that. Makes sense. Well, there was one big yin, with hair like a hay stook – you could just put him in at the front of the regiment and let him shelter the rest of them.'

'Grandad,' said his granddaughter, warning. 'He's that excited we're at war again. Talks of nothing else.'

'You wait,' said Mr. Allan, but it was not quite clear what for. 'Aye, well, so there was that one. Then there was the wee fellow, in a dark suit, so sharp he'd cut himself. No hay stooks about him, but I tell you, if he came up to me in the street and offered me a pound note I'd be looking behind me to see what was going on.'

Cattanach thought he understood.

'And what were they doing?'

'Sort of watching,' said Mr. Allan. 'Whiles they'd go up and talk to someone, and I think they chapped at a few doors. I canna see the fronts of the houses from here, but my granddaughter said a few people had said they'd had them call. But that would have been a bit later. At the beginning, when I first saw them, they were just kind of hanging around, if you get my meaning. That's what you say, isn't it, Mary? Hanging around, young fellows at street corners. Only these ones wasna that young – maybe their thirties.'

'You'd think they'd have something better to do,' said Mary briskly, brushing down her skirt with one hand and pouring a last cup of tea with the other.

'A' course, there was three of them to start with,' added the old man.

'Three of them?'

'Aye, mind I told you?' he asked Gauld. 'The Three Musketeers, ken?'

'What did the last one look like?'

'Sort of dumpy. Big, but shorter than the other one. He had a hat on so I couldna see the colour of his hair, but when they came down this way I saw he'd one of those daft wee moustaches, hardly worth the effort, just get in your way when you sneeze.'

'And you're sure he was with the other two?'

'Oh, aye, walking along with them, talking with them, watching with them an' all.'

Cattanach felt a prickle run up his spine.

'When did you last see him with them?'

'Well, now …'

'That's me off,' said Mary, back at the parlour door with her coat and hat on and her respirator case slung over one shoulder. 'I'll be back for tea.'

'I'll have it all ready for you!' Mr. Allan called back, and she laughed as she disappeared. 'That'll be the day,' he added, when the front door had shut. 'I can barely get to the kitchen. But she's a good girl, looks after me well.'

He pondered for a moment, then, just as Cattanach thought he might have to remind him where they were he said,

'Friday afternoon. Early evening. That like of a time.'

'Last Friday?'

'No, no, the one before. The one with the funeral.'

'What was he doing?'

'Well,' said the old man, frowning, 'I think it was him. He was in a wee van – black, or dark green, and he drove past.'

'Which way?'

'Oh, that way,' said Mr. Allan, pointing down the road towards the huts and tents. 'If he'd been going the other way I dinna think I could have seen him. I think it was him,' he added again. Cattanach nodded at Constable Gauld, who brought out his manila folder.

'I've a few pictures to show you, Mr. Allan, to see if any of these men's in them. Would you be able to see?'

'Oh! Aye, a' course. My eyesight's no bad. It's only my legs.'

Cattanach moved a little out of the way and Gauld came and squatted beside Mr. Allan's chair, using the folder to prop up the photographs one by one, deftly covering the other people in each picture and letting him see only the man that looked most like Stevie Tennant.

'It's like a card game. Yon memory one,' said the old man happily. 'I was always good at that. Now, let me see …'

Constable Gauld got his money's worth out of the photographs, Cattanach thought. Mr. Allan subjected each one to the closest of examinations, poring over each detail, staring at the faces as though they might speak to him. Then he sat back, pleased with himself.

'Aye, I recognise him, right enough.'

'You do?' Cattanach tried to sound calm. 'Which one is he?'

'That one there – no two ways about it, Inspector. Do I win a prize?'

As far as Cattanach was concerned, yes, he did. He had picked out Stevie Tennant.

'What does that mean, sir, though?' asked Constable Gauld, when they were back out in the street. They had reunited Mr. Allan with his broth and made him some fresh tea, and the man was in a cheerful mood as he waved goodbye from the window. 'How can Stevie Tennant … it's like a big circle, is it no?'

'That's what it feels like, Constable, I agree. Stevie stole the van and the whisky, and he knew Jock McKinstry who was seen about with Mabel Campbell, and then Stevie was seen with two men apparently looking for Mabel Campbell. I think we need to talk to Jock again, find out whether or not Stevie knew Mrs. Campbell.'

'Do you think she was in with a bad crowd, sir? Before she married Mr. Campbell, I mean.'

'It wouldn't surprise me, no,' Cattanach agreed. 'Though she and Campbell aren't married, apparently. Campbell was her name already – and Billy's, of course.'

'Plenty of them about, I suppose, sir,' said Gauld.

'Well done with the photographs, by the way. I think that was a very reliable identification.'

'Thank you, sir.' Gauld's ears, constant signals of his emotions, turned pink. He had the makings of a good policeman, though, Cattanach thought. He wondered if Gauld would sign up, or stay where he was. He was the prime age for the call-up. And how many others would they lose, too, leaving the older men like him, like Inspector Cochrane, to deal with whatever the war would do at home? He swallowed, thinking of all their young constables. How many of them would come back?

'What would you like me to do now, sir? Do you want me to try the photograph on a couple of other people, get some confirmation?'

'That's not a bad idea – did anyone else mention a third man?'

'Not really, sir, but that's not to say that they might not pick him out. And if he did know Mrs. Campbell, maybe he had even been here before this whole thing started.'

'What time is it?' Cattanach looked at his watch. It was past three o'clock, and he was not sure he had had any lunch. 'Try Mrs. Hawthorne first.'

'She definitely didn't mention a third man, sir,' Gauld objected.

'No, but her daughter should be home for her tea by now, and she's a smart child. She might have seen him.'

'I don't suppose there's any way he might be Billy Campbell's uncle, sir?' Gauld suggested tentatively.

'Good grief. That would turn things round, wouldn't it?' He stared across to the links for a moment, working it through in his head. 'I don't think so, but let's put Constable Leggatt on it, shall we? He's getting good at all this paperwork.'

'Aye, sir, he's beginning to fear he'll never be let back on the street again.'

33

CATTANACH LEFT CONSTABLE Gauld to his further investigations, and walked along the road to the Campbell flat. Already the garden was looking a little neglected, and the ornaments on the windowsills had a dusty appearance. Mabel Campbell had certainly looked after the place, whatever her background. In the brief time he had known her, he had had the impression that she was proud of her home.

The door opened sharply. Robert Campbell must have seen him from the window, for he looked not in the least surprised.

'Any news?' he asked at once.

'We haven't found her yet, I'm afraid.'

'Then what are you here for?'

'Robert, dinna speak to the mannie like that,' came a solemn voice from the kitchen. Tommy Campbell, the leader of the family, appeared, still in his working clothes from the shipyard. Robert, by contrast, was positively dapper: he had a well-fitting suit, clean shirt and collar, and a woollen tie neatly knotted. His boots gleamed.

'Come in, Inspector – I canna mind your name,' said Tommy, 'but do you want a fly cup?'

'Only if you're making one, Mr. Campbell,' said Cattanach, but he stepped inside the doorway quickly before the brothers could change their minds.

'Go on in and sit down,' said Tommy, evidently returning to the kettle. 'Robert, it's no going to make a difference if we go now or half an hour's time. Away in and talk to the mannie. To the

Inspector, ken.'

Cattanach gestured to Robert to precede him into the parlour, and found the youngest brother, Arthur, already there at the table. He, too, was dressed as if he were about to go out.

'I'm sorry, I've clearly interrupted. Were you off out somewhere?' Cattanach asked politely.

'Only for a walk,' said Robert, too stiff to sit easily.

'And maybe a drink,' said Arthur.

'They're coming to my place for their tea. Big job starting tomorrow, him and me got sent home, so we came up here to see him,' said Tommy, appearing in the doorway with two mugs of tea. He handed them to Robert and Cattanach, and went back for more.

'You looked as if you were off somewhere grand,' said Cattanach lightly. 'Or maybe to see your bank manager.'

Robert glared, but Arthur laughed.

'No, he's always gey smart, except when he's working. It's only Tommy looks like he's just come out of the yard, even when he's off out. The rest of us – well, you'll ken Edward.' He made a face. 'And Sam's the same. He's a steward. When he's in his uniform, he's like something from the American films.'

Mabel did like her men to look smart, it seemed. That was some kind of a pattern, perhaps. Was it helpful? He was beginning to wonder if anything was helpful.

'Why are you here, then, if you havena found her?' Robert demanded, as Tommy returned with two more mugs, and sat with Arthur at the table. 'You're no here to give us fashion advice, are you?'

'Robert!' said Tommy. 'Dinna be rude. If the Inspector's here and not out looking for Mabel, he'll have his reasons.'

'Aye, and a wheen of men all out looking for her on his behalf,' said Arthur.

'We are looking, constantly,' said Cattanach. 'And we've sent word to the neighbouring forces, too. Everyone is keeping an eye open for her. I'm here to ask you a couple more questions, I'm afraid, and the first one is whether or not you've thought of anything else at all that might help us? Anything particularly about her background, or anywhere you think she might have wanted to go, perhaps to feel safe? To hide from someone?'

'She never wanted to go anywhere,' said Arthur, when

Robert said nothing. 'She never wanted to leave the town. See, we all thought we might have a day out last summer, all the family, maybe down to Stonehaven or along to Banchory. On the train, ken, the lot of us. It would be a laugh. But she'd not think of it. Made a load of excuses, then started talking us out of it, said Duthie Park would be fine, we'd no need to go any further than that for a grand day out. Well, Duthie Park's all well and good, but some of us fancied a wee bit of an adventure, ken? But no, not for Mabel!'

'I think she'd have gone for Banchory, in the end,' said Tommy thoughtfully. 'It was Stonehaven she took exception to. But you're right: she didna ever want to leave the town. But there's plenty like that, all over.'

So she was more reluctant to go south, down the coast, than west and inland, Cattanach thought, if Tommy was right. Just as Lovie had said, too. Should he be searching to the north?

'I thought maybe Montrose,' said Robert suddenly. The other two looked at him. 'Montrose,' he repeated. 'Where I found her. I thought she might have gone back.'

'Except that's even further than Stonehaven,' said Arthur, practically. Clearly the cancellation of his day out still rankled.

'We've sent word to Montrose,' Cattanach assured Robert.

'I'd thought I might go down myself.'

'I'd rather you didn't, sir,' said Cattanach. 'For one thing, if we get word of Mrs. Campbell from somewhere else, it might be hard to contact you.' He saw Tommy look at him, and understand. The police in Montrose would not want someone coming in and ploughing around interfering in any sightings they might have.

'Aye, you'd be better staying here, Robert,' Tommy said, then added reluctantly. 'Or maybe one of us could go down.'

'Aye, we could send Betty and Lizzie!' said Arthur with a grin. 'They'd work it all out in no time!'

Tommy laughed, though his heart did not seem to be in it.

'She had money, didn't she?' asked Cattanach.

'What about it?' asked Robert.

'She'd have the means to stay somewhere independently, wouldn't she?'

'Aye, I suppose.'

'Had she a cheque book? A bank account?'

'What would she want those for? She had cash, that's all I

know.'

'Do you know how she came to have money?'

'I suppose it was from her first husband.' He glanced at Cattanach suddenly, waiting to see if he would pick him up on that, remind him that he had said they had not married. 'I suppose he left it to her.'

Or she took it, thought Cattanach. He set the thought to the back of his mind. He thought it might prove useful.

'Do any of you know a man called Jock McKinstry?' he asked. Blank looks around the room. 'Albert Lovie?'

'Ha!' said Arthur, 'that's the name of a jeweller's in Thistle Street.'

'What do you know about jeweller's?' asked Tommy. 'You need to settle down and get yourself a wife, not spend your money on fripperies.'

'That's no fun,' said Arthur, smoothing back his shiny hair.

'Do you know the man? The jeweller?'

'No,' admitted Arthur, 'I just looked in the window, and someone I was with made a joke about the name.'

'Well, then,' said Cattanach, not wholly surprised. 'What about Stevie Tennant?'

But again, they all shook their heads.

'Are these the fellows you think my wife's scared of?' asked Robert, scowling.

'They're just names that have come up in the course of the enquiry,' said Cattanach. 'It's possible Mrs. Campbell had never even heard of them.' Well, of one of them, anyway, he said to himself, to qualify the lie.

'Well, I've no heard of them, anyway,' said Robert. 'No even your jeweller friend,' he added sourly to Arthur. Arthur grinned at him, unabashed.

'Just one last thing for now, then,' said Cattanach, 'and I'll let you get on. Did Mrs. Campbell ever mention a brother? Or a married sister?'

Robert frowned.

'You asked that afore,' he said. 'I hadna heard tell of any then, and I havena heard of them since.'

'Did she say anything to either of you?' Cattanach opened the question to Tommy and Arthur, but they both shook their heads.

'She never said anything about her family,' said Tommy. 'Not to me.'

'No,' said Arthur.

'Well, I'm sorry to have disturbed you. Thank you for the tea.'

'Aye, you're welcome,' said Tommy.

'Just get on and find her,' said Robert. Neither of them stood, but Arthur got to his feet.

'I'll see you out,' he said.

It was not far to the front door, and he took a few steps down the path with Cattanach before saying suddenly,

'See, she was a great one for the men, was Mabel.'

'Was she?' asked Cattanach.

'Oh, aye.' He shifted a bit, not looking at Cattanach at all. 'She tried to be pally with me once or twice. Nothing much, ken, just … ach, you know.'

'What did you do?'

He made a face.

'Just made a joke of it, ken? What else could I do? But there was one thing – just with you asking about brothers and sisters there. We were laughing about – what had happened, or what hadn't happened, and she said something … I'm trying to think exactly what it was. But it was something along the lines of an only child marrying into a big family – she was joking about getting all the brothers muddled up, I think that was it.'

'But she said she was an only child?'

'That was what she said. Or what she sort of said. So I always had the impression of that – that she was an only child.'

'So,' said Lieutenant Moffat, supervising the painting of the windows of the new extension – unofficially. A squad of Robert Gordon's College boys in rugby jerseys and shorts were filling sandbags, already piled high up the sides of the old building. 'So, Stevie Tennant, with no previous particular record, is at once the thief of a vanload of whisky – with the van – an associate of two characters suspected of having an interest in the whereabouts of missing woman Mabel Campbell, and a murder victim.'

'A short career but a glorious one, sir.'

The Lieutenant gave him a sideways look.

'Aye.' He stopped for a moment, watching a man hanging out at a particularly awkward angle to reach the top of a frame.

'Have you any idea who might have killed him, then?'

'Not yet, sir. They're going through his – well, the stolen van, to see if there's anything useful to pick up. And Constable Gauld found a penknife at the scene – not the murder weapon, definitely, but it hadn't been there very long.' He fished the sketch out of his pocket and showed the Lieutenant.

'Mother-of-pearl, eh? Nice wee thing. A woman's knife?'

'Could be either, sir. It's a bit big for the kind of thing sold for a woman. The hallmark is Edinburgh 1840.'

'A family piece?'

'Or bought from an antique dealer, perhaps. Or stolen, of course.'

'Of course. Aye,' Moffat sighed, 'that's the kind of people we're likely to be dealing with, I suppose.'

'I think so, sir.'

'No idea who these fellows are, the short smart-looking one and the big fellow?'

'No. I'd almost have said that Jock McKinstry could fit the role of the smart-looking one, but he's been in one of our cells for slightly too long, and he's not quite that charming.'

'The housewife, aye. If she didn't fall for your blandishments but she favoured him, he must be a charmer.'

Cattanach was not quite sure what to make of that, and said nothing.

'Well, get Leggatt to check Stevie Tennant's known associates. Any information on new people in town – people of interest – that would be useful, too.'

'He's already working on it, sir.'

'He's bored, that's the trouble. Keep him working, Cattanach. How's Gauld doing?'

'Very well, sir, very intelligent.'

'Aye, I thought he would grow into it.'

'There's one more thing, sir,' said Cattanach, sensing the Lieutenant was about to dismiss him. 'Maybe you remember that young Billy Campbell had a kind of nature diary?' And he told Moffat about his discovery down at the mouth of the Don.

'More petrol hoarding, eh?' Moffat made a face. 'New rules

make new crimes make new criminals. Aye, well, they want us to crack down on this kind of thing. I'll see what I can do about setting some sort of a watch on the place. But I can see the time coming we'll not have the men for this. It's going to get bad, Cattanach, It's going to get bad.'

34

CATTANACH TURNED UP at the laird's club in Albyn Place ten minutes before the appointed time, and was greeted at the door by the doorman.

'I'm here to meet Gordon of Glenfindie,' he said.

'Of course, sir: Mr. Gordon said he was expecting you. If you'd just like to take a seat in the library I'll let him know you're here.'

'He's probably in the library already,' said Cattanach with a smile, and without needing direction he went into the room to the left of the entrance hall. And there was the laird, angular in a comfortable chair, engrossed in some leather-backed tome he would almost certainly have memorised, effortlessly, and quote from in a month's time.

'Sir,' he said softly, mindful of the other library occupiers. 'Sir?' No reaction. 'Grandfather?'

The laird looked up, and set the book down at once.

'Alec, dear boy.' He stood, and they shook hands warmly. 'How are you? Hungry?'

'Always.'

'Then let's go in to dinner straightaway. I find these wretched Council meetings make me quite starving.'

They talked generally over the soup about the prospects of war, and Cattanach automatically checked over the other diners and the waiters, estimating, too, how much of what they said might be overheard. Not much, he thought: the tables were well-spaced. He was pleased, for he sometimes found his grandfather a useful confidant.

'How has the City Council dragged you in, sir?' asked Cattanach.

'Just for advice, I think – or perhaps to keep some of the excitable businessmen in check. A title would work better, but even a laird still has a certain amount of clout.'

'What about the shire? Doesn't that council need you?'

'Oh, yes: it's meetings nearly every second day.' The laird sighed heavily as the waiter removed the empty soup plates. 'Whether you sign up or not, the war is full time work, I'm afraid. Are you going to?' he asked, almost casually.

'Sign up?' A cold finger of dread touched his stomach. 'Well … not immediately. There's so much to be done at home.'

'At least you know you're doing something useful.' The laird seemed satisfied for now. 'Like this case you're working on just now – that hallmark. Did it help?'

'I think it's indicative, anyway.' Cattanach had expected him to ask, and had brought his drawing. 'Here, this is what it was on.'

The laird squinted at the drawing in the soft light of the dining room, much as Lieutenant Moffat had out by the building works.

'Very charming,' he said. 'Yes, 1840 fits very well, I'd say. Stolen?'

'We don't know yet. Found, near to a body, stuck in a gorse bush.'

'The murder weapon?' The laird looked disappointed that anyone would use something like that for so sordid a task.

'No, too small. It's very clean and well kept, even though it might have been there as long as a week.'

'So it should be,' said the laird. 'The thought of leaving that outside for a week – dear me.'

'And now we're testing it for fingerprints.'

'Oh, dear.'

A police officer was not quite what the laird had expected of his only grandson: to be presented with delightful antiques associated with distasteful crimes was just another layer of unpleasantness. But the laird was a realist.

'Have you found the missing woman yet?'

'Not yet. I think she's in hiding.'

'From someone with a taste for antique penknives?'

'There's a chance of it, yes.'

'And did he also kill the – well, the body?'

'I'm not sure yet. But definitely not with the pretty penknife.'

They exchanged a grin. The fish arrived, so fresh it might have swum to their table unaided. The laird tucked in with undisguised enthusiasm.

'My favourite course,' he said. He was not, as far as Cattanach had ever seen, an excessive eater, but he had always enjoyed his fish.

The fish plates and cutlery had just been removed, too, when someone near them spoke.

'Mr. Gordon! Good evening to you.'

'Ah, Dr. Mackay! Good to see you.'

Cattanach turned, and saw that Mrs. Mackay was with her husband. They must just be arriving for dinner: she was swathed in some kind of thick, shiny material in a kind of muted pink that was not quite her colour any more, though it would have looked perfect on her daughter. He and the laird rose to their feet, dropping their napkins on the table.

'Mrs. Mackay, you are looking extraordinarily well this evening!' said the laird. 'May I introduce my grandson, Alec Cattanach?'

'We've met,' said Dr. Mackay, though his eyebrows were dancing in surprise. Mrs. Mackay, recovering fairly quickly, extended a gloved hand to be shaken.

'Mr. Cattanach! There, I knew you were teasing us!'

'Teasing you, madam?'

'When you said your uncle was a policeman! How silly!'

'But he was a policeman, Mrs. Mackay. If it helps I can give you his number.'

There was a tiny silence. Then the laird smiled.

'I'm afraid we're already past the fish, or I should ask you to join us. I had no idea you knew Alec, Mackay. Through work, I suppose?'

Mrs. Mackay opened her mouth to speak, but Dr. Mackay returned the laird's smile and nodded.

'That's right. I've been standing in this week on the old Casualty Surgeon role. Makes a change, you know?'

'We're very grateful, sir,' said Cattanach. 'It can't be much fun to be summoned in the middle of the night to stand in a gorse patch.'

'How wonderful to be so useful!' said the laird. 'I quite envy you both, really doing good, you know? And Mrs. Mackay, speaking of doing good, how is life at the W.V.S.? You must be tremendously busy just now.'

'Busy? Yes, yes, we are. You can have no idea the work that is coming our way! If you know of any ladies with time on their hands please, do say they would be made very welcome. Any ladies at all,' she added pointedly. Cattanach had a notion she was making a careful probe for information. How on earth, she was clearly thinking, could Gordon of Glenfindie have a grandson like that?

'Alas, I am on my own – and rather far out of the town for the servants to be of any use in their spare time, though no doubt there will be local opportunities for them, too. But if I come across any friend whose wife or daughter might be interested, I shall be sure to pass on your invitation, Mrs. Mackay.'

'That's more than good of you, Mr. Gordon. More than good of you.' She nodded, glanced at Cattanach again, and added, 'I always feel it pays to have the right sort working for us. They have more sense of – well, of what has to be done.'

'I must bow to your expertise, Mrs. Mackay,' said the laird. 'But I'm sure you could find a good use for anyone who was willing to help.'

'Oh, of course, of course! We should not wish to turn anyone away. Not when there's a war on.'

'Now you must excuse us, please, Mr. Gordon,' said Dr. Mackay, taking his wife's elbow. 'I'm still on call, and would like to have eaten before anyone tries to contact me. You'll know the feeling, no doubt, Mr. Cattanach.'

'The disadvantage of being useful, no doubt, sir,' said Cattanach.

'Indeed. We'll not keep you back from your dinner!'

The Mackays made their way, led by a patient waiter, to their table. Their own waiter seized the opportunity and presented them with two plates of beef, in a gravy that even the cow would have been gratified by.

'So how did you meet them, Alec?' asked the laird quietly, not looking anywhere but his plate. 'I daresay Mackay does not take his wife out on call to look at dead bodies.'

'No, thank goodness. That would certainly complicate crime scenes. No, it was their daughter, Anna, who told us that Mabel Campbell was missing.'

His grandfather looked up at him.

'Isn't she from … oh, near the bridge …'

'Seaton, yes.'

'Does she work on the estate?'

'No – no, there are new houses on the beach side of King Street now. Nothing to do with the Seaton estate, just called after it.'

'I see. But how did Miss Mackay know her?'

'They were volunteering together for the blood bank.'

'I see.'

'Miss Mackay is a medical student.'

'I believe there are two sons, as well, and they are already doctors.'

'I think so. The family business.'

The laird chewed for slightly longer than necessary on a mouthful of tender beef, then asked,

'Do you think you're being assessed as husband material?'

'I'm being assessed, certainly. I don't think Mrs. Mackay approves of the police – certainly not in her home.'

'Oh, Alec, didn't you wipe your boots?'

Cattanach laughed.

'Three times – and again on the way out.'

'What's the daughter like, then? Is she worth the risk?'

His grandfather had never spoken to him about women when his grandmother was alive. But then, his grandfather had not said much about anything when his grandmother was alive.

'She's intelligent, and decisive, and observant. I suspect she'll make a good doctor.'

'Hm,' said the laird. 'Pretty?'

'Handsome, yes,' said Cattanach, after a moment. 'Used to telling people what to do.'

'Including you?'

'She does seem to think I have just the one enquiry to work

on, yes.'

'So you have no intention of troubling Mrs. Mackay with any kind of social invitation to her daughter?'

'Anna Mackay is work, not social.'

'Perhaps you're right. Dr. Mackay is a good man, though.'

'And Mrs. Mackay?'

'Mrs. Mackay works very hard, I believe.' Even now, the laird had difficulty in saying anything against a woman. But he caught Cattanach's eye, and made a face. Indeed, what more could one say?

They had talked of other things after that, including the statutory discussion of whether or not the laird would call his driver out to take Cattanach home, or whether Cattanach would walk. As usual, Cattanach won, mostly because the laird understood him quite well – a good walk after dinner needed no excuse, and was often a perfect opportunity for turning over the problems of the day - in this case, Cattanach planned to spend the half hour or so contemplating the puzzle of Stevie Tennant. After all that, though, it was simply irritating that his thoughts should instead be full of Anna Mackay.

He walked up the leafy brae of Craigie Loanings to Rosemount, wondering where she had been this evening, since she was not out with her parents: perhaps she was dining with friends, or with a particular friend. Or she might just be working late: the older medical students sometimes did, he believed. Did she think he, too, worked long into the night, walking the town, searching for Mabel Campbell? It did come to that sometimes, but he could not see how it would help here. He needed to have a better idea of where Mabel might have gone – he should concentrate on that, not be thinking about Anna Mackay.

He wondered if she were continuing with the blood bank volunteering, perhaps with a different colleague. He crossed Rosemount and set off downhill again, with the pink granite terrace of Argyll Place on his left – lightless, all nicely blacked out – and soon the shrubby darkness of Victoria Park on his left. He could smell the damp earth behind the railings, hear the midnight rustlings of whatever called the park its home – cats, perhaps, after a late evening snack.

Who had mentioned the blood bank volunteering recently?

Someone in Seaton Place … Gladys Hawthorne, that was who. The smart-looking man who had charmed information from her – she had told him about Mabel Campbell and the posh girl she had volunteered with.

She had told him about Anna Mackay.

For a moment his heart caught in his throat. And just then, ahead of him, he heard a heavy grunt and a short cry of alarm. A woman's cry.

35

HE WAS RUNNING before he realised it, towards whatever was ahead. His feet in their leather-soled evening shoes slithered on the smooth granite pavement. And now he could hear sounds of a struggle, a woman's voice.

'Get off me! Help! Help!'

And then he was on them.

A great lump of a man, shadow on shadow, had a woman in a tight embrace from behind. Cattanach hurled himself at the pair.

'Police! Let her go!'

But the man paid no attention. Cattanach hauled on his left arm, struggling to pull it from around the woman, then kicked at the man's ankles, trying to hit his Achilles tendons. The man was wearing tough boots. Cattanach aimed higher, and struck the back of the man's knee, hard. The man went down, staggering, trying to use the woman for support. She, breathless, gave a little cry of triumph, and the man fell, swearing extravagantly.

'She bit me, the witch!'

Cattanach dropped to his knees and took his chance to try to turn the man over, to secure his arms, but he was twice Cattanach's width if not his height, and shoved back hard, knocking Cattanach over. The man scrambled to his feet and sprang, one-handed, over the park fence, disappearing at once into the leafy darkness.

'Damn,' said Cattanach. 'Forgive me. Are you all right, madam? Did he hurt you?'

'I'm a bit squashed,' said the woman crossly, 'but otherwise unharmed. Wait.' She seemed to be casting around on the ground for a moment, as Cattanach got to his feet, then gave a little satisfied noise.

'There we are! Now, then.'

A torch came on, one of the new ones being sold as blackout torches. It was nearly useless, but she turned it on Cattanach's face.

'I knew it!' she said. 'Inspector.'

'Miss Mackay!' He had that moment of readjustment when someone you've been thinking about suddenly appears, and bit his tongue to remind himself to watch what he said. 'What on earth are you doing here at this time of night?'

'I've been working late at the hospital,' she said. 'We had a case I wanted to see to – well, to the end, sadly. I usually feel safe enough walking home, even on my own.'

'Perhaps you were wrong,' he said. 'Here, let me walk you the rest of the way now.'

She had started to shake, he could hear it in her voice. She needed warmth, and a hot drink. All he could offer her here was his arm, but she declined it.

'But I'll accept the offer of company, all the same,' she said. They turned to go back up the hill Cattanach had just run down. Her parents' house was not that far from the laird's club.

'What happened?' he asked.

'He just sprang out of the bushes – there's a gap in the fence just near there. In full view of that terrace of houses, too.'

'They all have their blackout blinds down,' said Cattanach with a smile. 'Seeing no evil. Did he try to rob you? Or worse?'

'Do you know,' she said, 'I don't think it was either?'

'What do you mean?'

'He grabbed me from behind – as you probably saw. It was like being grabbed by a grizzly bear, I imagine, and he put his hand over my mouth. Then he said, "Need to ask you something. Don't scream." But I could already hear footsteps – your footsteps – so I sort of nodded. Then he said in my ear – ugh, I can still feel his breath – he said, "Where is she?" Then you shouted "Police!" and he didn't say anything more. Apart from swearing, of course.'

'You're positive that's what he said?'

'It wasn't a detailed conversation. I can remember it.' They walked on for a pace or two, nearing the crossroads at Rosemount again. His mind was busy. 'Did he mean Mabel Campbell, do you think?' she asked.

He half-turned to look at her, but it was too dark to read her expression clearly.

'Yes, I should think so,' he said. He wondered whether or not to go on, then decided she was better off informed than not. 'A couple of men have been going about near where she lives, looking for her.'

'Looking for her? Then they don't have her?'

'I'm inclined to think she's in hiding. She may be with friends, she may not, but whoever she was running from – for whatever reason – has not found her yet.'

'And how did they know about me?' Her tone was slightly accusing.

'One of the neighbours mentioned Mrs. Campbell had been volunteering for the blood bank. With a posh girl,' he added, smiling.

'And of course I'm the only posh girl in the town,' she responded, not as amused as he was.

'Well, they found you.'

'Are you sure this is one of those men?'

'I'm not sure how many men there might be trying to find Mabel Campbell,' he said mildly, 'but one was described as a large, yellow-haired man. With your attacker I think we can agree he matches the first part of that description, anyway. What was his voice like? You heard more of it than I did.'

And he wanted to see if they had both had the same impression of him. She was quick to give her opinion.

'A little high-pitched, for a big man,' she said. 'Scottish, but not local, I thought.'

'I agree,' he said.

'Not Edinburgh or Glasgow or Highland, either,' she added.

'Well, that narrows it down, I daresay.'

'Perhaps you shouldn't have let him get away,' said Miss Mackay, waspish at last. He wondered when it might come to that. 'I thought the police were trained to fight people. Or, you know, get them under control. Arrest them.'

'We are. It doesn't always work.'

'Clearly. Didn't you have a whistle?'

'I was out to dinner – it didn't occur to me to take it. Sorry about that.'

And back down Craigie Loanings, its old stone walls and leafy overhang almost romantic, in the right company. He should have taken the laird's offer of a lift. And then what would have happened to Anna? What lengths would the big man have gone to to find out that she really did not know where Mabel was?

He wondered if Dr. and Mrs. Mackay would be home from the club yet. Probably, as the doctor was on call: hadn't he said they were in a hurry? He had no wish to be interrogated once again by Mrs. Mackay, but at least he could hand Anna over to their safekeeping.

'Was I right about the jeweller?' she asked, after a longish silence. He hesitated.

'Yes, you were. But he has no idea where she is.'

'So she really was seeing another man when her husband was at sea?'

'It seems so,' he said. There was no need to go into Mabel's fabrications. Anna seemed quite shocked. Half Cattanach's mind was on what had happened, trying to gather what information he could. The other half was divided between listening to make sure the big man was not following them, and wondering what would happen when they reached Anna's house. Would he go in if invited by her parents? Would he make his excuses and flee? That would not, perhaps, look very professional.

'Where did you dine?' she asked.

'Sorry?'

'You said you were out to dinner. Somewhere nice?'

'Your father's club, as it turned out.'

Even though she had not taken his arm, he felt her jolt of surprise.

'My father's club?'

'I was dining there with a friend, and met Dr. and Mrs. Mackay.'

She took a few more paces.

'Quite a coincidence,' she said.

'That's what I thought. But then, why not, I suppose? It's a small town, in its way.'

More thoughtful paces.

'Are you a member?'

'A policeman? No, no.'

'Well, here we are,' she said, as two granite pillars loomed out of the darkness, and she sounded heartily relieved. He could sympathise. 'I'm home.'

'If you don't mind, I'll just see you to the door,' he said. 'I assume Dr. and Mrs. Mackay are home, too. You'll need to take more care, just for now,' he went on. 'Get a friend to drive you home, or at least walk with you. Don't be on your own, especially after dark.'

'Until when?'

'Until we catch them.'

'That could take a while. You haven't found Mabel yet.'

They walked, with him two paces behind, up the gravel driveway to the door. She brought out a key, and opened it.

'Will you be all right?' he asked at the last minute.

She looked round at him. A blackout curtain inside the doorway dutifully blocked any light from the hall.

'I'll be fine.'

'Please contact the station if you think of anything …'

'Of course. Good night, Inspector.'

'Good night, Miss Mackay.'

He sat at his desk the following morning – Wednesday, he noted, on his revolving calendar – and tried to write a report on the previous night. He had written the best part of a penny shocker on this case already: he did not feel that it needed another episode. He wanted to reach the point where he could write – 'And then Mabel Campbell walked into the police station and told us she had taken the train to Brighton for the week, and said she'd sent us a postcard, and hadn't we got it yet?'.

At least he had the office to himself. Early that morning Inspector Cochrane had taken it upon himself to make comparative measurements of some of the sandbags stacked against the station walls, and had found that the lengths varied by up to two inches. Cattanach had no idea how that might make a difference in the event of a nearby bombing, but if it kept Inspector Cochrane busy and out of his way, he was all for full scrutiny.

Two weeks and a day since the lorry crashes. A week and a

half since Mabel Campbell had disappeared. Was Anna Mackay right? Were they getting nowhere?

He had had a word with the beat constables around Albyn Place and Victoria Park, explaining what had happened and asking them to keep an eye open. In a moment or two he would go over to Victoria Park himself, and see if the big man had perhaps left any trace of himself behind. He did not hold out much hope. How long had the man been waiting there, though, ready to pounce on her? Or had he followed her from the hospital, slipped into the park by the corner gate and walked along almost beside her until he reached the hole in the fence – perhaps he had intended to drag her into the park, away even from the blacked-out eyes of the local residents, for some more intensive questioning? It didn't bear thinking about.

What else? He made a list in his head. Stevie Tennant's murder, first of all: he needed to follow up the matter of the penknife, see if there had been anything on it. Then he needed to ask a few of the city antique traders if they had ever sold such a thing. He needed to find out if the soldiers up at the Battery had seen or heard anything odd, though he thought they were not yet there at night. Maybe they had disturbed some last resident up there, though, who might have seen something. He needed to find out.

Mabel Campbell's disappearance. She had come from the south – it made her sound like something exotic from the South Seas – and had no wish to go back south, not even so far as Stonehaven, fifteen miles down the road, for a day out. If she were fleeing, had she gone north? He needed to press his County colleagues in Peterhead, Ellon, Fraserburgh, see if they had anything to report. And he needed to make sure that Anna Mackay was safe. If she were the only clue the big man and the smart man had to Mabel's whereabouts, even if in truth she knew nothing, then they would try again to interrogate her.

The lorry driver and his empty lorry, the one that had crashed into the tram. He needed to prod Dundee City, see if they had found out anything about the owner of the lorry. He needed to check with the hospital, and make sure Sandison was still too badly injured to move, or to escape.

And then there was the hut at the Don mouth, and the barrels of, he was sure, hoarded petrol. What was he going to do about that?

36

VICTORIA PARK LOOKED a good deal more tame in the daylight. It was not a large park, though combined with Westburn Park across the road it gave a touch of greenery accessible to those in the more industrial and commercial areas around George Street and Rosemount, a border of trees and shrubs to block the noise of traffic, sedately broad paths curling up the gentle slope, a glasshouse in one corner, a grand granite fountain as a focus. The park keeper lived in a tiny cottage on the other side of the park from where Anna Mackay had been attacked. Not unreasonably, he said he had seen and heard nothing last night.

'Dinna ken what I'm supposed to do in the blackout, any road,' he said huffily. 'You'd no find an egg in a saucepan with one of they wee torches.'

'You don't usually get much trouble here, though, do you?'

'Aye, but that's when I can get out and look. In the blackout, there could be a'body in those bushes. The Germans could invade and be hiding in there.'

Cattanach took a moment to try to picture this.

'And this morning?' he tried.

'Well, there's nobody there now, a' course. Why would there be?'

Cattanach wondered where the Germans would go in the daylight.

'But did you notice anything unusual? Broken branches, rubbish dropped, anything like that?'

'There was big footprints in one of the beds by the fountain, right enough,' said the man, considering. 'They werena there last night.'

'May I take a look?'

'Oh, aye. I'll show you where I mean.' He shouldered his long-handled brush like a musket, and pointed where they were supposed to go.

One of the flower beds by the fountain had had a display of pelargoniums, rather faded now as autumn came on. And indeed, the arrangement was not helped, either, by a line of heavy bootprints from one end of the bed to the other, in a line, Cattanach reckoned, from where the man had run from them at the hole in the fence, to the other side of the park, not far from the keeper's cottage. But by then, likely, the big man would have slowed down and begun to move more quietly, looking for a way out, or finding somewhere to hide himself until Cattanach and Miss Mackay had gone and he could use the hole again to leave. But here, across the flowerbed, it seemed the man had still been running.

'Have you anything I could cover these with, until our men come out and take some details?' he asked.

'I could get you a bit of sacking.'

'That would be perfect,' said Cattanach. There was no imminent sign of rain. He waited while the keeper went to fetch the sacking. The prints were definitely heavy, and long, too: he placed his own long foot delicately beside one and found it a good inch longer, and wider, too. There seemed to be nothing extraordinary about the pattern on the sole: these were good practical sturdy boots, ideal, like policeman's boots, for much standing about and a bit of walking. Only the size of them was out of the ordinary.

He saw to the spreading of the sacking over the bed, then asked if the keeper would guard them while he himself went to use the police telephone box across the road from the bottom park gate.

He did not have long to wait until the experts arrived, and when he had talked over the prints with them, he left them to their own operations. Inspector Cochrane always claimed that such investigators worked much better if he stayed to supervise them: Cattanach found the opposite was true for him.

On his way back through the town, he called at as many jewellery shops and antique traders as he could think of, to show them the drawing of the penknife.

'It's a nice wee thing,' was the usual response, 'It's a pretty item, but not one I've seen. No, that wasn't bought here. No, nor here, sir. I'd be happy to have it in the shop, mind.'

'Have you looked at the hallmark?' asked Albert Lovie, whose eyes had filled with alarm at the sight of Cattanach at his counter again. He was more relaxed now, spreading the paper out on the surface with his plump white fingers, fingering it as if it were the penknife itself.

'Edinburgh 1840.'

'Nearly a century old,' Lovie murmured, apparently pleased at the thought. 'Yes, a fine little thing. I'm sorry I can't help you with it. Maybe Edinburgh is where you should be looking, in fact. Yes, Edinburgh. I'd look there. Ahm,' he went on, clearing his throat, 'is this by any chance connected with Mabel? You'd tell me if you'd found her, wouldn't you, Inspector? I've been – I've been very worried.'

'I'm afraid we still don't know where she is, Mr. Lovie. Have you thought of anything else that might lead us in the right direction?'

'I've been wracking my brains, Inspector. I cannot think of anything.'

'Did she ever say anything about anywhere outside Aberdeen? Did she express a desire to go somewhere or visit somewhere, or an aversion to anywhere?'

'I still think she had come from south of here, Inspector,' said Lovie. 'But she certainly didn't mention going back south. I mean, I think at some point I suggested a day out in the car, you know? But then days out were much more difficult for her than evenings, with Billy to look after and her husband … well, wherever her husband was.' The words clearly still hurt him. Cattanach wondered if he had actually brought himself to believe yet that Mabel had lied to him so comprehensively. Lovie folded his drawing of the penknife lovingly flat again, and passed it to him. 'If I think of anything else, I promise you, Inspector, you will be the first to know.'

'Thank you, Mr. Lovie.' Cattanach returned the drawing to his pocket, and took up his hat. Days out in the car … a pleasant thought. 'Have you thought any more about your motor? Are you going to keep it on the road?'

'For now, yes, I think so. I'll see how things go. I don't have anyone to take about now,' he said sadly, 'but it's sometimes useful for the business. And of course, rationing doesn't start until Saturday, does it?'

'I met a petrol hoarder recently,' said Cattanach. 'It's against the law, of course, but it must be tempting.'

'I should imagine so! But there, life is full of temptations, isn't it?' He gave a smile that was almost friendly, though his eyes were still sorrowful. Cattanach bade him goodbye, and left him to his worries.

Back at the station, his office was still mercifully free of Inspector Cochrane. He took the opportunity to put a call through to the Dundee City Police, and found that the inspector he had spoken to previously was also at his desk, about, apparently, to telephone him.

'Aye, we've had a bit of fun with our Mr. Kitchener,' he admitted. 'No sign of him at his house or at the yard, and the other lorry – he has the two, or he had before your tram got in the way – the other lorry was away. So we thought we might make up a wee reception committee for him, see, to welcome him back from his journey. And today he appeared, and do you know what?'

'What?' The Dundee man was clearly enjoying his story, and Cattanach had no wish to put him off.

'He must have kenned we were coming, for he'd got the whisky in for us. Was that not good of him?'

'More than generous, I'd have said. The good stuff?'

'Oh, aye, awful fine. We were so impressed we took the lot, and himself and the lorry and all, and offered him our own brand of hospitality.'

'Did you find out where it was from?'

'Aye, and we've been in touch with the lads up in Highland to have a few words up there. Seems your fellow was heading that way, and when he had his wee incident with the tram his boss decided to go and collect the stuff himself. So if you don't mind, we could come and collect your Mr. Sandison just any time it's convenient for you.'

'He's still in the hospital, of course. I'll have a word with the ward sister, get her to give you a call, perhaps.'

'Aye, aye. We'd like to match the set. Unless you want him for dangerous driving?'

'If you get him for the whisky, he's not going to be driving anywhere for a while. Take him and welcome, as far as I'm concerned – you seem to be throwing quite a party down there.'

The Dundee man snorted, thanked Cattanach, and promised to keep in touch.

The next call was to the ward sister.

'I hope you still have Mr. Sandison there, Sister?' he asked.

'We do indeed, Inspector. Despite what you might think, we're not in the habit of letting our patients see themselves out!'

'Not at all, no. Well, the Dundee City police are very interested in Mr. Sandison, and very keen to come and collect him. Would you have any objections? Would he be fit to travel?'

'I'll carry him to the car myself,' she said. 'And if you could find anywhere further away than Dundee, that would be better still. When do they want him?'

'I think they're just organising transport. He's not able to abscond, is he?'

'People do some remarkable things, but I don't think so, Inspector. And I won't say anything to him about this, if you like – that'll mean he'll have less incentive to hurry off.'

'Excellent. Can I give you the Dundee inspector's telephone number? Then you can talk to him yourself and come to some mutual arrangement, if you like.'

'That would be perfect. I have a notebook and pencil just here, when you're ready.'

Cattanach gave her the name and number, and she repeated it back to him, as careful as with a dose of medicine. Then she asked,

'I don't suppose you've heard anything of the patient that did escape our clutches? The man with the dark hair.'

'Nothing at all.'

'I worry about him, you see. He really wasn't fit to go off like that, I'm sure. What if some accident happened to him?'

'I suppose no news, on that count, is good news, Sister. No bodies found, no one calling to say they've seen him wandering in confusion.'

'As long as he hasn't gone into the harbour, or something like that. Aye, well … I just worry.'

'If we find out anything, one way or the other, we'll be sure to let you know.'

'Speaking of worrying,' she added, as he began to think of ending the call, 'did you hear one of our young medical students was attacked last night by Victoria Park? One of the lassies.'

He stopped.

'I did, actually, yes. What's she saying?'

'She's not saying much, but she asked a couple of people to chum her after work today and word got around when she explained. What's the place coming to, Inspector? Criminals driving lorries into trams and good respectable drivers near destroyed, and now girls being attacked in the street? Is it the war, do you think?'

He could not tell her about either case, beyond what she already knew.

'You know what it's like, Sister, especially working where you are. Sometimes bad things happen in bunches, don't they? Unconnected. Maybe we just notice the second because we're already thinking about the first, and so it seems worse.'

'I suppose.' She was too sensible to allow herself to dwell on it for too long, anyway.

'Any problems with Mr. Sandison or the Dundee City people, let me know.'

'Aye, I'll do that.'

He ended the call, and sat for a moment staring down at his desk. At least Anna Mackay seemed to be taking care, taking it seriously. Should he do more?

And what would happen if and when the man found that Anna knew nothing? Where would he and his smartly-dressed charming friend go then?

37

'A WORD, INSPECTOR Cattanach?'

He refocused rapidly as Lieutenant Moffat stuck his head around the door. He stood at once.

'Sir. Do you want me to go to your office?'

'Where's Inspector Cochrane?' The Lieutenant looked around, as if concerned that Inspector Cochrane might be hiding behind his desk.

'I believe he's supervising the sandbag construction,' said Cattanach. 'I've been out a good deal of the morning, so I'm not sure.'

'Has he been gluing memoranda into that ledger?' the Lieutenant asked, edging around the door. Cattanach hesitated. Was he about to get Inspector Cochrane into trouble, wasting so much time on something a clerk could do? But he had the impression that Inspector Cochrane had been obeying orders over the ledger. When in doubt, try the truth …

'Yes, sir.'

'Good, good.' Moffat advanced entirely into the room, and propped himself firmly against Inspector Cochrane's tidy desk. 'Sit down, Cattanach.'

'Thank you, sir.'

'Any progress? I heard something happened last night, though I haven't seen anything official yet.'

'No, sir, I went to the site – edge of Victoria Park, by Argyll Terrace – this morning to see if there was any other evidence to add before I sent it up.' He gave a quick account of the attack on Anna Mackay. 'There are footprints across a flowerbed I'm having recorded, but nothing else of much interest. The park keeper heard nothing, but his cottage is on the other side of the park.'

'You just happened to be passing?'

'I wasn't even passing: it happened down ahead of me, by chance. I was walking home from the west end.'

'And this is Dr. Mackay's daughter this happened to?'

'That's right, sir. She was coming back from working late at the hospital. You know she's a medical student.'

'Aye, of course. A very medical family.' He gave Cattanach an odd look. 'He's a useful man to have on our side, Cattanach. I hope this isn't going to cause any problems.'

Cattanach frowned.

'I made sure Miss Mackay reached home safely, advised her on taking other steps with regard to her personal safety – which I gather she is doing – and asked the local constable to keep a particular eye on the house.'

It was Moffat's turn to frown.

'Well, all right, but that maybe seems a wee bit excessive. Is there more to this than I thought?'

'Oh, sorry, sir, I mustn't have made it clear. When the man seized her, he asked her to tell him where "she" is – we both thought he must have meant Mabel Campbell.'

'Mabel Campbell? It's connected with that?' Moffat was taken aback.

'I broke into the altercation before Miss Mackay could make it clear that she had no idea where Mabel Campbell was. And the attacker fitted the admittedly vague description we have been given of the larger man looking for Mrs. Campbell around Seaton.'

'Did he indeed? Aye, that puts a different perspective on it, right enough. I suppose,' he said tentatively, 'I suppose Miss Mackay really does have no idea where Mrs. Campbell is?'

The idea had indeed touched the edges of Cattanach's mind, but he shook his head.

'I'm sure she doesn't. She has just the right level of impatience with our continued lack of success in finding her. It would be hard to fake. If I can be allowed to suggest even the possibility that Dr. Mackay's daughter would do such a thing.'

The Lieutenant nodded, with half a smile at the thought.

'From all you've said, it would be odd if Mrs. Campbell suddenly decided to confide in someone who was only an acquaintance.'

'And a woman at that, sir. I think it's a sign that the two men trying to find Mrs. Campbell are growing desperate. If they find out that Miss Mackay knows nothing, where will they turn next?'

'Do we know anything else about Mabel Campbell that might help us find her first? Anything at all?'

Cattanach sighed.

'Not really, sir, no. There's speculation that if she has left the city at all – which has generally been against her inclination, even to go to Stonehaven or Banchory – she would go north rather than south, but that's more a reported aversion to going south rather than any particular link to the north.'

'No known friends in that direction?'

'No known anything,' said Cattanach, shrugging. 'She might not even be Mabel Campbell. She told Robert Campbell that was her name, but who knows?'

'Maybe better give our friends further north a prod. In case the first enquiry has been lost in the post.'

'I will do, sir.'

'Now, Stevie Tennant – any progress?'

'Lots of people like the penknife. But it's not the murder weapon, and it might not even be connected. I showed it to Albert Lovie, Mrs. Campbell's man friend, and he suggested a connexion with Edinburgh. It's where it was hallmarked, but I think he felt something of that quality must belong to the capital.'

'Hm,' said the Lieutenant, offended. He was a proud Aberdonian. 'Anyway, his father couldn't tell you who he was working with?'

'No, he had no idea. He doesn't get out much, and I think Stevie could have told him anything he liked and Mr. Tennant might not have known the difference.'

'You still think he might have been the third man at Seaton?'

'The third man matches the description – particularly the moustache – and he hasn't been seen since around the time Stevie must have been killed. Around the Friday that Billy Campbell was buried.'

'That's the day Mabel Campbell disappeared?'

'That's right, sir.'

'Do you think there's a chance she killed him?'

Cattanach thought about it.

'Maybe it was Stevie she saw at the funeral. He represented some kind of threat to her – she looked frightened. She waited until after the funeral, packed her things, and went after him. How did she know where to find him?'

'He could have left her a message.'

'No one has mentioned such a thing, either verbal or written.'

'Maybe they had an old arrangement – maybe they'd met at Torry Battery in the past. Didn't Constable Gauld say it was used by courting couples? That it was a courting couple who found Stevie?'

'That's right, sir - maybe not the kind of courting place that would have appealed to Mabel Campbell. She seems to appreciate the finer things in life.'

'These days, yes,' said Moffat wisely, 'but who knows what she might have done in her youth?'

'Maybe, sir, but in her youth Stevie Tennant would have been a child. He was a good ten years younger than her.'

'And what about four or five years ago, before she came to Aberdeen but after Billy was born? What would she have been – late twenties? And Stevie would have been seventeen or eighteen?'

'Even by then she was, if I have the pattern right, picking up men in tea shops, not on gorsy hillsides, sir.'

'All right, then, so that was not the nature of their association. But he dies and she disappears – that often means guilt, wouldn't you say?'

'I would, yes, sir. But we have no proof, and we still don't have her. And where did she learn to stab a man horizontally, between the ribs?'

'Well … clearly we don't know the company she's been keeping.'

'True.' Cattanach rubbed his face and groaned. 'Any ideas gratefully received, sir.'

The Lieutenant made a face.

'Just have to hope something turns up,' he said. 'And make sure that nothing happens to Miss Mackay. Now, something we could do something about – what about that stash of petrol by the Don mouth?'

'It seems a small thing beside the others, sir.'

'Aye, I know, but it's something we need to nip in the bud. It's all very well one fellow, like that fool of an antique dealer in Loch Street, trying to hide petrol in the back green. But if we ignore it, then we'll have racketeers on the case in no time. Things will get out of hand, and we'll be like something in a gangster film.'

Cattanach blinked: he had not thought of Lieutenant Moffat as an enthusiast for the talkies.

'What do you want to do, then, sir?'

'I want to set up a watch at the place. You said there's plenty of cover?'

'A fair bit, yes, sir, though it's not obvious what direction anyone might take to get there. There might be a danger of the criminal tripping over one of our men before we can link them with the hut.'

'I think we'll have to take the chance.'

'And we could be there for hours. Days, even. There's no knowing when the criminal might come back to the hut.'

'I think we have a good chance he'll be back soon. When does petrol rationing start?'

'Saturday now, sir, unless they postpone it again.'

'You've applied for your ration book, I hope?'

'I have, sir.'

'Good. Saturday … How many barrels would you say were in the hut?'

'Three, I think, sir. Quite large.'

'Room for any more?'

'I think they could fit in two more, if they were lucky. The walls are – well, flexible, sir.'

'It's a risk to public safety,' said Moffat, 'if nothing else. I think there'll be activity there before Saturday, don't you? He'll be buying up before the restrictions start, and topping up his supply as much as he can.'

'That makes sense.'

'Any other reason why a man might be wandering about there in the daylight? Carrying, presumably, some kind of petrol can?'

Cattanach thought, picturing the site.

'He might have a boat with an engine down by the water, sir.'

'So he might. He might even be a fisherman, I suppose. But if he's constantly pottering down to a non-existent boat he's going to feel a bittie conspicuous, I think. I would say we could maybe have our men in position around dusk, do you think? And watch till morning?'

'How many, sir? And will you want them in two watches?'

'You'll be one of them, of course. I daresay you know more about the wild than most of our men.' Cattanach thought he would hardly designate the area by the Don mouth as wild, but he nodded. 'Let's see – who else?'

They discussed for a while who to ask to join them: a mixture of older and younger men, ones with less family responsibility in the evenings, ones who did not mind a tussle with a reluctant captive. Enough to cover the ground, not too many so they were less likely to be noticed. In the end they had something like a rota for the next few nights.

'If we have nothing by Saturday, I'll have to think again,' said Lieutenant Moffat. 'But that's a working plan to start with.'

Inspector Cochrane still had not appeared by the time Cattanach pulled on his coat that evening, his desk cleared of paperwork for once, enjoying the sense of very temporary satisfaction such a sight brings. He literally had his hat in one hand and the other hand on the office door handle, when the telephone rang.

'Bah!' he exclaimed, and reached out for the receiver instead. 'Cattanach?'

'Sir,' said Sergeant McAulay, 'I thought you'd want to know. You sent the details of yon wee penknife out round the place, aye?'

'I did, yes. Has there been a response?'

'Aye, sir, from a Sergeant Collier in the Edinburgh City police. Let me see, now,' he paused, and Cattanach could hear the rustling of paper. He knew how organised McAulay always was – he must be spinning out his story for effect. 'Aye, here we are. Identified as from amongst a number of items stolen from a New

Town jeweller six months ago, and never recovered. So, see, while they canna tell you who might have had it recently, they'd like fine, our Edinburgh pals, to find out how it came to be up here, and where the other bits and pieces might have gone.'

38

CATTANACH TURNED UP that evening to see the first watch in place and to take another quick look at the hut – he would look a fool if it turned out that the petrol had been moved and they were watching an empty hut. The drums were still there, just visible through the crack in the wall, and in fact one of their clever technicians had gone along earlier, opened the lock, made sure it was indeed a store of petrol, and fastened the lock again. Cattanach was glad he was on the side of the police.

He went home for some hot soup, took a nap, then changed into rougher, darker clothes and good boots, and headed back out again in time to relieve the first watch.

It was past one in the morning, and about a week to full moon. He shivered, even though he was wrapped up warm, and hurried more by memory than by the feeble light of his blackout torch up to the top of his road where, in daylight, he would be able to see the sea, then down and across to King Street once again. Then it was a march all the way up to the Bridge of Don, hoping he would find his colleagues, hoping they had not all gone home without telling him, hoping they were safe.

The switchover turned out to be easy: the four men detailed to do the first watch slipped away towards the boulevard along the beach, where they could quickly pretend to have nothing to do with the mouth of the Don. Cattanach and the others stepped into their places, any sound covered by the running of the river and the more distant waves on the shore, and a soft wind from the sea in the stubby tree branches above them.

Cattanach settled down to wait, as he had done on many a hillside at this time of night. He was warmed, comfortable, and awake. He could last several hours if need be.

But as it happened, he had only to last a few minutes.

For a moment, he thought it was one of the early watch, stupidly coming back for something. Then he realised it was not any of their familiar shapes shifting quietly along the path from the road. Was this someone heading for the hut? Whoever it was, the figure was breathing heavily, panting a little, probably from the effort of carrying something. Cattanach could sense the effort, but could not quite see shapes. He watched, spine tingling, feeling as if his eyes and ears were out on stalks, as the figure slipped and wobbled towards the hut.

A large person, most likely a man. Anna Mackay's attacker? Would he be armed? Whoever he was, he was a known associate now of Stevie Tennant, and Stevie had been stabbed. He and Lieutenant Moffat had gone over this risk, but had come to no firm conclusion, only warned the men to be careful.

He was the officer stationed nearest to the hut. He needed to see if the person was actually going there. But was the man alone, or was his smart little friend with him, or watching out for him?

There was a dull double thud from up ahead. It sounded as if the man had deposited whatever he was carrying, perhaps so that he could unlock the hut, perhaps so that he could see he had not been followed. Listening all around him as best he could, drawing his whistle from his pocket, Cattanach stepped noiselessly on to the path, blood fizzing in his veins, and followed the man towards the hut.

The man had a slightly brighter torch than Cattanach's, probably thinking he would not be seen down here so far from any houses. The light was shining on the lock, steadily, though the man had not yet calmed his own breathing. Cattanach eased forward, watching. The lock sprang open with a clatter, and the man pulled it – hands gloved, Cattanach saw – away from the hasp, and swung the door out. He propped it open with a stone which he must have known already was there, kicking it in the darkness, then bent to heave whatever he had brought into the hut. He straightened, caught his breath again, and stepped inside.

'Men!' Cattanach yelled, and blew his whistle. 'To the hut!'

He dashed forward, grabbed the hut door, kicked the stone free, and shoved the door closed. No sense in taking risks until the others were with him.

Constable Gauld was first on the scene, since it was his area. The other two men were not far behind.

'He's in the hut,' said Cattanach, and indeed at that moment something in the hut clanked and fell over. The smell of petrol increased. 'Are you ready?' He flung open the door, and they all shone their torches inside.

There, jammed between two great drums, with petrol spilling from a jerrycan over his well-polished shoes, was Albert Lovie.

Lovie maintained a rigid silence all the way through his arrest, all the way through the wait for the police car which had been hidden some distance away, all the way through the journey to the police station. Occasionally he shifted his feet, and seemed almost relieved when his shoes and socks were removed in the interviewing room, but he did not speak. Yet it was not, Cattanach was sure, the silence of the hardened criminal, or even of despair. It was the silence before the storm.

He sat Lovie down at the table, and offered him a cup of tea.

'I can't say it will be a good one, but it'll take the chill off, even if you just hold the cup,' he said encouragingly. Lovie gave a quick shake of his head. 'Did you understand everything we said to you by the Don mouth?' he asked. 'You understand you're being arrested for petrol hoarding? Other charges may follow.'

Even as he said the last four words, he could almost see them hovering in the air. His whole brief acquaintance with Lovie spun past him. 'He called me Uncle Albert'. 'He said he had found out his uncle was a criminal.' Other charges may follow. He opened his mouth to speak, but at that moment the storm broke.

'I didn't touch Billy! I'd never do him any harm! I didn't touch him! I had nothing – I never even knew he was dead until you told me!'

'But you said he called you his uncle, didn't you? And he told someone, the day before he died, that he had discovered that his uncle was a criminal. What did Billy know about what you were doing in that hut?'

'Nothing! I'm sure he knew nothing!'

'Did Mrs. Campbell know?'

'I never said anything to either of them. I never told them – I didn't want them to know.' He took a few deep, gasping breaths, shuddered, then steadied himself. 'I was ashamed, if you want the truth.'

'But desperate enough to keep your big car on the road that you hoarded petrol? How long have you been hoarding? There's enough in there to keep even your motor going for what? A couple of months? More? Those barrels are big.'

'It wasn't my idea –' said Lovie quickly, then broke off.

'Whose idea was it, then?' Lovie pursed his lips but stared at the table. 'Where did you buy the petrol?'

'What?'

'Where did you buy it? You must know that garages are looking out for people just now who seem to be buying more than their fair share.'

'Oh! I bought it – I bought it in various places,' he said primly, pleased with himself. It was an obvious lie.

'Like where?'

Silence again.

'Like where, Mr. Lovie? You know we can check, make sure you've got it right.'

'I can't remember,' he said, his gaze once again fixed on the table. His shoulders were sagging.

Not his idea. Ashamed of what he was doing … Lovie was a jeweller, and the silly man in Loch Street had been an antique dealer – two not dissimilar trades. No doubt there were others across the city, people who, like him, were tempted to keep their motors running for as long as possible. But people who yielded to that temptation, and had put some aside, gradually, over the weeks. But Lovie's stash was more than a little put aside. The Loch Street man's barrel had been a fair size, too. Was there something more organised going on here? Were the racketeers already in the city? That would not please Lieutenant Moffat.

'Well, then, let's try a different angle. Who brought you the petrol?'

Lovie flashed him a look of alarm, much like the one he had turned on Cattanach in his shop that morning – the previous morning. It was well into Thursday now. Had Lovie thought then that Cattanach had found the petrol? Or was it something to do with Mabel Campbell? There were knots here it was going to take some time to undo.

Into this silence, the silence of Cattanach waiting, Lovie eventually spoke.

'They brought it to the flat, this time. After dark, of course. Sometimes they have a lorry, just a small one, covered over, but I think this time they parked the lorry somewhere and brought it in the two jerrycans. The lid didn't work properly on one of them. When you came into the shop this morning, I thought you knew.'

Cattanach looked at him, waiting again.

'His name's Tommy Wilson. He's the one in charge. He's the one who – who got me to do it.'

'What does he look like?'

'Shorter than me,' said Lovie, on a long outward breath. 'Black hair, smartly dressed.'

'And the other?'

'I don't know his real name. Wilson calls him Eck, Muckle Eck. And he is muckle – he's very big. And quite frightening, to be honest. But he's just, you know, muscle. Wilson is the brains, and he's much more terrifying than Eck.'

Cattanach's head spun. It looked as if he had names at last for the two men looking for Mabel Campbell, the two men who might know more about the death of Stevie Tennant. Tommy Wilson and Muckle Eck. Eck was usually Alexander – surname or Christian name?

'Where were they from?'

'From Dundee, I think. Somewhere that direction.'

South … had they known Mabel Campbell before, or was it this, this connexion with Albert Lovie that had caused her to run from them? He wondered if Dundee City police would appreciate a telephone call at three in the morning: he was not sure he would be able to restrain himself till it was daylight and normal working hours.

'Do you know if the petrol came from Dundee, too?'

Lovie shook his head.

'I don't think so. They've been up here for a while, now. They must be getting it somewhere locally, or they'd be using a lot of petrol bringing it here.'

Cattanach smiled: Lovie was not a stupid man. But that made it all the more surprising that he had become involved in all this. And why did he think it had anything to do with Billy Campbell?

But Billy Campbell had walked down by the Don mouth on Sunday evening before he died.

'Did it always come in jerrycans?'

'No, that was a small delivery. The barrels came first, two of them full and one just part-full, to be filled up. They met me down at the hut – Wilson came first, to see what the place was like, and then the others carried the barrels down. Just as well. I don't think I could have managed – I don't know how they did.'

'Others? You only mentioned one.'

'There were two big fellows at the beginning. I haven't seen the other one for a while. I suppose that's why they've started using jerrycans.'

'What was the other man like?'

'It was dark. He was biggish, I mean wide, but not so tall. Shorter than me. I heard them call him Stevie.'

Cattanach kept his face expressionless.

'You said then they delivered to your flat? How? Where did they park?

'No, that was only this time that they brought the jerrycans. The other times they went straight down to the Don mouth. Wilson wanted to see where the stuff was stored, make sure I was doing it properly. And that, you see, was when Billy turned up.'

39

'WHAT HAPPENED?' ASKED Cattanach, after a long pause. Lovie's head was down, his face almost invisible.

'We were at the hut, outside it, you know? It wasn't really dark, and the hut's too small for all of us to be inside, of course. Particularly that Eck and his friend. They could hardly squeeze through the door to shove the barrels in. I thought the hut might fall down.' He glanced up for a moment, as though checking to see that Cattanach had the situation clear. Cattanach nodded again.

'Well, one of the barrels wasn't quite in, to be honest, that was the problem. And Billy appeared, just up the way, and I could see him sniffing. There must have been a reek of petrol.'

'Go on.'

'He's – he was a bright lad, read all the papers, knew well all that was going on. I think he realised straightaway, or realised it was something he shouldn't be seeing, anyway. He turned and he ran.'

'And they went after him?'

'No, not then. I think that Stevie one would have, but Wilson held up a hand and he just stopped, like that.' He tapped the table sharply. 'And he said, "Not now, the lad will be running off to his ma. We'll be away before he might come back, and I'm in a hurry to get home. Find out who he is, and deal with him tomorrow." And Stevie just stood there, like a light switched off, and Billy disappeared.'

'And that was that?'

Lovie nodded miserably. His head was low, but Cattanach saw a tear fall on to his plump hand. He could sense the surprise of the constable standing guard at the door behind him, but even criminals could cry.

'I thought so. I didn't see how they could know who he was. He wasn't even in school uniform. I hadn't said anything, and they never thought to ask me if I knew the boy. And I mean, it was only petrol hoarding. What were they going to do, if anything?'

But he was squirming, and Cattanach knew there was more. Once again, he waited.

'I turned round, back to the hut, and I saw Wilson was looking after him, with a funny wee look on his face, I thought. As if he was wondering something – maybe wondering if he should have sent Stevie after him straightaway, after all. Wondering if he had made a mistake, which I'd say wasn't like him. But then the light was going, so maybe not.' And maybe it was Lovie's memory playing tricks, now that he knew what had happened to Billy. Tricks invented by a guilty conscience. 'Inspector, what … what came next?'

'Billy went home,' said Cattanach flatly. 'He said nothing to his mother, but next day he mentioned you to a friend. And the day after, when he was out on King Street in the early morning, he fell in front of a lorry.'

'He was pushed?'

'We have no proof.'

'By Wilson? Or one of his men? Wilson's not the kind to keep a dog and bark himself,' he explained, in case Cattanach might have thought otherwise, from his account.

'We don't know.'

'The schools are closed,' said Lovie, 'so he wasn't going there. You don't think he was coming to see me, do you?'

'I don't suppose we'll ever know.'

'Did he … did he live long?'

'He was killed instantly,' said Cattanach. 'But the lorry driver will never be the same again. And I've a constable who attended the scene who is probably still having nightmares.'

Lovie's shoulders shifted. He was sobbing now. Cattanach let him be for a while, sorry for his loss, and angry with him for causing it, in his own almost innocent, one-step-aside way.

'Why you?' he asked at last. Lovie blew his nose on a large handkerchief, and hunched even further, fiddling with his fingernails.

'He caught me out,' he muttered.

'With Mabel Campbell?'

Lovie looked up in surprise.

'No, he knew nothing of Mabel. I don't think he was the least interested in my personal life. No. No, it was something else I'd done … I don't understand, Inspector. I'm a very respectable man. I don't want any trouble. I hate the idea of crime – of Billy thinking I might have been a criminal. I've just been, you know, very unlucky.'

'It happens,' said Cattanach, doing his best to sound sympathetic. 'What happened?'

'It was – well, it was a few things that someone sold me, you know? That kind of thing happens in a jewellery shop. Curios, I suppose you could call them, and a ring or two. Nobody minds buying old jewellery unless it's an engagement ring, and then you can reset the stones, re-use the metal. You can make something really lovely out of something no one wants.' He was beginning to sound enthusiastic. Cattanach reined him in.

'I suppose what you were trying to sell was stolen?'

'It was the most unfortunate coincidence. I had no idea they were stolen, I assure you, Inspector. I know one has to be careful, but it never occurred to me to question – and they were very nice pieces,' he finished a little pathetically. Presumably selling stolen goods that were ugly was much more of a crime.

'So you were resetting,' said Cattanach. 'We'll leave aside the source for the moment. How did this man Wilson find out about it?'

'That's where the coincidence comes in. He wandered into my shop oh, a couple of months ago, taking a good look round. He looked respectable, very smart, and I thought "Here's a likely looking customer!" I wish I'd never set eyes on him.'

'Go on.'

Lovie sighed heavily.

'He said he was interested in something from the window – there, Inspector, would I have put it in the window if I'd known it was stolen?'

'Maybe. It depends where you thought it had come from, perhaps.'

'Well, anyway,' said Lovie, flashing him a sudden look of resentment. 'Anyway. He wanted to look at it, and in the end he bought it, and I gave him a receipt. And then he told me he knew it was stolen, and he told me exactly where it had been stolen from, and when.'

'That must have come as something of a shock.'

'I was shaking, I tell you. My first thought was that he must be a policeman, though he looked far too smart – I mean, well, the policemen I had seen before had not been … I mean …'

'All right, I take your point,' said Cattanach. 'But presumably he told you he was not a policeman?'

'He did – well, he made it clear, anyway. He knew something about the original theft – a housebreaking in Edinburgh – and by chance he had recognised the goods in my window.'

'That's quite a chance, isn't it?'

'I suppose so.'

'You don't think he was the one who had stolen them?'

Lovie made a face.

'I suppose it's possible,' he said. 'I certainly didn't ask.'

'No, quite right.'

'Anyway, he said the police would have a record of them, and that he could now prove he had bought one of the items from me. Of course I wanted to snatch back the receipt, but he already had it in his pocket. So I asked him if he was going to go to the police, and he said no, he wouldn't, but only if I would help him with a plan he had. He said he was from out of town, and he wanted to find somewhere to store petrol. That was when I first heard mention of petrol rationing, if there was a war. I hadn't thought about it before. And he said wouldn't it be sensible to get some of it laid by in case of shortages, and I thought well, yes, it would be sensible. It was only later that I read in the newspaper about penalties for hoarding, but by then it was too late: he'd have had me for that, too.'

'And he started with two barrels of the stuff?'

'He did, yes.'

'That sounds like more than one person might hoard for his own use.'

'To run his lorry, perhaps?' Lovie suggested.

'He'd get special commercial rates for his lorry. That's a different thing from you and me for our motors.'

'Is it? I try not to think about it,' said Lovie, shivering.

Well, he might not, thought Cattanach, but Lieutenant Moffat would. And the first word he would think of would indeed be racketeering. Almost certainly this petrol had been stolen to sell on illegally, to those who would pay above the odds to be able to keep using their cars. But where had it come from? He had not heard of any petrol thefts – perhaps that was something else to check with his counterparts in Dundee.

Then again, a professional criminal – even if he were newly branching out from housebreaking, if that had been him – would probably need more than two or three barrels of petrol to keep his customers happy. Was it possible that Albert Lovie had been just one of Wilson's unwilling collaborators? Assuming that Lovie had indeed been unwilling. Could there be other hoards of fuel around the city and its outskirts? The man in Loch Street, for example?

He yawned, and glanced at his watch. Nearly five o'clock in the morning: the crime scene experts would soon be on their way to record whatever evidence they might be able to find at the dismal hut by the Don mouth. Lovie looked grey, like the sky before dawn. Cattanach did not feel much better.

'Let's leave this for now,' he said. 'The sergeant will show you to your accommodation: I'm afraid it's probably not what you're used to.'

Love muttered something. It sounded like 'It's better than what Billy's got'.

'I really didn't tell Wilson Billy's name,' he said, more clearly. 'Honestly, I didn't. I'm not a quick thinker, but I wouldn't have done that.'

'It looks as if he found out somehow, though. When did you last see Wilson?'

'Is this Thursday?' Lovie smoothed back his hair absently. 'Yes – I saw Muckle Eck on Tuesday night when he brought the jerrycans. Wilson … when? Last week some time, I think. He was in a terrible hurry. He popped into the shop to say there would be more petrol coming on Tuesday, that's right. But I thought at the time he had his mind on other things.'

'I don't suppose he said what?'

'No … He looked – well, less sure of himself than usual, I thought. I wondered if maybe he thought the police – you people – were after him. I don't know. He didn't look as if he'd been sleeping well, that's for sure. I suffer that way myself,' he added virtuously, 'so I know what it's like.'

'Right, well, you can go and try to sleep now, anyway.'

He stood, and the constable who had waited patiently behind him went to help Lovie to his feet. Cattanach turned to leave the room, then thought of something else.

'The thing you sold Wilson, the curio, I think you called it.'

'Yes?' Lovie was braced for something.

'It was that penknife, wasn't it? The one I showed you the drawing of.'

'It was, yes. I lied to you, Inspector. I'm sorry.'

Cattanach turned back to the door to hide his smile. It was not often that anyone being questioned in here apologised for lying.

He waited at the front desk while Lovie was taken away, not ungently, to his temporary residence in the cell that had recently contained an impressive quantity of whisky. Cattanach toyed with the idea of telling him that the man in the cell next door, Jock McKinstry, had also had some association with Mabel Campbell. Then he felt that on the whole, Lovie had had a bad enough night. He said good morning to the sergeant, and went home.

40

'TOMMY WILSON, MUCKLE Eck, and Stevie Tennant,' enunciated Lieutenant Moffat, like a school roll call. 'And only Stevie Tennant a local man.'

'Dundee, Lovie thought the others were from. I haven't been able to catch my contact there yet.'

'A fresh city, fresh ground for a new venture?'

'That's what it looks like, sir,' said Cattanach. 'With Stevie as their local contact, a go-between, perhaps.'

'They mustn't have needed him anymore,' said Moffat.

'It seems an extreme way of disposing of his services,' said Cattanach. 'Perhaps they had an agreement that he should just work for Wilson, and not do any business on the side. Wilson found out about the whisky theft, and took exception.'

'Again, a little extreme,' said Moffat. 'Particularly when they don't seem to have found a replacement for him. It's still just been Wilson and Eck, hasn't it?'

Cattanach nodded.

'Any time they've been seen, yes, sir. And Eck on his own, apparently, on Tuesday night when he attacked Anna Mackay.'

'Maybe someone objected to this Wilson's taking over a bit of Aberdeen territory, and killed Stevie as a warning?'

'Who do we know who would do that, sir?' Cattanach objected. 'Can you think of any local villain who might go that far?'

The Lieutenant considered, tipping his chair back behind his desk, but Cattanach could see that he was having no success.

'Wait, though,' he said. 'What about your lorry driver that's in the Infirmary?'

'He couldn't have killed him, sir: he's stuck in his bed.'

'No, not him personally. But that's another Dundee fellow up here and up to no good. What if Wilson is not the only man trying to take Aberdeen as new territory? What if your lorry driver's boss – what's his name? Down in Dundee?'

'Kitchener, sir.'

'Aye, him. What if he's in competition with this Tommy Wilson? He sounds a harder nut.'

'He does, sir.'

'But?'

'But I'm not sure we can assume all our problems come from Dundee.'

'That's maybe true,' admitted Moffat, after a moment. 'But it just looks satisfying. Parcel them all up and send them back down there.'

'Speaking of down there, or further, did Sergeant McAulay report to you that the penknife was stolen in Edinburgh?'

'I heard tell, yes.'

'And then turned up here, too.'

'I don't know about you, Cattanach, but this business is starting to make my head hurt. Every time you find out one thing, it branches into two others, and they're both connected with branches you've found before. My son used his train set to make a knot like that once, and had two engines going round it, in and out. They very near hit each other half a dozen times on one circuit. Watch that doesna happen to you, Cattanach.'

'I will, sir. I know what you mean.'

Moffat sighed.

'Any word on Mabel Campbell?'

'No, sir, not a thing. The trouble is, though,' he went on, 'it looks to me as if she has done this kind of thing before. She goes somewhere new, sits in a tea shop until a smart-looking man turns up and latches on to him. She lies about her past, and sometimes just moves on from it. She moved on to Robert Campbell, and told him nothing, and she lied to Albert Lovie. She might have moved on with him, too, given the chance. Now she's gone, and I suspect that somewhere there's a man who has just met a woman in a respectable tea shop and is growing very attached to her, despite knowing very little about her.'

'Good point,' said the Lieutenant, giving it some thought. 'Good point. But there might be one small difference this time.'

'What's that?'

'She's lost her son.'

'That just makes her more free, surely?'

'Ah, Cattanach, you're not a parent, though, are you? She's left Billy behind. What I want to know is – will she be able to leave him behind without some kind of token, at least?'

Some kind of token – what? Flowers on Billy's grave? He would have to ask Robert, and go and see the grave himself. He was not wholly convinced that Lieutenant Moffat was right, but then, he did have children and Cattanach did not. Perhaps even Mabel, despite her apparent detachment, mourned for her son. Poor Billy.

There were plenty of florists in the city, and it would be a relatively simple task for a constable to go round them by telephone and ask if they had been sent money to put flowers on that particular grave. He should probably set it in motion, anyway. But was there something else? Something that might lead them to Mabel? He was sure Mabel would be more careful, son or no son.

But if they could not find her, then the chances were that Tommy Wilson and Muckle Eck could not find her either. Their trail, starting in Seaton, had gone cold with Anna Mackay, even if they did not know it yet. Though he supposed they had done quite a good job in tracking down Anna herself: Mrs. Hawthorne had not even known her name. Anna had joked that she was the only posh girl in town, and of course she was not. But she was working for the blood bank – perhaps that had been the key. And perhaps, just perhaps, the blood bank office had more information on Mabel Campbell, too.

He paused for a moment. It was clear now why Wilson and Muckle Eck had been looking for Billy Campbell, even why they might perhaps have had a hand in seeing him pushed under a lorry. But why would they be looking for Mabel? Did they think that Billy might have told her what he had seen? Had they found out about her connexion with Albert Lovie? That would be no reason to chase her, and she had had ample time now to go to the authorities about the petrol. It did not seem that she had. Why were they looking for her?

He went to talk to Sergeant McAulay about the florists.

'You ken Jock McKinstry's coming up before the magistrates the day, sir?'

'Oh, blow! Do you know a time?'

'It's most like to be this afternoon, sir. They're trying to get things tidied up, I reckon, while things are still quiet.'

'It is still quiet, isn't it? I don't know what I expected, but that's nearly three weeks now since war was declared.'

'I hear they're starting to call it the Bore War, sir,' said Sergeant McAulay, with a hint of a smile.

'Well, long may it continue,' said Cattanach. 'Magistrates this afternoon … right, I'm heading out just now.'

'Right you be, sir.'

Cattanach walked up King Street to St. Peter's Cemetery, still pondering the mystery of Mabel Campbell. She might not have left Aberdeen at all, but if she had not, then someone must be sheltering her, for she had not been seen since that Friday afternoon. But if she had left Aberdeen, how? Easy enough, he supposed. At that point, no one was keeping an eye on her. Staff questioned at the Joint Station could not remember her, and nor could any bus drivers heading out into the county. But all she had to do, if she was clever, was to make herself a little more dowdy, less noticeable. Cattanach had a feeling that in that respect, anyway, Mabel Campbell was indeed clever.

The cemetery was quiet, on a Thursday morning. A funeral was taking place up at the top, not in the oldest part but next to the Merkland Road gate, a long way from Billy's grave. Cattanach walked along peaceably parallel with King Street, and found the spot easily. There were no flowers on the earth, though leaves had fallen across it from the trees nearby. There had been no changes to the headstone yet, he saw. Given that Billy had not been Robert's son, he wondered if the boy would even be acknowledged. But he thought he would, sooner or later. Billy had been liked.

He walked on up to Seaton, making the most of reflective time out of the office, away from Inspector Cochrane. There was nothing quite like setting one's feet off in a particular direction, and just letting them get on with it, even in the town. But Robert Campbell was not in to tell him whether or not Mabel had been in touch. He hoped Robert was safely with his brothers, and took the tram back down into town.

The magistrate remanded Jock McKinstry in custody to await the next stage in the judicial process. Jock, very close to neat again in his hosed-down suit, made the magistrate a polite bow as if he were being presented to the Lord Lieutenant, and was returned to the cells. He and Albert Lovie had passed each other in the corridor and glanced at each other without interest: neither seemed to have a clue who the other was. Cattanach chose not to enlighten them: if Mabel Campbell had been more deeply involved in criminal activity than he had thought, it might be useful later to be able to say that McKinstry and Lovie, at least, had not worked together.

When he returned to the station, drained of energy in a way that only an afternoon in court can achieve, he found Inspector Cochrane and Sergeant McAulay in the midst of a disagreement at the front desk.

'I am perfectly capable of taking a note up to my office and laying it on a colleague's desk,' Inspector Cochrane was explaining in clipped tones.

'I'm under instructions to hand the note only to Inspector Cattanach,' said the sergeant, not reluctant to stand his ground to a senior officer.

'Under orders from whom? I cannot imagine the Chief Constable has been down here, telling you not to let me take someone else's note for them.'

'No, sir. From the young lady herself, sir. She was very particular, and seeing her father's who he is, sir, I thought it better –'

'Do you mean Inspector Cattanach has received another message from Miss Mackay? Extraordinary,' said Inspector Cochrane, then saw that the sergeant, wincing in embarrassment, was looking past him. Cattanach, fascinated, stepped forward.

'A message for me, Sergeant?' he asked, putting his hand out.

'That's right, sir. It's all in there.' He had already given away more than he intended, letting slip Anna Mackay's name. The note was closely folded from prying eyes.

'Thank you, Sergeant. Good afternoon to you, Inspector.' He wanted to linger, just to try Inspector Cochrane's patience, but his own was stretched. Had Anna been attacked again? Had she seen the big man – Muckle Eck – somewhere around her home or the hospital? He took the note outside quickly, and unfolded it.

'Matter of urgency,' the sergeant had written. 'Please contact her at the hospital. But not the big man.'

Cattanach folded the note again and went back into the station.

'Off to the Infirmary,' he told Sergeant McAulay, and left again at once, before Inspector Cochrane could decide to follow him, or make some inane remark. And what was he doing, lingering about the front desk when Cattanach was run off his feet with three different investigations? Irritation overcame him for a moment, and sped him along the street to the tram stop. He would walk from the far end of Union Street this time. At least, if he understood the note correctly, Anna had not been attacked.

He asked for her at the reception desk by the main entrance. Anna must have been waiting nearby, for she emerged almost at once, in a bottle-green tweed skirt and twinset that made her hair glow. For once, she smiled when she saw him, a smile of slight uncertainty.

'I'd thank you for coming so quickly, Inspector, except that I suspect it's you that will be grateful when you see what I have,' she said. 'At least, I hope so.'

'What is it, then?'

'I have news of Mabel Campbell. I believe I do.'

41

SHE HAD POCKETS in the skirt, and from one of them drew out a grubby white, thin-looking envelope, rather crumpled.

'I'm sorry, I daresay you'll be thinking of fingerprints and such. I had no idea who it was from, so I pulled the letter out right away, but once I saw it I did try to be more careful. As for the envelope, well, who knows how many people have handled that?'

He took it from her, squeezed the corners of the envelope to open it, and peered inside. There was a banknote – a pound – and some writing on a piece of paper very similar to the envelope.

'I can tell you what it says,' said Anna, 'if you want to know straightaway without handling it again. I have a good memory. There is no address at the top, just a date – Monday the eleventh. The note says,' – she closed her eyes to focus – "Dear Miss Mackay, may I ask you a favour? Enclosed please find a pound which please give to my husband to pay for Billy's name to be put on his stone. It is not fair to ask him to do it when Billy wasn't his son. Yours faithfully, Mabel Campbell." And the banknote is there, too.'

'So I see.' He turned the envelope over. It was addressed to Miss A. Mackay at the office of the bloodbank, here at Foresterhill, near the Infirmary itself. He squinted at the postmark.

'It was posted on Monday the eleventh, too. When did you get this?'

'Just at lunchtime. The clerk from the bloodbank came up here to give it to me. He said he had no idea how long it had been there – you know they had a break in? The place was a mess afterwards.'

Cattanach looked at her blankly for a second. A break-in at the bloodbank … he remembered two constables talking about an odd break-in – mistaking it for a real bank, wasn't that what one of them had said?

'That would have been on Monday, yes?'

'That's right. You had heard about it! For a moment I thought perhaps no one had mentioned it.'

'I haven't seen any recent reports,' he said, a little sideways at the absolute truth. 'Was there much taken?'

'They don't think so. Just a glorious mess. Files and letters and everything everywhere. I think they've only just got it halfway straight.'

He would talk with the constables: he needed to know if they had any suspects in mind, or even better, in the cells. But he wondered if the thieves had been after information – perhaps the name and address of the posh girl who had done the rounds with Mabel Campbell? Otherwise how had Muckle Eck found her?

And if they had found an address for Anna Mackay, what might they have found out about Mabel Campbell herself?

'But the main thing,' Anna was saying, still standing confidently in the middle of the foyer, in charge of the situation, 'the main thing is the postmark. Not when it was posted, of course, but where. For once it's actually quite clear. Did you see?'

He looked down again at the envelope, mentally kicking himself for his slowness. Nearly two weeks of wondering where Mabel Campbell was, and he almost let the first real clue pass him by. He held it up closer.

'Peterhead?'

'I'm sure that's what it says, yes. Peterhead.'

North. Of course, she could easily have moved on by now. But a week and a half ago, she had been in Peterhead, a bus journey up the coast. A town big enough to be missed in, just about. Big enough to hide in, with a bit of cash. He dared say there might even be a respectable teashop or two, where Mabel might make a new friend. Was it possible that she was still there?

'By the way,' said Miss Mackay, 'my mother has decided you are now almost respectable. I gather you were dining with some suitable companion at Father's club?' She was teasing him.

'I'm not at all sure that policemen are at any advantage in

being respectable,' he replied. 'We have to spend a great deal of time in quite the wrong kind of company. We should be very short of conversation if we wanted only to be respectable. Or almost respectable.' He could not help adding that. Mrs. Mackay clearly still had her reservations. Not that he particularly cared. 'Any more sign of our large friend?'

'Nothing. I've asked a couple of my fellow students to walk me home after dark, but as it happens I haven't been working late since.'

'He goes by the name of Muckle Eck, apparently.' He was dawdling now: he had slipped the letter from Mabel Campbell into his inside pocket, and part of him was eager to get back to the office and telephone someone in the County Police at Peterhead. Part of him, though, seemed determined to linger.

'Descriptive,' Anna Mackay agreed. To be fair, she was not rushing off either.

'But watch out for his boss – his name is Tommy Wilson. He's a charmer, apparently. Small, neat, smartly dressed, black hair.'

'Ha,' said Anna, 'that sounds like our mystery man!'

'You have another mystery man?' He felt his heart sink.

'No, the one you know about – or the police know about. The one who was knocked out in the tram crash, and then discharged himself on his own recognizances.'

He blinked at her. She was right.

'Wait,' he said, 'the man had a wristwatch with an engraving on the back.' He summoned the memory – he was sure he was as good at that as she was. '"To T from your Belle". That's what it said.'

'T for Tommy?'

'Maybe. Quite a coincidence otherwise. Did we have a photographer come to see your patient?

'I believe so. Surely you can check.'

'Of course: I was thinking out loud. We don't have a photograph of Mr. Wilson, but we know a few people who have seen him.' Was this another loop of the knot? 'Right, well, I've kept you back long enough, Miss Mackay. Many thanks for this.' He tapped his inside pocket. 'And look after yourself.'

'Every intention, Inspector,' she said smoothly, and raised a hand as he headed for the door.

The bloodbank was, as he had thought, on the vast hospital site. By comparison with the maternity hospital, the children's hospital, and the Infirmary, it had the look of a temporary hut, not the headquarters of a medical advance and major contribution to the war effort. One of the four windows was boarded up. The door already looked shabby.

Inside, a weary clerk was sorting stacks of loose papers into different stacks. He had probably been there since the police had left on Monday afternoon.

'Yes?' he said, torn between a welcome distraction and the desire to get the job done.

'Inspector Cattanach, City Police.'

'Aye, well, your lads are away long ago.'

'So I gather. I'm looking for some information you might have held here.'

'Good luck with that,' said the man, waving a hand at the stacks of paper around him. 'If you find anything useful, let me know.'

'I suspect the information is in your head, though. I wanted to know what kind of details you keep about your volunteers – you know, name, address, that kind of thing.'

'Aye,' said the man slowly, 'aye, I could tell you that, I suppose. You don't mean you want to know about a specific volunteer, do you?'

'No – well, not unless what you tell me is interesting.'

'I rarely have anything interesting to tell anybody.'

'This should be quick, then. You keep information on your volunteers, yes?'

'Yes, of course.'

'What information do you keep?'

'Name, address, like you said. Telephone number if they have one. Age, if they're willing to tell us – we really just want to know if they're over twenty-one and under, well, ninety, really.'

'Anything else?'

'Whether they've any relevant experience or qualifications. We've a retired doctor or two, and several nurses.'

'Date of birth? Place of birth? Nationality?'

But the clerk was shaking his head.

'No, none of those. What would be the use?'

'You might want nationality soon.'

'I suppose. But then soon we can look at their identification cards, can't we?'

And Mabel had been concerned about identification cards, hadn't she? About registration, and what she would have to tell the authorities, and who might be able to look at it.

'So if I had broken in here, say, to try to find out about someone – one of your volunteers – all I would get would be their name, their current address, and an approximate age?'

'Unless they'd been a nurse or a doctor.'

'Yes. And unless they had a telephone.' The Campbells did not have a telephone. Mabel had gone to a call box to contact Anna Mackay. Cattanach drummed his fingers briefly on a spare inch of desk, making the nearby papers tremble. The clerk tensed.

'So was that interesting, then?'

'What?' asked Cattanach.

'You said you'd maybe want to ask about a specific volunteer if what I told you was interesting?'

'Oh, yes. Well, it was interesting, but not, I'm afraid, interesting enough.'

'That's good,' said the clerk, 'for the information on the volunteers is the worst bit of the whole mess. You'd think someone had something against them – or against good honest paperwork.'

'It's a terrible thought,' Cattanach agreed, and left him to his task.

If Muckle Eck had found the letter to Anna Mackay at the bloodbank, Cattanach was very sure he would not have left it there for anyone else to find. No doubt all he had done was to find out Anna's details, then wreck the place for a distraction. It would certainly keep the clerk distracted for a while. And there seemed to be no other way of tracing Mabel Campbell's current whereabouts from the papers the bloodbank would hold. Maybe, just maybe, the police were one step ahead of the villains. He paused just for a moment as he walked back towards Union Street, pulled his shoulders back, and took off his hat to let the wind sweep through his hair. One step ahead of the villains – a rare and precious feeling.

'Peterhead?' asked Lieutenant Moffat. 'Well, I suppose. As you say, she could be long gone. But it looks as if people's thoughts were right – she's heading north. Where is there after Peterhead?'

'Fraserburgh, various villages. Inverness. Then up into Caithness and Sutherland – no very big settlements to hide in. Thurso, maybe, or Wick?'

'She might double back south.'

'She might at that, sir. She can't go north for very much longer – not on the mainland, anyway.'

'Could it be a bluff? She'd know that there would be a postmark on the letter.'

'You said yourself, sir: she left a connexion behind this time. She needed to deal with the headstone.'

'Why Miss Mackay?'

'I think that was where she was being careful. She knew Anna Mackay would do what she asked, but that she would not be over-curious: she would probably be surprised to know that it was Miss Mackay who raised the question of her disappearance.'

'You'll be calling Peterhead, anyway.'

'I already have, sir. They'd seen the news that we were looking for her, but my contact up there – they've had a lot to do since war was declared, and he admits it slipped through the net.'

'Do you want to go up yourself?' asked Moffat.

'Can you clear it with County?'

'I should think so. Anyway, you met her: you know what she looks like. They're just going by a description in the Blue Toon.'

'Then as soon as they're happy, I'll go.'

'Take Constable Gauld with you,' said Moffat. 'It'll do him good. Will you take your own motor?'

Cattanach hesitated.

'Of course, sir.'

'Keep a note of the mileage. I don't know yet what we're doing about rationing for that, but if I can I'll make sure you get it back.'

42

'WHAT WAY IS it called the Blue Toon, sir?'

Perhaps Constable Gauld was trying to distract himself from the fear of imminent death. He had clung on to the dashboard, the door handle, the seat, and once, alarmingly, the gear lever, constantly since they had left the police station. Cattanach speculated that he had never actually been in a motor before.

'Apparently the fishermen used to wear blue stockings, Constable.'

'I thought it was maybe for the polis that was in it,' Gauld tried, with a weak laugh.

'That would be helpful, but unfortunately I don't think so.'

'Aye,' said Gauld, 'there's plenty fishers in Peterhead. Whalers and all, or there used to be. I hear it's a fine wee town.'

'It used to be a spa town, too.'

'What like of a thing is that, then, sir?'

'A place where people came to drink the waters, and bathe in them, for the good of their health.'

'I'd no fancy drinking the waters around Peterhead, though, sir.'

'I think it was from a spring, not from the sea. But I'm not sure. It was very fashionable, for a while.'

'Aye, well,' said Gauld, with a prophetic turn, 'all things pass.'

He glanced through the side window, perhaps alarmed at the rate all things seemed to be passing. Cattanach thought he heard a faint groan. He hoped Gauld was not going to be sick.

Gauld swallowed noisily.

'So what are we going to do when we get there, sir? Do we have to talk to someone from the County police?'

'It's always considered polite, if you cross the borders. They might even have found her by now. Even if not, we can find out where they've looked, where the most likely places are – the lie of the land, generally. Maybe they'll have some idea of someone who might have helped her, or be harbouring her.'

Gauld considered.

'What do you think she is, sir?'

'How do you mean?'

'Is she a criminal, or a victim? Or both?'

'I'm not even sure that Mabel Campbell is her real name.' Though he was beginning to wonder about at least part of that name – something had occurred to him to make him think part of it was real.

'Then what's she up to? Is it fraud, or what?'

'I can't put my finger on a crime she's committed, unless she did kill Stevie Tennant. But I think our smart little Tommy Wilson did that, or had Muckle Eck do it for him. That was a skilled job.'

'Has she tricked anyone out of money, sir?'

'Only if you count telling Albert Lovie lies about her husband – well, about Robert Campbell – and going about with him under slightly false pretences. I don't suppose Lovie would have grounds for taking her to court – not even for breach of promise.'

'So if we find her, sir, and she doesna want to come home – what do we do then, sir?'

'Nothing we can do, except to reassure ourselves that she's safe. She's a grown woman, and she's not even Robert Campbell's wife. We can't force her to do anything.'

'I suppose …'

'She might well just have gone away somewhere to come to terms with Billy's death.'

Constable Gauld tutted.

'You could almost forget Billy was at the back of this, couldn't you, sir? I mean, I dinna think I'll ever forget Billy – not that day he died. But it's all gone all over the place since then, has it no?'

'That's very well put, Constable. It has indeed gone all over the place.'

They fell silent as the outskirts of Peterhead laid arms along each side of the road. Constable Gauld sat up and looked about him, taking in an unfamiliar town with interest.

'That's the prison, over there,' said Cattanach, pointing to the right, towards the sea. Gauld nodded.

'I've heard of that, a' course, sir.'

Cattanach negotiated the main streets into the centre of the town, then turned right on narrower roads between grey granite buildings not at all unlike the city they had come from. He pulled up beside a corner building on Merchant Street, and pointed again.

'The police station.'

'It's like a bairn's version of our own one, sir,' said Gauld, clambering out of the car and looking happier than he had for the whole journey. 'Just a wee one.'

'They've plenty to do, all the same. And now we're at war – well, all of us along the east coast will be looking out for trouble, I daresay. Come on, let's go and see if we can find someone to help us. I have a … Sergeant Schivas, I think, knows how things are going.'

Gauld hurried to hold the door open for Cattanach, then followed him in to the front office. Cattanach could sense him relaxing by the minute: this all looked like home territory, even if it was a different police force.

Sergeant Schivas turned out to be a thin, red-haired man with a full moustache and eyebrows that seemed to be of more substance than the man himself.

'Aye, we saw in the *Gazette* she was missing,' he said. 'But you ken how it is: when it's no local sometimes it goes to the back of your mind. I'm that sorry, though, sir.'

'Well,' said Cattanach, 'now that you've remembered her – and now that we've a closer link with Peterhead with this postmark – have you any information you can give us?'

'A woman matching her description stayed in a hotel just off Broad Street for near a fortnight – let me see, now, that would be the eighth to the nineteenth.'

'The Friday to the Tuesday of the week after – or do you mean she stayed the night of the nineteeth?'

'Aye, sir.'

'So, to the Wednesday. The day before yesterday. She posted the letter on the Monday of the first week.' Cattanach saw that Constable Gauld was taking notes. 'And after that?'

'No idea, sir. We had a word with the hotel owner, but I could take you there and you could talk to him yourself.'

'That would be very good of you, thank you. Just to confirm – you've had no other sightings matching this woman?'

'None, sir. There was no photograph, mind.'

'No, I know – we couldn't find one.'

'And I might say, by the way, that the woman that stayed in the hotel didna call herself – what was it now? Mabel Campbell. No, she was Mabel Christie.'

'Was she indeed? Very interesting. Christie – did you write that down, Constable?'

'I did, sir,' said Gauld, looking put out. Cattanach sensed that he was not impressed by the Peterhead sergeant.

They had passed through Broad Street on their way to the police station.

'You'd have been quicker going along the shore,' said Sergeant Schivas, 'but then I suppose if you didn't know you wouldn't know.'

'Probably not, no,' Cattanach agreed.

'Here we are. Man's name is Hardie.'

Mr. Hardie was agitated, but not by a visit from the police.

'Soldiers! Soldiers everywhere. Where am I to put them all? Where can I put real guests? And who's going to pay me?'

Sergeant Schivas did his best to be a steadying influence, and introduced the Aberdeen men.

'Mr. Hardie, can you leave off for five minutes? These officers have come all the way fae Aberdeen to hear about yon quine that stayed here lately.'

'She arrived about two weeks ago,' put in Cattanach. 'She was here from the eighth to the morning of the twentieth, apparently.'

'Aye, right enough, that's two weeks to the day she came here. Mr. Hardie?'

'Oh, aye? The one you were asking me about? A constable came round asking, and a' course I remembered her. Fine woman like that, all on her own. Said she was a widow. Tragic,' said Mr. Hardie.

'Indeed, sir,' said Cattanach. 'Did you see how she arrived at your hotel?'

'She walked in the door.'

'With her bags with her? Did anyone bring them in for her?'

'She had only the one bag, Inspector, and she was carrying it herself.'

'Had she a car? Did you see anyone wave her goodbye, or drop her off? A taxi, perhaps?' But Hardie was shaking his head.

'No, she just walked in off the street, just like that. You can see for yourself it's no a wide entrance. If someone's coming in, it's no that easy to see past them. But I dinna think there was a car.' He looked towards the door himself, and scowled at the sight of three soldiers heading out into the bright midday, laughing as they went.

'I see. A single room?'

'Aye.'

'Did anyone call for her, visit her, leave anything for her, while she was here?'

'Not a bit of it.'

'Were there any telephone calls for her? Did she place any calls herself?'

'None.'

'Did she go out at all?'

'Oh, aye, she went out near every day. I think she must have taken her lunch out somewhere. We do evening meals every day, but we only do lunches on Sundays.'

'Did she say anything about where she had been when she was out?'

'Not to me, any road.'

'Did she mention where she had come from, or where she was going to?

'No …'

'What about the Sundays? Did she go out on Sundays?'

'I never saw her go out. Nor come back in.'

'Did she take her lunch in the hotel on Sundays, then?'

'She did, aye.'

'And her dinners?'

'Oh, aye. The lass that serves might know something about

her, but I never heard her say much.'

'And Wednesday? The day before yesterday?'

'Aye, she went out on Wednesday again. Then she came back, after lunch, this would have been – if she had lunch – in fact it was later than that. It must have been about four. Anyway, she said she was moving on, and could we make up her bill.'

'Was that a surprise? Had she said how long she planned to stay?'

'I suppose not. I mean, I think she sort of mentioned a week, but she was still here, so …'

'Did she seem – different at all? What kind of mood would you say she was in?'

This baffled the hotel owner.

'What mood? What like?'

'Did she seem pleased to be leaving? Dissatisfied with her stay?'

'I dinna ken …'

'Worried? Frightened? Excited?' Cattanach looked at Gauld, who frowned, and contributed,

'In a hurry?'

'Oh, aye, she was in a hurry, all right. I thought maybe she was in a – in a good mood?' he tried, eyeing them to see if he had it right. 'I'd no go so far as to say she was excited, but she looked happy enough. But right enough, she skipped out of here like someone who hadna paid.'

'But she did pay. Did she pay in cash?'

'Oh, aye.'

'But she said nothing about where she was moving on to?'

'Not a thing, no. She went about four o'clock, and this time I can tell you – she had a taxi and she must have ordered it while she was out, for the driver turned up here at the front desk and asked for her.'

'Did he, indeed?' Cattanach clutched at the straw. 'Was it a driver you knew?'

'Oh, aye, I know all the drivers in the town, I think, pretty much. In this line of business, you get to.'

'I'm sure you do. Tell me, Mrs. Christie's room – it was Christie, wasn't it, her name?'

'I can show you the register.'

'Please do.' Hardie turned away to fetch it. Cattanach went on.

'Her room, did it face the front or the back?'

'The front,' said Hardie at once. 'She asked specially to be at the front.'

'Did she say why?'

Hardie frowned.

'I dinna think so. She just asked if she could, and I said we could. Here, here's where she signed.'

The writing was the same as that in the letter to Anna Mackay, but the name was Mabel Christie. For her permanent address, she had just put 'Aberdeen'. There was no other information.

'You'll no get away with this kind of thing now,' said Sergeant Schivas sternly. 'There's a war on, you ken. It'll be registration this, identification cards that, all the way.'

'Aye, if the place is no full of soldiers,' muttered Hardie, unimpressed.

'We'll need to speak to the taxi driver,' said Cattanach.

But the taxi driver had only taken Mrs. Campbell, or Christie, as far as the main railway station. The officers walked on to it. It was unremarkable.

'Where to from here, sir?' asked Constable Gauld.

'This is nearly the end of the line. There's just the harbour station that way, for the fish trains,' Sergeant Schivas explained.

'And the other way, sir?' asked Gauld. He was definitely looking cross.

'The rest of the world,' said Schivas, with a shrug. 'She could be anywhere, your woman.'

'Let's think,' said Cattanach, walking over to where timetables were displayed on the wall. 'This line takes you back to the junction at New Maud. From there she could go north to Fraserburgh, or south to Dyce, another junction. From Dyce, indeed, the world would be her oyster. But she came here first, didn't she? And she would have known that this was the end of this line – so there must have been some reason for her to come here. The question is, did she fulfil that reason in the few days she was here, or did she, from her carefully chosen front room window, see something that made her take to the road again?'

'Sir,' said Gauld, tentatively, 'maybe there's another possibility?'

'Go on.'

'Maybe she came here to the station, but she never left Peterhead at all?'

43

CATTANACH NODDED, ACKNOWLEDGING the possibility.

'You mean she came here and changed her mind? Or came here, perhaps, to make it look as if she had left?'

'I just wondered, sir, if she might have doubled back, as they say. I mean, we know she's been good at leaving her past behind before. She could have a few tricks she could play, and this would be a good one.'

'My!' remarked Sergeant Schivas, and Gauld once again blushed irritably.

Cattanach thought it through.

'Is there a left-luggage office here?'

'Aye, sir, over yonder.'

In a moment the left-luggage clerk had confirmed that he had in his possession a small case under the name of M. Christie, and that though he had not been on duty at the time, he believed it had been deposited on Wednesday, his day off.

'We'll come back for that later, I think,' said Cattanach to Gauld. He turned to the sergeant. 'Have you many tea shops in Peterhead? Tea rooms, perhaps? Something respectable, not too cheap.'

'And maybe not too far from the harbour, sir.'

Gauld was using his head again. The sergeant raised his eyebrows, but Cattanach waved him on.

'See – sorry, sir, but I've been thinking – see we first know that she turned up in Montrose, in a tea shop where Robert Campbell found her, and she stayed with fishing people in Aberdeen. And when she left, she went to Peterhead. We know she picked up Lovie in a tea shop, too, and that was down near the harbour. I think she goes towards the fishing, as well as the tea shops.'

'It's a fair guess,' said Cattanach. 'Certainly a good place to start. Well, Sergeant? What do you have by way of tea shops near the harbour?'

'There's one I could think of, sir, that's near there and respectable. Are you wanting to go there now?'

'Yes, please.'

'Then it's this way.'

Tea shops did not seem to be Sergeant Schivas' native habitat. This one, with its polished glass windows and neat table cloths, looked exactly the kind of place they sought, but the sergeant approached it like an elephant trying to hunt a mouse, all awkward tiptoes and anxious glances.

'Will you be going in, sir?'

'Not only will I go in, Sergeant, but I'll stand you both a pot of tea and a fancy piece, if they have any. Come on.'

It was still a little early for lunches, so the tea shop was not overly full. The waitress was happy to find a table for three larger than average men, two of them in uniform, and Cattanach guessed that the girl lived a blameless life. She took their order – Sergeant Schivas asked for a fruit scone, in a moment of extravagance – and agreed, too, to fetch the manageress.

The manageress was slightly less welcoming, perhaps concerned about the impression potential customers might have that this was a police canteen.

'We'll not take up too much of your time, madam,' said Cattanach. 'We're looking for a missing woman, and there's a possibility that she might have come in here recently.'

'How recently, then?'

'Any time from two weeks ago to the day before yesterday.'

'My, that's a whilie. Have you a photo, or a description?'

Cattanach recited from memory the official description of Mabel Campbell – or Christie. The woman was not sure, and called over the waitress.

'It could be – I mean, she could have been here. That could fit lots of people, sir,' said the waitress.

'I think she was probably here in the afternoon, and had left by four.'

'Aye, well, we close at four, so she would have had to go.'

'She wasn't a local.'

The two women looked at each other.

'That could be the new woman, could it no?' said the waitress.

'New woman?'

'Aye, she's been here a few days recently. And you're right – I think she was here the day before yesterday, an' all.'

'Did you see her talking to anyone? Maybe meeting a friend?'

They shook their heads as if pulled by the same string.

'She might have met a man here around that time. I don't mean an assignation,' he added quickly – he could see the manageress about to leap to the defence of her respectable establishment – 'I mean that they might have got talking, perhaps, on adjacent tables. Something quite innocent like that.'

'And you say she's missing?' asked the waitress. 'Did she meet – I mean, did he murder her, this man? Is it like one of those things you read in the papers?'

'Dinna be daft, Aileen!' exclaimed the manageress, but she looked worried.

Cattanach smiled, reassuring.

'I don't think so, no. We just think they might have fallen into conversation here, and it's possible that he knows where she is. We don't think that any harm of that kind has come to her.' Not until Tommy Wilson and Muckle Eck had caught up with her, anyway, and he could not see how they might have traced her so quickly to a Peterhead tea shop.

'There was someone …' The waitress was frowning now. 'Let me think … who's that man that comes in on a Wednesday sometimes? He has a shop on Marischal Street, I think, but it doesna open on a Wednesday. Mind?'

'I ken who you mean. Och, what's his name? He's a bittie lonely, ken? He'll chat to a'body.'

'What's he like?' asked Cattanach.

'He's – he's a nice man. Well-dressed, an' all. Nice manners. Lived with his mother for years, and I think that's why he's no married, but he has an eye for the ladies. And right enough, he was here two days ago. He was there,' she indicated a table at the far corner of the tea shop, 'and I mind him leaning over to talk to a quine at the next table. That's extraordinary,' she added, giving Cattanach a suspicious look. 'Were you watching, or what? How did you ken about him? Frank Fraser, that's the fellow's name.'

'And he has a shop in – was it Marischal Street, you said?'

'That's right,' said Sergeant Schivas. 'Now you've the name, I ken the place. It's a hairdressers, though, no a shop.'

'That's the man!' said the manageress, as if she had the winning card in Snap. 'That'll be him. Aye, well, he'll have done her no harm, anyway. He's a gentleman.' She looked sideways at Cattanach, suddenly awkward.

'I'm sure he's entirely innocent,' Cattanach said. 'But it's good to know that our missing woman was able to have a friendly chat while she was here: and she might have said something to him about her plans. Thank you, ladies, you've been extremely helpful.'

They finished their tea quickly, and Cattanach left a generous tip.

'Marischal Street, then?' he said to Sergeant Schivas once they were outside. 'I hope we're not taking up too much of your valuable time, Sergeant.'

'Not a bit of it, sir,' said the sergeant, brushing scone crumbs from the corners of his moustache. 'It's always a pleasure to help our colleagues from other forces.' The scone seemed to have improved his mood tremendously, and he swung out with enthusiasm back towards the centre of the town.

'Do you know anything of this man Fraser?'

'Not much more than they quines could tell you, sir. He's no come under our notice, but he cuts my wife's hair.'

'She must like him, then.'

'Aye, I suppose. She likes what he does with her hair, any road.'

The hairdressing establishment was much busier than the tea shop had been – Frank Fraser would have little chance of popping out for a fly cup this afternoon. But he did despatch an assistant to wash a customer's hair while he stepped into a tiny room at the back to talk to Cattanach and Gauld. There was no hope of another body fitting in there, and Sergeant Schivas took up a stand in the crowded main room, thus feeding local gossip as effectively as a zoo keeper flinging half a sheep into the lions' cage.

'How can I help you, Inspector?' Fraser asked at once. It was hard to take him in in the limited space, but Cattanach could smell hair oil and scented shampoo, and see the well-shaved jaw and clean, trimmed fingernails. He named the tea shop, and saw Fraser nod with familiarity.

'Were you there, by any chance, on the afternoon of Wednesday the twentieth? The day before yesterday?'

'I was, yes. I often pop in on a Wednesday. The scones are excellent.'

Cattanach was sure that Sergeant Schivas would agree.

'Can you remember if there was anyone else there that afternoon? Did you perhaps talk with any of the other customers?'

The first hint of discomfort played suddenly over Fraser's smooth features. He paused very slightly.

'May I ask, Inspector, what this is in connexion with? You're with the City Force, you say?'

'We're looking for a missing woman,' said Cattanach. 'We believe she's safe at present, but we'd like to make sure.'

'She's not a criminal of any kind, is she?'

Cattanach did not catch Gauld's eye.

'Not that we're aware of, sir. We'd just like to assure ourselves of her safety.'

'So she's already missing? I mean, when did she go missing?'

'She was reported missing on Monday the eleventh, sir, in Aberdeen. Now we know she was here in Peterhead from the previous Friday afternoon until at least Wednesday afternoon. We haven't yet traced her beyond that, so if you can tell us anything of what she said to you, any indication of what her plans might have been …'

'I see.'

'After she left the tea shop, she returned to her hotel and asked for her bill, and left in a taxi for the station. Did she say anything to you? Anything that might take us another step forward?'

Fraser shifted a little in the cramped space, doing his best to look anywhere but at Cattanach.

'This is very awkward, Inspector. I don't quite know what to say.'

Cattanach waited. The chatter from the salon filled the silence between them, and you might have thought that Fraser was listening to it, waiting for some voice amongst the customers to tell him what to do. Then he sighed.

'I'd just like you to know, Inspector, that what I'm about to tell you – it's not something I'm in the habit of doing. And I'm sure, I'm really positive, that it was not something Mrs. Christie had done before, either. We're talking about a very respectable woman here.'

Mrs. Christie – the name under which Mabel Campbell had registered at the hotel.

'Of course,' said Cattanach.

'She was at the table next to mine in the tea shop, and she dropped her napkin, and I bent to pick it up, as you would do.'

'Indeed.'

Fraser nodded, as if he felt he had established a connexion, something in common with Cattanach.

'She thanked me, and we just fell into conversation. She's a widow, and had just moved here from – from somewhere further south, I think she said. She was staying in a hotel, she told me, and feeling – well, very lonely. She hadn't made any friends yet. Well … one thing led to another, and I found myself inviting her to dine with me. At my home.'

'Alone?'

'Well … yes.'

Cattanach refrained from pointing out that that was scarcely the action of a very respectable woman. And even if it had been, the respectable women in question would not necessarily leave their hotel with all their luggage, just to go and join a man for dinner. Was it Mabel Campbell who, having deposited her luggage safely, was presuming more than dinner, or was that what Frank Fraser had intended, too?

'So you went home, and she left her hotel … then what? You met at your house?'

'No, Inspector.'

'Then where?'

'No, I mean we didn't meet.'

'Go on.'

Fraser shrugged.

'There's nothing more to say. I went home, picking up some bits and pieces on the way for dinner – I'm quite a good cook, you see.'

'Right.'

'And I made a start on the dinner, tidied up a bit. You know. And I waited. But she never appeared.'

'Did you think to look for her?'

'I did go out, after a bit, and walk up and down.' Fraser looked a bit shame-faced. 'But I wasn't very sure where she was coming from, or how. There was no sign of her.'

'And so you put it down to experience, and moved on?'

'I thought I'd been tricked, you know, led up the garden path. I felt like a fool. I went back inside and checked I still had my wallet, if you must know.'

'Where do you live, Mr. Fraser? I'm afraid that we'll have to go and take a look.'

'I was afraid you'd say that.'

Frank Fraser lived in what had been his mother's cottage, along a narrow road north of the town. Similar cottages lined, sporadically, one side of the road, while on the other side only a steep bank of gorse and scrub separated the road from the beach.

'The third house on the left,' said Frank Fraser, waving ahead. But they were not destined to reach it just yet. A skinny constable, overtopping Gauld by a good eight inches, was suddenly in front of them.

'I canna let you pass, sir – oh, Sergeant!' He saluted with one stringy arm.

'What's going on here, then, Constable?' asked Sergeant Schivas. 'Go on – you can say in front of these ones.'

'It's a body, sir,' said the constable. 'A woman's body, down the bank.'

44

THE EXPERT TEAMS of the Peterhead police were not far behind them.

'If I'd popped into the station we could have saved ourselves the walk,' grumbled Sergeant Schivas.

'I think I'd have wanted to come up here anyway,' said Cattanach. The wind straight off the grey sea whipped at them and at the coats of the photographers and medical men as they struggled to reach the body from the road and from the beach below. Whether it was Mabel Campbell or not, the body seemed to have been deposited in a very awkward place. There was no question for the moment of his seeing her. Sergeant Schivas did not seem keen to wait out in the cold.

'You could come into the house,' said Frank Fraser, reluctantly.

'I'm afraid not, sir, not yet,' said Cattanach. 'I think if this turns out to be your Mrs. Christie, the police will want to take a look at the house, too.'

'Aye,' said Schivas. 'Our Inspector's on his way an' all, sir. You might be wanting to think if there's somewhere else you can stay. And dinna think of heading out of town without telling us, eh?'

'What?' Fraser looked bewildered.

'Just in case, sir,' said Sergeant Schivas comfortably. 'Just in case.'

'Am I a suspect?' His voice shook.

'You'll see we need to check, don't you?' said Cattanach.

'Apart from the hotel keeper and the taxi driver, you're about the last person known to have talked with Mrs. Christie, and you had an arrangement to meet her up here. You've been very generous with your account of that –'

'I wish I'd never mentioned it.'

'If it is her, and it was found out afterwards that you'd invited her here – anyone could have overheard you in the tea shop, couldn't they? – it would have looked much worse for you, sir.'

'Mr. Cattanach?'

He turned at the sound of his name being called. One of the photographers, clinging to his hat, was perched halfway up the bank, visible only from his chest up.

'They're asking if you can come and take a look at her now, sir.'

'Right, I'm coming.'

He began to slither down from gorse bush to bramble down the bank, and found his heart skipping. A dead body, perhaps dead a couple of days – not pleasant. A woman's body, perhaps worse. But was it her? Was it the woman they had been hunting all this time?

He followed the photographer's directions a few yards further along the beach, and met the local Casualty Surgeon. Brief introductions, and then he was waved up the bank again, feet placed carefully in the indicated spots, hands clinging to sharp sheafs of tough grass. A shoe first, brown, with a little impractical buckle and a moderate heel. Then a stockinged foot and leg, the nylon ripped and laddered. He tried to stand straight, to lean back slightly to see along the length of the lightweight blue coat, stained and dark in the centre, crumpled into the gorse at the sides, past gloved hands that seemed to reach up, out of the scrub, asking to be pulled out and rescued. He had a sudden recollection of Stevie Tennant's body, the same gorse bushes, the same sickening stench of decay fighting the fresh sea breeze. Was it a coincidence?

A hat, tilted against a rock, and then the face. Just like Stevie Tennant's, abandoned to the elements. But it was not so damaged yet, and the hair was right, the eyebrows, the look of her. They were too late.

'Yes,' he said clearly. 'Yes, I believe this is the body of the woman going by the name of Mabel Campbell or Mabel Christie.

Or very, very like her.'

'Thank you, Inspector,' said the doctor.

Despite the short distance, and all his experience, he made a hash of backing down on to the beach. He brushed his knees and stood for a long moment, staring out to sea. Mabel Campbell was dead. He would have to wait until cause of death had been established, until the Peterhead police had searched Frank Fraser's cottage and questioned him, until the suitcase at the station had been examined, until someone – Robert Campbell, presumably – could be brought up from Aberdeen to make a formal identification. And then what? Co-operation with the Peterhead police and the Aberdeenshire force – Lieutenant Moffat would love that. He was entirely dependent on them for the next move.

He had sent Gil Gauld home on the train, but he himself had spent the rest of the day in Peterhead. Understandably the local inspector wanted to know why Cattanach had been searching for the missing woman, and why he thought she might have ended up dead in his town. There had been plenty to do and say, and cups of tea to drink. He had gone with the Inspector and Sergeant Schivas to pick up Mabel's case from the station, and they had opened it together to find very much what Cattanach had expected: some carefully selected smart clothing, make-up, and evening shoes. There was nothing at all to distinguish it from any other woman's suitcase – no letters, photographs, bank book. The only thing of any real note was tucked under everything else – a plain cloth bag, filled with a roll of fifty pound notes. No doubt someone would check the numbers. She had brought money when she came to live with Robert Campbell. He would ask Campbell if it had been in notes then, or if she had changed it since.

'Strange woman,' the local inspector had said. 'Where did she keep all her clutter? Her handbag was almost empty – just make-up and such. Didn't she even have a photograph of the boy?'

'Maybe the murderer took it,' Sergeant Schivas had said.

'Maybe,' Cattanach had said. 'I don't think she went in much for photographs, though. There weren't any in the house. And she was a good-looking woman, but there weren't even any of her.'

'Unencumbered,' the local inspector had remarked.

'It looked that way,' Cattanach had agreed. 'But I think she was encumbered, all right. I suspect that's why she's dead.'

He had waited, drinking yet more tea and eating sandwiches for which a constable had been sent out specially, while the local inspector interviewed Frank Fraser. There had been no sign of anything suspicious in his trim little cottage, no evidence that Mabel Campbell had ever set foot in it. After an hour or more the inspector had emerged, shaking his head.

'If you ask me – and no doubt somebody will – yon's an innocent man. And there's never been the least word against him in the town. He's started thinking it's his fault now, inviting her there and not escorting her himself. A judgement on him.' He had nodded solemnly, and Cattanach was not entirely sure if the inspector really thought Frank Fraser's current discomfort was a direct result of divine displeasure.

He left the station in the early evening, and found a late-opening garage. While the attendant filled up the tank he flicked through his grandly-titled 'Motor Spirit Ration Book'. It would come into force at midnight: he was not surprised that there were a few cars queuing behind him as he paid and left. How many stashes of fuel were there about the county and city – a gallon or two here, a bottle there. There would be other fires, no doubt, though maybe not as bad as the one in Loch Street had been. Lovie's hut was at least secluded – and was now well guarded, until they worked out what to do with all that petrol.

Tommy Wilson had blackmailed Lovie into storing the petrol. Tommy Wilson had seen Billy Campbell at the petrol store, and Billy Campbell had died. Tommy Wilson had been looking for Mabel, and now Mabel was dead. He was not the least surprised that the Peterhead inspector had concluded that Frank Fraser was innocent. But how had Tommy Wilson found Mabel before they had? He and Muckle Eck had still been looking for her as late as Tuesday evening. How had they found her between then and Wednesday evening?

He drove away from Peterhead with the sea darkening down to his left, the shadows long. He would need his headlights before he reached Aberdeen, and he remembered that the special blackout covers he had bought for them were still, usefully, under the front passenger seat. He saw the turn-off for Foveran and Newburgh, and took it, finding a field gate to pull in and fit the covers.

They were fiddly, but he managed it to his satisfaction, standing back to consider the funny little slits. Could they really be safe? He was not at all sure.

The sound of a tractor surprised him, and he glanced over the gate to see one approaching up the field, hauling behind it a trailer stacked with bales of hay. He waved, to acknowledge he would move out of the way, and slipped back behind the wheel to drive off. Tractors were rare enough here: he wondered if the farmer were cursing his luck, modernising just in time for petrol rationing. On the other hand, the army had commandeered horses in the last war, so maybe the tractor was safer in the end. And anyway, hadn't he read that farmers' petrol wasn't rationed yet, because of the harvest? No doubt the regulations were somewhere in Inspector Cochrane's ledger of memoranda – indexed and numbered neatly. What was it that Inspector Cochrane did to justify his presence on the force? What had he been doing over the last two weeks, while he himself had been rushing round investigating lorry accidents and all that had followed? He allowed himself to be faintly resentful for a moment or two, then reminded himself that he liked to keep busy: he would much rather be out hunting missing women than spending his day gluing memoranda into a ledger, never mind indexing them.

Feeling invisible with his dimmed lights, he pulled cautiously back out on to the main road, and turned towards Aberdeen.

At home, he found a message shoved through his letterbox by Mrs. Walker next door, asking him to call and take the dogs out if he was back by nine. He peered at his watch, and found it was five to.

'Aye, you'll be busy enough,' said Mrs. Walker when she answered the door. 'I hear on the wireless there was a mannie in the town found hoarding petrol.'

He was about to make a non-committal remark – Mrs. Walker was an excellent neighbour, but she could not resist an occasional prod for gossip – when she surprised him.

'Aye, a fellow in Rosemount. Has a wee watchmaker's there – I've taken my husband's old pocket watch to him in the past. You'd have thought butter wouldna melt, but there it is. Nice wee fellow, too. I'd no idea he even ran a motor.'

He headed off, the terriers at his heels as he walked up the road in the darkness, eyes straining to see anything of the familiar street. He needed to talk to the man in Loch Street, whatever his name was – Sutherland – and now to this new fellow in Rosemount. Were they freelance hoarders, as it were, or had they both also acted as – what, agents? Victims? – of Tommy Wilson? Or possibly of someone else at the same game, though Cattanach was not yet willing to think that there could be two racketeers competing on the same ground in the city at once. Aberdeen was, on the whole, a law-abiding city. Where had Tommy and Muckle Eck appeared from? Was it really Dundee? Stevie Tennant might be home-grown, but they were not.

He drew to a halt, letting the dogs nose about the grassy patch at the end of the road past the school. Letting thoughts nose around inside his head. Mabel's body lying under the brambles, her stockings torn, her make-up smudged, the almost empty handbag tossed in after her. How had she died? Who had actually killed her? All her moving and meeting and moving on, all her secrets and lies – all over. Would he ever find out who she really was?

45

ON SATURDAY MORNING he went into work at the usual time, not quite sure what was going to come in from Peterhead or from Rosemount and the new petrol case, but determined to be there when it did. He had a feeling that the knots of the whole affair were gradually easing out into a usable piece of rope, but the end was not in sight yet.

'You might want to see the fellow we have in custody, sir,' suggested the duty sergeant when he stopped at the front desk. 'It'd be like your man Lovie there.'

'It would indeed,' said Cattanach. 'What's his name?'

'Simpson, sir.'

He had heard of Simpson's, considered to be a reliable watchmaker and mender of the middle sort.

'I'll happily have a word.'

'Where did you get the petrol?' he asked Simpson. The man was small and wildly short-sighted, probably from years of peering into the workings of watches. Cattanach shuddered to think of him behind the wheel of a car. Simpson was shaking.

'From a garage,' he said, not looking anywhere near Cattanach.

'Which one?' The questions he had asked Lovie, too. Simpson's stash had not been so large: a neighbour, trying to find her cat on Thursday evening, had ventured up the lane beside Simpson's shop and wondered at the smell of the barrel by the back door. It was very like the set-up in Loch Street.

'I don't know, sir,' said Simpson miserably. 'I don't know anything about petrol, or motors. I just … I like clocks, sir.'

'Then what inspired you to make up a barrel of petrol and keep it behind your shop?' He waited. 'Whose idea was it, Mr. Simpson?'

'A man,' Simpson breathed, almost inaudibly. 'A nasty kind of a man.'

'What happened, Mr. Simpson?' Cattanach kept his own voice gentle, soothing. 'Did the man find out something you wanted kept quiet? Was that it?'

Simpson, after one shocked flash of a look at Cattanach's face, nodded.

'Did you know the man before?' He thought this might be an easier route than discovering Simpson's secret, for now, and probably more important. Simpson was shaking his head.

'No, sir. I'd never seen him before. But he seemed to know all about me. Though he had a lovely pocket watch …'

Cattanach could sense Simpson's disappointment that an unpleasant character should have a good watch, a kind of betrayal.

'That's interesting. What did he look like?'

'Very smart. Very well turned out, sir. A dark suit and tie, dark hair.'

'What line of work did you think he might be in?'

'Maybe a clerk, or a junior bank manager – a lawyer, maybe, even? Though I didn't think he was quite there. He asked if I could clean his watch, and then I filled in the receipt – he gave his name as Thomas Wilson, sir. And then, after everything, he said he knew – he knew about – about a lady I sometimes see. That I'm very fond of.'

'A married lady?'

Simpson nodded miserably.

'He just sort of mentioned her. And then … then he asked if I would look after a barrel for him, maybe behind the shop. He came back that night, sir, with a lorry and a big fellow, and they put the barrel in the yard, and I just sort of tried to forget it was there, sir.'

It seemed all too like Lovie's account not to be true. So Cattanach had been right: Wilson was more widely involved in hoarding than they had thought. Where else should they look?

He had noted down some dates and details, though doubtless these had already been taken. Simpson would be fined, calculated on how long he had had the petrol. Then a thought struck him.

'Can you describe the watch?'

'Of course, sir.' Simpson began on a lecture of extreme technical detail, of which Cattanach understood approximately a quarter. He listened politely, ready to learn something. Then he asked,

'Was there any inscription on it, at all?'

'Oh, yes, well, that's of minor importance,' said Simpson, much more confident now on his home ground.

'Do you remember it?'

'I think so. It was something like 'To T, from your Belle'.

The same as the anonymous victim of the tram accident. Another loop of the knot freed.

So.

He went to his office – mercifully free of Inspector Cochrane this weekend – and stood staring out through the window at the Saturday business of Lodge Walk, and the almost completed extension.

So Tommy Wilson had seen Billy Campbell at the petrol hoard at the Don mouth on the evening of Sunday, the third of September. Whatever he had done on the Monday, on Tuesday morning he boarded a tram, somewhere up Woodside, and was involved in the accident that rendered him unconscious and in hospital. An hour or so later, Billy Campbell was hit by another lorry, and killed. Tommy Wilson had an unshakeable alibi for a direct involvement in Billy's death – but he had two men who would undoubtedly be prepared to follow orders, Stevie Tennant and Muckle Eck. Tommy Wilson kept his head down and discharged himself from hospital on … he riffled through his memories of the past three weeks … on the Thursday, the seventh. So he could have appeared at Billy's funeral on Friday the eighth, the purpose being to frighten Mabel.

But was that his purpose? If he had only intended to frighten her, why would he then pursue her and kill her?

And why, after all, would she be frightened, so suddenly? Even if Billy had told her what he had seen, even if he had described the men he had seen in minute detail, would that really have caused that panic in Mabel? No, there had to be more to it than that.

Oh, Mabel, what was it? Why had he not found her in time?

Mabel Campbell, Mabel Christie. He suspected that Mabel was her real name, if she clung on to it like that. A common enough name, though. Mabel. Ma belle, my beautiful one.

Your Belle.

Mabel had known Tommy before. And whatever their relationship had been – cordial at the very least to start with – it had clearly turned sour. And Mabel had fled.

Knots loosening … He lifted the telephone receiver and asked to be put through to the inspector, Geddes, in Peterhead.

'Are you calling for any progress?' Geddes asked warily.

'No, not this early! No, I was calling to say that Robert Campbell should be on his way to you for the identification – I sent a car round for him. And it looks as if our man, who might or might not have been involved, knew Mabel of old.' He explained about the watch.

'And you think he's a racketeer?'

'We have another bit of petrol hoarding he's involved in. He can't have been keeping it all for his own use. He must have planned to sell it illicitly.'

'Sounds like it, for sure. Where's he getting it from?'

'Good question. That'll be the next thing.'

'Right, well, I'll leave you to it. If a'thing happens I'll let you know.'

'Thanks, Geddes.'

It was a question that Cattanach pondered for a few minutes, before thinking that he should probably complete his report on the matter of Sandison and the whisky before Sandison was removed, complete with broken leg, to Dundee. It was quiet enough in the station – though there was little sign of war yet people were still subdued and anxious, and it seemed that few were out to cause trouble, not on an autumnal Saturday morning. He wrote quickly and neatly, according to the formulas expected of him, and then took the time to type duplicate copies for Lieutenant Moffat and for Dundee. He rarely typed when Inspector Cochrane was in the room – it seemed to irk him.

The report finished, he sat back and considered. Outside the weather looked damp and fresh. He wondered if the laird was shooting today, if his father was out nodding at beaters and offering quiet words of advice to some of the guns. No use thinking about all that, and the wind and the dogs and the wide sky. Not here.

He would have to tell Anna Mackay about Mabel, he thought suddenly. At least it meant that Anna would not be attacked again, presumably, but she would be saddened, and possibly angry that they had not found Mabel in time. Two days too late. What had happened, anyway? Muckle Eck had attacked Anna on Tuesday night, trying to find out where Mabel was, and on Wednesday night Mabel was dead. How had they found her? The awful thought that it might just be coincidence, that someone else had killed Mabel while both the police and Tommy Wilson were looking for her was too dreadful to contemplate. How had they suddenly known where to go?

Anyway, he would not tell Anna Mackay about Mabel until after he had received official confirmation that it was in fact her. Where would Anna be on a Saturday? Out with friends? Playing golf? Shopping? He realised he had little idea of her beyond being a medical student. He could see no reason why that would change.

He spent some time catching up on memoranda, seeing how already some of the directives sent out in the first few days of the war were reversed. Schools were likely to reopen. There was talk of cinemas not staying closed, too. He had heard that one or two of the children evacuated from the town to the country, a couple of days before war had been declared, coming back already, homesick. He entertained a fleeting happy thought of evacuating the police force to the country, complete with their name labels around their necks, then quashed it. What he wanted just now was a telephone call from Peterhead.

It came, at last, at four o'clock.

'It's definitely her,' said Geddes, without much in the way of preamble. 'Mabel Campbell, or Christie.'

'How did Robert Campbell take it?'

'Philosophically,' said Geddes. 'I think he'd decided a whilie ago that he was no going to get her back.'

'Any sign of the two fellows I described to you? Wilson or Muckle Eck?'

'No yet. We're working on it. We've let Frank Fraser go, though.'

'Fair enough. I wonder if she tried picking anyone else up in that tea shop?'

'I dinna ken about that, but I have got something for you. You mind those nice big crisp fifty pound notes in her luggage?'

'I do indeed.'

'Well, in the course of our investigations – which as you well know, means something we came across by accident when we were thinking about something else – we found out that your Mrs. Campbell tried to change one of them. In the Commercial Bank on Broad Street, last Tuesday.'

'Tried to?'

'Aye, the manager was away for the day and the assistant manager's a cautious creature. He wasn't sure about the look of her in the context of a fifty pound note, and asked her to come back when the manager was there, the next day. She seemed a bit put out, and said she needed cash, but there was nothing he could do for her, so off she went.'

'Did she come back?'

'No, but it made me think. You'd said she had plenty of jewellery, and right enough, there was a fair bit on her and most of it good. So I took myself off to a couple of pawn shops, and in the second one I got her.'

'She'd popped some jewellery?'

'A brooch – gold, apparently. It was the pawnbroker's wife was affa keen to tell us all about it. The pawnbroker himself maybe not so much – he was looking daggers at his wife the whole time we were there.'

'Mabel Campbell was quite an attractive woman. Maybe the wife was getting her own back for the husband's attention to his customer.'

'Aye, maybe!' Geddes laughed. 'But see, what you might like to know is that yon pawnbroker is no frae round these parts.'

'Oh, aye?'

'No, he's frae Dundee. And he keeps up with his old pals, as it turns out. I took a wee look in his telephone book, and there was the name of Wilson, with a Dundee number crossed out. A common enough name, you might say, but I thought you'd like to know.'

Cattanach drummed his pencil on the desk, just briefly.

'And this was Tuesday?'

'Aye, lateish Tuesday. The shop was away to close, and she just got in in time. Listen, Cattanach, I'm dead sorry we dropped the ball on this one. We should have found her a week ago, when the thing came up in the *Police Gazette*. I've no excuses, only the damned war heaping paperwork on us like you wouldn't believe. Only you would, I should think, as you'll have the same.'

'We do. Look, can't be helped, Geddes. Thanks for all you're doing.'

A word or two more and the receiver went down, leaving Cattanach putting another piece in place.

A pawnbroker – could that fit in with jewellers, watchmakers and antique dealers? Part of Wilson's network? If so, could this pawnbroker, perhaps provided now with Wilson's Aberdeen address, have picked up the telephone on Tuesday evening, and told Tommy Wilson where to find Mabel Campbell?

46

ANOTHER TELEPHONE CALL, this time to Anna Mackay's home, provided the information that Miss Mackay was that afternoon paying a visit with other students to the Mental Hospital. Since Cattanach spoke with Mrs. Mackay, he was also provided with the information, unspoken, that she did not quite approve of her daughter visiting the Mental Hospital, and also that she had still not quite made up her mind about Cattanach himself: if he had not made it clear that his reasons for seeking Anna were entirely police business, he had a strong sense that she would not have told him at all.

The Mental Hospital, until not long ago the Lunatic Asylum, a little further into town than the Infirmary but also, in its day, built on the edge of the countryside, was on a generous site, with a mixture of tall grey buildings full of once stern wards, and newer residences on a smaller scale about the grounds. There was a back gateway as well as a front, but both were guarded by porters. Cattanach, at the front gate, took the opportunity to ask the porter where he thought the student visitors might be.

'Aye, well, if it's the students you're seeking, I was told they were going to be in the board room in the main building. But they should be due out soon. You canna keep students in for long on a Saturday, in my experience. Though with all the sports matches off, they might be less eager to get out.'

It was true: on the rare occasion when Cattanach was at home on a Saturday, his day tended to be enlivened by the many students, in shorts and rugby jerseys or cricket whites or carrying hockey sticks marching muddily up and down the road outside, but since the war restrictions had come in, the place was a good deal quieter. Memorising the porter's directions, Cattanach made for the main entrance door and had to explain himself to another porter there, who looked at him with a good deal more suspicion than the first one. In the end, though, Cattanach managed to persuade him that he was indeed a real police officer, and the porter informed him that the students were still in the boardroom but were expected out within the next quarter of an hour or so: if Cattanach chose (and the porter's tone implied that his opinion of Cattanach, already not very high, would not be helped if he did choose) – if Cattanch chose he could take a seat on a bench in the entrance hall, and wait for the students to appear.

Cattanach settled on the bench, resigned to the continued scrutiny of the porter. But the porter was busy enough, for it seemed that visiting hour was beginning, and a number of people had now turned up at the main door seeking admission to see various patients. Some looked furtive, or embarrassed. Some were weary or resigned, and one or two actually frightened. Cattanach leaned back, making himself unobtrusive, and watched them with interest. He had never ventured in here before, not even for work, and wanted to learn while he had the opportunity. One or two faces he vaguely recognised: Aberdeen was a smallish city, and he saw a good number of its inhabitants. Then, to his astonishment, a man came in whose face and name he knew very well indeed.

Inspector Cochrane, dressed a mile away from his usual style in a collarless shirt and a V-necked handknitted sweater, approached the reception desk, leaned in and clearly mentioned a name. His face, when he turned away again, was set and white. He walked past Cattanach without remotely seeing him – never a glance to left or right – and disappeared through double glazed doors along a corridor, and out of sight. Cattanach blinked. What had he just seen? Was Inspector Cochrane here on a case? But which one – and why was he so casually dressed?

'Inspector!' He heard his name spoken nearby, and rose at once to his feet, shaking all questions of Inspector Cochrane from his mind for now. It was Anna Mackay, letting her fellow students hurry past her to their Saturday afternoon freedom while she stopped and stared at him. Only one, a red-haired rugby forward with a watchful eye, stepped back towards her.

'Anna?' he said. 'All well?'

'All well, thank you, Matthew.'

The man paused, then nodded and went on, leaving them alone.

'One of my bodyguards,' she said with a smile. 'I think he's looking forward to a scrum. Are you by any chance waiting for me, Inspector?'

'I am, yes. But shall we leave the premises?'

'By all means, Mr. Cattanach. But you're quite safe here, you know.' The smile turned to a mischievous grin.

'I'm sure I am, yes,' he said, ushering her ahead of him through the main door. 'It's only – in my line of work we meet many different people, and I've just seen someone I know. I'd not like to disturb them.' It was true in all its facts: it perhaps created a slightly false impression, but no matter. It was none of Anna Mackay's business who he might have seen.

'Of course – pleas of unsound mind, and so on,' she said at once, well aware already of cases that might not be discussed. For a few moments they exchanged only perfunctory enquiries until they had reached the main gate, and walked out on to Westburn Road.

'I need a word, I'm afraid,' he said then. 'Would you prefer a stroll in Westburn Park, or perhaps if there's a café in Rosemount?'

She looked straight at him, assessing him. He thought she perhaps knew what he had come to say, already, and that was no bad thing.

'The park, I think,' she said, and began walking briskly towards it. Once inside, she selected the first unoccupied bench, and sat gracefully. Today her twinset was dark blue, and her skirt and coat a blue-green plaid, straight and smart, with a navy hat. Whether she had the training to be a doctor yet or not he did not know: he knew that she had the authority down pat.

'Well?' she asked.

'I have bad news, I'm afraid.'

'Mabel Campbell.'

'Yes. We were too late.' He explained, in minimal detail, following the clue she herself had discovered to Peterhead, and his theory about the information that had taken Tommy Wilson there two days faster.

'You think the pawnbroker called him?'

'It seems to be the circle he moves in. I have no proof yet, but the Peterhead police are working hard.' He did not mention their lapse in concentration earlier – there was no sense, at this stage, in placing blame. She sat for a moment in silence, and he wondered what she was thinking – did she blame him?

'How did she die?'

'They hadn't held the post mortem when the officer there called this morning. He might be able to call back this evening – I'll need to go back to the office.'

'And you're sure this man she – she picked up in the tea shop was not to blame?'

'I didn't think he was, and the police there have interviewed him and are pretty sure. He blames himself, of course, for not accompanying her.'

'Ah, well, Inspector, we all know that sometimes women walk along darkened streets for the most innocent of reasons, and sometimes it does not end well, don't we?'

'Indeed we do.' Victoria Park was only across the road from them: if he had not happened to be walking down the side of it, what might have happened to Anna that Tuesday night?

'Poor Mrs. Campbell,' she sighed. 'And her poor husband – the little boy and now his wife.'

'He has a good family about him,' he said. 'They'll look after him.'

'And – and the jeweller? Albert Lovie?'

'I think he'll get over it. He has other things on his mind.' He shifted to look at her. Her face was stony. 'Will you be all right? I'm sorry to be the bearer of such awful tidings.'

She turned, and smiled, and her face relaxed into courtesy.

'It is awful, yes. Though one cannot say one did not half-expect it, with everything that has happened. But thank you for coming to tell me, all the same. It would have been horrible to find out over the telephone, and I'm sure you're busy.'

He felt dismissed. She stood, too, and brushed down her coat, then put out a hand to be shaken. He took it dutifully, and watched her go, heading for Argyll Place and home. Her attack had left no lingering fears, then, or at least not by daylight. The park was bright, leaves just beginning to turn, catching the autumn sunlight.

Anna Mackay was a dark figure striding through yellow and green, walking away.

He gave himself a little shake, and wondered if there would be any news of the Peterhead post mortem yet, and tried not to imagine Mabel Campbell on the mortuary slab. He began to walk back towards the police station.

'A knife wound to the chest,' Inspector Geddes told him glumly, around five o'clock.

'Front or back? Cattanach was thinking again of Stevie Tennant.

'Front. Biggish blade, double-edged, removed – we've not seen a sign of it around the site.'

'Hm.' Someone had stabbed Stevie from behind, taking him by surprise. Mabel Campbell would have seen it coming, seen her attacker's face. He wondered if it had been the same knife, but they would only have an idea of that when they could properly compare the two reports. So far all he could say was that they sounded similar. 'Anything about the wound?'

'Wounds,' said Inspector Geddes. 'Aye, three of them. Two deflected by the ribs, so it seems it was the third one that killed her.'

Cattanach swallowed hard. So she had seen that, had she? Three blows, someone determined to destroy her. Had it hurt, or was the shock too much? She must have been terrified. Had she tried to argue? To defend herself?

'Defensive wounds?'

'Aye, there were marks on her gloves and her sleeves, right through.'

'It's a wonder nobody heard what was going on.'

'Well,' said Inspector Geddes, 'we reckon it happened down on the beach, and the murderer then shoved her up into the bushes, not dropping her down from above. The embankment there would have masked a lot of the sound, and anyway, the cottages along that road are quite wide apart. We've asked all the people along there, and no one says they heard anything. Nor saw anything. But after dark, these days, that's not exactly unusual, is it? Or it isna up here – maybe in the big smoke you've still people coming and going all hours.'

'Not so much,' Cattanach admitted. 'So they must have lured

her, or taken her, down on to the beach. I doubt a woman going out for dinner would choose to walk along there.'

'Aye, that was what I thought, an' all. You still reckon it's this Tommy Wilson and his pal?'

'I think so, yes. Though … well, the other victim, if they killed him too, he was killed much more professionally.' He explained about the neat single stab wound, horizontal between the ribs. And then he added his thoughts about Tommy and his Belle. There was silence for a moment from Geddes.

'I see, I think,' he said. 'Your idea is that the first one was business, but this was more like a crime of passion?'

'That's what I'm wondering. Otherwise I can't see why Tommy Wilson would pursue the mother of the boy who saw him, as well as the boy himself.'

'If it was him at all.'

'If indeed. Have you come across any sightings of him? Or Muckle Eck?'

'None yet. You?'

'Not since last Tuesday evening, no.'

'Well,' said Geddes, 'they have to be somewhere. I doubt the pair of them have done us all a favour and thrown themselves into the sea. But I suppose they could have moved on by now. You've no idea where they came from?'

'South, is my best bet. Possibly Dundee. But Tommy Wilson has invested quite a bit in his petrol hoarding in Aberdeen. We've found three so far, and I suspect that's just the unlucky ones. There'll be more, and he's not going to abandon that.'

'Then where is he? How are you going to find him? I mean, we'll keep looking here, a' course. Nothing else to do,' he added, wearily.

'You do that. But there must be more here. They must have stayed somewhere.' Somewhere in Woodside, perhaps? Otherwise why had Tommy Wilson been on the tram that morning? But Stevie Tennant and Muckle Eck had not. Woodside … 'I'll find them,' he said, as much to himself as to Geddes. 'I'll find them.'

47

'WAS THAT PETERHEAD?'

Cattanach jumped as he put the telephone down. Lieutenant Moffat's head poked round the office door.

'It was, sir, yes.'

'Good to see they're working on a Saturday. Not sure they've worked any other day this week.'

'He did apologise, sir. Swamped with war stuff.'

'Aye, well, I suppose. Any news?'

'Cause of death, sir, and a possible way that Tommy Wilson might have found Mabel Campbell before we did.' He explained about the pawnbroker, and the post mortem results.

'So you're still working on the idea that it was Tommy Wilson who killed her? Is that not a bit of a leap?'

'There's his watch, sir. The inscription that Tommy Wilson had on the watch he gave in to the Rosemount watchmaker for cleaning matches the inscription on the watch belonging to the man knocked cold in the Woodside tram crash. It's marked "To T from your Belle.' He spelled it for clarity. 'I think that might be a pun, if that's the right word, on Mabel. *Ma belle.*'

'If the villains start speaking French I think it's time I retired,' said the Lieutenant. 'Right, well, if Peterhead get anyone who saw a couple of fellows matching the descriptions of Wilson and Muckle Eck, it's more than worth getting them in.'

'We want them on the petrol hoarding, anyway, sir.'

'And have we any place to start looking?'

'I suppose Woodside might be a possibility, sir. After all, witnesses place Wilson on the tram that morning, before the accident.'

'Then best get – is Constable Leggatt back on the beat?'

'I think he's to start on Monday, sir.'

'Fine. He's a thorough man. He can make enquiries, but he'll probably need help there, too. I'll sort it out.'

'Yes … And then there's the petrol angle, I suppose. Where else is he storing it?'

'Good. Two angles are always better than one. How is Miss Mackay, by the way? Have you told her about Mabel Campbell?'

'I have, yes. Sir – I went to find her at the Mental Hospital because she was at a class there, and I happened to see Inspector Cochrane go in. Is he investigating something there?'

'Hasn't he said?'

'No, sir. He doesn't say much about what he's doing.'

Moffat mulled something over briefly, eyes on the window, then found the words.

'His wife's been taken in. If he's been behaving oddly lately, that's probably why. Not a happy situation. Very difficult, in fact. I've been keeping him on, well, lighter duties, just in case.'

'I see, sir. I'll bear it in mind.'

'Aye, well. Keep hunting for Wilson and Muckle Eck. That's the thing.'

Cattanach held out very little hope for the Woodside angle, he realised, when Moffat had gone. No one had recognised Wilson on the tram, so he was presumably not a regular. No, the petrol angle seemed more promising, and at this point more likely to lead to a conviction.

But how could they trace where else Tommy Wilson was hoarding petrol? Lovie had never heard of any other men in his position, and nor had silly Mr. Sutherland in Loch Street. They could hardly go round the rest of the jewellers and antique dealers in the town, asking them if they were hoarding motor spirit. Nor did they have the manpower to watch them all – and that was even assuming that Wilson used the same kind of man each time.

He drummed his fingers on the desk, staring out at the backs of buildings, granite precipices blocking the sky. Hills … he wished he were out of the town, up a hill somewhere, his tent pitched for the night, his stove lit for a cup of coffee. He closed his eyes, conjuring up the smell of heather and gorse and peaty water, the feel of springy turf under his boots, the cry of the birds above him. When would he be able to get out again? Next week? It felt like a month since he had come back on the train from Oyne, back from his weekend on Bennachie.

If they could work out where Tommy Wilson was acquiring the petrol, they could go to the other end of the supply chain and find him there. But where could that be? And now that petrol was actually finally rationed, was he going to change his means of supply? Had Lovie been right, even accidentally, when he pretended he had bought extra cans of petrol from several different garages? Even if so, Tommy Wilson would not be able to do that now. Did he have enough hoarded petrol for his plans? In Cattanach's experience, no criminal ever thought they had enough. Many of them were caught simply because they had no idea when to stop.

He wondered how Inspector Cochrane was spending his weekend. What were visiting hours like at the Mental Hospital? He had no idea. The place had changed so much over the years: it looked a pleasant place now, with some of the patients house in little pavilions in smaller groups, not in great grim wards. Different ideas of how to treat the disturbed – there used, he had heard, to be a farm for the asylum, where patients could in theory subdue their mental distress with good physical labour, and provide food for the hospital at the same time.

Farms … Somewhere in his head, something clicked into place like a cog tooth that had been misplaced. Farms. Farmers with tractors. Agricultural fuel was not yet rationed, because of the harvest – might never be rationed like ordinary petrol. Now, there was something else … what else had he been thinking about? Mental cases, asylums … Inspector Cochrane … spending weekends doing what? Spending weekends walking on Bennachie, taking the train to Oyne … taking the train back from Oyne … he had got it.

From the train last Sunday, he had seen that farm steading. The two men, and the lorry with barrels. What could be in those barrels? Could it possibly, possibly, be petrol intended for Aberdeen?

He closed his eyes again, pressing on his memory. He knew he could conjure it up again if he focussed hard. Oyne ... leaving the station, the farm there after a few minutes down on his left, the north side of the line. The road was near the line there. The train, slowing slightly, and – was there a lamp of some kind in the farmyard? There must have been something, contravening the blackout, for he could see the yard framed in his mind. A small lorry to the left, tilted slightly – there must have been a bit of a slope to the yard. Two men he had thought were farmhands lifting metal barrels into the back – one of them, he thought, was struggling a bit, finding the load a heavy one. The other, the man with his back to him, was big, though, and seemed to lift the barrel effortlessly, swinging it up and in. The struggling man definitely had a country look to him, but the other – he was not so sure. All he could really see was a dark coat and trousers, and a hat, dark too, perched on the back of the man's head. He scanned over the image in his head, looking for the other characters on this little stage. There: the farmer, no doubt, in long boots and a flat cap with grey hair curling out from the sides, hands deep in his pockets, fitting into the farmyard as if he belonged there, which he probably did. But beside him, the man Cattanach had immediately thought of as a tounser, not a country man. Why? He had been smaller than the farmer – not really relevant – but smartly dressed, in Cattanach's memory. He was wearing a dark suit, white shirt and a dark tie, hat neatly on his head. Cattanach had dismissed him as perhaps the lorry's driver, but now that he thought about it, the man looked more like a well-paid clerk. Smart. Could it possibly be that Cattanach had actually seen Tommy Wilson?

He set that possibility firmly to the back of his mind, but the general idea was a good one. If anyone was trying to hoard petrol in Aberdeen, agricultural fuel was probably a very good bet. But in that case, he would have to talk to Lieutenant Moffat: it was time to liaise with the County force again.

'He's certainly a man who works to a pattern,' Moffat agreed, leaning back in his chair. 'Find a certain kind of tradesman – maybe we should say 'merchant' – then find out something about them that can be used.'

'I think with our man in Loch Street it was pure greed, sir,' said Cattanach. 'But yes, all the ones we've found so far have been very, well, couthy. I wonder if Stevie Tennant gave Wilson the local gossip? His father said he was interested in people, and there were the remains of a notebook in his pocket.'

'So Stevie gave Wilson the means of blackmail, but we don't have Stevie's list. And sadly, when we've found the hoarders, it's been accidental, hasn't it? So as you say, our chances of rounding them up are slim.'

'That's why I thought going to the source might be the answer, sir. If we can find the source.'

'I take your point about agricultural fuel, Inspector. But the county's a big place, with a gey lot of farmers. And that's just to the north and the west – there's Kincardineshire, too, to the south, and plenty farmers there.'

'That's where local expertise comes in. They'll know who might be likely, or where there's been suspicious activity, won't they?'

'Well … I'll give it a go. It might take a whilie, though.'

'I know, sir. Thank you.'

'There's something more, then, is there, Inspector?'

Cattanach reflected, once again, on what he had seen from the train. How could he be sure, when he had never knowingly seen Tommy Wilson, or even Muckle Eck very clearly? All he could say about Muckle Eck was that the man in the farmyard, with his back to Cattanach and wearing a hat, could have been the man he had struggled with briefly by Victoria Park the night Anna Mackay had been attacked – there were no obvious differences. Should he even mention it? It could be an unnecessary distraction from the real source of the petrol. Though, if it had not been petrol in those heavy barrels, what had it been?

'Well, sir … it's vague.' And he described the scene.

'You're right,' said Moffat, 'that's remarkably vague. Do you want the County police to look there first, based on that?'

'Not really, sir. No, it was just – you know, an image that lingers.'

Lieutenant Moffat frowned.

'Why don't I mention to the County force that we've had a tip-off – nothing too definite – in the area of … should we say maybe Insch to Inverurie? Along that road? Garioch or thereabouts. That way we're not leading the witness, if you like, but if anything was going on there we might get to it sooner. How does that sound?'

'That sounds like a good idea, sir. Thank you.'

Moffat nodded, settled on his plan.

'I want to get these fools before something else catches fire. They were lucky in Loch Street – next time it might not be so good. No point in going to war with Germany, and then blowing ourselves up, is there?'

There was nothing to do now other than wait. How much the county force might do on the Sabbath he was not sure – there was no word from them, at any rate – but on Monday morning Cattanach returned to his desk and took out the Post Office Directory, turning to the trades section.

'What are you doing?' asked Inspector Cochrane, who regarded the reference books in their shared office very much as his own domain.

'Looking at lists. Jewellers, watchmakers, antique and curio dealers, that kind of thing.'

'I hope you aren't thinking of buying a ring,' said Inspector Cochrane, in what Cattanach hoped he thought would pass for humour.

'It's for a case.' He sighed. He had grown out of the habit of sharing any thoughts with Inspector Cochrane: it was like sharing them with an empty corned beef tin. 'The fuel hoarding. We're working on the theory that the hoarders are connected, and the ones we have so far are, well, a jeweller, an antiques dealer, and a watchmaker.'

'How very interesting!' said Inspector Cochrane. For a glorious moment, Cattanach thought his colleague was about to come out with some astonishing revelation, or vital inspiration. He waited, holding his breath. But nothing came.

48

HE HAD SPENT an hour or so plotting the various jewellers, watchmakers, and related trades, on a rough sketch map that also showed the beats that might cover them. It might be most efficient to have the local constable take look first and report back, bearing in mind that in only two out of their three hoarders so far had the petrol actually been on their premises. He made a list of constables he would need to talk to, and a note of what he should tell the sergeant giving them their daily briefing – he had started early, and he should be in good time if he headed down to the muster room now.

He returned to his office as quickly as he could, and found Inspector Cochrane on the telephone.

'Oh, aye, indeed. Is that a fact? My, my.' Inspector Cochrane's ponderous tones could make any conversation sound dull. Cattanach, reminding himself to be sympathetic, wondered about his wife. There were many kinds of madness, he knew. What kind was this? The ungenerous thought crept into his head that either Inspector Cochrane had driven her mad, or she was faking it to get away from him. Not the latter, surely. Even Inspector Cochrane could surely not drive a woman to that length of desperation.

'Oh, did he? Did he indeed? Oh, he's a gey busy man, aye, he's that all right. Rarely in the office, to be quite honest with you. Aye, aye. Well, you're in luck, though, because he's just not that long walked in. Do you still want a wee word with him? Aye, right you are, I'll pass you over. Inspector, here's a mannie from the

County Police wants a news with you, aye?'

Struggling to keep his face straight, Cattanach took the receiver from Inspector Cochrane.

'Good morning, Cattanach here.'

'Oh, good morning, there, Jim Middleton here, inspector at Inverurie. I'm sorry to interrupt your busy day …'

'I'm delighted to hear from you. Is this about petrol, by any chance?'

'It is, it is. You ken, your boss talking to my boss, and then there was that wee extra thing to see if it helped to narrow down the search. That's the thing.'

'And had you any luck?' Cattanach tried to breathe normally, but he could feel his pulse speed up. No, he told himself, surely it was nothing. If it was anything exciting, surely Inspector Cochrane would have handed the receiver over faster.

'Aye, well, no so much luck as good steady policing, you ken?'

'Luck on my part, then, that I should happen to be looking for something you've already found!'

'Aye,' laughed Middleton, 'that's more like it! Well, there's a fellow we're interested in near Oyne – do you ken the place?'

'A little, yes.' Was it the same place? Oyne would be surrounded by farms, of course.

'An old farmer who's not that keen on company, but his neighbours say there's been a deal of coming and going there this last couple of months.'

'So not just harvest, then?'

'A City polis that's heard of the hairst! My. No, not just harvest. The neighbours are all farmers an' all – they'd know what was usual and what wasn't.'

'Do you think it could be something illicit?'

'That's our thought, anyway. So yesterday, when we got your message, well, this fellow's name was at the top of our list, and we sent a couple of fellows round – without benefit of uniform – yesterday evening when it was a bittie darker. They say there are a couple of men staying there just now, and they don't look like long-lost sons or billeted soldiers. They've a lorry. I'd say it's worth taking a closer look – maybe this evening, before they decide to move on?'

'Would you like the company of a few ignorant but willing tounsers?'

'Have you a couple of cars would be ready to go at short notice, at all? Our boss says it's fine and your boss has already offered, so everything's agreed among the high heidyins.'

'Well, then, all we can do is obey, I should think,' said Cattanach. 'We'll try not to get in your way.'

'It'd be later on today. If you could be ready maybe the back of five?'

They made tentative arrangements, and Cattanach promised to confirm them once everything was in place. He liked the sound of Middleton, and looked forward to meeting him. He ended the call, and returned to his desk, ignoring the fact that Inspector Cochrane had watched him intently through the call and clearly wanted to hear the whole story. In Cattanach's view the story was not yet complete.

The day passed slowly, with occasional flashes of interest. Two constables had found a suspicious quantity of fuel behind two shops in the city, one a jeweller's and the other an antique dealer's barely a step up from a junk shop. Both traders were brought in for questioning, and one readily gave descriptions that matched Tommy Wilson and Muckle Eck. The other, the junk shop owner, seemed to have been acting on his own initiative, and was quickly fined and released.

At five, after a quick call to Inspector Middleton, Cattanach took Constable Gauld in one car, and a sergeant and constable in the other, and headed out to the north-west once again, along the road towards Inverness and Inverurie and Oyne. In Woodside, at the busy Haudagain junction where the lorry had hit the tram that dreadful morning, almost three weeks ago, they pulled in at the side of the road where Constable Leggat was waiting, his bicycle propped against a police call box. He saluted smartly when Cattanach climbed out of the car, clearly delighted to be back on duty at last.

'Belt and braces, Constable, I'm afraid,' Cattanach said with a smile. 'Is everything in order?'

'Yes, sir. Well, it's hard to tell from this end with the bicycle receiver, and to be honest sometimes you're as likely to get a call from Glasgow as from Aberdeen, sir, but the call box is all fine – I tried it five minutes ago.'

'Good, thanks. I suppose in that case all we can do now is wait.'

But they did not have to wait for long. The bicycle, with its blackout-shielded lights and shiny saddle, had a small box strapped just over the back wheel, from which more wires than were necessary on an average bike ran along the frame. Ten minutes later there was a buzz from the contraption, and Constable Leggat, at a nod from Cattanach, lifted a small receiver from the box.

'That's the message through from Inverurie, sir,' he said at once. 'They're ready.'

'Then send a message back to say we're off,' said Cattanach. 'We'll be with them as soon as we can.'

'As far as we can see,' said Inspector Middleton, pointing on a map, 'there are still barrels in the yard, and a truck – a smallish one. No one about, but we think they're in there, in the farmhouse. There's a possibility they'll shift under cover of darkness, so we thought it best to go in tonight, just when it's properly dark.'

'What do you know about the farmer?'

'No' the friendly sort. Lives on his own there and seems to like it that way: casual visitors are not welcome. I think the place has barely changed since his father's time, maybe his grandfather's. Except only the lads in the bothy are always changing, never stick him for long.'

'Harvest all in? Will they be working up to dusk?'

'No, they finished two days ago, I'm told. I dinna think any of the lads is of interest to us, but we could bring them in for a wee word, see if they ken a'thing.'

'Dogs?'

'One, elderly, not thought to be a threat. There's a single track up to the farm, but then it splits in two and the steading has two entrances. We've men up there watching the place - they'll go straight to the house when they hear us coming, stop anyone getting out that way. We'll put a car across each of them, though I doubt they'd get the lorry through the far one. Then get the men out and spread about, catch a'body trying for a run.'

'You want help with that, then?'

'Aye, that'd be grand. Just hand them over when you've caught them, eh?'

'Happy to.'

The County man gave the sky an assessing look.

'I think it might be time to go. If we leave now, we'll get there just in time that we can still see something without torches. You see well at night?'

'Not badly.'

'Grand. Let's go.'

The county cars led the way, and when they had set off Cattanach followed, glancing back to make sure the other city car was behind them.

The luminous figures on the mileometer were starting to shimmer into life. Cattanach glanced down and just at the mile point he saw the car ahead slow for a right hand turn. In a moment they were all in the lane, dykes and hedges close enough to touch on each side. The farm buildings were a dark hulk not that far ahead, as far as he could judge. Inspector Middleton's description had been closely accurate so far.

The county cars, slipping ahead in the darkness, disappeared to left and right, but anyone on the premises would surely by now have heard the four motors approaching. Cattanach felt his heart accelerate a little as he pulled up just clear enough of the lane's head to let the other City car squeeze through behind him. As soon as the car was stationary he was out, Constable Gauld only a second after him. All four engines died, and for a moment the silence surged around them. Then they heard running footsteps. Fugitives, or officers running to form a barrier? He knew he should stay out of the way of the County men, but he edged around the stopped cars, trying to get a view into the farmyard. He gave a little grunt of surprised satisfaction when he saw that it was indeed the yard he had seen from the train. A typical steading, with one arched entrance through the buildings forming a kind of stone passage five or six yards long, wide enough for any farm vehicle.

It took him a moment to realise that the reason he could see that clearly was that the lorry parked in the yard had its headlights full on, and another lamp was shining high on a wall. They lit a cramped tableau in the centre of the yard, not that different from the scene he remembered from a week ago. Several metal barrels stood over to one side, the lorry was near the far wall, poised to go, perhaps, to squeeze past the barrels to the gate, and in the centre, almost behind the barrels, were four men and an elderly dog. He recognised the farmer, in his shabby tweeds with his shotgun – a museum piece, from what Cattanach could see – broken under his arm, his other hand already reaching for it. A farmhand looked as if he would rather be anywhere else in the world, his arms folded across his chest in self-defence. The nearest to the lorry was a big fair haired fellow in a dark suit, the cheap fabric stretched over taut muscles. And the fourth, standing close to the farmer, his white shirt crisply catching the light, his black hair neat – it had to be Tommy Wilson.

For half a second, no one moved. With the lights on them, the four in the yard must have had to squint to see what was happening out in the lane. Then Inspector Middleton stepped out on to the stage from the darkness, framed in the gateway, and everything happened at once.

'Nobody move, please,' called Middleton authoritatively.

But Tommy Wilson did not obey orders. He snatched at the farmer's shotgun, snapping it shut with an echoing click. The farmer cried out, reaching a hand as if to grab the stock even as Tommy Wilson raised it to his shoulder, aiming it at Inspector Middleton. The farmhand vanished behind the barrels. The dog, so unsteady looking a moment ago, was gone. And Tommy Wilson pulled the trigger.

Not an experienced shot, thought some distant part of Cattanach's mind. Snatching the trigger like that.

The pellets sprayed high and left. A cry came from a constable half in the darkness. The big man by the lorry swore. Inspector Middleton was on the ground. And a little trio of sparks, thrown from the ancient firearm, drew a delicate arch through the air, and fell on the nearest barrel.

49

THE AIR WAS beaten flat by a double explosion.

The flash burned into Cattanach's eyes an image of three men on the ground in the yard, fire leaping from the ruins of two barrels, Inspector Middleton struggling to get to his feet in the yard's gateway. Cattanach ran towards him, crouching down.

'Stay down!' he bellowed, but he could barely hear himself. 'There were three barrels!'

But the drain down the cobbled yard led straight towards them, and now it was a little river of flame as the petrol ran and burned at once. Both men scrambled clear. The heat was tremendous.

'Push the cars away!' Middleton bellowed, waving his arms. Cattanach tried to keep track of what was happening in the yard.

The largest man on the ground hauled his great bulk to his knees, lurching and crawling as fast as he could towards the lorry. Glowing debris thudded about him, and maybe that made him think twice. He spun awkwardly on his knees and began to head towards the gate and the two inspectors. The other two men had not moved. A line of police officers, broken up by the blast but now reforming, stood ready at both gates to the yard, eyeing the fire warily, eyeing the victims with even more caution. Cattanach saw Gil Gauld among them, and the other City men, and prayed they'd get home safely tonight.

The hot air stank with burning petrol. Middleton sat up warily, but at that moment the third barrel seemed to fold in on itself as flames shot skyward like flags in a strong wind. Cattanach shook his head sharply, trying to clear it. Middleton was mouthing something at him, but he had no idea what it was. He seemed uninjured. Cattanach remembered hearing one of the constables yelp when the shotgun was fired, but he had no idea where the man was.

Muckle Eck had stopped, but he was still on the ground, maybe trying to catch his breath after the last explosion. Then he straightened, up on his knees, holding something long in his hands, turning it to point it in their direction. It was the shotgun.

'Let me get away, or I'll shoot!' he cried, his voice wildly unsteady. The gun swayed: there was no telling what he might hit. Instinctively, every policeman ducked, and Muckle Eck gave a desperate grin, teeth glinting red.

Except that the shotgun was a single-barrelled type, and Tommy Wilson had fired the one cartridge in it.

'Come on, now, Eck,' Cattanach shouted back. 'There's no sense in that.'

'You ken who I am?' came the puzzled reply. He still seemed to be whispering, but gradually Cattanach could feel his ears begin to work again. The roar of flames grew louder.

'Of course we do,' shouted Middleton, pulling himself to his feet by the stonework of the gatepost. 'Now, come on out of this, before the whole place goes up.'

'Where's the farmhand?' Cattanach asked.

'He was behind the barrels. Be careful!' Middleton raised a hand as if to stop him, then stepped forward himself to bar the way for Muckle Eck. Cattanach, as he passed, saw the moment when Eck considered fighting, just before the spirit went out of him and he admitted defeat.

But Cattanach was already halfway up the yard, coat collar pulled up to shield his face from the heat of the fire. He reached the farmer first, thrown forward on to the cobbles. If he was not already dead he would be very shortly: one arm had been ripped off, trailing bright red blood that glinted in the firelight. A jagged slice of barrel had hacked into his chest. Cattanach left him and cautiously rounded the fire, only to see what was left of the farmhand thrown against the wall of the farm building, entangled in what looked like a rusty harrow. Two dead. What about Tommy Wilson?

He had kept Tommy Wilson at least at the corner of his eye

as he checked the others, and now he approached the final body with even more care. The blast had thrown him sideways, half-rolled him, and knocked him out. There was no other sign of injury. Cattanach needed to move fast: the fire must have caught the wooden rafters, and broken slates like knife blades were being hurled into the air, smashing on the cobbles. leaned down towards him, and looked for a pulse. It was there, and even as he moved his hand away, Wilson shifted, groaned, tried to sit up and gasped.

'This one will need an ambulance,' Cattanach shouted. 'Are you fit to move, sir? We need to get away from this fire.'

'The ambulance is supposed to be on its way,' Middleton called over. Cattanach could just hear him. 'It should have been just behind us. We didn't think of a fire engine, though,' he added ruefully.

Tommy Wilson was trying to get up. He sagged for a moment, coughed, then gave a scream of pain.

'Ribs?' asked Cattanach, almost sympathetic. 'Come on – let's get you out of here, anyway.' He shoved a hand under Wilson's arm, and helped him to his feet, Wilson breathing noisily with every move. 'There's a man over here would very much like to arrest you. I think he's been practising on your friend Muckle Eck.'

It was hard to tell if Tommy was scowling at the pain or at him, but the flames helped him to move, maddeningly slowly. Cattanach thought his face would melt before they reached the gateway. Every breath seemed to hurt – and he was painfully aware of the lorry, waiting in the yard behind them, ready to blow. It seemed a lifetime before he and Wilson fell past the gatepost, Wilson staggering and falling to the ground again. Cattanach knelt beside him, stupidly grateful for the damp earth under his knees.

He looked about, trying to take stock. Inspector Middleton was issuing instructions to his men. One constable was propped against the police car, a handkerchief clutched scarlet to his cheek, presumably the one who had caught the pellet from Wilson's ill-fated shot. A distant bell seemed to be nearing now, and the constable sighed in relief.

'Ambulance, sir,' he said. Middleton nodded his thanks, saw Muckle Eck folded into a police car, and turned his attention to Wilson.

'I'm arresting you for attempted murder of a policeman, and

for motor spirit hoarding with a possible view to racketeering – though what evidence there might be left for that one after your idiotic bit with the gun is a'body's guess. What did you think you were doing, you fool? I'll think up some more charges when my head's stopped ringing, but if I could have you charged with gross stupidity I think the judge would just wave it through on the evidence. You're a bloody dunderhead.'

Cattanach almost wanted to laugh as Inspector Middleton instructed a constable to take Wilson to the ambulance, and guard him until relieved. But there was a nasty look in Wilson's eyes, even as he clutched his broken ribs, that said he was not accustomed to people calling him stupid, and was unlikely to tolerate it. But then the look faded, and a baffled expression replaced it. He stopped, though the constable had a firm hold of him.

'Where's Mabel?' he said, and he sounded genuinely confused.

'Mabel?' asked Middleton. 'Who's Mabel?'

Cattanach opened his mouth to tell him, but Wilson was becoming agitated.

'Where's Mabel? Where's she gone? Is she all right?'

One of the ambulancemen hurried over, seeing Wilson's state.

'Did he pass out?' he asked. 'Or hit his head?'

'Probably,' said Cattanach. 'The blast caught him and he was unconscious when I found him.'

'Come on, now, son, let's get you into the ambulance,' said the man. 'He's concussed, I reckon. His eyes look bad.'

'That would be the second time in three weeks, then,' said Cattanach, and the ambulanceman turned to look at him.

'The second time? How long was he out for before?'

'We're not sure,' said Cattanach, taken by surprise, 'but a couple of days, probably.'

'A couple of days?' The ambulanceman looked not only alarmed, but also disapproving.

'He was in the hospital,' said Cattanach, sure he was going to be blamed for mistreating Wilson.

'It's not going to help,' said the ambulanceman sourly. 'Who knows how it might affect him?'

'Where's Mabel?' Wilson demanded. 'Where is she?'

'Is she around?' asked the ambulanceman, but Middleton shook his head.

'No Mabel here.'

'Come away over here with me, son,' said the ambulanceman. 'Maybe she's over here somewhere. Will we go and see?'

Both of them ignoring the large constable with his hand firmly on Wilson's arm, the ambulanceman led Tommy Wilson over to the ambulance, and packed him gently inside with the injured constable. They remained long enough only for the ambulanceman to return and take a quick assessment of Muckle Eck, then the doors closed on the strange, greenish interior, darkness returned, and the ambulance disappeared into the night.

'I've sent one of the men to call the fire brigade, too,' Middleton told Cattanach. 'My sergeant can take yon big yin in the car back to Inverurie, and get him organised. I'd better stay here. Do you want to come back again in the morning and sit in while we question the fellow? Who knows, by then we might have the wee one back, an' all.'

'Not the farmer and the farmhand, though,' said Cattanach sadly, looking back at the farmyard and the body of the farmer, still lying in the flickering light from the burning steading. In fact there had not been so much for the fire to take hold of, it seemed, and it was already beginning to die out. The County photographers were hovering at the edges of the scene, contemplating light levels and comparative risks, and muttering to each other about the effect of heat on film. A mortuary van was also expected to come and collect them, when the experts had finished with the miserable scene.

'Ah, go on home, Cattanach,' said Middleton. 'I'll see you in the morning. Thanks for your help.'

'Wait,' said Cattanach, and stepped over to the shadow of the steading wall. A furry bundle lay there, pressed into the corner where wall met earth. Cattanach felt for the old dog's nose and ears, then tugged gently on his collar. The dog shifted, and came warily out into the light. He did not seem to be wounded.

'Found yourself a pal, have you?' asked Middleton. 'Well – you couldn't take him away with you just now, could you? It'd be one thing off my plate. We could let you know if a'body claims him – or the fleas that are on him, no doubt.'

'I can do that,' said Cattanach, 'if he'll come.' But the old dog must have assessed the situation as quickly as he had fled from the flames. He went easily with Cattanach to the city car, and hauled himself in when invited.

They left the police vehicles at the police station, and Cattanach shook hands with each of the City men before saying good night. The smell of burned petrol was in his nose and mouth, and lingered nastily in his clothes and hair: he was sure they all felt the same.

He walked home slowly in the darkness, the dog on a length of string at his heel. It would not be a hot water night, he remembered: he would have to boil the kettle a few times, possibly for both of them. Images of the farmer, the farmhand, Muckle Eck's defeat, Tommy Wilson's switch from unpleasant to confused, spun in turn in his mind's eye. That switch – how genuine had that been? Two bouts of concussion in three weeks was not going to be good for anyone, but had Wilson just taken the opportunity to pretend he was unwell?

But then, he had mentioned Mabel. And until that moment, they had had no firm proof that he knew anyone of that name. He could have denied it, and they would have been struggling to prove it.

He let himself in to his terraced house, and went about thoughtfully, closing the curtains, before lighting the stove and setting his first kettle to boil. The dog sniffed warily around the kitchen, not straying too far from Cattanach's ankles. He found a tin of meat and a bowl of water, setting them on the floor not far from the stove. Everything was coated with the beginnings of an autumnal chill, and it was going to take a while – in fact, he thought, it would probably be weeks before he really felt he had soaked the smoke away. He left the kettle to warm up, found a rug for the dog, and went to the telephone in the hall. It was late, but then it was police business, and the man was acting as the Casualty Surgeon. He had to expect calls at odd hours.

'Dr. Mackay?' he asked.

'Mackay here.'

'Sorry to disturb you at a late hour, sir,' Cattanach said at once. 'It's Alec Cattanach here. We've just arrested a man and I need a quick opinion on something.'

'Where is he?'

'He's in Inverurie. I don't need you to come and see him: I'd just like to ask something about concussion.'

'His or yours?' asked Mackay, without emotion.

'His. Three weeks ago, near enough, this man was knocked cold, and appeared to have been unconscious for about forty-eight hours.'

'Appeared? Was he not in medical care?'

'He was. He was unconscious at the Infirmary, and the next thing they knew he had picked himself up, dressed, and discharged himself. Anna – Miss Mackay knows about him, I believe.'

'Is this the man who was knocked out at the tram crash in Woodside?'

'Yes, sir. We've now arrested him, after he was knocked out in an explosion.'

'An explosion? Good Lord.' There was a long silence. 'Do you mean, um, enemy action?'

'Not exactly, sir. An illicit fuel store.'

'Right. I see. Right. So,' Dr. Mackay seemed to pull himself back to the matter in hand. 'The man was knocked out in the explosion.'

'He was thrown across a farmyard, sir.'

'How long was he out this time?'

Cattanach reflected. Time had moved oddly at that Oyne farm.

'No more than five minutes, I think.'

'Still … What do you want to know?'

'First, will the effects be worse if he's concussed twice in quick succession like that?'

'They could well be. It can take a good deal longer to recover from concussion than we realise.'

'Thank you, sir. And the second thing is – could someone concussed appear quite unaffected at first, and only then seem muddled?'

'Oh, yes, of course. Yes, that can happen.'

'And if he's muddled, but gives us information that is actually helpful – do you think that would be admissable in court?'

'You mean if he inadvertently admits something …'

'Not quite admitting, sir, not to a crime. Admitting to knowing someone, demonstrating an acquaintance that we had not yet managed to prove.'

'I see. I'm not sure, Inspector. I think you'd have to talk to the Procurator Fiscal about that one.'

'Oh. Well, I suppose that makes sense, sir. Sorry to have taken up your time.'

'That's perfectly all right, Inspector. I hope you find what you're looking for.'

So do I, thought Cattanach, as he ended the call. Because what I'm looking for is proof.

50

TUESDAY, AND THE early train to Inverurie. Three weeks ago this morning, Tommy Wilson boarded a tram in Woodside, and spent the next two days in the Infirmary. Three weeks ago this morning, Billy Campbell headed out on to King Street on a busy footpath, and fell in front of a lorry.

The dog was with Mrs. Walker for the day, contentedly lying with her terriers by the kitchen stove. But Cattanach was heading back.

Woodside and Dyce chugged past now in the autumn morning, mist lingering over allotments and airfield, and over the low curves of the River Don, sweeping slowly through the pastureland on the approach to Port Elphinstone. Here you could see where the old canal had been, before the railway came along. Cattanach was nearly at Inverurie and he had not managed to focus his mind on Tommy Wilson or Muckle Eck at all. Inspector Jim Middleton would have had an even later night than he had had. He hoped one of them was awake enough to make the most of the day.

Inverurie's station was very central, depositing visitors almost directly behind the town hall. It was only a short walk from there to the police station, where Middleton, as red-eyed as he was from smoke and lack of sleep, was waiting for him.

'Any developments?' asked Cattanach, as they shook hands.

'Aye, I found if you put the bacon and the egg between two slices of bread, you can have breakfast and get out the door faster. What about you?'

'Coffee in a flask.'

'Aye, we'll have the Germans beat in a month, you and me. What first? The big yin or the wee one?'

'Is the wee one fit to be questioned?'

'Aye, that's a fair point. They say he has concussion, but they'd no wish to keep him in the hospital for he was struggling to get out, fighting off the nurses and the constables like a good 'un, yelling for Mabel. So he's in a cell here, but the doctor's going to come and see him again in …' he looked up at the regulation station clock, '… about twenty minutes. So we could have a cup of coffee, or we could go and have a wee word with yon big fellow.'

'Let's see what he has to say. I thought he looked ready to talk, last night. Ready to admit defeat, anyway.'

'I'm with you on that. I'll do the questioning, but pass me a note or something if you think I'm missing a'thing.'

There was not much need. Cattanach was impressed at how well Middleton had read the notes on the case, and had his finger on most of the details. Muckle Eck, it transpired, had the Sunday name of Alexander Davidson, and hailed from Dundee. He had no fixed abode in Aberdeen, and admitted that he had been doing some work, in a casual way, for the man named Tommy Wilson. Middleton looked sorrowful.

'Aye, well, you'll have seen last night that Tommy Wilson's no a well man. Did you hear him? Looking for some lassie called Mabel?'

Eck gave a sickly look.

'Who's Mabel?'

'Well, that's the question, is it no?' He sat back. 'It's worrying, right enough. I mean, if I was in your shoes, I'd be worried.'

'Why's that?' Eck looked more confused than worried.

'Well, you say you were working for him, Eck, and he's like the boss.'

'Aye, that's right.'

'Well, people are likely to listen to what he says about what happened, more than to you.'

'I suppose …'

'And the way Mr. Wilson is talking, it sounds to me as if he'd say just a'thing. The daftest things. And if you haven't got your story in first, there could be polis that'll think it's him that's telling the truth.'

'Well …'

'And he could blame you, then, for a'thing that's happened. Whereas you and I know fine, Eck, that he's the boss and he telt you what to do, did he no?'

'I suppose …'

'So what about you tell me, Eck, all about Mr. Wilson's big idea about the petrol, eh?'

What came across in the next few minutes was that Muckle Eck did not totally understand Mr. Wilson's big idea about the petrol, but was well enough paid to do his bit.

'He said he was going to make sure a'body had enough petrol, after the rationing started,' said Eck, nodding at the good sense of it. 'So he took petrol to people to store.'

'How did he know what people to take it to?'

'Oh, I dinna ken that,' said Eck. 'That was partly what he got Stevie for. For *local information*.' He nodded again, having produced what he felt was an important phrase. 'Stevie was the one knew all the stories, and he told Mr. Wilson, and Mr. Wilson went to see people and then he took them petrol.'

'And did all the petrol come from farms?'

'Aye, that's right, sir. Cause, see, the farms are no rationed, and they have loads, so it all made sense. And I can drive a lorry, and I can load the drums in the back and take them out again – I'm a gey important part of the whole operation.' He said it with quiet pride, and Cattanach wondered if he had ever felt so important before. Wilson was a charmer, even to his hired strong man.

'So tell me about Stevie. Stevie who? Where's he these days?'

'I – I dinna ken.'

'He's not helping Mr. Wilson any more? Not like you?'

'No. Stevie did something wrong, and Mr. Wilson was cross with him.'

'What did Stevie do?'

'He made a mistake, that's all. He thought Mr. Wilson had told him to do something, and he hadna. Or he hadna really. Stevie shouldna have done it.'

Eck was turning red, and Middleton stepped back a little.

'Where were you last Wednesday, Eck?'

'Wednesday?' Eck did not seem quite to know the meaning of the word.

'Aye, Wednesday. You were in Aberdeen on Tuesday night, and then you left town. Did you take your lorry out for a drive somewhere?'

'Oh, aye.' Eck brightened. 'We went up to Peterhead. I've never been that far before. I wanted to stay a wee while, see about the place, but when you work for Mr. Wilson you have to shift yourself. That's what he says.'

'So how long were you there?'

Eck considered.

'We went up the morn, and we come back after dark. I dinna like driving with they wee things over your headlights, but Mr. Wilson said we had to get back to Aberdeen, and like I say, you have to shift yourself.'

'And what did you do when you were in Peterhead, son?'

'Me?' Eck shuffled on his seat. It groaned. 'What did I do?'

'Aye, son. I don't suppose you drove all that way to buy a bit of fish, did you?'

Eck laughed, then looked dismayed.

'I didna do nothing, sir.'

'Really? Nothing at all?'

'Not that time, sir, no. I did nothing, honest.'

'Maybe you did nothing yourself, Eck, but did you help Mr. Wilson at all?'

'Help him?' Eck was reddening again, and starting to sweat. Cattanach could almost smell his fear. 'How could I help him? I didna understand what he was doing. I never understood it. He took my knife from me. It wasna me, not that time. See a woman? I couldna kill a woman, sir, honest.'

'Are you saying that Tommy Wilson killed a woman? In Peterhead?' asked Middleton, with severe clarity.

Eck nodded hard.

'He did, sir, aye. I heard him call her Mabel. He took my knife and he lashed out at her. I mean, it was no way to stab a'body at all. And then he got me to pick her up and put her into the bushes.' Tears were running freely down his red cheeks. 'A woman! And just leave her there!'

'What else did he do?' asked Cattanach suddenly, earning himself a scowl from Middleton. 'Did he do something else? While you were lifting her, maybe?'

'Aye, sir. He went through her handbag. And then he swore, like, and he said something about betraying him. And he threw the bag up into the bushes an' all. And then we left.'

Cattanach shot a look of apology at Middleton, but he had another piece of information. Mabel had left her case, with all the money, at the station. Had Wilson been looking for that? The picture was starting to take a definite shape.

Middleton settled down again, glancing at the constable who was taking notes, making sure he was not lagging behind.

'I suppose you know better how to stab someone, Eck?'

'Well,' said Eck, 'I ken you dinna lash out like that. You hold the knife flat. That's what I was taught.'

'And so when Mr. Wilson told you to kill Stevie, that was how you did it. Efficient, aye?'

'Aye … well.' Eck's face fell, hollowing out in a flash. Then he sighed. 'Och, I knew I'd find myself telling you. You'll aye be cleverer than me. It was Mr. Wilson tellt me to do it, a'course.'

'Why?'

'Why what?'

'Why did he want Stevie killed? You said Stevie was giving him local information. Was he afraid Stevie would inform on him? Or was it the whisky? Was he angry that Stevie had done a job on the side?'

'What?' Eck looked completely bewildered. 'What whisky?'

'Never mind,' said Middleton. 'Why did Mr. Wilson tell you to kill Stevie?'

'Oh,' said Eck, looking relieved. 'That was easy. It was because Stevie made sure that wee lad had an accident.'

'The wee lad?' Middleton glanced down at his notes, making sure, though the name was leaping in Cattanach's head. 'Billy Campbell?'

'Aye. Billy Campbell.' Eck's eyes had dried, but now fresh tears followed the old tracks down his face. 'The wee lad.'

'Because he had seen you all at the Don mouth?'

'That's right, sir, aye.'

Middleton paused. Cattanach did not make a sound. They

could both sense that there was more to come. Eck swept a tear from his cheek, and cleared his throat.

'The wee lad came on us, and ran off. And Mr. Wilson said something like 'Oh, that'll have to be dealt with,' but he gave the wee lad a gey odd look, ken? And Stevie thought he meant the boy would have to be got rid of, ken? So the next day – no, he had to wait, for he thought he'd get the lad on his way to school, but then the schools were closed. So on the morn's morn he went to do it.'

'And Mr. Wilson was angry?'

'We didna see Mr. Wilson for twa-three days. Then he came back, and he said he'd been at a funeral, and then he said there'd be another one soon. And so we went and looked for Stevie, and that was that.'

'Your knife?'

'Aye, sir.' He looked weary now.

'And your hand.'

'Aye, sir.' He rubbed the heel of his hand into his eyes. 'I liked Stevie, right enough: he was a good laugh. But when Mr. Wilson tells you, you have to shift yourself.'

'So have you all the mannies that had the petrol?'

Maggie Hawthorne, solemn and serious, needed to clear up the details of the story she had started.

'We have. The big man gave us a list of the places they had delivered petrol to.'

'That's good. And it wasna Billy's real uncle that was doing it?'

'It was a friend of Mrs. Campbell's,' said Mrs. Hawthorne quickly. Her eyes darted about the parlour, as if checking to see that there was nothing of which the Inspector could disapprove. 'See, if you're naughty they'll catch you in the end, Maggie.'

Maggie gave her mother a disappointed look.

'What do you want to be when you grow up, Maggie?'

'It's no use me going into the police, is it, Mr. Cattanach?'

He shook his head.

'There aren't very many opportunities for a woman, Maggie.'

She tutted.

'Then I'll be a doctor.'

'People like you aren't doctors, Maggie,' said her mother, with an embarrassed glance at Cattanach.

'I will be,' said Maggie simply, and Cattanach believed her.

He could tell more of the story to Anna Mackay, though. After all, she had condescended to join him for lunch at the Palace Hotel.

'And he's still not right? Wilson? Foolish man, leaving the hospital like that.'

'He spent some time asking for Mabel, then cursing her. I think we have something like the full story now.'

'They were married.'

'They were. In Dundee. And had a child.'

'Billy.'

'We have all the certificates. She was Mabel Carter, if she was telling the truth then.'

'But she left. Bolted.'

'I think bolters abandon their children, don't they? She took Billy with her. We think he would have been two or three at the time. And perhaps just as importantly, she took the proceeds of Tommy Wilson's very successful criminal business.'

'Hence the money. And then – did he recognise Billy?'

'I think he must have seen something about him. And I think perhaps Albert Lovie let slip the Campbells' first names, anyway, whatever he says. Wilson spent the Monday investigating, and then, I think, he was heading into town to find Stevie on that Tuesday morning to make sure he was not going to do anything to – well, to his son.'

'And then the tram crashed, and he was knocked out.'

Cattanach nodded.

'And Wilson didn't find out until he went to Mabel's house on Friday that, in fact, Stevie had gone ahead and killed Billy.'

'Horrible.'

'And we probably wouldn't have pieced it all together if it hadn't been for two intelligent women.'

'Really?' He could see that she already assumed that she was one of them.

'You reported Mabel missing. But before that, Billy's friend told us about his criminal uncle, and her worry that his death had not been an accident. She's only ten, but she wants to be a doctor, too.'

'Tell her to come and see me.'

Yes, ma'am, he thought.

'I shall. You'd like her.'

The waitress arrived with coffee, and nothing was said until she had left again.

'So, Inspector Cattanach,' said Anna, pouring milk into her cup. 'Is your grandfather really Gordon of Glenfindie?'

'He is.'

'And your uncle was a police sergeant?'

'He was.'

'And you have no intention of talking about that interesting arrangement, have you?'

He smiled.

'No intention at all.'

A laird and a police sergeant. It made for a fine, if awkward, mixture. Always in the wrong place.

Cattanach sat at the door of his little tent, drinking coffee from a flask. It might not have been as fine as the coffee at the Palace Hotel, but it was hot and sweet. And the view was a good deal better. The elderly dog had turned out to be more lively than he had thought, and sat at his feet, nose twitching happily at the mountain air.

He wondered if Billy Campbell had ever managed to get out into the countryside, up into the hills, and what he would have seen. He had been an observant lad – maybe he would have ended up in the police, too. Or gone to war. Nothing was sure.

But at least he might have had a chance – if he had not been in the wrong place.

Cattanach shook out the last drops of coffee, and turned to pack up and strike his tent. It was time to go back to the city, and to work. There was a war on.

About the Author

LEXIE CONYNGHAM IS a historian living in the shadow of the Highlands. Her historical crime novels are born of a life amidst Scotland's old cities, ancient universities and hidden-away aristocratic estates, but she has written since the day she found out that people were allowed to do such a thing. Beyond teaching and research, her days are spent with wool, wild allotments and a wee bit of whisky.

We hope you've enjoyed this instalment. Reviews are important to authors, so it would be lovely if you could post a review where you bought it!

Visit our website at www.lexieconyngham.co.uk. There are several free Murray of Letho short stories, Murray's World Tour of Edinburgh, and the chance to follow Lexie Conyngham's meandering thoughts on writing, gardening and knitting, at www.murrayofletho.blogspot.co.uk. You can also follow Lexie, should such a thing appeal, on Facebook, Pinterest or Instagram.

Finally! If you'd like to be kept up to date with Lexie and her writing, please join our mailing list at: contact@kellascatpress.co.uk. There's a free novella to be claimed, and a quarterly newsletter, often with a short story attached, and fair warning of any new books coming out.

Murray of Letho

We first meet Charles Murray when he's a student at St. Andrews University in Fife in 1802, resisting his father's attempts to force him home to the family estate to learn how it's run. Pushed into involvement in the investigation of a professor's death, he solves his first murder before taking up a post as tutor to Lord Scoggie. This series takes us around Georgian Scotland as well as India, Italy and Norway (so far!), in the company of Murray, his manservant Robbins, his father's old friend Blair, the enigmatic Mary, and other members of his occasionally shambolic household.

Death in a Scarlet Gown

The Status of Murder (a novella)

Knowledge of Sins Past

Service of the Heir (An Edinburgh Murder)

An Abandoned Woman

Fellowship with Demons

The Tender Herb (A Murder in Mughal India)

Death of an Officer's Lady

Out of a Dark Reflection

A Dark Night at Midsummer (a novella)

Slow Death by Quicksilver

Thicker than Water

A Deficit of Bones

The Dead Chase

Shroud for a Sinner

Hippolyta Napier

Hippolyta Napier is only nineteen when she arrives in Ballater, on Deeside, in 1829, the new wife of the local doctor. Blessed with a love of animals, a talent for painting, a helpless instinct for hospitality, and insatiable curiosity, Hippolyta finds her feet in her new home and role in society, making friends and enemies as she goes. Ballater may be small but it attracts great numbers of visitors, so the issues of the time, politics, slavery, medical advances, all affect the locals. Hippolyta, despite her loving husband and their friend Durris, the sheriff's officer, manages to involve herself in all kinds of dangerous adventures in her efforts to solve every mystery that presents itself.

A Knife in Darkness

Death of a False Physician

A Murderous Game

The Thankless Child

A Lochgorm Lament

The Corrupted Blood

Orkneyinga Murders

Orkney, c.1050 A.D.: Thorfinn Sigurdarson, Earl of Orkney, rules from the Brough of Birsay on the western edges of these islands. Ketil Gunnarson is his man, representing his interests in any part of his extended realm. When Sigrid, a childhood friend of Ketil's, finds a dead man on her land, Ketil, despite his distrust of islands, is commissioned to investigate. Sigrid, though she has quite enough to do, decides he cannot manage on his own, and insists on helping – which Ketil might or might not appreciate.

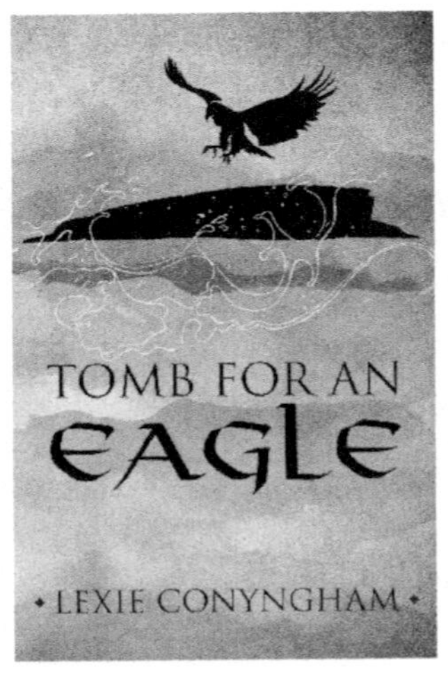

Tomb for an Eagle

A Wolf at the Gate

Dragon in the Snow

The Bear at Midnight

Other books by Lexie Conyngham:

Windhorse Burning

'I'm not mad, for a start, and I'm about as far from violent as you can get.'
When Toby's mother, Tibet activist Susan Hepplewhite, dies, he is determined to honour her memory. He finds her diaries and decides to have them translated into English. But his mother had a secret, and she was not the only one: Toby's decision will lead to obsession and murder.

The War, The Bones, and Dr. Cowie

Far from the London Blitz, Marian Cowie is reluctantly resting in rural Aberdeenshire when a German 'plane crashes nearby. An airman goes missing, and old bones are revealed. Marian is sure she could solve the mystery if only the villagers would stop telling her useless stories – but then the crisis comes, and Marian finds the stories may have a use after all.

Jail Fever

It's the year 2000, and millennium paranoia is everywhere.
Eliot is a bad-tempered merchant with a shady past, feeling under the weather.
Catriona is an archaeologist at a student dig, when she finds something unexpected.
Tom is a microbiologist, investigating a new and terrible disease with a stigma.
Together, their knowledge could save thousands of lives – but someone does not want them to …

The Slaughter of Leith Hall* and *The Contentious Business of Samuel Seabury

'See, Charlie, it might be near twenty years since Culloden, but there's plenty hard feelings still amongst the Jacobites, and no so far under the skin, ken?'

Charlie Rob has never thought of politics, nor strayed far from his Aberdeenshire birthplace. But when John Leith of Leith Hall takes him under his wing, his life changes completely. Soon he is far from home, dealing with conspiracy and murder, and lost in a desperate hunt for justice.

Thrawn Thoughts and Blithe Bits **and** ***Quite Useful in Minor Emergencies***

Two collections of short stories, some featuring characters from the series, some not; some seen before, some not; some long, some very short. Find a whole new dimension to car theft, the life history of an unfortunate Victorian rebel, a problem with dragons and a problem with draugens, and what happens when you advertise that you've found somebody's leg.

Printed in Great Britain
by Amazon